THE SENTINEL

Hamish Spiers

The cover art for this book features the following images used under standard license from shutterstock.com: 1395120767 (Digital Storm), 353060375 (Songquan Deng), 338314844 (Maria Starovoytova)

ISBN: 978-0-6485479-3-8

First published: 2012
This edition published: 2024

6 5 4 3 2 1

Books by Hamish Spiers:

Star Frontier
Star Frontier: Beyond the Veil
Star Frontier: Dangerous Games
Star Frontier: Descent
Star Frontier: Intrepid

The Sentinel
Fringe City Nightfall

The Sun Always Sets

The Martian Archaeologist

The Veya Child

hamishspiers.com

This book is dedicated to my wife Erin, my son Jason and finally to my brother Rob for all his feedback and advice on this story and others.

WELCOME TO

FRINGE CITY

THE TRAIL

"*THIS IS MARIANE O'HARA, FOR FRINGE CITY Central. Today's top story—sixteen people shot dead in a café in Fringe City's central business district.*"

"*The commander of the operation has cordoned off the neighborhood and despite fears that there may be innocent bystanders still in the vicinity, the national guard is moving in at this very moment. We are now crossing live to our reporter on the scene.*"

"*And yet once again, the perpetrator of this horrendous crime, the Bandit, has disappeared without a trace.*"

"*Hundreds of families are on the street, and fifty-three people have been confirmed dead, after the inexplicable collapse of an inner city apartment block earlier this evening. Investigators on the scene believe that explosives very similar to those used in standard demolitions caused the accident, but so far, there is no clue as to who was responsible.*"

"The latest theory, according to police experts, is that there are several organizations supplying these gangs."

"Kingsford residents are becoming increasingly impatient over the continued delays in repairing their local subway station."

"The siege finally came to an end at 11.20 p.m. last night when Lady Vice and her associates left the premises via a rear stairwell and police were able to enter the building and secure the area. Although thankfully no one was harmed, for the twenty-three hostages, it was a terrifying ordeal."

"Once again, the police were unable to prevent the Specter killings."

Shaking his head, Jason Harding climbed up from the sofa and flicked the television off. After a long day at work, the last thing he needed was to see the Fringe City news. With a slight groan, he rubbed his forehead just above the temples, walked over to the sink and splashed some cold water over his face. It always helped. However, what he really needed was a bit of air, even Fringe City air.

Angie would be back soon, he knew, but she

wouldn't mind him being out for a little bit. Grabbing a piece of paper, he scribbled a note: *Going for a walk.* He slid the edge of it under the fruit bowl on the kitchen bench and grabbed his keys.

The night was hot and humid, without the slightest breeze to alleviate the sensation of the clammy air. Within moments, Jason was drenched in sweat. He wiped off what he could with his thin white shirt, and for a moment he thought about going back to the apartment. But as he was already on the street, he decided that he might as well have a little stroll. He could always have a cold shower when he got back home.

He ambled along, keeping on the main roads. From everything that was going on in this place that the rest of the country had given up on, he was probably taking his life into his own hands every time he stepped outside the door. But even so, one could take precautions.

All the same though, with the oppressive heat combining with his weary state, he was rather out of things for a couple of blocks. Then some voices ahead of him brought him back into the world of the living.

Up ahead, he saw three men by a parked car. One of them was holding the trunk open and the other two were lifting a body out of it. It was wrapped in what looked like an old bed sheet or somebody's unwanted curtains, but it would have been just as obvious without the shroud that this was a very limp, very dead body.

Panicking, Jason ducked into a small alcove at the base of the apartment building beside him and pressed himself into it, as far out of the light from the street lamps as humanly possible.

He had to remain calm. These men were either killers themselves or working for one, and he was the only witness on the scene who could identify them. He looked at the license plate on the back of the black sedan beside the men: GCD 1647. As he repeated the number a couple of times in his head, the men dumped the body in a dumpster and climbed back into the car.

Jason waited several minutes after they'd gone before he stepped out again and decided what to do. He wasn't going anywhere near the dumpster for starters—that was obvious—and he wasn't going to go back to the apartment just yet either. If those men were hanging around nearby, he sure as hell didn't want them finding out where he lived. And there was another problem.

He had to call the cops but he didn't want to get involved in this any more than he had to. An anonymous call from a payphone would do the trick.

He'd give them the street where the dumpster was, along with the license plate number from the car, and then he'd go back to the apartment. He nodded to himself as he thought it over. It was a sound plan. He'd sort this out, go home, see Angie and try to forget the whole thing.

As he stepped into the phone booth, he took a moment to compose himself—not so much for the benefit of whoever would pick up the phone on the other end but because he didn't want any onlookers figuring out what he was doing. Thankfully, there didn't seem to be anyone standing too close.

Eyeing the street, glancing at the café across the road, he picked up the handset and dialed the number for the emergency services. The dial tone rang twice before someone picked it up.

"Police," he said quickly before the operator said anything.

"One moment," came the curt reply, followed by a click and a different dial tone as the call was diverted.

"This is the Fringe City Metropolitan Police," a gruff voice said. "How can I help you?"

"Who am I speaking to?" Jason asked. He frowned; he didn't know why he'd started with that line. He must have been running on autopilot.

"This is Sergeant Hemming speaking. What's the problem, sir?"

"I wish to report a murder," Jason said, his voice wavering. He glanced down at the receiver. His hand was shaking.

"All right. Now, I want you to stay calm. When and where did this happen? I realize this is difficult, but try to be as precise as you can."

"I—I didn't see it," Jason stammered. "But I just saw three men throw a dead body in a dumpster... the car was GCD 1647... I mean, its plate..."

"I'm sorry, sir," Hemming interrupted. "Could you repeat that a little more slowly?"

Jason took a breath, and another few glances around the street. Thankfully, no one was in earshot.

"I saw three men throw a body in dumpster," he repeated, as slowly as he could. "On Seville Avenue... I don't know exactly where... but it was on the corner of one of those little streets that crosses over to Merrill. The apartment building next to it was one of the smaller ones... looked like something out of the seventies."

"And you got a license plate number?"

"Yeah," Jason said. "They left in a black sedan. The license plate number was GCD 1647."

"And when was this?"

"Just a few minutes ago. I don't know. Maybe ten or

fifteen minutes."

"All right." There was a slight pause. A long pause actually. "Where are you now?"

Jason hesitated. He didn't like the sound of this. For a moment, he contemplated hanging up. He'd given this officer everything he knew.

"Um, I'd rather not say if it's all the same to you. I don't want these creeps to find out I called you and then come knocking on my door."

"That's precisely why I'm asking," Sergeant Hemming replied. "It's possible these men might have seen you already, and if so, you might be in danger. Are you at home?"

"No, I'm in a phone booth opposite some café on Merrill Avenue." Jason looked across the street and read the bright tacky lettering that hung over the door. "The Rio Café."

"All right, sir. Listen to me very carefully. We respect people's rights to remain anonymous in these situations, so don't panic. I'm going to send a car to pick you up for your safety. You don't have to tell the officer in the car who you are, but he or she will take you wherever you want to go and make sure you get there safely. Do you understand?"

"Um. Yeah, sure."

"Good. When you hang up, go across the road and wait in the café. It's best to stay somewhere public and visible. And if there are other people around, you'll be that much safer. Just wait there and a car should be there in five minutes."

Including the two staff members running the place that night, there were twelve other people in café.

Sipping his coffee, Jason glanced at the clock on the wall. He'd been there now for seven minutes, and there was still no sign of a car. For a moment, he thought about just heading home. This Sergeant Hemming character had all the information he needed. It was annoying having to wait for a ride. He should have hung up and left as soon as Hemming had suggested it.

Then, with a screech of car tires, a black sedan pulled to a stop outside and everyone in the café looked up as three men leapt out of the vehicle. For a split second, Jason couldn't believe his eyes. He knew this stuff happened all the time in Fringe City. He just never imagined it could happen to him.

He dived for cover as the café windows blew inwards, showering glass everywhere, and as the furniture exploded into burning splinters. For a moment that seemed far longer than it really was, he heard screams—screams that cut through the deafening barrage that was drowning out everything else. Screams that briefly cut through it and then, just as briefly, ended.

As he lay dazed on the floor, Jason realized he'd been injured. He felt a burning sensation in his upper right arm and glancing at it, saw it was drenched in blood. The second thing he realized was he was still alive. However, his next observation was the most important. The men outside hadn't got back into their car yet, which most likely meant that they were going to make sure everyone in the café was dead before they left.

Without making a sound, Jason smeared the blood from his arm over his chest and his neck and then laid still, his head under a stool so he could see the killers without them realizing it. He saw their legs as they came in and inspected the place. There were three of them, in black dress trousers and leather shoes. Jason didn't move a muscle.

As they turned to leave, he noticed something else. The back of their car, along with the license plate GCD 1647, the car he'd reported to Sergeant Hemming.

If the men in the car had seen Jason, then they could have waited until he came out of the café and jumped him then. However, they had opted to kill everyone in the café instead, which meant they had no idea what he looked like. All they knew was that one of the people in the café had seen them dumping that body earlier and there was only one way they could have known that.

Jason was angry. He'd seen three men dump a dead body, twelve innocent people had just been killed and someone on the police force had orchestrated it.

One of the men then came back with a fuel can and poured its contents all over the place. When he was done, he threw the container into a corner, lit a match, dropped it and left.

Jason watched the flames climb higher and higher, and when the fire and smoke had fully obscured the view of the street outside, he moved. Kicking open the kitchen door, he saw a window with some louvers on the back wall that would get him to the little alley behind the café. He pulled each louver out of its metal catch and threw it aside until he had an opening he could just fit through. By the time he was done, the fire was coming through the kitchen door.

He looked outside, hoping against hope that there wasn't anyone waiting for him, and he saw the alley was deserted.

He climbed through the window, darted across the alley and, using a sturdy drainpipe, hauled himself up three storeys and onto a roof. He crossed the roof and repeated the process several times, substituting fire escapes for drainpipes where possible, but keeping off the street. He didn't dare go back to his apartment. Not until he got cleaned up. Being covered in blood was likely to get people's attention and right then, he needed attention about as much as the world needed HR consultants and property speculators.

Spying a public restroom, he climbed back down to the ground and ducked in. Washing the blood off his neck and his chest was easy enough but his arm was a mess. It didn't hurt too much anymore but that was probably more down to the adrenaline than anything else. He guessed it'd be pretty sore in the morning. For now, he tore a section of his shirt off and made a little tourniquet around the arm to stem the bleeding.

Then, since no one else had come into the restroom, he risked staying a little longer to wash his shirt. After taking it off, running it under the tap and wringing it out, he got it to a dirty orange color, which was better than nothing. Now, he was ready to head home.

"Jesus Christ, Jason! What the hell happened?"

All was most certainly not right in the world just then but the fact that Angie was there for him made it easier to deal with.

Jason shook his head. "I… uh…" Then, giving up on the exercise of speech for the time being, he took his shirt off, scrunched it up and threw it into the bin. Aware that he was pretty much leaving Angie in the dark, he walked straight to the bathroom, shut the door and had a long cold shower.

When he came out, he was clutching his wounded arm again. He moved for the bin and tried to lever it open with his foot.

"Hang on," Angie said, rushing to his side. "Let me help you. What are you doing?"

He winced. "Honey, can you get the shirt out? Tear off a strip for me, will you?"

"Jason, we've got bandages."

Jason nodded and leaned back, sliding his legs out over the tiles of the kitchen floor. It felt so good to relax for a moment. So comfortable. The place really wasn't much, and it wasn't spacious by any stretch of the imagination, but it was home. And right then, it was the embassy for the little-known independent country of Sanity.

He felt Angie move his hand off his injury. He closed his eyes as she washed it with cold water, kept them closed as she dried it with careful patting motions and smiled as she wrapped a nice clean bandage around his arm.

"Come on," she said, helping him to his feet. She guided him across to their little sofa and they sat down together.

She watched as Jason rested, leaning back and closing his eyes. She watched him for several minutes and then tried to have a rest herself.

After a while—maybe a few minutes, maybe an hour—Jason started to talk to her. She didn't interrupt him. She just listened and when he had finished, they were both quiet for a few minutes as it all sank in.

"So this cop told these gangsters about you?" Angie finally asked.

"Yeah. And now a whole lot of people who were simply just having an evening coffee are dead."

"But we've got to tell someone. There must be someone we can trust."

"Maybe," Jason muttered. "But until I know for sure who's bent and who's not, I'm going to have to handle this on my own."

"Handle what?"

"I'm going to find out who those thugs were," Jason told her. "I'm going to find out who they killed in the alley. I'm going to find out who they're working for and who's working with them on the police force and I'm going to make every last one of them pay for what they did."

"Yeah," Jason said after the laughter died down. "Hilarious." He shook his head at the kid and turned back to the board. "A motif," he explained, writing it in nice big letters with perhaps more force than was necessary. "A symbol that recurs throughout the text—" He winced and looked at his arm. The wound had opened up and blood was seeping through his shirt.

"I think Sir's straining it with all that whiteboard writing!" some wit called out to more of that moronic laughter that only the most juvenile of adolescent males made, a sort of animalistic grunting noise.

Jason sighed. Trent Frederickson again. He wondered how long it'd be before he snapped and gave in to his primal urge to smack the kid's head in.

"Thanks, Trent. Your concern is truly touching."

Caitlyn, the nice young lady from the library showed somewhat more sympathy when she joined him and the others in the department staffroom for lunch. It was nice there, better than going to the main one with admin and half the teachers at the school.

"Oh, it's all right," he assured her. "I just slipped on some stairs." He turned back to his computer.

"What you up to?" she asked. "You seem distracted today."

"I just want to check an online transaction. That's all."

She nodded with a little smile and took a sip of

coffee. "I'll leave you to it then."

He smiled back. "Don't worry. Won't be long."

As she turned away and started chatting to Daniel, Jason found the site for the vehicle registration department.

Generally, when there wasn't some goddamn department meeting, Jason would knock off work with Angie straight after school. If there was any curriculum development, marking or reports to be done, they did it at home. Sometimes, he'd meet his friend who worked at the nearby university for a drink and as he went off on his own, he wished he'd told Angie *that* was what he was doing. When he had told her he was going to the local library, it didn't look as though she'd bought it.

Not that it mattered. It was just a white lie—well, probably more the conventional kind—and as long as he came home in one piece, she'd be fine.

Once she was out of sight, he went straight to the nearest payphone and dialed the number he'd found.

"This is the Fringe City vehicle registration department. How can we be of assistance?"

It was show time. "Hello, this is the metropolitan police. We need you guys to run a search through your system for us. We've just found an abandoned car outside the city limits and we need to contact the owner. The license plate is GCD 1647."

He took a quiet breath. Either this was going to work out just the way he had planned it or he was going to hang up really quickly.

Fortunately though, unlike Angie with his library story, this guy bought his bull.

After getting the details, there were a couple of things to check before he headed home. After a short bus ride—just one stop past the one where he usually got off—he reached his first destination.

He'd been pretty certain of what he'd find there, and he wasn't surprised, but it felt good to confirm his suspicions as it meant he wasn't going crazy. The dumpster he'd seen the night before was now empty. Whoever he was dealing with wasn't taking any chances.

After that, he headed down to the nearest subway station. Thirty-five minutes and two transfers later, he reached his second destination where he was pleased to learn the information he'd been given by the vehicle registration department was accurate. Whoever owned that car could change the plates now or sell the thing and it wouldn't make a difference. He had an address and it wasn't on wheels.

· · ·

"You were quite a while," Angie remarked as he came in through the door, "at the library."

"Yeah, all right. I was tracking the whereabouts of that car from last night."

Angie nodded. "Any luck?"

"Yeah, as a matter of fact—" He winced as sudden pain rushed through his arm.

"Oh, Jason," she sighed, coming over and inspecting his injury. "We'd better go and get that looked at right now." She grabbed the house keys from the bench. "Come on. Let's go."

Jason put his hand out to stop her. "Wait a minute. If I see a doctor, they're bound to figure out what happened and I don't know if I want that kind of attention. I might get implicated in the killing of those people at the café last night by virtue of simple association."

"Say it was a random mugging on the way home," Angie told him.

"All right. By the way, was there anything in the news about last night?"

"Yeah, of course there was. Twelve dead in a café shooting. No one's going to cover something like that up."

• • •

"Some dumb punk mugged me on my way home from work yesterday," Jason told the doctor. "I ran down a side street and he got me as I was going around the corner. But anyway, I got away from the little bastard and that's the main thing."

"Good lord. And you didn't think to tell the police?"

Jason shrugged. "What would be the point? I probably couldn't even pick the punk from a line up. It'd just end up as another statistic in the books."

"If you say so," the doctor said as he stitched up the wound. "Now, I don't suppose I have to tell you not to get these wet?"

"No, it's all right. I know."

"Good. Now these particular stitches will fall out by themselves in about a week, by which time the wound will have largely closed. Fortunately, your injury was fairly minor all things considered."

"I'm glad to hear it."

"Minor all things considered, you understand," the doctor repeated. "And you definitely shouldn't go to work for the rest of this week. You were shot for heaven's sake."

Jason tried not to smile. No school for the rest of the week. He wondered how he'd manage. "Well, grazed really but yeah, I guess you're right. I probably shouldn't have gone in to work today then either, right?"

The doctor frowned. "No. You should have seen me as soon as you could. However, better late than never, I suppose. Now, before you go home, I want you to get some high grade antiseptic ointment from the pharmacist and apply it liberally and often. At least for the next week, maybe two. It's very important to keep the area sterile."

"All right."

"And come back and see me after the stitches are gone so we can check up on it."

Angie was much relieved when Jason came out of the doctor's consultation room with a proper bandage around his arm and a medical certificate in his hand. After paying at the reception and picking up the antiseptic ointment, they took a bus home. They didn't say anything about what had happened until they came through their door.

"All right," Angie said, as they sat down on their sofa. "What was it you were going to tell me earlier?"

"I found those gangsters."

"And there's no way they'd know that?"

"No. They don't know what I look like and as far as they're aware, I'm dead. I found them through the vehicle registration department."

"You didn't go in person, did you?"

"Of course not. I called them from a payphone."

Angie nodded. "All right. So now what do you want to do?"

"I want to find some way to observe their place. You know, see who comes and goes during the day. But it's got to be something that isn't risky. Like a small CCTV camera on a roof or something."

"Why don't you talk to Geoffrey? He'd know all about that stuff."

"Yeah, I might do that. Maybe I can meet him at the university for lunch tomorrow. After all, I've got the rest of the week off."

Angie gave him a wry grin. "Don't rub it in when you call the school tomorrow, will you?"

Jason smiled back. "Would I do that?"

Jason had known Geoffrey since university. They had done some core education subjects together in their first year, despite having different majors, and they had been friends ever since. In Jason's case, he had followed through with his course and gone on to teaching. Geoffrey on the other hand had dropped everything related to education and had focused on anything and everything related to the practical applications of science. Somewhere along the line, he had gotten himself a job at the university's science faculty and the upshot of it all was that he had never left. And this was where Jason met him the next day.

"Hey, Wolfman," he grinned, shaking his hand as Geoffrey came out of the lab building; the nickname had come about because of the combined effect of his friend's slightly protruding ears and long sideburns.

"Hey, Jason. How's it going?"

"Good, Geoffrey. How about you?"

Geoffrey nodded. "Yeah pretty good…" He trailed off, looking puzzled. "Isn't this a weekday?"

Jason laughed. "Yeah. No one would accuse you of being out of it. It's Thursday. I've got the rest of the week off."

"Cool."

No questions. No apparent interest in the reason why. That was Geoffrey to the core. The real world was something he came into contact with from time to time but he rarely paid it too much attention.

"Let's go and grab a bite. I've got something I want to talk to you about."

"Is it lunchtime yet?"

"Yeah. It's one-thirty."

Geoffrey nodded again. "Cool."

A lot of people were a bit fazed by Geoffrey. With his spiky hair and the t-shirts he'd been wearing since high school, he didn't look like the kind of person you'd go to with a problem. But under it all, there was a very sharp guy. You just had to know the secret door knock to talk to him.

"Jeez," Geoffrey muttered after Jason had finished. He took a sip of his drink and was quiet for a while. Jason didn't say anything either. He knew Geoffrey. His friend was working everything over in his mind.

"You know," he said after a little while. "I've got a friend who works in one of those hi-tech companies. They manufacture a whole lot of this CCTV stuff and coupled with some transmitters and recording equipment, I think I could put something together for you. Also, this guy's company has pretty good discounts for employees so I could probably get it for you for a good price. It wouldn't be cheap exactly but it wouldn't break the vault either."

"Nice."

"I used this guy another time as well. Got a good deal from him for some friends of mine who mind the computer labs here after hours. By the way, what are you going to do about these guys when all's said and done?"

Jason shrugged. "I'm not really sure yet. Somehow, I've got to work out a way to put the scare in a few of them and find out who was behind all of this."

Geoffrey grinned and shook his head. It wasn't a typical reaction to a statement like that but then again, Geoffrey wasn't a typical person. "Yeah, well. That's all well and good but I think there are a couple of flaws in the plan."

"Such as?"

"Well, basically, if you try to put the scare into anyone, then A, it won't work, and B, you'll get yourself killed."

"Thanks for your support."

Geoffrey shrugged and took another sip of his drink. "Don't mention it."

"Well, you've got a point," Jason conceded. "But don't worry; I'm not crazy. And I'm not going to do anything yet. I want to do some other things first. Make some gear that I can wear that'll offer some protection. Maybe have a face concealing helmet as well."

"*Now* you might have something," Geoffrey told him. "And I might be able to help you out as well."

"Good. What can you get me?"

"How about some of that Kevlar body armor that S.W.A.T. teams use? I could make something just as good as their gear. Maybe even better."

"Where in the hell are you going to get Kevlar from?"

Geoffrey shrugged. "The science faculty here has

access to suppliers for all sorts of things you can't find in your local hardware store. We do a lot of manufacturing and experimentation, you know. Just recently, we built our very own wind tunnel. Just like the ones you find in car factories. Really cool stuff." He paused for a moment. "Um, anyway. And you see, it's easy to write off expenses in the budget because when you're experimenting, it's inevitable that certain things don't work and end up getting thrown by the wayside."

"It might be a problem though if someone comes in asking why someone in your lab placed an enormous order for Kevlar."

"Come on. The only reason why any of those big shots would come looking around the lab would be if we're not getting any work done or if we've gone noticeably over their annual budget." Geoffrey smiled. "Give me some time. I'll get you something really snappy."

At the Fringe City police headquarters, Captain Diane Reilly downed a cup of cheap vendor machine coffee. She knew should probably try to get out later and have something—anything—that resembled a proper meal but it was always so busy around this time of the evening. Why the scum who plagued the city couldn't keep their extra legal activities scheduled between the hours of nine and five, she didn't know.

However, the shift was nearly over... even if the work wasn't. Glancing around the busy room — with cops left, right and centre, and a dozen phones ringing — she noticed Sergeant Rodriguez heading for his office. She threw her paper coffee cup in the wastebasket and followed him. Her other work could wait a few moments.

"Rodriguez, wait up."

He turned around, mildly surprised, but happy to see her. "Hello, Captain."

"Have you got a minute? I want to talk to you about something."

He nodded. "Let's talk inside my office. It'll be quieter."

It was, Diane thought as she closed the door behind her, but that wasn't the real reason why they had so many of their conversations this way.

"So, what's up?" Rodriguez asked.

"A breakthrough," Diane told him. "I've just found out that Sergeant Hemming is on Lamont's payroll and that he helped Lamont cover up a murder."

"How?"

"Someone saw Lamont's men dumping a body and called the department. And Sergeant Hemming took the call. Then he told the witness to wait in a café and told Lamont's men where he was."

Rodriguez's expression was grim. "And was this the Rio Café on Merrill Avenue?"

"That's the one."

The sergeant took a long breath. "Jesus. How did you find this out?"

"I had my suspicions a while ago so I contacted the District Attorney and asked him for a warrant to wire-tap Hemming's phone."

"That's crafty work. Does Commissioner Levings know about any of this?"

"No," Diane replied. "Faulkner's not sure if we can trust him."

"Does he think he's one of Lamont's men?"

"He hasn't said. All he's said is that we need to be very careful about who we trust when it comes to sharing these things. Both of us."

"He's right about that," Rodriguez agreed. "We'd better get these tapes of yours to Faulkner as soon as we can. He'll know what to do. Have you got them here?"

"In my office."

"Good," the sergeant replied, looking at his watch. "I get off in twenty minutes. How about you?"

"Fifty."

"Well, if you give 'em to me, I'll run them over straightaway."

. . .

Twenty minutes later, Rodriguez was on his way. It wasn't a long drive to the D.A.'s office. He just hoped the man would be in. But he would be. Charles Faulkner worked longer hours than anyone else he *knew*.

Up ahead, a light turned red. As he pulled to a stop, he reached down to flick the radio on. However, just as he was adjusting the dial, there was a short burst of static and a call came through.

"Car 27, come in."

So much for being off duty. With a sigh, he picked up his police radio. "This is car 27. Go ahead."

"Sorry, Rodriguez," the operator at the station said. "I know you just got off but there's a break-in at 237 Adamson. A couple of teenagers and they might be armed."

"Back-up?" he asked, more in hope than expectation.

"We're making some calls but it may be a few minutes."

"All right," Rodriguez replied. "I'm on it."

The light turned green as he put the radio down but as there was no one behind him, he took the opportunity to flick on his GPS display and find the place. It wasn't far away at all, no more than a block.

Although as he pulled away and turned right at the next intersection, he didn't know whether that was a blessing or not. Sometimes, although he hated to admit it, it was a relief getting to a break in after the perpetrators were gone.

Barely thirty seconds had passed when he reached the place. As he pulled up to the curb and got out, he frowned. There were no broken doors, windows or anything like that. And the only other thing that looked out of the ordinary was the other police car.

"I was told there was a break-in," he said as he walked over to the two officers standing beside it, one of whom was Sergeant Hemming. It didn't look as though they'd just arrived either.

"Yeah, sorry about that," Hemming told him. It was the last thing Rodriguez heard. Before he even knew what was happening, the other officer had whipped out a gun that he'd been holding out of sight and shot him in the chest.

"It's shocking, these street kids and their guns," Hemming said as his partner cleaned the barrel of his weapon and put it away. The other man snorted in amusement. Hemming kicked Rodriguez out of the way, rolling him onto his front, and leaned into his car. The glove compartment was unlocked and a second later, he found what he was looking for.

His partner grinned. "You know, we ought to put in

a commendation for Sergeant Rodriguez. He gave his life protecting the city from these thugs."

"Absolutely," Hemming said, shoving the tapes he'd found into his pockets.

"Is that them?"

"Yep." He walked back to his own car and got in as his partner climbed into the driver's seat. "These squealers aren't too bright, are they? Getting a warrant to perform a wire-tap? No wonder they're always two steps behind."

His partner shook his head. "Yeah. I have to say our way's a lot easier. Now, what are we going to do about Reilly?"

"Nothing yet," Hemming said, warning his overzealous friend. "She doesn't have her precious evidence any more so we don't have to worry about her for the moment. Also, it might be a bit suspicious if she turns up dead right after her partner does."

"Yeah, good point."

"Well?" Jason asked.

Angie looked at the two TVs, each with their own DVD recorders. One was of course the TV set they had already owned. The other was a model of similar vintage. Neither of the things would ever be mistaken for components of a home theatre system, being rather on the small size, but that was okay. They never invited friends around for movie nights anyway and as Angie looked at the set up, she decided this was just as well. Given the not so legal nature of spying on neighborhoods, it wouldn't do to have visiting friends asking questions about Jason's little CCTV network.

"It looks… well, dodgy… but in a good way. So, run it by me. How is this all going to work again?"

"Well," Jason said, pointing to the screens of the televisions even though there was nothing on them yet, "I'm getting a remote signal from a long-life battery powered camera that I placed on a roof adjacent to those gangsters. All the footage is automatically recorded so I can check it later if I miss anything. So when I get home from school for example, I can stop the recording and watch the DVD on our old TV to see if anything happened while I was away—and at the same time, I can keep an eye on the other TV to make sure I don't miss anything that's happening right then."

"It seems pretty excessive but if you really want to do this…" Angie sighed.

Jason tried to give her a reassuring smile. "I'm almost ready now. Geoffrey says the suit should be ready within a few days so now I just need some way to move around the city easily without being seen."

"I'm worried about you, Jason."

"I'm worried too," Jason told her. "But until I can get to the bottom of this thing, I'm going to have a hard time taking it easy. Anyway, I'm not planning on doing anything really drastic just yet."

It was another two weeks before he got a look at the suit Geoffrey was working on. Although considering the time it took to order the various bits of material needed and put it together, it was fast work. When he got his first glimpse of it in one of the basement rooms of the university's science block, Jason was well and truly speechless.

"How's it look?" Geoffrey asked him after he'd had a minute to take it all in.

"Awesome."

"It should," Geoffrey said, one of his characteristic smiles firmly in place. "I made it." He gave his handiwork an affectionate pat. "It still needs a bit more work though and if you're serious about going out in it, I really have to insist on testing it first."

"I understand," Jason replied. "Thanks."

"Anyway, the armor should give you quite a bit of cover, although you'll have to watch your sides, the armpit areas and several other places. But still, you've got to be able to move, right?"

"Right."

"And you'll love the helmet too," Geoffrey said, removing it from the rest of the suit and handing it to him. Jason put it on. It was a snug fit but it didn't inhibit head movement. Suddenly, there was a click from his left and the view through the visor completely changed; he was now looking at the room as if through a green tinted lens. Geoffrey was still talking. "With a flick of a switch, you've got infrared, night goggles, binoculars… the works."

Jason fiddled around with the settings himself, quite enjoying the zoom function he discovered. "I don't know how you do it," he said as he focused on some boxes at the other end of the room. "You're amazing."

"Well, that's how," Geoffrey replied. "And I still get all my work done here too. That's probably why I've got an open-ended offer for an associate professor position in Boston."

"Jesus." Jason took the helmet off, its multitude of gimmicks forgotten. "I didn't know that. What are you waiting around here for? You should get on the next train and take it."

Geoffrey waved a dismissive hand. "Nah. This is my neighborhood. Besides, I think Boston's too up-market for me. I'd have to dress properly and all that. Anyway, the offer's open-ended. And right now, you really need my help."

"Within reason," Jason pointed out, placing the

helmet back with the suit "I don't want to hold you back from doing something that could really change your life."

"I know," Geoffrey told him. "But, believe it or not, I'm kind of happy where I am. I've got all my friends in the faculty. And there's you and Angie."

Jason nodded, his thoughts drifting back once more to his own plans and ideas. "Well, if you're going to be here anyway, I wonder if I could trouble you with something else."

"What's that?"

"What do you know about harpoons?"

In another part of the city, Captain Diane Reilly of the Fringe City Police Force put a few quarters in a public telephone and dialed. She didn't have to wait long.

"Hello." The voice on the other end was that of the city's district attorney, Charles Faulkner. And she had a direct line to his office, a privilege reserved for a very short list of people.

"It's me," she said.

"Where are you?"

"In a relatively safe street as far from the police station as I could find," Diane replied "Did you hear what happened to Rodriguez the other week?"

"I did," Faulkner said. "And I'm really sorry. He

wasn't just a fine officer. He was a good friend."

"It was Hemming, I'm sure of it," Diane said. "Rodriguez was bringing you some tapes of his phone conversations when he was killed. I've just pieced this thing together."

"So Hemming *killed* him?"

"I checked out Rodriguez's office later. Hemming had it bugged. It all fits."

"I could charge him for that. Wire-tapping without a warrant."

"Perhaps later. We have to be careful 'cause we don't know what lengths Hemming will go to to cover his tracks. If he's prepared to kill once..."

"Right," Faulkner agreed. "Anyway, what did you get on those tapes? I mean if he killed someone for them, they must have been pretty incriminating."

"Two phone conversations. In the first one, a man called up after seeing Lamont's men dump a dead body in a dumpster. Hemming told him to wait in a nearby café and that he'd send a car to pick him up. In the second one, Hemming called the men who dumped the body and told them where to find the witness who'd called it in."

"Merrill Avenue," Faulkner murmured.

"Yeah," Diane agreed. "Still though, I think we've got to keep quiet for a while until we can figure out a way to fix this."

· · ·

During the next few days, particularly attentive citizens of Fringe City might have noticed a few subtle changes to the place as, with a harpoon and coils of wire, Jason Harding was assembling a network of flying foxes that would allow him to move throughout the city while keeping out of sight.

And every afternoon, when he wasn't doing that, he reviewed his CCTV footage. After a while, he made a slight change to his surveillance arrangements by relocating his street camera to a position where he could record people coming and going from the city's main police headquarters. Then after accumulating a couple of days' worth of that footage, he ran it side by side with some of the footage he had taken of the gangsters' base of operations, looking for anyone who appeared at both locations. It took him a while but eventually he found what he was looking for: a clear shot of what Sergeant Hemming looked like.

Not long afterwards, Geoffrey called to tell him that the suit was ready.

With a paper bag full of cash, Sergeant Hemming stepped out of the old run down building and crossed the street to his car. His private car, that was, as he never came near this place in his patrol vehicle. He had to keep *some* distance when he was on duty.

Climbing in, he locked the money in his glove box, turned the key in the ignition and pulled away. He got about a block before he felt the cold sensation of metal on the back of his neck.

"Take the next left," came a voice from behind him.

Every part of his body went rigid. "Who are you?"

"Just do as I say."

Hemming swallowed. He followed the man's first instruction and several others over the course of the next five minutes until he pulled up in a dark street next to what appeared to be a derelict warehouse.

"Put both your hands on the steering wheel," the man behind him ordered.

Sergeant Hemming did so. The person in the back seat reached over his shoulder, found his gun and took it... and in a moment of panic, Hemming tried to snatch it back. With a loud bang, the windscreen shattered and his right hand was a bloody mess of bruised tissue and broken bones. He clutched it in anguish. "Goddamn it!"

Then the back door opened, then the front, and before he could turn around, his assailant grabbed him by the scruff of his neck, hauled him out of the vehicle and slammed him into the pavement.

"What part about keeping both hands on the wheel

didn't you understand?"

Grimacing, Hemming turned to look at the man and flinched. This wasn't an ordinary mob enforcer or private investigator. With his strange Kevlar suit and helmet, this was someone who operated far outside familiar channels.

"Jesus Christ! You're a goddamn psychopath!"

"You're one to talk, Sergeant Hemming," the stranger replied. "Now, get up."

"Make me."

"All right." The figure grabbed Hemming's injured hand and squeezed. Hemming was on his feet a moment later, stumbling as the stranger dragged him into the derelict building he had parked next to—only now Hemming saw it wasn't a warehouse. It was an abandoned wharf building, complete with a lot of really old maritime gear.

There was also a massive chunk missing from part of the floor on the other side and this is where the stranger dragged him.

Hemming swallowed again. It didn't take a genius to work out what was going on.

"You're one sick cop, Sergeant Hemming," the stranger told him. "Someone reports a murder and you, a man who's supposed to be upholding the law and protecting the lives of citizens... You orchestrate his murder and the murder of everyone in the Rio café to cover the criminals he reported. Now, I can leave you tied up in front of the police headquarters where your friends on the force can find you or they can dredge your body out of the harbor. Your choice."

"All right, all right," Hemming stammered. "Just tell me what the hell you want."

"Answers. I have a few questions for you, Sergeant."

A few hours later, a body dangled in front of Fringe City's central police station, stopping a few feet above the ground before dropping the rest of the way with a loose end of wire following.

Several cops who had been chatting by the main entrance walked over to have a look, while a couple of others headed for the roof to see who had dropped it— although all they found for their troubles was a dislodged drainpipe.

While they were gone, the remaining cops rolled the body over to see the face of Sergeant Hemming. A bit battered and bruised but otherwise recognizable. His hand was a mess and he was barely conscious, but he was alive. And around his neck was a loose piece of string with a note attached:

This is the man who orchestrated the Rio Café massacre.

• • •

"I think this was the witness who called Sergeant Hemming. I think he survived when Lamont's men opened fire on the café and he tracked Hemming down."

Sitting across from Charles Faulkner in the D.A's office, Diane Reilly thought the sunlight coming through the window somewhat belied all the excitement at the station the night before. There'd been a lot of talk, and of course some bright spark who wanted to make a few bucks out of the thing had called a reporter. And once one news van had rocked up, it wasn't long before a whole fleet of the damn things were parked outside the station. If dramatic impact had been the intended effect of dumping Hemming unconscious in front of the police headquarters, this guy had got his money's worth.

Faulkner considered the statement for a moment. "Based on?"

"Based on the fact there's no other way he could have known about Hemming's role in what happened," Diane explained. "Now we've got an outside witness statement that correlates with what I've already told you."

"We've also got a witness who's not going to come in," Faulkner pointed out. "He's crossed a pretty major line, if he is who you say he is, and he'd know that."

Diane sighed. "Yeah, I know. But we can't let

Hemming get away with everything he's done."

"It's a pity there was no surveillance footage of the shooting. If there was some evidence at the crime scene that could prove Lamont's men did this, we could approach the case from the other way."

A pensive mood came over Diane. "Actually, there is," she said after a moment. "The officers on the scene who investigated the Rio Café massacre didn't mention it but I was able to access their reports this morning. After last night, it was decided they should be brought out again. Anyway, the killers came in a car as you know, but what wasn't made known the first time around was that they had left tread marks on the road as they pulled up."

"Sudden braking to give them an edge of surprise?"

"I guess so."

"So if you had a suspect vehicle in mind, you could check whether there was a match?"

"That's right and when I listened to the tapes, I took the liberty of writing down the license plate of the car that Lamont's men were driving when they dumped that body. Given the brief time between that and the café shooting, I'd say it'd probably be the same car."

"All right, " Faulkner said. "I'll get you a warrant to check that out. Take a good-sized unit with you however. That way if there are any crooked cops among the group, there will hopefully be enough honest ones to cover your back. And I think we can still use this mystery witness as well. Now, I can't really use his word as proof but I think I can use it as sufficient cause to issue a second warrant, to look at transactions in Hemming's bank account. If Lamont's men have made any payments either directly or through subsidiaries, then I think we can nail him."

"But we'll never get him for Rodriguez's murder," Diane told him.

Faulkner smiled. "Oh, I don't know about that. You see, I'm planning to get you *one more* warrant as well, to search Hemming's office for illegal recording equipment. If I'm right, we might get a tape of that conversation you had with Rodriguez about Hemming's role in the Rio Café shooting. Now, we might not get a lot of solid evidence but I think I can still prepare a pretty strong case against this man. I'm absolutely sure he'll never work as a police officer again. I'm also pretty certain I can put him in jail and I think I can put him away for a while."

When Jason watched the news that those responsible for the Rio Café massacre had been arrested, it was with mixed feelings. Faulkner made a public promise they would be put on trial as quickly as possible, guaranteeing they would remain behind bars for the rest of their lives. The reporter then discussed Hemming and how subsequent investigations revealed he'd played a major part in the incident. How allegedly someone had called him about a murder and how Hemming told the men who were associated with it where he was so they could silence him, leading to the massacre. The reporter then stated it was believed that Hemming had murdered another police officer who knew about the conspiracy while he was attempting to bring evidence to the D.A. Something that Jason hadn't known about.

"Faulkner expects Hemming will receive a similar sentence to that of the men responsible for the café shooting," the reporter continued. *"However, there are still several matters that remain unresolved. Firstly, police do not yet know who the original murder victim was and as yet, the body has not been found. Secondly, while Hemming and these other men were allegedly linked to Martin Lamont, the prominent businessman's involvement is unclear. And finally, nobody knows who it was who brought Hemming in to the authorities and Hemming has remained strangely silent on the matter. Those who were on the scene when he was dumped in front of the police headquarters say that — and I quote — whoever he was, he gave him a hell of a good scare."*

Jason smiled at the last remark and turned the TV off. He turned to Angie. "Well, there you go."

She shook her head. "That's incredible. How did you pull it all off?"

"I just had to follow the crumbs on the trail," Jason said. "The license plate of that car, the name of the officer I talked to, that address I found through the motor vehicle registration department... a bit of amateur detective work. Although, there was a lot of luck involved too. I would have had a hell of time trying to do any of it without Geoffrey's help for starters. Also, it seems there are some good people working in the police force too, not to mention the D.A."

"Yeah, Faulkner's a good guy," Angie agreed. "But anyway, what now? You've put those bastards away. Was that what you were after?"

Jason frowned. "I'm not sure. This city's still falling apart. When visiting LA cops say they'd never want to work here, when the national guard's called in every second week and when our state governor writes us off as beyond salvage, then we've got a real problem. And right now, I've been given the chance to do something about it."

"What?" Angie scoffed. "Fix this whole city? Right now, I'd say I agree with the governor."

"I didn't say I'd fix the whole thing overnight," Jason said. "But I think I can make some inroads and get the ball rolling. And I'm not finished with this

Hemming thing either. Hemming and those men who shot up the café are small fries. There are some really sick bastards behind all this and if we don't do something about them, we'll just get a whole lot of other Hemmings later on down the road. But I've got some more bread crumbs that might help me find them."

"What exactly did Hemming give you?"

"I asked him who the man Lamont's guys dumped in that alley was," Jason explained, "and he said he was from the mayor's office. One of his assistants or something. Anyway, he had apparently taken issue with something the mayor was doing and was going to take it to the press. So the mayor asked Lamont to sort him out."

Angie shook her head. "Reggie Burges and Lamont, working together. Did Hemming know what this guy had found out?"

"No," Jason answered. "Like I said, Hemming's pretty far down the ladder and if this secret's as sensitive as it sounds then I'd say that only a few people at the top know about it."

"So what are you going to do?"

The first thing was surviving the week. When Friday night came around and he and Angie had a chance to relax again, Jason was almost exhausted.

"Sarah said you really went off at those ninth graders today," Angie told him.

Jason shrugged. "They had it coming."

Angie looked concerned. "She thought you sounded a little more stressed out than usual. Are you sure you're all right?"

"Yeah." Jason had another mouthful of tuna casserole. "I guess I'm a bit preoccupied."

"That's understandable," Angie replied. "However, I think you really ought to stay in tonight and get some rest. I know you want to get straight back into your evening job but the fact is you need your day job to pay the bills and you need time to rest at night. Maybe you'll get better at managing this double life in the future but since you're just starting out, why don't you just ease into it gently for now?"

Jason nodded. Angie was right again, as always. "Good idea. I've got to talk to Geoffrey again before I do anything else anyway."

"More toys?"

Jason smiled. "Something like that."

"Fair enough." It was clear Angie wasn't really comfortable with Jason's new vigilante gig but she didn't say anything else about it.

"By the way," she said, changing the topic. "Thanks for getting everyone out of that meeting on

Wednesday. We all appreciate it."

"Oh. Your co-workers knew about that?"

"Yeah, they know the routine. Every time Gary schedules one of those staff detention sessions, you remove all the notices and put them back in his drawer so he thinks he's forgotten to send them out. Much appreciated."

"Well, I'm glad everyone thinks so."

Angie gave him a smile. "There you go. You've got *some* people on your side."

"Still though," Jason said, "hopefully I'm a little more subtle when it comes to my evening job."

On Saturday morning, he met Geoffrey for coffee.

"You're insane," Geoffrey said, "you know that?"

Jason gave him a funny look. "What did you think I was going to do with all that equipment you gave me?"

"I don't know…" Geoffrey shrugged. "Trail a few people. Take some photos. You're insane."

"I got results though," Jason pointed out.

"Hey, I'm not arguing. But I hope you're careful out there."

"I am, believe me. But I've got to do something about the mess this place is in."

Geoffrey shrugged again. "I'm not going to stop

you. Angie might but you've got my full support."

"Yeah, I guess this can't be easy for her," Jason admitted. "But she's taking it fairly well, all things considered."

"She's not hauling you off to make an appointment with a shrink then?"

"No, not yet. Although she could change her mind."

"Yeah."

"By the way, I have another favor to ask."

"What is it?"

"I need something I can use to tag and track a car."

"Why? Your stint with the motor vehicle registration department worked last time."

"I was lucky last time. I don't want to push my luck too far."

"Fair enough. Well, I think I can rig something up."

"Knew I could count on you."

"Anything else you want?"

"Yeah, I've got a few items actually. They're not urgent but I think they'd make life easier." Jason pulled out a piece of paper. "Here, I drew up a wish list."

Geoffrey looked it over and gave Jason a smile. "I'll see what I can do."

THE BLACK BARON

FOR CAPTAIN DIANE REILLY, SEEING THE MAN who had murdered Rodriguez put away had certainly lifted her morale but the reprieve had been all too brief.

She looked at the chaos around her. Numerous residents of the neighborhood were wandering outside in confusion. Some were sharing their woes with other police officers. Some were sharing them with the media. All of them were bewildered.

She turned to a lieutenant who had arrived at the scene twenty minutes before her. "So what's the story? Every electrical appliance in this neighborhood just shorted out or fried up at the same time?"

"Sounds like it."

Diane shook her head. "What a nightmare. All right, I want the electrical company to assess the area and see if there are any dangers. You know, loose live wires… that sort of thing. And then I want them to cut the power until the damage can be repaired."

"That could take a while."

"You're right about that. Well, I suppose I'd better

get in touch with the mayor's office and see about arranging some temporary public shelter."

"Good luck getting any help from the mayor."

Diane sighed. "Yeah. Tell me about it."

When night fell over the city, Jason Harding took to the streets again. This time to move his CCTV surveillance equipment to a rooftop looking across a large square towards Grand Central, the huge eyesore in the middle of Fringe City where the mayor had both his private office and a penthouse suite. Positioned behind the camera and operating it manually, Jason zoomed in on the office as this was what interested him the most. Once he was satisfied that he had the whole room in frame and that the resolution of the image was clear, he headed home, where Angie was watching the evening news after a late dinner.

"Police all along the eastern seaboard are staging a massive man hunt for Alex Grigorie, wanted for his attempt to destroy a major New York subway station last night. Police claim that if the bombs Grigorie had put in place had not been disarmed, thousands of people could have been killed.

"Although Grigorie's whereabouts are currently not known ..."

Just then, Jason came through the door.

"You're back early," Angie remarked. "I thought you might have been having an all-nighter."

Jason smiled. "No, I was just re-positioning the camera."

"So what's your plan now?"

"Well…" Jason dropped a big bag on the floor and opened it up. Inside, the gear that Geoffrey had made for him was visible, along with some other bits and pieces. Among them were two folders, which he pulled out and put on the table. However, he ignored them for a moment and pointed to the TV that was playing his remote CCTV footage.

"I'm looking for someone who I can shake down for information," he said. "I'm not planning to confront Burges or Lamont just yet, as I want them to know about me first. You know, build up a healthy dose of fear in them and have them looking over their shoulders."

Angie picked up the folders. The name Reggie Burges was written on the front of one and Martin Lamont was written on the other. "So I see. What's all this?"

"I went to the public library after I met Geoffrey this morning and I found everything I could on those two characters. I found newspaper articles and public records, including a few that Faulkner released. I'm doing my homework."

"Moving up from the little fish to the big fish?"

"Something like that. Anyway, I'm planning to start my investigation with someone fairly small. One of Burges' lackeys, I think. I'm sure he's got a few who could help me. So I'm watching his office for the time being to see if I can find someone who looks like he can tell me what I want to know."

Angie curled her lip as she realized how nuts it all was. "My god, your parents would freak if they knew what you were doing."

"Probably. But they probably freak every time they see the news from Fringe City too."

"I suppose," Angie conceded. "I imagine things are a little quieter in San Francisco."

"You're not freaking out though, are you?"

Angie took a breath as she thought about it. "Well, I'm trying not to."

Then something on the television grabbed both of their attention. Jason got the remote and turned the volume up.

"- some kind of electronic pulse basically overrode the current in every electrical device in the vicinity. All over the neighborhood, we're hearing the same reports. Everything's shorted out. Lights, refrigerators, hot water systems, microwave ovens... they've all fried their circuits."

· · ·

The next week was relatively painless for Jason. At least by the standards one set when working at a public school. With frustration, irritation and exhaustion all part of the daily grind, there was a limit on how painless the school week could be but there were no attempted assaults or vicious brawls so by public school standards, it counted as a good week.

Each day, after coming home from work, Jason also checked his CCTV footage of the mayor's office and by Tuesday night, he had identified his man.

On Wednesday night, he re-positioned his surveillance camera in order to record cars leaving the parking lot under Grand Central. Then on Thursday night, he had a look at the footage he had recorded so far and found what he wanted without too much difficulty. The man he wanted left the parking lot in a black sedan around eight p.m. the night before, not long after he had re-positioned his camera.

On Friday morning, he got up a little earlier to check the previous night's footage and saw that the man once again had left at eight. Luck was with him. The man was a creature of habit.

That night, as the man pulled out of Grand Central, he nearly hit Jason. He blasted his horn in annoyance at the stranger who had walked across the exit ramp without bothering to look first.

Jason made an apologetic gesture, feigning embarrassment, and stepped out of the way. As the car went past him—far more slowly than it had originally been travelling—Jason slapped a magnetic device on the trunk. Then as the car pulled into the traffic on the main road and disappeared, Jason pulled another device out of his pocket, a device about as small as a cell phone with a tracking display. It was working beautifully.

Shortly afterwards, he came through the door to his apartment, his disappointment evident in his slumped shoulders and his expression of frustration.

"You're home early," Angie remarked. "What's wrong?"

"I couldn't find any place to grab the guy," Jason replied. "He went straight home to his expensive apartment complex where there are security cameras in the underground garage and..." He sat down on the lounge and sighed. "I'll try again tomorrow night."

"Well," Angie said, "you had a bit of beginner's luck when you were starting out so a little setback's not a bad thing. Think of it as a reality check. If this were easy, wouldn't everyone be doing it?"

"True," Jason agreed. "But it should get easier once

I'm better equipped."

"I hope you're not pushing Geoffrey too hard. You realize that it's the Faculty of Science that pays his wages, not you."

"Yeah, but he likes the challenge. And anyway, if he's offering..." Jason pulled something out of his pocket and put it on the table.

Angie stared at it. "Is that the tracking display?"

"Yeah, although I doubt you'll get much of a demonstration at the moment. The target vehicle's just sitting in a garage."

"The 'target vehicle'? You've gone all military on me. Wait..."

"What?"

"It's moving."

A little later, the man from the mayor's office stumbled out the back door of a fancy licensed restaurant and lurched over to his car. Fumbling around with his keys, he tried to fit them in the door lock.

"I hope you're not thinking of driving like that," came a voice from behind.

The man whirled around. "Who's there?"

His answer came in the form of a quick shove to the ground. Groaning, he had little time to react before he was gagged and his hands were bound.

"Allow me," his assailant said. The man got only a brief glimpse of the stranger as he was manhandled into the trunk. Flashes of black synthetic material with armored plating.

The first thing the man saw when the blindfold came off was a rather long drop.

"The car park at the restaurant was a little public," his assailant told him. "This will be better suited to our purposes."

"What purposes?" the man stammered. "Throwing me off a roof?"

"Why would I drag you all the way up here just to throw you off?" the stranger countered. "I just want to talk."

"Well, goddamn it, I'll talk! Just tell me what you want to know!"

"Your boss and Lamont had someone from your office murdered because they were going to leak something to the press. You're going to tell me what that was."

"I wasn't in on all of it but Burges and Lamont were working under the table with some nut job called the Black Baron. Clearly a dumb pseudonym but don't ask me what his real name is. Anyway, he's some weapons designer who approached Burges and

Lamont and made a deal with them. They'd finance his research and give him the means to manufacture his weapons. And in exchange, he'd provide Lamont's organization with a steady supply of high-tech arms." The man was babbling now. "This guy's a nut. That building that was blown up a few weeks ago and this electronic pulse thing in the news... they've got his prints all over 'em."

"So why is your boss letting him do it?"

The man laughed. "Wha—? No one's letting him do anything. That's the problem. The guy's gone rogue. He's moved off with all our manufacturing equipment, along with the millions that were given to him, and he's relocated in another part of town. I can tell you that Lamont was pretty damn pissed at Burges about the whole thing since it was Burges' idea to do business with him in the first place. But anyway, now they're out of pocket with nothing to show for it and there's this psycho with a whole lot of high tech weaponry running around out there like a ticking time-bomb. And it was Burges and Lamont who gave him everything he needed to set up shop! Can you imagine the kind of press the mayor's office would be getting if that leaked out? It's no wonder Burges had that guy shot."

The stranger grabbed him by the scruff of his neck. "You goddamn idiots! How long has this guy been rogue now?"

"Uh…" the man stammered. "A couple of months?"

"And you have no idea where he's relocated? A weapons manufacturing plant is not a florist."

"No one's looked for him because there's too scared. The guy's got a personal stockpile of military grade weapons. But we know how he moved it though."

"Go on."

"He's got half the S.W.A.T. units in the city working for him. They moved his gear and if the rumors our guys in the police are hearing are right, they're guarding it as well."

Jason released him from his grip. He had gotten everything he wanted out of the guy and then some. And he'd found out a whole lot of things he'd been happier not knowing. Shelving the train of thought, he untied the man, shoved him onto the roof and threw him his car keys. "All right. Your car's on the street and there's a fire escape on your right. And between you and me, I would seriously consider changing employers."

He then strode to the other side of the building and leapt into the night.

Scrambling to his feet, the mayor's assistant ran over to the ledge in disbelief. Leaning over the side, he saw no trace of his assailant. Just the side of the building and the street below. He shook his head and headed for the fire escape.

About a minute after he was gone, Jason pushed himself out from under a window sill two floors down. Using a wire attached to his waist, he pulled himself back up to the rooftop, feeling rather pleased with his deception. It would give that lackey something to think about.

He walked to the other side of the roof and watched as the man drove away. Once he was out of sight, he pulled out a bag from behind an air conditioning vent, got out of his armored gear and packed it away with his harpoon lines. All in all, it had been a very interesting evening.

The next day, while she was getting some forms from the main office, Diane Reilly was approached by a lieutenant.

"Captain, I was wondering if I could speak with you in private for a few moments."

"Sure," she replied. "Come into my office and we'll talk there. So, what's up?" she asked as she closed the door behind her.

"Commissioner Levings has been trying to keep this under wraps," the man told her, "But we've received an anonymous tip that members of our S.W.A.T. units are moonlighting for some crazy called the Black

Baron."

"Never heard of him."

"I hadn't either until today. But our source believed this guy was responsible for blowing up that apartment block a few weeks ago as well as the electronic pulse attack the other day."

"We don't know it was an attack."

"No, but it was damn peculiar."

"True."

"Also, we've talked to some of the guys in the S.W.A.T. units who have clean records and they said they've heard the name thrown around a bit as well... all in a hush-hush kind of way."

"I wonder if this is the same guy..."

"Sorry?"

"Well, this is the second time in a fairly short space of time that an ordinary citizen has supplied us with pretty substantial information like this. Could be the same guy."

The lieutenant shrugged. "Could be."

"All right," Diane said. "I'll start talking to our S.W.A.T. guys and see what I can find out."

David Merlon, personal assistant to the mayor of Fringe City, was not a happy man and he let his employer know it the first chance he got. Sitting in

Mayor Reggie Burges' office, he sipped some scotch to calm his nerves.

As he sat behind his desk, Burges didn't look much happier. "So you've had a run in with the new player in town? What did he want?"

"He wanted to know why you got Lamont to kill Marshall."

"And what did you tell him?"

Merlon sculled the remaining scotch in his glass and wiped his mouth with a shirt cuff. "I told him Marshall was going public with the fact you supplied funding and equipment to the Black Baron before he went rogue."

"Why the hell did you tell him that? Marshall didn't *know* about the Black Baron."

"Well, I had to tell him something!" Merlon shot back. "The guy was going to throw me off a goddamn roof! Anyway, I'd figured that was better than telling him you were harboring Alex Grigorie."

Burges thought this over, clasping his hands together to ease out the tension. "Yeah, all right. Actually, this might turn out nicely. Let this nut go after the Black Baron and whatever the outcome, it'll be a win for us. If he gets the Black Baron, that's one potential embarrassment we don't have to worry about. And if the Black Baron gets him… Yeah, you did all right."

"Glad to hear it," Merlon replied. "Now, are you going to tell Lamont about Grigorie at some stage? I mean, after all, the operation requires both of them."

"I'll tell him when the time's right," Burges replied. "Right now, he's panicking over the fact that the Black Baron's gone rogue after we gave him all that gear and money. I don't know but I think paranoia must be a common affliction with mob bosses. Anyway, if I told him I was harboring a guy wanted all over the country, he'd lose it completely. Let's just wait until this nonsense with the Black Baron blows over. We've still got some time. Vincent's boys are only just setting up."

Merlon shook his head. "I don't know. If Lamont finds out you've turned a blind eye to these guys making themselves at home in his city…"

"First of all, despite what he thinks, it's not his city," Burges corrected him. "It's my city. Second, he's not going to find out. I can pretend I discovered them any time I want to. Relax, David. Everything's going to work out fine."

"Well?" Geoffrey asked as he and Jason met for drinks after work mid-week. "What is it you need this time?"

"I was wondering," Jason asked, "if you might be able to get a few more of those magnetic tracking devices for me."

"I suppose I could. How many do you need?"

Once Jason had acquired the additional devices, he made a few trips to the central police headquarters and planted them on the roofs of some S.W.A.T. vans.

In the meantime, Captain Diane Reilly had been doing her own investigating, talking to members of various S.W.A.T. units to get her own information about what was going on. After nearly a week of this, she was called into the commissioner's office for a little chat. It was 6.00 p.m. on Saturday and she had a big night ahead.

Commissioner Levings frowned as they sat down opposite each other—she in the small chair in front of his desk, he in the considerably raised chair behind it. "Captain, I hear you've been shaking down our S.W.A.T. boys over some tenuous connection to this 'Black Baron' character. A man so notorious, I've never even heard of him. I'm ordering this to stop."

"With respect, Commissioner," Diane replied, "those officers I've spoken to who are playing straight say they've heard some pretty worrying rumors."

"Rumors!" Levings scoffed. "Rumors are worthless. And as for these guys 'playing straight', if they were really playing straight, they wouldn't be selling out their fellow officers. We stick together here, Captain

Reilly. We don't snitch on our friends for making a little money on the side. Hell, you know the pay's not that great."

"That's no excuse for getting in bed with the mob."

"That's enough of that, Captain," Levings told her, raising his voice. "You're out of line. You've already turned one of my cops over to that son of a bitch Faulkner. You're not turning over any more. Breaks my heart knowing one of my boys is rotting in prison when he should be—"

Diane rose to her feet. "Don't you dare defend Hemming, Commissioner, or I'll start checking your record."

"Watch yourself, Captain. And leave our S.W.A.T. units alone."

"Fine," Diane replied, getting to her feet. "Good night, Commissioner."

At 7.00 p.m., the following news bulletin was aired:

"The man hunt for Alex Grigorie, who attempted to bomb a New York subway station, continues without any end in sight. It is believed that Grigorie has already crossed several state lines, all the while eluding capture. Should any member of the public have information on the whereabouts of this man, they are urged to come forward.

"In other news, it appears that members of our own

Special Weapons and Tactical police division here in Fringe City may be involved with another urban terrorist, a weapons manufacturer hiding in our city who calls himself the Black Baron.

"Little is known about this man but it is alleged that during the past month or so, he has been carrying out weapons tests on local neighborhoods. Some say that he destroyed the Sundown Apartment Building last month and that another weapon of his caused that electrical disruption that destroyed every electrical device in West Henley, leaving hundreds of residents without lighting and refrigeration and in some cases, injuries from fire incidents.

"If this is indeed the case, then Fringe City must be wary. And questions are being asked. Who is this man? Where is he manufacturing and stockpiling his weapons? How large is his operation? And finally, if he is indeed testing weapons and expanding his operation, what is he planning?

"These are the questions that Fringe City's police are grappling with and hopefully, they will be answered before it is too late. In the meantime, anyone who knows anything that may help police with their investigations are being urged to come forward. For Fringe City Central, this is Mariane O'Hara."

"Meanwhile," a male reporter with a phony TV grin said, taking over, *"those who like to party in Fringe City are getting ready for the mayor's annual charity masquerade. As in previous years, all proceeds will go*

toward..."

"Well, it's out there now," Jason told Angie, pulling out a map of the city and laying it out on the kitchen table. "And I think I've got the answers to a few of those questions."

"Your work tracking all those S.W.A.T. vans has paid off?"

"I'd have to check to be sure," Jason told her, pointing out a particular block. "But a lot of S.W.A.T. vans have been going here over the past few days. I think they're transporting stuff back and forth."

"I don't like the idea of you checking out a possible weapons manufacturing plant," Angie told him. "This isn't like putting the scare in the mayor's man or Sergeant Hemming. Also, so far, you haven't had to test whether your Kevlar gear will stand up to a gunshot and I think we'd both be happier if things stayed that way."

"I'll be careful," Jason said, picking up his bag. "But I'm worried. I don't know what this guy is up to and I don't know how much time we have before we find out."

"Jason," Angie called after him as he turned to leave.

"Yes?"

"I just wanted to say…" she trailed off as she saw a red glow around the edges of the front door. "Get down!"

They both hit the floor as the door half splintered and went flying off its hinges. A wall of flame tore through the apartment, igniting wooden surfaces and blowing up several electrical appliances.

A silhouette appeared against the flames and Jason looked up to see an elegant looking figure in black drab and a flowing trench coat.

"I believe you've been looking for me," he announced as he circled Jason. "So I thought I'd make things easier for you. I take it you're the one who's been shaking down bent cops and officials and tagging my S.W.A.T. vans."

Jason didn't reply.

"I have to say, you've done a commendable job," the man continued. "However, I've worked hard getting everything ready for tonight and I can't have you spoiling the surprise."

Walking past Jason now, he picked up the map from the burning table and looked it over. "Yes, quite commendable. You found the place." He scrunched it up and threw it into one of the many fires that were now burning in the room and, presumably, the rest of the building.

"So you're the Black Baron," Jason muttered.

In reply, the man performed a sweeping bow and smiled. "At your service."

"How did you find me? If you don't mind me asking."

"Actually," the Black Baron said, pulling out one of Jason's tracking devices from his pocket, "you led me here. I noticed on my surveillance cameras that a lot of my S.W.A.T. vans were coming in with these little devices on their roofs—" He laughed in almost boyish delight as he inspected the item in his hand. "Ingenious devices, aren't they? Well, I analyzed the signals they were transmitting and traced them back to you. You see, a weapons designer, if they're any good, is first and foremost a scientist." He threw the tracking device to Jason. "You'd be better off using this on a mob boss." With the performance over, he nodded to Jason in a gesture of parting. "Now, if you'll excuse me, I must get ready for the ball."

"The ball?"

"The mayor's charity masquerade," the Black Baron replied, as if surprised Jason had to ask. "Everyone who's anyone is going to be there. It would be wrong of someone of my social standing not to attend. However, I personally have to as when the clock strikes nine, I must unveil the big surprise. It's a pity you won't be able to come."

Jason didn't have any time to react. One moment his

assailant was simply standing there and the next, he struck him across the head with a baton he'd whipped out from his trench coat.

"You're so worried about all the bent cops in this city," the Black Baron said to the now unconscious man at his feet. "Well, after tonight, there won't be any."

He looked at Angie, lying trapped under a fallen cupboard half in flames, and tapped his brow. "Ma'am."

In his office in Grand Central, Reggie Burges was getting ready for the aforementioned ball when his assistant came in. "Mr. Mayor, we've got a concerned citizen outside who wants to talk to you about the Black Baron."

"Oh god," Burges groaned. "Fine. Send Lamont in."

The mob boss must have been standing by the door because he didn't wait for Merlon to relay the message. "Reggie," he said, striding into the room, "the public seems to know a lot about our rogue weapons manufacturer. I don't think I like it."

"I don't much like it either," Burges told him. "But there's nothing out there that can pin him on us, so don't worry about it."

"What if the cops get him and he squeals? Tells them we gave him all the money and gear he needed to get his operation going so he could supply me with high-tech guns to guard your interests? This could bring the whole house crashing down. We don't have enough cops on the payrolls to cover up this. And now this son of a bitch is buying his own guys off the cops using our money."

"Look, Lamont," Burges replied, fixing the mob boss with a glare. "I didn't force you to go along with this. You wanted those guns for your guys too and if you didn't, then you should've said no."

"Save it, Burges," Lamont cut him off. "I didn't come here to argue about who's to blame. I want to discuss whether we should reconsider our decision not to go after this guy."

"The decision was the right one, trust me. We don't want to mess with him and we don't have to. If I'm right, he wouldn't squeal on us. He'd go off to prison telling everyone how he did all by himself. He's not like us. He's a showman. And showmen are idiots."

Lamont sat down, considering it. And, Burges couldn't helping noticing, helping himself to the scotch on his desk. "Maybe. Although I'm not just worried about him squealing on us. I don't know what this guy's planning to do but if it's big enough, it might affect everyone. Including us."

"Maybe, but I can't see what difference worrying about it will make," Burges told him. "Now, do you mind? I've got to get ready for the big charity masquerade. It's on in less than an hour."

"Right," Lamont muttered. He finished the glass he'd poured for himself and made his way out. "And all proceeds will, as usual, go to the Burges Retirement Fund."

"Hey, that's a very important cause," Burges told him as he adjusted his tie.

As burning fragments of the roof collapsed and parts of the floor began to give in, Angie was terrified. Realizing how little time she and Jason had to get out of the apartment, she tried to dislodge the burning cupboard that had her pinned up to the waist but it was too heavy. Trying not to panic, she thought over her options but unless the fire department was right around the corner, there didn't seem to be many.

She grabbed at the floor, trying to pull herself toward Jason. "Jason," she murmured. "Jason... you've got to wake up."

From the slight movement of his chest, he was still breathing but he was definitely out of it—and Angie saw the Black Baron had left a nasty gash on his forehead when he'd struck him with that baton.

With tears in her eyes, she tried to stretch out to Jason again when the floor collapsed at one end of the room, dragging her and several other miscellaneous things from around the apartment back with it. Angie screamed, clutching at anything she could, but somewhere in the back of her mind she realized she was no longer pinned down by the fallen cupboard. Summoning reserves of determination she hadn't realized she had, she kicked it away into a gaping hole where half the floor had been and clambered to her feet. She was free.

While every second counted, for a moment all she could think to do was hug Jason as their home collapsed around them. Briefly, she wondered if there were any point in trying to get out now. Now that the entrance to the apartment had been disintegrated in the blaze, she saw the corridor outside was engulfed in flames and choking smoke as well. The entire floor of the building was burning.

Then Angie's gaze fell on Jason's bag, the one where he kept all the gear Geoffrey had made him. Only minutes ago, he'd been getting ready to go out the door with it and it was now lying open a foot away from her. She looked over harpoon lines and bits of armor and formed a plan.

She dragged Jason and the bag to the window, got out one of the harpoon lines and tied one end around his waist and looped it around his shoulders for good measure. That done, she leant out the window and looped the the line around a metal protrusion a little bit above her—some kind of drainpipe fitting—and tied the other end around her own waist.

With her makeshift pulley system in place, she hoisted Jason up and carefully lowered him out of the window. However, as cautious as she was, he still got away from her and for a few terrifying moments, she struggled with the wire to slow his descent as well as trying to keep her own footing.

Once she had lowered Jason to the street and he was actually on it—not hovering half a foot above it—she unwound the wire from her waist and threw it over the protrusion and onto the street too. She then set up another pulley system with a second wire in order to lower herself down, mindful of the flames closing in. If she had a minute left to get out before she was overcome by smoke inhalation, she'd be lucky. However, despite the urgency and the oppressive heat, she had to remain calm. A mistake made in panic from three flights up would be fatal.

She wrapped the second wire around her waist in methodical fashion and secured it, then looped it over the same protrusion she had used for the first pulley system. She then felt around in Jason's bag and pulled out his gloves. After putting them on, she grabbed the wire and gave it a solid pull to check the grip. It was firm. Then she slung Jason's bag over her shoulders and abseiled down, feeding the wire through her hands with the gloves protecting her palms. When her feet were firmly on the ground, she pulled the wire free from the protrusion and sighed. The worst was over.

Next, she had to get herself and Jason a safe distance from the building as the fire had now spread to the floors above and below their apartment. Lifting Jason onto his bag to cushion him, Angie glanced back at the building just in time to see the protrusion she'd used for her makeshift pulley system break off and fall to the street. Somewhere above, glass shattered and flames were now pouring out of several windows. It was time to now put a bit of distance between themselves and what was left of the building.

Angie dragged Jason and his bag across the asphalt until she reached the stairs of an apartment block a bit farther down and across the street. She slumped on the bottom step, resting against Jason's bag, and caught her breath. Across the street, their five storey apartment building began to crumble. Angie saw some of their neighbors in the street. She hoped the rest of them had gotten out in time.

Beside her, Jason coughed and spluttered.

"Jason!" Angie exclaimed, cradling him to see if he was awake. "Are you all right?"

He blinked at her, his head still swimming from his concussion. "Angie?"

"Yeah," she smiled. "It's me."

"How did you—?"

She hugged him. "Later, later. I'm just glad you're all right."

"What about you?" Jason asked, trying to sit up and sliding back down again. "Are you hurt?"

"I was trapped under a cupboard for a while there. But I'm all right. Just a bit sore."

The sound of sirens grew louder in the distance and many of their neighbors were now gathered in the street. There was also a growing crowd of onlookers and people trying to help out.

"Come on," Jason said, taking Angie's hand and staggering to his feet. "We weren't here."

Angie frowned. "What are you talking about?"

"There'll be too many questions," Jason replied. "Awkward ones. We don't have time."

"Time?" Angie exclaimed as she realized what he was thinking. "No, no. Jason! You can't seriously be going after the Black Baron. You were unconscious a minute ago."

"Well, I'm not now."

"And we just lost our home, in case you didn't notice."

Jason sighed. "But you heard what the Black Baron said. He's going to unveil a big surprise at nine o'clock. And I doubt it's going to be a box of chocolates. We'll have to deal with our home, the insurance claims and all that. I know that and I'm not looking forward to it. But we've got to deal with this first. Come on. We can get changed at Geoff's place."

"All right," Angie told him, giving in. She frowned as another thought struck her. "Oh, there was something else... before I forget. After he knocked you out, the Black Baron mentioned all those bent cops you were concerned about. And he said that after tonight, there weren't going to be any."

At 8.15 p.m., an officer answered an emergency call at the police headquarters. "Police."

"I need to talk to the officer in charge of the Black Baron investigation right away," came the voice on the other end of the line. "Tell him it's urgent."

"That would be her," the man replied. "Captain Reilly. Hold on."

He put the line on hold and called Diane at her office. "Captain Reilly, I've got someone on the line who wants to talk to you about the Black Baron case. He says it's urgent."

"Put him through," Diane replied. She waited while the call was transferred. "This is Captain Reilly. You wanted to speak to me?"

"Whatever the Black Baron's got in mind, it's

happening tonight. I had a run in with him earlier this evening."

"You did, did you?"

"You're going to have to trust me. I was right about those S.W.A.T. teams working with him, wasn't I?"

"So it's you," Diane said. "All right. What do you know?"

"The Black Baron says he's going to the mayor's charity masquerade and he's going to unveil a big surprise at nine o 'clock. He then mentioned all the bent cops in the city and he said that when tonight was over, there wouldn't be any. You can read that any way you like but I think he's planning to blow up your headquarters."

"What? Why would he want to do that?"

"I don't know. Maybe so you guys can't stop him from doing something else. He's also got that electronic pulse weapon or whatever it is. And I can think of one thing he might use *that* for."

"Disabling security systems," Diane replied. "Some kind of heist."

"And he's got a whole lot of S.W.A.T. teams ready to assist him."

"And a whole lot of armored vans," Diane said, following his logic. "He's going to steal a stack of money, while some of our S.W.A.T. boys are going to help him transport it."

"You should get a bomb squad to go over the police headquarters and find out where all your S.W.A.T. teams are. And if you find a stack of S.W.A.T. vans near a major bank, then you've got trouble."

"I understand," Diane replied. "I don't know you who are but thank you for all your help. And before you go, what does the Black Baron look like?"

"I didn't get a good look at him. But black hair, a goatee, black clothes, black trench coat. The works. Dressed up like he's cosplaying someone. But I assume if he's going to that ball, he'll be wearing a mask."

With that, the caller hung up.

Moments later, a youngish officer opened the door. "Captain Reilly? We traced the call to a payphone. We can have a squad car there in three or four minutes."

"Don't bother," Diane told him. "We've got more important things to worry about."

"If you say so."

As the officer left, Diane called the bomb squad. "It's Captain Reilly here. We have reason to believe there may be explosives somewhere in the station."

"Did you receive a threat?"

"Not exactly. More of a tip. But I want you and your men to search the premises right away."

"I'm on it."

"Thanks. I'll keep regular contact on the radio. And be careful. From what we've gathered, it's likely there'd be a timer on these things. And my guess is that if they're there, they'll go off by nine, if not earlier." She hung up and made another call, this time to get some helicopters in the air to search for any S.W.A.T. vans parked outside major banks. This was a little more difficult as any time the police helicopters went up, there was always an extra load of paperwork for someone. In the end, she had to persuade the man on the other end of the line that she'd assume all the responsibility if it turned out they got the helicopters in the air for nothing.

Then she left the office and got a squad together of her own, eight other officers in all.

"Where are we going?" one of them asked.

"We're going to a ball," Diane replied, checking her watch. "And we've got about thirty-five minutes to stop all hell from breaking loose."

At 8.40 p.m., Jason arrived at the mayor's charity masquerade. Not wanting to part with the two hundred dollars he needed for a ticket—and wanting even less to line the mayor's pockets with the money— he made his own way in. It wasn't difficult.

The venue was a luxurious hotel built along Spanish architectural lines with large bricks and pillars, all in an elegant white, with ivy leaves cascading over the sides of its balconies. The building was five storeys and the masquerade was of course being held in the magnificent hall on the top floor. Attendants were manning the doors, checking the tickets of everyone who entered, but only the doors inside.

After scoping the place, Jason shot a harpoon hook onto the balcony. He listened a few moments for any indication that someone may have noticed it but there was nothing. And given the fact that the hook was probably nicely concealed by the ivy, it wasn't surprising. Then it was just a simple matter of hauling himself up by using the harpoon line and packing it somewhere out of sight.

Angie in the meantime, being a reasonably attractive woman, had a much easier time getting in without paying.

"Excuse me," she said to a man at the door, while looking frantically in her purse. "I wonder if you could help me." She feigned embarrassment, fumbling among her contents. "I just ducked out to use the phone in the lobby downstairs. It was a little too loud inside."

The man smiled in understanding.

"Anyway, I seem to have misplaced my ticket," Angie continued explaining. "Is there any way perhaps—"

"Don't worry about it," the man told her, stepping aside and waving her through. "It happens."

"Oh, thank you," Angie told him, lifting the hem of her dress and making her way in. "Sorry about that."

"Not at all," the man replied with a polite nod of his head. "Enjoy your evening."

"You look stunning," Jason remarked when they met. And she did. All things considered, the two of them had scrubbed up very well, but Angie really looked great—and the mask she'd chosen complimented her well.

"You said before," she reminded him, with a little smile to conceal her nervousness. "And you look... well, as long as no one looks too closely at you, you'll be all right."

Jason on the other hand was wearing his armored gear, along with his helmet, underneath a cheap tuxedo that was several sizes larger than his own in order to accommodate the extra bulk. And to hide the helmet, he had donned a ridiculous turban with more feathers than a peacock.

Clasping Angie's hands, he began to sway to the slow number that was being played. If it weren't for the Black Baron's threat, he could have almost succumbed to the mood that had taken many other couples in the room…

They turned in an apparent lover's waltz, both of them eyeing the sea of masks around them, looking for any sign of the man who had just assaulted them and burned their home to ashes.

As they surveyed the room, Jason brushed past an attractive dark skinned woman in a glittering silver mask with neat shoulder length hair. He had no way of recognizing her as they had never actually met, but he had spoken to her on the phone just a half-hour before.

Oblivious to the fact that she had just brushed past the man who had tipped her off about the Black Baron, Captain Diane Reilly lifted a small radio out of the view of the people around her. "Anything?"

"Not yet," came the reply. "But frankly, there are a lot of people at this party."

"Keep it short, Lieutenant," Diane replied. "Over and out." She went to the balcony and radioed headquarters. "What have you got?"

"We've found a stack of explosives in the basement and around the perimeter," the head of the bomb squad told her. "Enough to blow the station to pieces."

Diane glanced at her watch. "How long would it take to go over them for timers or radio controlled detonation devices?"

"Um. There are a lot of them so…"

"Forget it," Diane told him. "You won't have time. At best, our suspect is going to detonate those things in sixteen minutes. Evacuate the building. Get everyone out and cordon off the surrounding area. Take whatever precautions you have to."

"Should we alert the commissioner?"

"Later. Cordon off that area first." Diane flicked the radio off. "Stuff the commissioner," she muttered. She changed the frequency and called the officer in charge of the helicopter search. "How's it going up there? Anything?"

"We've found them," the man replied. "Twenty S.W.A.T. vans in the vicinity of the Alliance Bank near Grand Central."

Diane paused for a moment as that set in. At the most, she had expected they'd find two or three. "All right," she said. There was no time to worry about it then. "Don't engage them. But leave a few choppers in the air so you can keep watching them."

"What are you going to do?"

"Pile our resources and hope they're enough to do the job," Diane told him. She looked at her watch again. It was 8.46 p.m.

Back inside, Jason was still searching the place with Angie. "I can't see him," he told her. "But I think I've seen a few of his S.W.A.T. guys."

"Wait, we don't know that. They could be Captain

Reilly's men."

"Or a mix of the two..." Jason murmured. "Yeah, this could be tricky."

"Wait," Angie said, nodding over his shoulder. "That guy going to that door beside the stage. That's him."

Jason saw the man, an elegant man in black drab and an all-too familiar flowing trench coat. "All right. Why don't you stay here and mingle for a while?"

He headed after the man and got to the door just in time. The Black Baron had locked it behind him but Jason caught it before it swung shut, then followed his quarry up some stairs and checked the time. 8.53 p.m.

When he reached the top of the stairs, he discarded the tuxedo, the mask and the turban, shoving the gear into a corner of the dark room. To his left were some more stairs leading up into a sound room right above the ballroom. Through the back window of this room, he saw the Black Baron fiddling with a PA system.

Downstairs, Diane got a call on the radio. She checked the frequency as she held it to her ear. It was from one of the officers in the choppers. "Go ahead."

"We've spotted a foreign object on top of the Alliance Bank near Grand Central and some of my men have rappelled down to the roof to investigate it."

"What was it?"

"We think it was the Black Baron's electronic pulse generator," the man replied. "We shut it down and removed its built-in battery operating system."

"First good news I've heard all night," Diane told him. "Good work. All right. Now the device is disabled, there's no urgent need to engage those S.W.A.T. guys. If we don't have to have a bloodbath, then let's not. However, if you can do it without endangering yourselves, identify those guys and report back to me later."

"Understood."

She checked her watch again. 8.55 p.m.

Jason strode up the remaining set of stairs into the sound room, grabbed the Black Baron by the scruff of the neck and slammed his face into the PA system.

"You?" the Black Baron muttered.

"That's right," Jason replied. "It looks like I could make it after all. Now where are the remotes for your weapons? The one for the electronic pulse generator on whatever bank you're robbing and the bombs in the police headquarters?"

At this, the Black Baron laughed so hard, tears came to his eyes. "Oh, that's too good!" he said, rubbing them with a free hand, still chuckling. "You honestly think I'd have remotes for these things. Seriously, I've got this all planned to the wire. Why would I need remotes?"

"There must be a way to stop the devices," Jason insisted, feeling the situation slipping out of his control.

"Of course there's a way," the Black Baron replied, glancing at his watch. "It's just time that's your problem. Now, do you mind?" He reached for something out of Jason's peripheral.

Beneath Jason's feet, the floor gave way and a moment later, he was clinging to one wing of a trapdoor—dangling six yards over the ballroom below to the shocked gasps of several hundred guests, one of them Angie.

"This is how they move heavy PA equipment in and out of this booth," the Black Baron told him as if Jason cared right then. The Baron then picked up a microphone and down in the ballroom, his face filled a large projector screen behind the main stage.

"Good evening, ladies and gentlemen," he announced, his amplified voice bouncing off the walls. "The time has now come for the main event of the evening as I, the Black Baron, rob you blind and leave the police helpless to do anything about it. Any second now. If you look out the windows to the right side of the stage." He chuckled, clearly enjoying his moment in the sun immensely. "That's your right and my left."

There was a deafening bang and the sky lit up in an orange glow. "That there, ladies and gentlemen," he boomed over the terrified cries that followed, "was the Fringe City police headquarters, where your city's finest have been wasting your tax dollars for all these years."

Holding her radio right to her ear and shouting to be heard over the chaotic din, Diane called the head of the bomb squad. "We heard the explosion! Did you get everyone out?"

"Everyone's safe," the officer replied, his voice strained in equal measures by stress and shock. "But... my god, the whole building went up!"

"And although you can't hear it," the Black Baron continued over the loudspeaker, "I have just completely disabled the security systems of the largest branch of the Alliance Bank in this state and right now, my men are taking every last cent out of it. So if you happen to bank with them, then I guess this isn't your night."

There was an understandable commotion on the ballroom floor, although for many of the patrons there, the reasons for their panic were now somewhat mixed. And more than a few were conflicted with guilt as they realized that the loss of their money had, however momentarily, upset them more than the deaths of several hundred police officers.

"In fact," the Black Baron added, "I believe the organizer of this wonderful evening owns a sizeable portion of Alliance shares. Isn't that right, Burges, you clown? However, since you were planning on keeping the proceeds of tonight's ball for yourself instead of helping out families in need, I don't think you can really complain."

In the midst of the chaos on the ballroom floor, one of the masked patrons grimaced under the glares of those around him.

Above the crowd, Jason climbed up the trapdoor flap. People saw him of course but they were smart enough not to bring attention to it.

"In fact, ladies and gentlemen, everyone's getting their just desserts," the Black Baron continued, almost ranting now. "A stack of the corrupt officers in the police force are dead and though they don't know it, the men who are robbing the Alliance Bank will get their comeuppance as well. Even now, a slow acting poison is working its way through their systems. An hour or two after they've transported my money, they'll be dead too. And if there are any Alliance bankers down there, you have all been supporting a company that makes its profits in the exotic timber trade, financing the destruction of irreplaceable rainforest eco-systems in the Amazon and Indonesia.

So you've simply got what was coming to you too."

"Yeah. You're a saint," Jason told him, emerging from the trapdoor. The Black Baron whirled around, right in time for Jason to haul him halfway across the booth by his collar. "I don't know how the hell you thought you could pull this public bragging nonsense and get away without being caught," Jason told him. "But it's not going to happen."

With the microphone still on, every word boomed over the ballroom as the Black Baron's boasts had.

"Well if you hadn't spoiled everything by climbing back up," the Black Baron replied, "then I could have left without anyone getting hurt." He kicked Jason to the floor behind the trapdoor and from within the folds of his coat, pulled out a live grenade, flinging it at the wall of the sound booth. With a deafening noise, it exploded, leaving the room as nothing more than an exposed platform above the ballroom, while the stunned guests looked on.

"Go on," the Black Baron said, pulling out another grenade and flicking the pin. "Save them!" With a contemptuous sneer, he lobbed it into the air.

Running forward, Jason grabbed a bundle of dead cables and leapt out. Below, Angie watched with a lump in her throat, almost too terrified to breathe. Swinging under the remains of the sound booth, Jason batted the grenade with one free hand—knocking it away from the helpless crowd below and right back into the rubble above. The job done, he continued on his pendulum swing, crashing through one of the great windows to the side of the room. He then clawed at one of the decorative ivy vines around a column and slid to a rough but otherwise safe landing on the balcony outside.

In doing so, he missed witnessing the explosion in the roof that took out the Black Baron and showered those below with debris that, while dangerous, was not life-threatening. However, he sure heard it.

Inside, there was a mass movement towards the balcony as hundreds rushed to see what had become of their mysterious savior, Angie among them. They were just in time to see Jason leap off the balcony and disappear. Out of their sight, Jason slowed his descent, digging his heels into a tangle of ivy as he dragged his way down the length of a stone column. Then, hitting the ground, he beat a hasty retreat. When the crowd reached the railings and leaned over the sides, he was nowhere to be seen.

About a week later when things had more or less calmed down, Diane met with Charles Faulkner in his office. "Well, we got confessions from pretty much everybody. Those S.W.A.T. guys weren't too keen on the idea of coming clean but they weren't that keen on dying from whatever it was the Black Baron had poisoned them with either."

"It's funny, isn't it?" Faulkner remarked in that objective manner of his that so many of his adversaries in legal circles mistook for emotional detachment. "In being as extreme as he was in his methods, this guy actually helped us in our investigations. Too bad the self-appointed guardian of the city had to kill him though. I would still like to have put this Black Baron up on charges to show the city that our system can deal with nuts like this."

"He didn't kill him," Diane pointed out. "The Black Baron killed himself when he flicked the pin on that grenade. Our 'self-appointed guardian' followed the only course of action that was available to him. If he didn't knock that grenade back, tens—possibly hundreds—of people in that ballroom would have been killed. And given that he barely had a second to act, he didn't have the luxury of deciding where to knock it."

"Hell, I'm not judging." Faulkner sighed and looked at Diane. "It must have been quite a night."

"It was," Diane replied. "Although hopefully, we won't get too many more like that."

"Hopefully," Faulkner agreed. "Although it could have been worse. And for once, the money raised by the mayor's charity ball is actually going to a charity rather than his own personal trust fund."

Diane chuckled. "Yeah, he was caught red handed this time." She shook her head. "The Black Baron may have been a nut but he did tell it how it was. And he's probably done more to expose the business practices of the Alliance Bank than the newspapers ever have."

"True." Faulkner then changed the topic. "By the way, how's the new station looking?"

"I think it'll be a bit hectic until everyone's settled in but it'll be good."

"And did Commissioner Levings give you any grief about the way you handled everything on Saturday night?"

"He didn't like being left out of the loop but he's not going to say anything. I've got the press on my side."

"Well, they were only telling the truth. You got everyone out of the police headquarters before it blew up and you stopped the Alliance Bank robbery. There was no exaggeration there."

"That's true, I suppose," Diane said. She shook her head and allowed herself a slight smile. "You know, I think things might just be looking up in this city."

"Maybe," Faulkner agreed reluctantly.

LAMONT

ANOTHER TWO WEEKS PASSED AND Saturday evening found Jason and Angie relaxing in their new apartment with the news on in the background.

"... *with still no clue to Alex Grigorie's whereabouts.*

"*In other news, this manhunt isn't the only thing that appears to be going nowhere. Right here in Fringe City, things are rising to a boiling point in Kingsford. For several months now, local residents of Kingsford have had to walk miles out of their way to access subway facilities, while their elected officials claim that the city cannot spare the necessary funding for the upgrades.*

"*However, last night, Mayor Burges was caught hosting an extravagant private party, costing tens of thousands of dollars, with the residents of Fringe City footing the bill.*

"*Residents of Kingsford, along with taxpayers all over the city, are furious, especially with this latest development coming so soon after the mayor's attempts to swindle the funds raised at his recent charity ball.*"

Jason shook his head and flicked the TV off.

"There's something really wrong with that. I just can't put my finger on it."

"With how the mayor's hanging those people out to dry while embezzling public funds?" Angie said. "Yeah, that's a tricky one."

"No, not that." Jason frowned. "It feels like there's some hidden agenda there."

He cleared the thoughts from his mind. They were going nowhere. "Well, I think I could get used to this," he said, looking around the new apartment. "Actually, being this close to work will probably make life a lot easier. I could do without the commuting time now."

"True," Angie said. "Although, how far are you planning to take this thing now?"

"I don't know," Jason confessed. "I'm glad we stopped the Black Baron but Burges is still sitting in his office, orchestrating all these things for his own ends, while the rest of the city's picking up the tab." He shrugged. "I don't know. I guess I'll know how far I'm planning on taking this when I get there. How did we go with the insurance claims by the way?"

"Well, the whole building burnt down and there were fires in the corridors before our apartment started burning so they were pretty understanding. It was a lot of paperwork though. I mean, it was nice having a week off school but compared to getting the paperwork done, finding this place and refurnishing, I think I'd rather be at work. And I'm sick to death of clothes shopping."

"Yeah, me too," Jason said "Although, I don't think I'd rather be at work. It wasn't that bad. And I think Geoffrey's had it tougher than we have. He's blaming himself for what happened and now he's busily working out how to trace radio signals and prevent them from being traced—"

"You did tell him it wasn't his fault though?" Angie asked, her voice laced with suspicion.

"I did," Jason replied. "But having devices that can send untraceable signals could be useful..."

"Poor Geoffrey," Angie shook her head. "Now you've got him making gas powered grappling hooks and untraceable cell phones. What's next?"

Jason pretended to wave the question off. "He likes the work."

"And do you?" Angie asked, the jokes over. "You nearly got killed that night."

"True," Jason agreed. "I wouldn't want to do that every night but I like to think I'm getting something done." He went to the kitchen counter and opened a file of bits and pieces on Burges and Lamont. After the fire, he'd wasted no time in writing out everything he'd previously gathered on them while it was still fresh in his memory. Then he'd gone to town—or rather to the public library—gathering anything else he could get.

"Now what are you doing?" Angie asked.

"I can't stop thinking about this business with Kingsford station."

Angie shook her head. "I swear you're obsessed with this."

"Maybe," Jason agreed in a distracted tone, only catching half of what Angie had said. "Look at this. I mean bright flashy casinos seem to get built without any hassles at all, while basic essential services for poor neighborhoods can go neglected for years. Wait... this is interesting."

"What?" Angie asked, leaning over him to have a look. Jason pulled out a map and showed her his discovery. "Check this out. It seems that a couple of years ago, Burges gave a green light for this new subway line here." He then grabbed another sheet of paper. "Now, according to these city planning proposals that no one seems to read, it's all finished and ready to go but it's never been opened. Now, check *this* out." He pointed to a nearby part of the map. "Here it runs parallel to Kingsford station. He could easily bring it into play and all the people in Kingsford would have easy access to the subway. But he hasn't."

"My god," Angie murmured. It was so perverse and yet so utterly plausible in their messed up town. "He's going to demolish Kingsford station. Then he can build a mall or some shiny new city blocks and bring his secret line into play right when he wants it."

"And potentially kill thousands of people in the process," Jason said. "Man, the Black Baron was nothing compared to this."

"But he wouldn't, would he?"

"Not personally," Jason agreed. "He'll get someone else to do it. But this is right up his alley. Maybe this was why he was working with the Black Baron in the first place. Maybe he was hoping to use him." He paused as he thought it over. "However, now that the Black Baron's dead, who else could he get to do the job?"

At the Fringe City Police Headquarters, Commissioner Levings was giving Diane yet another earful. "This self appointed guardian angel," he told her, waving a newspaper, "or the 'Sentinel' as these stupid papers are calling him… He's a menace. And since he's contacted you on several occasions, you're our best chance of bringing him in."

"Those were anonymous calls," Diane replied. "They could have been from anyone."

"Cut the crap, Captain. We both know they weren't."

"Fine. It won't do you any good though. Each time

he contacted me, it was from a public pay phone. Also, don't forget this guy saved a room full of people from the Black Baron at that charity ball, not to mention everyone at the old police headquarters since he was the one who warned us about the bombs. Oh, and that's right; he helped us stop the Alliance Bank from getting robbed. Personally, I'm glad he's out there."

"He's an urban terrorist. In fact, by turning up at that charity ball, he endangered everyone there. Or need I remind you that it was only when this guy drove the Black Baron to desperation that he threw that grenade?"

"Well, maybe he thought having someone like the Black Baron running loose around the city wasn't a good idea."

"You're no better than the hero worshippers who work at the papers. In fact, all this strange public goodwill is one of the reasons we've got to catch this guy. To show people that he's not some kind of hero. You know, this so-called 'sentinel' of yours recently abducted a prominent businessman from his office. And then he humiliated him by leaving him tied up in wire rope and dumping him in front of this building for everyone to see as they came in on the morning shift. Does that sound like someone you want running loose around the place?"

"That prominent businessman was a crook," Diane

pointed out. "If you read the reports we sent you about him a few weeks back, you'd know he was one of the major weapon suppliers to the local street gangs. Why don't you visit some of those neighborhoods where they hang out and see them for yourself?"

"I've read the reports," Levings muttered. "I don't need to see these places close up."

"Well, unlike you, I *have* seen these places close up and this businessman of yours came up in a lot of my investigations there."

"Fine," Levings replied, waving aside the argument as he so often did when he realized he wasn't winning the things. "But if I find out you're withholding anything on this 'sentinel', I'll have your ass in a sling."

"Eloquently put as always, Commissioner," Diane told him as she got up and left. There had been a time when she would have waited for Levings to dismiss her first but the memory was pretty hazy now.

With the amount of time he'd been spending in the mayor's office lately, Grand Central felt like a home away from home to Martin Lamont.

"I don't much care for these new guys," he muttered, sniffing the whisky that Burges had given him. He had always liked the smell. "Moving in on our market. I want you to pull whatever strings you have to and find out who they're paying off."

"Why do you think they're paying anyone off?" Burges asked.

"Things are going too smoothly for them," Lamont replied. "The amount of stuff they're hauling without any trouble from the cops... I was rather under the impression my organization had an exclusive deal here, Mr. Mayor. Unless you know differently."

"You do," Burges told him. "I don't know who's letting them move their wares but I sure as hell didn't authorize it."

"Well, someone with enough clout to do the job is smoothing the way for them. It's unheard of for anyone to open a market as quickly as these guys have."

"And you think I've got something to do with it?"

"Well, I don't see you doing anything to stop them."

"Well, I didn't know about these guys until a few days ago, you ungrateful son of a bitch."

"You'd better not have," Lamont said. "After all, it's my money that's been keeping you in office."

"Yes, how could I forget? But if you quit your whining and listen for a moment I think I can help you. In fact, I think we can help each other actually. We can get rid of these new guys and sort out a little problem of mine at the same time."

"I don't give a damn about your problems, Burges."

"But I should leap over fences to sort yours out, is that it?"

"Not at all," Lamont replied. "I can take care of these guys myself. All I need's your assurance that you can keep the cops from getting in the way."

"I'll do my best," Burges told him, his tone sardonic. "But all right. You go do your thing and I'll pin whatever charges come up on the neighborhood gangs. However, if you can stay away from the news cameras when you're shooting up Fringe City, I would deeply appreciate it."

"I'll do my best," Lamont told him, mimicking his words along with his tone. "How are you going to stick those charges, if you don't mind me asking? I understand Faulkner's making that kind of thing a little harder these days."

"I've hired some new help in the courts to mitigate the damage Faulkner's doing there," Burges said. "Even if they can't make such charges stick, they can at least bury anything you do in legal limbo for the next six months."

Lamont thought about it. "All right. Although, do you think you can come up with anything better than pinning charges on those kids?"

"What do you care about some stupid kids?"

"I don't give a damn about them," Lamont replied. "But one of our mutual acquaintances makes a good living selling weapons to those gangs and if the police haul them off, he'll be seriously out of pocket."

"I know the man," Burges told him. "And believe me, we're better off without him. Or hadn't you heard about his tangle with the cops? The Sentinel gift-wrapped him and dumped outside the new police headquarters."

"No, I hadn't heard."

"Read the papers a bit more," Burges told him. "Do you good. You can read, can't you?"

"My paper was late this morning," Lamont replied. "Maybe you could do a little more to fix the traffic congestion around here."

"Touché. Anyway, that man's an embarrassment. Forget him. And remember, I'm doing this for your precious organization."

"All right."

"Wonderful. Then that's settled. So go ahead. Duke it out with these new guys. Have a blast." Burges lifted the edge of a folder on his desk and glanced at the contents. "But if it doesn't work out for you, let me know."

"And in other news, residents at West Quay are reeling after a drive-by shooting last night..."

"... streets turned into an urban war zone today."

"... yet another drive-by shooting, this time in broad daylight."

"I tell you, Jim, when things are this bad you call in the national guard."

"I'm sorry, Henry, but surely you of all people must realize that such action would only serve to escalate the situation."

"Jim, you know me. In most cases, I would agree with you, but frankly speaking... right now, I can't see how you could escalate it."

"Now, Henry—"

"If I may, just one moment—"

"Sure, go ahead."

"Thank you. Now, Jim, this past week, we've had mobsters gunning people from their cars, bursting into bars and clubs all across town, shooting people dead, and innocent people are being caught in the crossfire."

"Well, that should suggest to you that moderation is the better course of action."

"Jim—"

"No, no, look. Henry, by your own admission, there is serious collateral risk here. If innocent people are being caught in the crossfire now, how many more will be if you have armed soldiers on the street?"

"I hardly think that's an appropriate thing to say about our own home troops."

"I mean no disrespect to our troops and you know that.

But do you honestly think these mobsters would sit back while the national guard moved in without a fight?"

"Yes! There would be absolutely no reason for them to gun it out with the armed forces. There would be nothing for them to gain. They'd have no choice but to go underground."

"All right. I see your point. However, what happens after the national guard leaves, if your assessment of the situation is accurate?"

"The national guard would stay long enough to ensure that the situation is under control."

"For how long? And you haven't answered my other question."

"I don't believe that's necessary, Jim. With the national guard in place, the local authorities can carry out thorough investigations and bring the perpetrators of these crimes in."

"You're sure of that? Why couldn't they disappear as they've been doing all week? So far, the police have been getting nothing but false leads indicating that the various youth gangs around the city are perpetrating these crimes, which is patently false."

"That's coming from their representatives in the legal department."

"In the legal department, right."

"And, if you consider that fact, these people are traceable. They have lawyers and—"

"Henry, that's absurd. Are you suggesting that while the national guard are patrolling the city—"

"Jim—"

"No, wait a minute. Hear me out. Are you suggesting that while the national guard are patrolling the city, that the police interview the members of every registered firm and independent lawyer and ask them if they have any criminal syndicates on their payroll?"

"That's not what I'm suggesting at all, Jim. I—"

"I think you are. You just said—and these are your words, by the way—these people are traceable. They have lawyers."

"The Lamont connection. The biggest crime syndicate in this city is being run by Martin Lamont. Everyone knows it—"

"But no one as yet has been able to prove it. And everyone has tried. His attorneys are too good at what they do, and even if the new D.A. could pin one of Lamont's boys, he'll never be able to pin the head of the operation."

"I think it's too early to make that call. Charles Faulkner's been making a lot of progress since he took over the position. Who knows? With the scale of this latest spree, maybe Lamont's outdone himself. Maybe he's left one loose end too many."

"I suppose anything is possible. However, I think we've drifted away from the main issue. And that it is what the best immediate solution is to bring this latest round of urban chaos under control."

"And I still say that the best way is to bring in the

National Guard. You need a deterrent to—"

"It never rains but it pours," Angie remarked, shaking her head as she and Jason watched the news.

"In this town, it seems to always pour," Jason replied. "But you're right. This is nuttier than it's been for a while."

"What do you make of it?"

Jason shrugged. "If those mobsters want to kill each other off, that's fine with me. They can do us all a favor. And as for those kids being picked up by the cops, if they don't want to be on a suspect list every time something like this happens, then they shouldn't play their stupid territorial games in the first place. But the problem is all the innocent people getting caught in the crossfire. If these guys could find an abandoned neighborhood and play their games there, then you wouldn't have anything to worry about."

They watched some more and the report cut to an interview with the mayor. Jason sat up and pointed at the screen of the TV they were watching. There was another beside it, hooked up to a DVD player recording CCTV footage of Grand Central; however, these days he was recording the news too with a second player hooked up to the main TV. It was almost a perfect replica of the dual recording setup Jason had made at the old apartment, and yet another expense Angie would have been happier without.

Jason stopped both players, ejected the DVDs and, using the second TV and DVD player, he watched the recording of the interview they'd just seen. After a few seconds, he paused on a shot of the mayor and his entourage and zoomed in on a man standing behind him.

"There!" he said.

Angie saw it too. Minus the long ragged hair and beard, the man Jason had spotted looked exactly like a man wanted all over the country.

"It's Alex Grigorie," she murmured.

"Yep. The guy who tried to bomb the New York subway. Seems almost natural that he'd end up here, doesn't it?"

Angie nodded. "I imagine he feels right at home."

"City hall," Jason said, recognizing the building in the background. "Angie, can you switch the DVDs back for me?"

"Sure."

"Thanks."

Jason grabbed his bag and raced out the door. It wasn't a planned outing for him but he'd been to City Hall often enough recently that he could get there soon enough.

. . .

Twenty-five minutes later or thereabouts, he was on a rooftop looking down at City Hall. He adjusted the visor on his helmet, bringing up the binocular settings and zooming in on the scene below. He watched as the mayor and his entourage went inside the building while the media dispersed and then he waited.

Over two hours passed. Then finally, Grigorie emerged alone and headed towards the nearest subway station.

When he got home, Jason was exhausted. Angie had been in bed for a couple of hours already, he'd been gone so long, but she woke up to hear his news.

"Well?" she asked, flicking on the bedside lamp and sitting up.

"I found where Grigorie's staying and moved the CCTV camera so I can keep an eye on him."

"Sounds like you've had a busy night."

"Yeah. Well, it wasn't anything too tricky. It just took a while. Anyway, I got some photos of him and I'll send them to Captain Reilly, along with a copy of the news footage we recorded."

"Captain Reilly specifically?"

"Well, she's the only cop I can trust for certain."

. . .

When Diane received her gifts, she reached the same conclusion Jason had and passed the information on to a superior she got along with fairly well.

"I think, Commander," she said, handing him the photos and the DVD Jason had sent her, "that these will carry a bit more weight for the commissioner coming from you than coming from me."

"Have you two been at it again?" the man asked.

"When have we not?"

"Fair enough."

"Hey," she called as he turned away. "You'll let me know what he's going to do about it, won't you?"

"You've got it."

Diane didn't have to wait long. About half an hour all told.

"Levings says higher sources know about him," the commander said, his tone despondent as he slumped down in a chair across from her. "Apparently he's a transport consultant from out of town who's working with the mayor—and the likeness between his appearance and the subway bomber Alex Grigorie is apparently just coincidental."

"The hell it is. You don't buy that, do you?"

"Not for a second," the commander replied. "But what can you do about it?"

The question was rhetorical but nevertheless, Diane found herself thinking it over. She smiled. "I'll tell you what I can do about it," she said, gathering the pictures and the DVD. "I'll make up some copies of these and send them along to the Federal Bureau of Investigation, along with a nice long letter about Commissioner Levings and his 'higher sources'."

Another day passed. After work, Jason reviewed the day's CCTV footage and observed that Grigorie had left and come back several times during the day but he hadn't gone far.

"I'm going back to Grigorie's place to keep an eye on things," he told Angie.

"Is something going on?"

"I don't know. But I kind of get the feeling he's been a bit busier today than he was yesterday and the day before."

"Be careful," Angie said as Jason picked up his bag.

"I will," he promised. "I don't know how long I'll be so don't wait up. But if I'm not home before you go to bed, I'll tell you all about it in the morning."

A late night train pulled into a station. A number of people got off, a number of people got on and then it was away again. One of those who had just got on was a man with a large piece of luggage. A bag full of all sorts of interesting things, including a costume of Kevlar armor and harpoons. To avoid unnecessary attention, he sat towards the back of the carriage behind the other passengers, including another who had gotten on at the same station. Jason watched that man closely. When his quarry disembarked at Grand Central, he did too. And once he was sure the man was heading into the building of the same name, he went his own way. He knew exactly where Alex Grigorie was going.

He scaled a neighboring building, one a little closer to Grand Central than the one he had used for his surveillance of the place. On the rooftop, he checked some climbing anchors he had put in place earlier. There was a wire running from them to some others on the rooftop of Grand Central, carefully positioned so as not to be visible in the offensive bright beams of light that projected from that eyesore into the night sky.

Jason then opened his bag and pulled out the pieces for his costume. He quickly changed into it and produced a flying fox contraption, and another little device, from the bag. He hooked the flying fox contraption onto the wire and swung across to the monstrous building where Grigorie would soon be meeting the mayor in his top floor office, if they weren't already.

Looking into the room was a little tricky but not

overly so, thanks to a bit of ingenuity on Geoffrey's part; the other device Jason had gotten out of the bag. The small and unremarkable looking piece of equipment had two functions. One was a fairly simple prospect: a reverse periscope that, after he affixed it on the roof ledge, allowed him to see what was going on in the mayor's office without being seen himself. The second function however was the trickier one, a sensor that amplified sound and cleared the interference of dampening effects caused by walls and windows. The device allowed him to both see and hear what was going on underneath him and the audio was transmitted directly into a receptor built into the left side of his helmet. It was probably illegal, as it basically espionage equipment, but then again so was vigilantism.

Jason then made himself comfortable as he listened and watched.

"Martin," Burges said, gesturing to the man who had just entered the room, "allow me to introduce Alex Grigorie."

Lamont gave the newcomer one look and turned to the mayor. "Are you nuts, Reggie?"

Burges smiled and clapped a hand on Lamont's shoulder. "Martin, Martin. Relax. No one's going to know. I've already cleared this with Commissioner Levings."

"What do you mean you've cleared this?"

"I've covered myself. I've covered us. The—"

"Us? Jesus Christ, you've roped me into this too?"

"The official story," Burges said, cutting him off, "is that this man is a transport consultant who's advising me and that the similarities between his appearance and that of the terrorist who's being hunted across the country are entirely coincidental. Does that work better for you or do you want me to write it down?"

"Shove it, Reggie," Lamont told him. "All right..." He took a moment to recompose himself and even managed to extend a hand to Alex. "It's Mr. Lamont to you, pal, until I get to know you better. I'm only Martin to my friends and this asshole here. Nice to meet you, comrade."

Grigorie ignored the lame joke, shaking his hand but not saying anything as yet.

"All right," Lamont said, turning to Burges. "Now, do you want to tell me what you're doing harboring this walking liability here?" He glanced back to Grigorie. "No offence."

The urban terrorist just glared in return.

"Grigorie here's the answer to our problems," Burges said. "Your problem and my problem that you didn't want to hear about."

"Get to the point."

"I will if you stop interrupting. I know about your rival organization. It's run by some guy called Danny Vincent who used to run an operation over in Detroit and they're currently holed up in Kingsford Station, that derelict station in the news. They're using it as a temporary warehouse to stockpile the drugs they're bringing in before they siphon them to the dealers."

For a moment, the tension in the room was stretched to breaking point and there was murder in the first degree in Lamont's eyes. "If you knew about these guys, why didn't you tell me this before?"

"Because you didn't want to hear it before."

"That's no answer."

"Well tough, Martin. I told you I had an idea that I wanted to run by you but you shot me down without giving me a chance to discuss it. You wanted to have your little rampage and you've had it. You got loads of publicity to boost your already inflated ego and you got your kicks. So I don't want any more of your crap."

"All right, fine. So what's the story now?"

"Here you go, Martin. A few weeks ago, I placed a mole in Vincent's organization and with the info he's gathered for me, along with the services of my friend Alex here, we can blow their lair of operations sky-high. And in doing so, we'll take out a sizeable portion of the organization as well as their stockpiles. Also, we can assume this mob has contracts with a number of suppliers here in the city and that they've already received down-payments from these guys. So if any of them manage to get out alive and they've got any sense, they're going to skip town before their clients come chasing up their orders."

"And what do you get out of this? I always feel suspicious when you say you're giving me things for free."

"You're as astute as always, Martin," Burges said, his tone sardonic. "What I get out of this is a chance to make some much needed upgrades to the area."

"Upgrades? You bomb Kingsford station and you'll take out half the neighborhood."

"Yeah. The crappy half. And here's a little something for you, Martin. You know how you've been pushing me for ages to give you a chance to put in another large legitimate business to help fund your illegitimate one?"

"Are you finally going to come good on your promises?"

"I never promised a damn thing but, anyway, with Kingsford leveled and swept up, that whole area's going to be prime real estate."

"Are you kidding me? That land'll be unserviceable for years until you can get another subway line in. I'm not going to waste good money setting up a business in a ghost town."

"I know that's what it looks like, but trust me. It isn't the case."

Lamont frowned. "What do you mean?"

"That other line you mentioned? It's already there."

"Come again?"

"I've been working on this for years. There's already a new line running adjacent to the one that's there now. And it's ready to open whenever I decide to bring it into play."

At this, Lamont warmed up and there was even a hint of admiration in his expression. "Jesus."

"So as you can see," Burges told him, "that land'll be worth a fortune. And you can have as much of it as you want. And you can *put* whatever you want on it too. A shopping centre, a football stadium, a casino. Or all three."

"All right," Lamont said. "So what do you need from me?"

Jason sat back and let out a long breath. "God, it'd be nice to be wrong for a change," he muttered. For a moment, he contemplated whether or not he could stop all of this nonsense by jumping in through the window and thrashing everyone in the room but two things stopped him.

Although confrontations were almost inevitable now, he wasn't sure he wanted to risk one with the three men together right then. The mayor probably wouldn't be a problem but Lamont was likely to be packing a hand gun at least and there was Grigorie to watch out for as well.

But more than that, he didn't have enough information to act on. If there were any other variables like timed explosives or more men on the mayor's payroll awaiting instructions, then premature action might be worse than useless.

"Well, I think we're all done here," Burges announced, clasping his hands and walking around his desk. "Mr. Grigorie will accompany you downstairs, Martin, and will discuss the rest of the details with you in your car."

"I'm going somewhere, am I?" Lamont asked.

Burges smiled. "Of course. You're not going to get anything done sitting around here."

"And where am I going, may I ask?"

"I can't say, I'm afraid. Mr. Grigorie will tell you on the way."

Lamont frowned, growing tired of the game. "Why can't you say?"

"For the same reason that Mr. Grigorie will be

discussing the rest of the details with you on the drive over. The less I know, the easier it is for me to lie about it to the press afterwards. I can act all shocked and condemn this act of senseless violence much more convincingly this way. Also, remember the Black Baron? If this got out, it'd be a hundred times worse."

"Great. That makes me feel better."

"Martin, relax. You're too tense. Just do what Mr. Grigorie says. You won't even need to go *near* Kingsford station."

"All right."

"Oh, and one other thing," Burges called out as Lamont followed Grigorie to the door.

Lamont turned around.

"When you're done, take our guest to the airport. He has a flight out of the country later this evening and he needs to arrive there... what is it these days? Two hours beforehand or something like that?"

"You know, Reggie, if I go driving around with one of the most wanted men in the country, I might get a whole lot of attention I can live without."

"How many times do I have to tell you, Martin? Just relax. I've got everything covered. Mr. Grigorie has the best forged documents money can buy and as you can see for yourself, without his beard and long hair, he looks nothing like the man on the national news."

"The resemblance is still a bit too strong for my

liking," Lamont muttered. He turned to Grigorie. "All right then, comrade. Let's go."

Reggie Burges waited a few moments after they had gone and reached for his phone. "David. Can you come into my office for a moment?"

"I'll be right there."

There was a click and Burges put the phone back down. He played with the paperweight on his desk, the mannerism a sign that he'd dropped the calm façade he had put on for Lamont's benefit.

His assistant David Merlon appeared at the door. "Yes?"

"What's the deal with this unwanted evidence that's been handed to the police?"

"I'd say it's our new friend again," Merlon replied. "This 'Sentinel' guy."

"Yes, and he's a right pain in the ass," Burges said hurriedly. "But what's been *done* about it? Did you talk to Commissioner Levings?"

Merlon shook his head. "The prick's screwed it up."

"But I told him what to say! Did he use our official line?"

"Yes, he fed the unit that B.S. about Grigorie being a transport consultant and the rest of it. How he was a resident of San Francisco who was going to assist the transport department in dealing with some safety concerns regarding the Kingsford station upgrade. But he clearly didn't do a good enough job of selling it."

Burges stamped in frustration. "Damn it, what's wrong with the man?"

"Do you want a short answer or a laundry list?"

"This could ruin everything," Burges muttered, ignoring the quip.

"I guess Levings just panicked."

"So how bad is the situation?" Burges asked.

"Someone tipped off the Feds that the police had received information on Grigorie's whereabouts," Merlon said, "that he was here in Fringe City and that the Police Commissioner had refused to pass the information on."

"So in a couple of hours, we're going to have Federal agents crawling all over the place?"

"I'd imagine so. You'd better let Lamont know and call the plan off."

"Why? They won't catch him."

"He's got Grigorie."

"I know," Burges replied. "But in a few short hours, he'll get him to his plane and get him the hell out of here. Then I can act all surprised that Grigorie was working for me as a transport consultant. It'll be fine."

"Lamont won't see it that way."

"He won't know. I'll tell him that I was just as

surprised as he was to learn that the Feds were in town." He reached for his phone again. "Which will be very easy once we cut Levings off. He's really dropped the ball this time."

Merlon frowned. "Cut him off?"

"Well, he can pin us," Burges pointed out. "We can't have anything to do with him."

"Hang on a minute. Do you honestly think you could get a more valuable employee on the police payroll than the commissioner?"

"We can't afford him," Burges argued. "And by your own admission, we're going to have external investigators all over the city in an hour or two. Besides, since he fumbled the ball so badly, he deserves to be left out on a limb."

"Great. And if you cut him off, do you think he's just going to sit there and take it? If you burn him, he'll burn you. And then what are you going to do?"

"Nothing because he's *not* going to burn me. I'm cutting him off permanently."

"You're out of your goddamn mind if that means what I think it means. If the Feds come and see that, the next group in town will be the national guard."

Burges shrugged. "They've come in before, haven't they?"

"Yeah, but—"

"David," Burges sighed. "You don't get it, do you?

Because contrary to what you think, if external investigators come and see what I've got in mind, they'll go running back to where they came from. You see, the beautiful truth is that the rest of the country thinks Fringe City is beyond salvage and they're not going to waste precious time and resources trying to stop its inevitable slide into the void."

"Well, if that's the case," Merlon countered, "if the rest of the country thinks this place is a write-off and that it's a waste of tax money sending the Feds in, then I guess no one will show up after all, right?"

Burges shook his head. "What the hell are you talking about?"

"The rest of the country is taking an interest right *now*."

At this however, Burges relaxed and even managed to smile. "They're not showing an interest in Fringe City, David. They're coming here because they're after someone who tried to bomb one of *their* subways. Now, relax."

"You know, you scare the hell out of me when you say that."

Burges nodded. "I know. Now, I've got to make a call. If you scare as easily as you do, then you won't want to be privy to this conversation."

"Who are you calling?"

"Someone a lot scarier than me."

. . .

In the back of his chauffeured car, Lamont eyed his new acquaintance with unveiled distaste. "You know, you don't talk very much."

Grigorie didn't look at him. "No. Maybe you should try it."

Lamont laughed uncomfortably. "Boy, did the mayor give us a frosty one this time."

Grigorie sighed. "Look, you know why I'm wanted all over the country. What do you expect me to be like?"

"All right," Lamont replied, raising his hands in a show of surrender. "Settle down."

Just then, his cell phone rang. His bodyguard, sitting next to the driver, handed it back to him. "I guess that'll be for you."

"Thanks." Lamont held the phone close to his ear just in case the call was about something private. "Lamont."

He nodded as he listened, digesting the news. "All right, thanks for the heads up. I'll call you back later."

"Trouble?" his bodyguard asked.

"Someone's tipped off the cops about Grigorie's rather close relationship with the mayor."

"That's not good."

"Oh and it gets better," Lamont smiled, giving the terrorist beside him a funny look. "Commissioner Levings covered it up with a bit of B.S. that Burges concocted, so someone down the chain went over his head and called the Feds in to investigate the whole thing."

The driver whistled.

"He's done it this time then," the bodyguard said. "He won't be able to talk his way out of this one."

"Yeah," Lamont agreed, still eyeing Grigorie to make sure the guy wasn't going to try anything stupid now that his connection to the mayor had been uncovered. "Another hour, tops, and the Feds are going to haul Levings off to a cell, with the mayor straight afterwards."

"Then we'd better lie low, right?" the driver asked.

"You mean call this thing off?" Lamont asked. "Forget it. Burges can't pin us. There's nothing on paper he can use. This is our chance to get rid of this 'Vincent' guy and his organization and I'm going to take it."

"But what about the Feds? They'll be crawling all over the place in an hour, if they aren't already."

"Great. Perfect cover. With everyone watching the city's main police headquarters, no one will be paying any attention to the docks or Kingsford station." He turned to Grigorie. "That is if you're still happy to go ahead with it, comrade. Mind you though, I don't like people who renege on their agreements."

"Why would I renege? You're my ticket out of town, remember?"

Lamont nodded, satisfied with the reply. "That's right. Anyway, I guess we should be at the docks pretty soon. So what happens then?"

"You're going to intercept one of Vincent's freight boxes as it's unloaded and kill all the guys he's got there."

"There's no part of that plan I don't like. Then what?"

"First of all, I'll just have to point out that you need to be careful not to shoot the mayor's mole. The guy's done his job well so far and in my business, you reward people like that. They might be useful later on."

"In my business too," Lamont agreed.

"Good. Now, the next part is that Vincent's boys have got the driver's carriage of a train, along with two cargo carriages there."

"So they can just shift their stuff straight from the docks to their headquarters at Kingsford station?"

"That's right. Direct. No unloading necessary. No middlemen. Nothing. Then they distribute everything from their base of operations at their own pace."

"Boy, I'd love to have a set up like that. All right

then. Let me guess. Once we secure that freight box, we load it up with explosives—"

"Well, *I* load it up with explosives but close enough."

"Got it. And then someone drives the train to the station, jumps off somewhere safe and watches the fireworks."

"In a nutshell, yes."

Jason headed for the docks as fast as he could. He was glad he'd put that bug on Lamont's car a while ago; he knew he wouldn't have had time to get down to Grand Central's basement parking lot and tag the vehicle before Lamont and Grigorie left.

He made swift progress, using the network of flying foxes he had set up across the city—quite an impressive network, he realized with some pride. He hadn't paid that much attention when he had been setting it up, just putting a few more wires in place every few nights, but now it felt as though he'd ended up covering a tenth of the city. He was overestimating the scale of course, but it still blew him away... until he hit a dead end.

He found the remains of a climbing anchor he had put in place earlier, the wire missing. "Son of a bitch," he muttered. He looked across the gap between him and the building opposite. A while ago, he had talked to Geoffrey about the possibility of getting some gas-powered grappling hooks and they were coming. But they weren't on hand now and he knew he'd just have to settle for one of his sluggish harpoon hooks instead.

He fumbled in his bag, mindful that time was precious if he wanted to get to the docks before Lamont did.

With the harpoon in his hand, he identified a point on the ledge of the building opposite. He'd done this plenty of times before but never under time restraints. He took aim and fired the hook. It looked like it worked but when he pulled on the wire to test it, the hook dislodged and he realized he'd shot it into a loose girder.

In frustration, he freed his end of the wire and not wishing to leave a hazard—or a highly visible dangling wire that might get people looking up and noticing his other modifications to the Fringe City skyline—he fixed it to another hook and shot it off so the whole tangled mess sat on top of the building opposite and out of sight. Then he dug one of his climbing claws into a drainpipe and slid down, the resistance of the tearing metal slowing his descent.

At the central Fringe City Police headquarters,

everything appeared to be ineffective as usual when all hell broke loose. One minute, everyone in the main office was going about their business and the next, a wall exploded, sending shrapnel everywhere along with a thick cloud of dusty smoke. From somewhere in the gaping hole, someone lobbed two gas grenades into the room.

Several officers nearby tried to grab their weapons but were overcome by the gas before they could get them out of their holsters.

Just out of range of the gas but not for long, Diane took her jacket off and used it to cover her mouth. When the gas cloud swept over her, it largely stopped the effects. She maintained consciousness and could still move without disorientation but the stuff bothered her eyes terribly, making it hard to even keep them open.

Unable to do much else under the circumstances, she kept her head down, while reaching for her drawer—for her gun and her portable radio inside.

A moment later, the officers of Fringe City's police force present were confronted with a sight few had seen and lived to talk about, as the city's most notorious hit man emerged from the hole in the wall. His face was concealed, his body entirely covered with high grade Kevlar body armor and in his hands, and strapped to his belt and his back, he carried more military grade weaponry than the average person had seen outside of a hyper-stylized action movie. Nobody knew who he was but his name on the street, the name he was known by in all the news stories he had generated over his checkered career, was the Bandit.

Immediately, he opened fire—gunning down anyone unfortunate enough to be in his field of view. A few officers tried to take him out but their shots, failing to penetrate his armor, only succeeded in drawing his attention.

Diane knew with that much armor, the hand guns she and the other officers were carrying were probably useless against him. Fortunately though, given the insane amount of noise, it was safe to assume that the Bandit wouldn't hear her place a call.

"We read you," came a voice from her radio a moment later.

"We need a S.W.A.T. team in the station right now! The Bandit's on the premises!"

"Shit!" The man on the other end knew what that meant all right. "Hold tight."

"Bring air support if you've got it as well. We know how good this guy is at vanishing."

"You've got it. That son of a bitch is not getting away this time."

She felt a small sense of relief knowing that a whole lot of heavy reinforcements were now on their way but not much. The Bandit could do a hell of a lot of damage in a short space of time, and he was notorious for getting out of the tightest spots imaginable. Risking raising her head above her desk to see where the killer was then, she saw him head straight for the commissioner's office... and as much as Levings deserved what was no doubt coming to him, in that moment she genuinely pitied him.

Through the doorway, she saw that Levings had prepared himself. She hadn't known he had an impressive long barreled shotgun hidden under his desk but she did then. Levings gave it his all, emptying every shell in a desperate display of defiance. The Bandit even staggered a little under the attack. For the briefest moment, Diane thought that maybe—just maybe—a bullet had penetrated. However, the moment passed and the Bandit recomposed himself, losing little of his forward momentum and—using two automatic weapons at once—blew the commissioner away.

Then, after shattering the outside window with a fusillade of bullets absurdly excessive to the task, the Bandit leapt onto the street one storey below.

As one, the remaining officers in the building raced to the window to see what would happen next. Already, a helicopter was overhead and S.W.A.T. vans were tearing up the street from both ends, but the

Bandit ignored them. Without even looking at the vans, he blew away the cover of a man hole and jumped down into the city's stormwater system. The first of the S.W.A.T. teams arrived moments later and went straight down after him but it was soon clear they had lost him.

Not content with being a spectator, Diane went downstairs to see what she could do to help.

"Not much, I'm afraid," one of the S.W.A.T. officers told her. "We've got teams moving across the city to cover possible exits in the nearby neighborhoods but frankly, there are a lot of interconnecting pipes down there. And we can't cover all the man holes in the city."

Just then, there was a commotion as a number of other vehicles pulled up outside the station.

"Damn," the officer muttered, looking back up the street. "Could the Feds have picked a worse time to rock up?"

Diane took a breath. "Oh, well. I'd better go and bring them up to speed."

She walked briskly to the agent stepping out of the car at the front of the line of new arrivals. "Officers, I'm Captain Diane Reilly. I'm the one who sent that information to you."

"Nice to meet you, Captain," the agent replied, shaking her hand. His eyes however were riveted to the scene of chaos in front of him—the S.W.A.T. vans heading off in different directions, the men on the radios, the officers climbing in and out of the man hole and of course, the billowing clouds of smoke pouring out of the police headquarters. Utterly dazed by what he saw, he forgot to introduce himself entirely.

"Um... we're here to arrest to the commissioner," he said, still staring at the chaos.

"I'm afraid that's no longer possible, officer," Diane said. "You've seen the Bandit on the evening news?"

"Yeah," the other replied. "'Only in Fringe City' as they say. He was here?"

"He's just shot up half the precinct and it looks like the commissioner was his intended target. He left as soon as he killed him."

"And what's going on now?" the agent asked, his voice almost dreamlike now.

"The perpetrator's escaped into the stormwater drains so our S.W.A.T. teams are attempting to organize an entrapment operation," Diane told him. "It might work. It might not. But we've got to try, right?"

"Right." The voice was still hollow and distant.

"Man," one of the agents behind him said, shaking his head. "No wonder no one ever wants to come out to this hellhole."

Diane gave him a quick glance but ignored the tactless remark. She needed these people but like any Fringe City resident, she didn't care for outsiders badmouthing the place. That was *her* privilege.

"Jesus," the first agent said as his brain began to catch up with him. "Well, I suppose some of us ought to go to Grigorie's place then, and I guess a few of us can try and help out here…"

"I can take you to Grigorie's place," Diane volunteered, taking charge of the situation. "Come on."

Totally unaware of the mess that was unfolding at the police headquarters, Lamont pulled up at a section of the docks. His bodyguard got out of the car first, letting him out next and allowing Grigorie out afterwards. In the meantime, a few other cars pulled up and the rest of the men he'd asked along joined him.

"All right," Lamont said to Grigorie. "Let's go."

"This way," Grigorie replied.

Lamont and his men followed him past a few crates, then a few cars doubtless belonging to Vincent's boys—which they eyed with disdain—and then for about another six hundred feet onto a large concrete loading jetty. Old railroad tracks ran off the jetty into a tunnel and sitting at the very end of them next to the freight boxes was a rather derelict looking old freight train that fit the description Grigorie had given earlier.

Vincent's boys were in plain view beside it. By the

looks of things, they'd just disconnected the second cargo carriage, presumably because they only needed one to transport whatever was coming in that night. A few more of the men were back on the jetty, inspecting some newly unloaded crates.

"They're just looking for their one," Grigorie explained quietly. "The mole said there's just the one tonight... and it looks like they've found it."

Lamont nodded as he saw one of the men climbing into a fork lift to move one of the things. "All right. Now, where's your mole?"

"The mayor's mole," Grigorie corrected.

"Whatever," Lamont muttered.

"He's standing the furthest away," Grigorie said, pointing out one of the men. "Hands in his pockets. Ugly cap. Fits right in, doesn't he?"

"Jesus, comrade," Lamont smiled. "You've got an ounce of humor after all."

"Flesh and blood like the rest of you," Grigorie told him, actually smiling as well. For once. "Now, the mole will drive the train to the station because he's done it before."

A short distance away, Jason observed all of them in silence. Lamont and Grigorie, the other men who were with them, Vincent's boys... all of them. But he didn't move in. He had a pretty fair idea of what Lamont and his men were going to do next, and while he didn't exactly approve of it, it would certainly make his work easier. And besides, they'd just be gunning down drug dealers and murderers.

But now that he was about to witness it all with his own eyes, he felt a sudden sense of apprehension, dread... and disgust. He was disgusted with himself.

He was waiting for Lamont's men to gun down Vincent's boys and worse, he was counting on it.

Watching in silence, he decided he just had to accept that he wasn't responsible for what was about to happen. All he was responsible for was using the knowledge he had gained to save the residents of Kingsford, who had no idea that the mayor of Fringe City was planning to kill them all for the sake of a bit of property development.

Then the sound of gunfire drowned out his thoughts. It was loud—louder than he had expected even though he had already expected it to be louder than that. It also brought back the terror from the café shooting where it had all started for him but he pushed the memory from his mind. That was the past; this was the present. Then, only moments after it began, it was over.

He observed the mole, who had ducked out of sight during the firing, as he moved out from behind one of the crates and met with Lamont. Vincent's boys meanwhile were down and they weren't getting up again. Satisfied that Lamont's attention was now entirely focused on rigging the train, Jason moved into position for the next stage of his plan.

"So you're the mayor's man?" Lamont said, shaking the hand of Reggie's mole. "Got a name?"

"No, and as far as I'm concerned, neither do you," the man replied.

"Fair enough." Lamont agreed. "So we load that train up with explosives and you drive it in?"

"Basically. Grigorie will set them up, I'll get the train going at the right speed and then he and I'll jump off and the whole thing will go off like clockwork."

"Great. Now where are these bombs of yours?"

The mole walked over to a crate a few yards away from the one containing Vincent's merchandise. "This crate here. Came in with the same shipment as Vincent's."

Lamont smiled. "Beautiful. By the way, you won't have any objections to my boys laying claim to Vincent's merchandise, will you?" There was no question in his voice.

"Do whatever you want with it," the mole replied, a little annoyed. Not because he wasn't getting a say in the matter but because of the nature of the remark. Lamont didn't need to throw his weight around with him. They were supposed to be on the same side.

"Now, let's hear the rest of the details," Lamont said.

"All right. Grigorie will set up the explosives on the train. I'll drive it towards the station and he'll be with me, as I said. Before it reaches the station, there's a short cantilever bridge with two tracks. Both unused. As the train gets there, I'll slow down and we'll jump off."

"What about the timing of the explosion?" Lamont interrupted.

"I was just getting to that," the mole replied, trying to keep a grip on his patience. "Grigorie's going to use a tracking device that'll let us know when the train reaches Kingsford station and then he'll detonate the explosives by remote. There won't be any automatic timers involved so we'll have complete control over everything at all points of the operation."

"Sounds good. Now what can my men do for you?"

"Well, they can help us load the train. But after that, we'll be fine. The only thing left for you will be to pick Grigorie up and take him to the airport."

"Great. Let's get started then."

With that, Lamont set his men to the task of unloading the explosives from their storage crate and putting them on the train under Grigorie's supervision. When they were finished however, Grigorie looked a little perplexed.

"Something wrong, comrade?" Lamont asked him.

"Yes," Grigorie scowled, pacing around the now empty crate and looking everywhere with searching eyes. "I'm two explosives short."

"Well, my men unloaded everything inside this box. You saw it yourself. Maybe whoever loaded the explosives at the other end screwed up."

"Not likely," Grigorie said. "I've worked with him before. But I suppose it's possible."

"All right then. Is it a problem?"

Grigorie shrugged. "I've still got enough explosives to make short work of everything and everyone in that do the job. It's just... I don't like missing hardware."

"So you're good to go then?" Lamont asked, suddenly impatient to get the whole thing over with.

"What, are you worried about the Feds all of a sudden?" Grigorie asked him. "What happened to your sense of cool detachment?"

"I just want to make sure you don't miss your flight," Lamont replied, matching his tone.

Again, Grigorie smiled. "I like you. Maybe we'll do business again sometime."

"Christ, I hope not," Lamont muttered. "All right. I'll go and wait by the bridge. With luck, we'll get there a few minutes before you."

"See you there," Grigorie replied and climbed into the driver's carriage followed by the mole. Suddenly, the mole went flying back from the doorway, landing on his side and rolling to Lamont's feet.

"What the-?" Lamont moved towards the train, drawing his weapon, but a few of his men waved him back.

"Grigorie's gone!" one of them called out, after looking in the doorway of the driver's carriage.

"Check the crates on the other side!" Lamont ordered. The men spread out and did a quick sweep of the area, but found nothing. "Where the hell could he have gone?" one of them wondered.

"I hope you boys can swim."

Everyone looked about in confusion. Lamont found his voice first. "Come again?" he asked, trying to work out where the voice had come from.

"I said I hope you boys can swim," the voice said again. "You should probably remove your shoes and coats. Clothes tend to drag you down."

"Who the hell are you?" Lamont demanded, turning around and waving his gun. "Show yourself!"

"You know who I am, Mr. Lamont, as I am sure you're also aware you're standing on a small concrete wharf and you're missing two explosives."

"You?" Lamont asked, beginning to sweat.

"Yes, me, Mr. Lamont," the voice replied. "The explosives are underneath you, one under each side of this platform. The water underneath isn't very deep but it's deep enough. And don't forget the other explosives on the train."

"You're crazy!" Lamont shouted.

"That's entirely possible," the voice agreed. "But I've got the detonator from your friend Grigorie and I'm deadly serious. No more games."

The Sentinel appeared standing on one of the nearby crates with Grigorie beside him, bound and gagged with wire. Then Lamont and his men noticed something they'd missed before: a wire rig running from a light post behind the crate to the buildings next to the wharf.

"You were planning to kill a lot of innocent people tonight," the Sentinel said. "And that's something I don't stand for."

He glided along the wire, with Grigorie tied to another flying fox contraption in front of him. A few of Lamont's men opened fire but it was too late. The others just ran for it and, a moment later, the wharf exploded, sending pieces of crates, twisted metal fragments from the train, concrete, wood and packets of drugs flying into the air. Lamont's men managed to get out of range of this meteor shower of debris but as the Sentinel had hinted it would, their footing gave way almost immediately and a second later, they found themselves swimming through the dark waters of Fringe City's harbor, Lamont as well.

The swim to shore wasn't far but weighed down by their clothes and having to fight their way through the now submerged rubble that was all that was left of the wharf, it was exhausting. When the men finally crawled out at the water's edge, coughing and spluttering, they were separated from each other and Lamont was alone when the Sentinel grabbed him by the collar of his shirt.

"You know," the Sentinel told him, "since I ought to feed you to the dogs, you should be grateful that I'm just leaving you for the cops."

Lamont looked to his right, where a few of his men were climbing out of the water, but his imploring gaze went ignored. The men, clearly frightened by the apparition that had its hands around their boss's neck, took just one look and ran.

Not long afterwards, the Sentinel held Grigorie over the edge of a building four storeys up, having now taken care of Lamont. The infamous subway bomber, hunted all over the country, was terrified.

"You're finished, Grigorie," the Sentinel told him. "And since there's no way out for you, there really isn't any point in protecting the mayor now, is there?"

Grigorie tried to nod his agreement, his gaze flitting between the drop below him and the man in the armored suit who was the only thing keeping him on the ledge.

"More to the point," the Sentinel continued. "If I find out that you do try to protect the mayor, then you'll find yourself removed from police custody and right back here."

A few minutes later, Diane and the Feds returned to the chaos at police headquarters, having found Grigorie's place empty and his few belongings cleared out. As they entered the main office, they overheard a commotion around a phone.

The man taking the call seemed flustered and the officers around him seemed to be waiting to see what it was all about. "Look. If you tell me, I can help you with the problem." He looked up and a wave of visible relief swept over him when he saw Diane. "Oh, thank god!"

Diane frowned. "What's going on?"

"This joker insists on talking to you and you only," the man said. "He won't talk to me."

"Here," Diane told him. "I'll take it." She had a fair idea who it was, and anything that pulled her away from the chaos that had taken over the station was a welcome distraction. "Hello," she said, taking the phone. "This is Captain Diane Reilly. I hear you want to speak to me."

"I'm calling from a pay phone."

"I figured that. What do you want to tell me?"

"I have Grigorie."

Diane drew in a breath. "Where?"

The man momentarily passed the question over. "I also have Lamont. And the two of them were collaborating with the mayor. You can pick them up at 422, 82nd street in the docks district."

"I'll be right—"

"There's more," the man said. "Lamont and Grigorie were planning to bomb the Kingsford subway station."

"What? Why?"

"A rival organization to Lamont's group is working out of it, stockpiling drugs there. If I were you, I'd send a S.W.A.T. team in to take care of that."

"How do you know all this?"

"Long story. You'll have to take it on faith. But you'll get your proof soon enough. You can trust me on that."

Diane took a breath to calm herself. "And are you who I think you are?"

"That depends on who you've got in mind," the

man replied and hung up.

Throwing his bag over his shoulder, Jason left the public phone booth, looking for all the world like a backpacker who had just stepped off the bus or a postgrad college student coming home after a football game. To the casual observer, there was nothing out of the ordinary about his appearance. And neither Alex Grigorie nor Martin Lamont were anywhere in sight.

Roughly eight minutes later, Diane and her adopted group of Feds pulled up beside three of Lamont's cars. The tires of all three vehicles were slashed and the drivers were missing, while the trunks were slightly ajar.

"Is this the place?" one of the Feds asked, confused.

"It has to be," Diane replied. "Open the trunks."

"All right," the man said. He gave a nod to the others. They opened the trunk of the car at the rear and found Lamont inside, bound and gagged. And in the trunk of the next car in the line, they found Grigorie.

Both men were hauled out of the vehicles, their gags removed, and shoved up against the side of the rear car, where they were cuffed properly and freed from the tangle of wires they were wrapped up in.

Diane ignored Lamont for the moment, walking up to Grigorie. "I've been told you have some information for me," she told him.

From a distance, the Sentinel watched—in his costume once more. When it was all over and the police cars pulled away, he left too.

GRAND CENTRAL

Angie rolled over, wondering what had woken her up. She blinked once and then she heard it again. The doorbell. She reached for the alarm clock and checked the time: 11.30. "What the hell?" she muttered, climbing out of the bed. She fumbled in the dark until she found the light switch and threw on a large shirt that went to her thighs.

Groggily, she walked to the door and looked through the peephole before answering. "Jesus," she muttered when she saw who it was. She slid back the lock and opened the door, glaring at the man standing there in distaste. "Damn, Geoffrey. Do you have any idea what time it is?"

More at home with his science than normal human interactions, Geoffrey brushed the question off and marched straight in. "Oh my god!" he exclaimed. Angie watched him as he headed straight for the kitchen, unable to help noticing the bag of microwave popcorn he was carrying.

"Quick, turn on the TV!" he told her.

"Why?" Angie asked.

"Why?" Geoffrey exclaimed as he set the microwave timer for the popcorn. "What do you mean 'why'? Where have you been?"

"I've been trying to sleep."

"Screw that," Geoffrey told her, brushing past her to flick on the TV. "The city's going to hell out there. The Bandit shot up the police headquarters, along with the police commissioner. Then FBI agents found Grigorie, right here in Fringe City. There's also been a bomb blast at the wharfs, and a major drug bust at Kingsford station that's still going. A S.W.A.T. unit's down there in a shootout with a mob group." He shook his head. "Man, you've got to love this town."

Despite the absurdity of it all, Angie could sort of understand his excitement. A lot of Fringe City residents had adjusted to the madness they put up with in their daily lives by just looking at it all as some kind of circus show. However, right then she didn't appreciate Geoffrey taking that attitude. If she was right, then Jason was out there in the middle of it.

Diane pulled up at Grand Central. The building was already surrounded by various police units, bathing the scene in the alternating strobe effect of blue and red lights.

"I don't know if you've got enough to convict your mayor," the Fed at her side said as they walked up to the officer who looked like he was in charge of the show. "But you've definitely got enough to arrest him. I mean, I've come across a lot of political corruption in my time but this just takes the cake."

"What's going on?" Diane asked the officer, who she recognized as Commander Harrington.

"What's going on is that I'm in charge here, Captain Reilly," he snapped. "So why don't you back off and stop acting like you're running the show. I know the Sentinel seems to think you're the only honest cop on the force, and you got to take in Grigorie and all that, but a lot of us take our jobs just as seriously as you do."

Diane grimaced. She didn't need this. Harrington was a good cop but he had a tendency to get defensive when it wasn't warranted.

Fortunately, she didn't need to say anything as the Federal agent beside her intervened on her behalf. "Look… "

"Commander Harrington," the man gruffly introduced himself.

"It's good to meet you, sir," the agent replied, shaking his hand. "I'm Federal Agent McLaughlin."

"Nice to meet you too, sir, but as you can see, I'm pretty busy so—"

"I just have to point out, sir, that Captain Reilly here

was the officer on scene when the call was made to arrest the mayor so she should be in on this operation as well."

"Jesus," Harrington complained. "Do I fly to Washington and tell you how to do your jobs?"

"Actually, I'm stationed in Richmond," McLaughlin said. "And I wouldn't presume to tell you how to do your job. We're not here to take over. We're here to help."

This cooled Harrington down somewhat. He sighed. "Sorry, buddy. It's been a rough night. And now it seems the mayor's got word of the arrest warrant we issued for him. So he's got *another* insider."

"How many bent cops have we *got* in our outfit?" Diane wondered aloud. "So what's the story? Has he barricaded himself in?"

"We can't tell whether he's completely blocked off all routes to the top floor," Harrington said, "but he's disabled the elevators somehow. I'd say he's probably tried to block the stairwells as well."

Inside the building, Burges was busy on his computer, bringing up the false identification he had given Grigorie. He swapped the photo with one of his own, printed it off and hastily assembled the fake ID. Even with the knowledge that half the police force of Fringe

City was outside the building, he did it with an ease borne from familiarity.

Once it was done, he set about transferring millions from his bank account to an offshore subsidiary of a company that didn't exist. Behind him, the paper shredders were running at full capacity as Merlon destroyed his collection of sensitive material. Soon, the sound of shredding ceased, and the only background noise was the hum of the machines as they'd been left on their automatic settings.

"Is that everything?" Burges asked.

"Yeah, that's everything."

Burges nodded, wiped the sweat off his brow and shot Merlon through the chest with a hand gun the other man never even saw he was carrying. He then gathered what was left of his gear, stuffed it into his briefcase and left the office, running for a staircase that led onto the roof.

Down below, the assembled police force watched as one of their choppers flew in. Harrington smiled. "We've got him now."

Diane nodded but for some reason, she didn't share his optimism. Something felt wrong to her.

Then there was a small commotion and several officers who'd been standing around one of the patrol cars ran over. "Captain Reilly, Commander Harrington! We were just on the radio to headquarters. Two of our pilots have just been found beaten up. They're alive but in bad shape."

Diane looked back at the helicopter as it hovered above the roof, preparing for its descent.

"Commander," she said to Harrington. "Grigorie was carrying false documents to get him out of the country. The mayor might try the same thing. We need to alert the airport and send a unit out there."

"Leave it to me," Harrington replied, pulling out his radio.

On the roof of the building, Burges watched as the helicopter set down. From the shadows cast by the rooftop air conditioning vents, the Sentinel also watched.

The rotating blades slowed and Burges ran from his position, ready to leap on board. The Sentinel however moved faster, bolting out into the open and tackling the mayor to the ground.

Inside the helicopter, there were two men aside from the pilot. Seeing this unwelcome intruder, one of them swung the door open and fired a shot that hit Jason in his side. The body armor absorbed most of the impact but it still hurt. With a grimace, he turned around and moved towards the door. Before the thug could fire his weapon again, Jason grabbed him by the back of his head and threw him face first into the concrete.

The blow left the man dazed and clearly in a bad way.

Jason then grabbed the second thug from the chopper and dragged him out too. Feeling exhilarated from a sudden rush of adrenaline, he slammed the second thug's head into the side of the machine before dropping him beside the first thug.

The pilot in the meantime, no doubt deciding his own skin was a lot more important to him than saving the mayor's ass, shoved Jason away from the door and tried to get the helicopter into the air.

However, Jason had other plans. He rushed past the two stunned men and the mayor—who was now trying to crawl away unnoticed—and grabbed his bag, which was next to the air conditioning vents where he'd been hiding. He then pulled out his harpoon, took aim, and fired a hook that caught onto the helicopter's landing gear. With that done, he anchored the other end onto the air conditioning units and watched the results of his handiwork; the pilot of the craft got about sixty feet off the roof before the line went taut. Seeing the danger, the pilot brought the vehicle back down.

As the helicopter landed again, the pilot grabbed a

hand gun and prepared to leap out and run into the open where he could cover the whole roof and shoot the bastard who was waiting for him out there.

However in mid-leap, a firm hand caught him off balance. Then, as he had with the others, the Sentinel threw him face first into the concrete. That done, he bound the man's hands with wire.

"Since wire can cut when drawn tightly," he told him, "I'd advise you not to struggle."

With the pilot taken care of, Jason stood up and looked around to see where the mayor had gotten to. The first thing he saw though was one of the other two thugs starting to climb up. Rushing over, he restrained him before he got the chance. While he was doing this though, the man who'd shot him earlier recovered his wits and drew his gun.

Having now had it with the guy, Jason knocked the gun from his hand and sent it sliding under the helicopter. Then he slammed him back onto the roof and pounded his face into the gravel a few times for good measure and personal satisfaction. He got some more wire and bound the thug's hands more tightly than he had with the others, and finished up by rolling him onto his back just to make him a little less comfortable.

"Now *stay* down this time, you son of a bitch!"

After that, there was only one thing left to take care

of.

Now, the perpetually cool, calm and collected Burges was a shivering wreck. Jason found him slithering on the concrete, practically whimpering in fright, and trying to back away.

"It's over, Mr. Mayor," he told him. "You're finished."

When the police finally broke through all the makeshift barricades of desks and chairs that the mayor had blocked the stairwells with and emerged onto the roof, the Sentinel was gone.

"So, where are we at now?" Diane asked the young lieutenant who had just come off the radio to bring them all up to speed.

The man looked at her and Commander Harrington and nodded to the Feds. "The gang in Kingsford station disappeared down the tunnels. They were smart enough to know the odds were against them."

"It's like the Bandit all over again," Harrington muttered. "You won't find them, believe me. And I guess the search for the Bandit turned up empty too, right?"

"Yeah. The boys in headquarters called it off ten minutes ago."

Harrington nodded. "Sounds like the sensible thing

to me."

"Anyway," the lieutenant continued, "while that gang got away, we seized an enormous drug stash so we've probably prevented a lot of headaches further down the line there."

"Yeah," Diane agreed. "Cut that stuff out of circulation anywhere you can. Anyway... Thanks, Lieutenant."

Behind her, Harrington took a call on his radio. He nodded a little, then shook his head in bemusement before turning back to them. "Well, I'd say it's almost academic now whether or not we had enough to put the mayor away. It seems that in trying to cover his tracks, the mayor shot his assistant. And we've got all the evidence we need to prove it."

"Right then," Diane said. "Well, I think it's time to pack this show in. I'm sure we'd all agree it's been a long night."

"Yeah, and I'm not looking forward to the paperwork for all of this," Harrington added.

"We might get going too," McLaughlin said. "Grigorie's wanted in New York."

"We want him here," Harrington protested. "Forget New York. Or don't you trust us enough to keep him?"

"I think such matters are above our authority," McLaughlin told him. "Yours and mine both. However, we'll get a full confession out of him before we take him and we'll give you everything you need. Tapes. A written transcript of the whole thing. Everything."

He started to turn away and then stopped. "One last thing though. This 'Sentinel' has obviously been a big help to everyone. I see that. But don't forget that you're still dealing with a vigilante and a dangerous one at that. I understand you might not want to bring him in and I'm not going to judge. But maybe you can just tell him that you appreciate what he's done and that you'll take over from here."

"Get him to back down?" Diane asked, her tone doubtful.

McLaughlin shrugged. "I don't know how. And I imagine it won't be easy. But if I were you, I would try to stop this guy before he gets carried away. Before someone gets hurt."

It was a couple of hours away from sunrise when Jason got home. He was exhausted as he came through the door and closing it behind him took his last reserves of energy.

"Oh, thank god you're home," Angie said, tears of relief in her eyes as she hugged him. She then noticed blood seeping through the side of his shirt. "You're hurt!"

"My first injury in the line of duty," Jason replied, walking over to the couch and collapsing in a heap. He turned his head to acknowledge his friend who was sitting at the other end. "Hey, Geoffrey."

"What happened?" Angie asked.

"Someone shot me," Jason replied. "But I'm fine," he added quickly. "The armor took most of the impact and the bullet didn't penetrate. I've just got an ugly bruise with a bit of bleeding."

"Oh, well done on a good night's work there, Jason," Geoffrey said. "We've been watching the live coverage all night. I tell you, they'll be replaying the highlights for weeks."

"I'm glad you found it so entertaining, Geoffrey," Jason told him, giving Angie a sympathetic glance; she'd probably been listening to Geoffrey go on like that for hours.

"Oh, you'll also be pleased to know I should have your gas-powered grappling hooks ready pretty soon."

"Cool. You know, I was thinking of them tonight actually. Now that you mention it."

Geoffrey paused. "They would have come in handy?"

"They would have but don't feel down about it," Jason told him. "Trust me. I couldn't do any of this without you." He yawned. "Anyway, what I need right now is sleep and lots of it."

Geoffrey smiled and got up. "Got it."

"Night, Geoffrey," Angie said.

"Night, guys," he replied as he left.

"Well," Angie said, sitting down next to Jason and leaning up to him. "Honey, I realize Geoffrey's been working hard on these grappling hooks and you're probably pretty fired up at the moment with all the progress you've been making. But you've got to the bottom of the mess you were trying to sort out. The mayor's being put away. Maybe we can put an end to all this now. You know, quit while you're ahead."

Jason didn't reply.

"Don't forget how close we both came to getting killed when you started this whole thing," she reminded him.

"I know," Jason murmured, the effort of speaking noticeable. "I made mistakes then... but you know... I've learned from them." He closed his eyes and yawned again, leaning back onto the couch. "Actually that thing with the Black Baron..."

"All right," Angie said. "You can't fall asleep here. Let's get you to bed." She reached for his arm.

"That tightened my resolve," Jason finished at last.

"Yeah?" Angie asked. "For me, it just tightened my wallet. Even with the insurance payments, losing the old apartment still put a rather large dent in our budget."

She helped him up and supporting him, walked to the bedroom. "Anyway, the Black Baron's dead and the mayor's being put away. So really, you've got what you wanted, right?"

"Maybe," Jason replied and let himself fall on the bed.

Angie sighed. So much for the conversation. "Let him rest," she murmured to herself. "He needs it." Carefully, she undressed him, rolled him into a more comfortable sleeping position and pulled the sheets up.

For a few moments, she watched him in silence. Then she leaned forward and kissed him on the forehead. "I love you," she whispered.

She discarded her shirt, flicked the light off and crawled into bed alongside him. Then she lay awake for a few more minutes, thinking about the events of the past few weeks before she fell asleep too.

THE FALLOUT

DIANE

THE GLARING LIGHTS OF THE NEIGHBORHOOD'S
neon signs were tacky and largely red. Some formed
words, some formed... other things. And on the corner
of a street, a slimy looking character covered in gold
jewelry was hawking his wares, a group of scantily
clad young women.

The jerk had been standing there a while and
business was slow. "I'm going inside," he told the girls.
"Got to make a call. Stay put!"

He shoved the door open to his little five-room hotel
and walked up the creaky wooden steps to his office
on the second floor. Absently trying to light a cigarette
in one hand, he flicked the light switch with the other.
It took him a second to realize nothing had happened.
"What the hell, what the hell..." he muttered, trying
the switch again and flicking it back and forth. He tried
the switch in the hall as well and nothing happened
there either.

"What the—"

Before he got another word out, someone threw him

across the room, landing him on his back in the middle of his desk. He groaned and as he tried to stagger to his feet, the window shattered.

The Sentinel knocked him down again. Then he leaned out of the window and fired a gas-powered grappling hook at the roof ledge. He waited a moment while the pimp climbed to his feet and fired a second grappling hook at him, which wrapped around him and pinned his arms to the side.

"What the hell are you doing, man?" the pimp demanded.

Not bothering to answer, the Sentinel yanked him to the window and used the first grappling hook to pull them both up to the roof by recoiling the wire.

"Holy shit! What do you want with me, man?"

"You're blackmailing your girls over minor infringements to keep them here. It ends now."

"Wha-?" the pimp protested. "What about Caprini around the corner? He's got this Russian girl. Holding her passport—"

"Had," the Sentinel corrected him. "I've already taken care of that son of a bitch."

"Jesus, man, what did you do to him?"

"That's his business. Worry about your own. The other night, a woman was found dead in the alley behind this establishment of yours. I'm looking for the guy who killed her."

"I don't know shit about that, man. I swear to God!"

"Well, the trail seems to keep coming back to you. One of your clients perhaps?"

The man nodded, visibly sweating. "All right, all right. The guy's a regular but I don't know his name or nothing."

"I suggest then," the Sentinel said, "that you tell me everything you *do* know."

It was nice being on the day shift for a change, Diane thought as she sipped a coffee and looked over the daily reports and listened to the gossip in the office.

"Who's the 'hard ass'?" she asked the guy next to her, nodding to the conversation at the next table.

The officer looked over, listened in for a moment and turned back. "Ah, they're talking about our new acting commissioner, Eric Hutchens. Some big showboat I hadn't even heard of until a couple of days ago."

"He was a commander in a nearby precinct, wasn't he?" Diane said.

The officer shrugged. "Maybe."

"So why's he a hard ass?"

"Apparently he's on some kind of one-man vendetta against the Sentinel for goodness-knows-what reason, saying he's a liability and this, that and the other." He shrugged again and stirred the coffee in front of him.

"That's insane. The Sentinel saved half the police force from the Black Baron. He caught Burges and if it weren't for him, several hundred residents of the Kingsford area would have been killed. Also, I bet this vendetta is nothing more than a smokescreen to draw everyone's attention away from the fact that the Bandit is still at large."

The officer beside her shook his head. "No, I don't think anyone's expecting Hutchens to bring that guy in. The way he always appears out of nowhere and vanishes without a trace... The Bandit's just something we have to live with."

"No, he's not."

The officer looked surprised by the strength of Diane's reaction. Then he sighed. "No, you're right. We just have to keep trying. I'm sure we'll get him eventually."

They were both silent for a while, he drinking his coffee and Diane flipping through the reports in front of her.

"What's this?" she asked, picking up a homicide report.

"Girl dumped in an alley a few nights ago."

"It looks like someone's just filled in a few blank spaces on the form and called it a day."

"Forensics looked into it and found some fingerprints and DNA but they don't match any of our records. And we've got nothing else to go on. The murder took place in a red light district where heaps of people come and go all round the clock." The officer shrugged again. "You could take the case if you want it."

Acting Commissioner Eric Hutchens looked up from the sidewalk, shielding his eyes against the glare. "Here," he said, turning to one of the men beside him. "Hand me those binoculars."

"Yeah," he murmured as he adjusted them and got a better look. "Right there."

"Where?" the man asked.

"Between those two buildings," Hutchens said, pointing. "Another wire."

"I see it. We'll take it down immediately."

"And make a note of the building addresses and see if there's any other gear lying about on the roofs. Climbing anchors or bits of junk. You know the drill."

"And shall I mark out some surveillance points nearby?"

"Yeah, we'll post another man up there somewhere tonight. That's nine locations so far, and maybe we can find nine more before dark. Who knows? Maybe tonight, we'll catch our man."

District Attorney Charles Faulkner shook his head as he walked down the hallway. "I can't believe Lamont walked. Our mystery friend messed that case up completely."

"How's that?" his assistant asked.

"He destroyed too much of the evidence," Faulkner explained. "If he left that train intact with all the explosives Lamont's men had loaded it with, we may have had all the proof we needed to back our case. However, now the police divers'll have to scour the harbor for ages before they can find anything we can use. And that leaves us with nothing but Alex Grigorie's word."

He laughed in despondent impotence. "And the defence had field day with that, I can tell you. The testimony of an urban terrorist as evidence. I can't say I blame them."

"But if the Sentinel hadn't blown the docks, then Lamont would have bombed that subway station, surely?"

Faulkner shrugged. "Maybe. Maybe not."

"Anyway, it's not all bad news. Burges is still going away for a number of years and we have that news footage showing how he was clearly on good terms with Grigorie while the manhunt was going on. When you think about it, the Sentinel really did try to provide us with the evidence we needed to prosecute these guys. There was also that conversation he recorded between Burges, Lamont and Grigorie in their office."

"Yeah, and it was a nice gesture sending it in. But still, even if he's not an expert on law, he should have known bugged recordings obtained without warrants aren't permitted as evidence."

The assistant smiled, trying to lift Faulkner's spirits. "Don't worry, sir. We still got one of our big fish and that's nothing to sneer at. And sooner or later, Lamont will screw up."

Sitting in one of his private bars, Martin Lamont glared at his men. "I don't know what I pay you for. I really don't. What a spectacular display of heroism that was. There I am being threatened by this Sentinel bastard and what do you guys do? Run for it."

No one was stupid enough to try to apologize. Lamont watched them until they all looked appropriately ashamed of themselves, then changed the line of conversation. "All right. New order of business. I've been giving it some thought over the past few days and it seems to me this fiasco with Burges's plan was not a complete waste of time. I talked to some of our men in the police department earlier today and they say those drugs they seized are top quality and will fetch a pretty good price on the street. However, if we're going to take advantage of this, we've got to move this stock quickly. These new arrivals and their boss… this Danny Vincent guy… they could be a problem. So I don't want to give them any time to find out their drugs weren't destroyed."

"You shouldn't try to argue with Gary," Angie told Jason as they stepped through their door and into their little apartment.

Jason shrugged. "What's he going to do? If he could get rid of me, he would've done it ages ago."

"That's not the point," Angie said. "It doesn't do you any good either to get yourself all riled up. Just try not to let it get to you."

Gary, the principal of East Somerset High, had figured out a new way of scheduling teacher's meetings by going around to everyone's staffroom to announce today's one in person. Jason's trick of putting the reminder notices back in Gary's office was ineffective against this new strategy and as a result, he and Angie were home an hour later than usual.

Jason sighed. "Yeah, you're right. I just wish he'd give these meetings a miss. We all know how to do our jobs. What's to talk about?"

"Nothing," Angie replied. "But... you know. Gary doesn't budge when it comes to these bureaucratic requirements. You know that. But I think the *real* problem is you're burnt out doing this evening job of yours. You can't keep this up forever."

"Yeah, I know that."

"So why not put the costume away and move on? Maybe we can move out of this town some day, settle down, have a kid... You know. Do normal things like normal people."

"I want to sort out this thing with that girl in the red light district. And I've already taken care of those pimps I read about in the *Inquirer*."

"The police could have done that."

"But they didn't," Jason said. "Even with the article that was printed."

"It wasn't a frontline story and the *Inquirer* isn't a major broadsheet," Angie countered. "They might not have known. You could have called up from that new cell phone that Geoffrey made for you and demanded to speak to your friend Diane Reilly. I'm sure she would have helped."

"Yeah, maybe, But the point is my way worked."

Angie sighed. "Yeah, but—"

"And now I think I might be able to catch the man who murdered that woman too."

"All right," Angie said. "So you'll clean up this messy red light district. But then what? Are you going to go off on P.I. mode every time you come across some unsolved crime in the newspapers? You can't carry all this on your shoulders."

"At least I've packed away the CCTV gear and put the other TV in the cupboard."

"Outstanding," Angie said. "And off-topic. I'm not worried about you wasting blank DVDs here. I'm worried about you literally burning yourself out."

Jason sighed. "I know."

"It'd be better all round to quit this thing while you're ahead. And while you're alive."

"You're right."

"Don't go out tonight, honey," Angie told him. "Have a rest. We'll stay in, have an early dinner... then we'll go to bed early as well and have a nice long sleep so we don't feel exhausted tomorrow."

"It's Friday tomorrow," Jason murmured.

"It's still a school day though."

"All right. You win, honey. I'll continue the hunt tomorrow night then."

"Well, I suppose that's a fair compromise," Angie said. "Deal."

· · ·

As Jason slept, Eric Hutchens' men waited on the rooftops. No one turned up wondering where their flying fox wires had gotten to and when the morning came around, they were all tired as hell with nothing to show for their all-night vigil.

For Jason however, he started the day well-rested and felt better than he'd felt on any Friday so far during the semester. The rest of the day wasn't too bad either. His least favorite class was nowhere in sight, and he had his senior history class that he actually *enjoyed* teaching. All in all, it wasn't a bad way to end the week.

"That was interesting, this afternoon," he said to Angie as they left for the day.

"What was that?"

"I had this girl who was working on a story written in first-person style from the point of view of three separate characters. And it cut between them without backtracking on the narrative once. She told me she got the idea from some books she read over the holidays. The girl actually reads at home."

"What on earth is she doing at East Somerset High?" Angie wondered in jest.

"Beats me. But it's nice to know there are kids who are actually interested in learning. It helps makes it all worthwhile. You know, every now and then I think of giving it all up and getting a job in a mail-sorting room somewhere—"

"Yeah, me too."

"But then I remember the occasional kids out there who actually give me some hope for the future and I start to see things a little differently. Suddenly, it stops being a soul destroying grind and becomes a chance to make a difference in people's lives."

"Wow. Jason, I'm impressed."

Jason smiled. "I know, I can't believe I'm saying this myself. Don't worry though. I'm sure this weird mood'll wear off soon."

When they got home, there was a message on the machine from Geoffrey. Jason played the tape. "Hey, Jason," came the familiar voice. "I thought it'd be nice to catch up this afternoon if you're interested. Also, I've got a present for you."

Angie raised her eyebrows. "Any idea what that might mean?"

Jason shrugged. "Not sure. It sounds like he's moving ahead of me now. Creating supply *before* demand."

"Anticipating whatever it is you'll need next."

"Yeah," Jason said. "So what do I want?" He picked up the phone and dialed. He didn't have to wait long.

"Hey man. Did you get my message?"

Jason grinned. "Loud and clear, Wolfman. So you've anticipated the next item on my wish list and gone ahead and made it?"

"I figure it saves time."

Jason laughed. "True. So what is it exactly that I want next?"

"Oh, it's more fun if I show you."

"Why don't you come around then?"

"What's the menu?"

"How about some take-away from Delhi Palace? My treat. Beef vindaloo, butter chicken and tandoori chicken, of course."

"I'm there. Oh, and don't forget the Tikka Masala."

"Beef or lamb?"

"Well, we've covered beef with the vindaloo, so lamb."

"And garlic naan?"

"Of course."

"All right," Jason told him, checking his watch and doing some quick thinking. "I'll order at five and we can have an early dinner. Come round anytime you want."

Geoffrey actually arrived before they ordered and with a big grin on his face, he opened up his bag and pulled out some very cool looking gadgets.

"If you liked the gas-powered grappling hooks I gave you before, then you're going to love these," he said, holding one up to show Jason. "Double-action gas-powered grappling hooks. Allow me to demonstrate."

He indicated the different parts of the device as he explained what it did. "You can fire a hook from one end onto the building you're on and then from the other end, you can fire a hook onto another building. *Then* hold the trigger mechanism down like this... and that cord retracts, while the other unwinds, allowing you to slide across the way you would with one of your old flying foxes. I also put in a little safety control mechanism that slows down the speed the cords retract at for the last foot of their length. That way they won't give you that whiplash effect you get from vacuum cleaner cords."

"Awesome."

"And unlike your old flying fox system, you don't have to leave wires everywhere."

Jason shook his head. "You know, you couldn't have timed this better. The acting police commissioner's busy taking down my old flying fox wires right *now*."

"Is he?" Geoffrey asked. "There's been nothing in the news about it."

"Of course there hasn't," Jason said. "He doesn't want me to know. But fortunately, I'm a little more observant than he gives me credit for. Also, he seems to think I'd be stupid enough to just rock up to one of my network points leaping from roof to roof in my Sentinel gear. I don't work that way. Well, okay. There was that one time when I was tailing Lamont to the dock district but it's not my usual modus operandi."

Geoffrey nodded. "Fair enough. Well then, in light of my excellent timing, I think I've earned something extra, wouldn't you say?"

"Well, we haven't ordered yet so all right. What would you like me to add to the list?"

"Beef Madras and pompadums."

"That's two items," Jason pointed out.

"Come on, indulge me. Besides, pompadums and riata are just extras."

"And now it's riata too."

Geoffrey reached for his bag and pulled out some more gadgets. "I also brought you some more regular gas-powered grappling hooks. And don't forget that other special order I put together for you."

"What's that?" Angie asked, frowning.

"Nothing," Jason said.

"Gas grenades to render people unconscious," Geoffrey told her with a gleeful grin.

"I'm not sure I like the sound of that."

"It's a good way to disarm dangerous people without risking my own skin," Jason pointed out.

"It sounds like it could be dangerous for other

reasons though," Angie said. "How do you know you won't kill someone with them? I understand that putting people out with chemicals or whatever the hell that stuff is is a delicate thing. If it wasn't, then any old Joe off the street could get a job as a general anesthetist, couldn't they?"

"Hey, it's me," Geoffrey protested. "I'm not any old Joe."

"All right. But I sure hope you guys know what you're doing."

"It'll be all right, honey," Jason assured her and turned back to Geoffrey. "All right, Wolfman. I'll throw in Beef Madras and pompadums for you."

"And riata," Geoffrey reminded him.

"And riata," Jason nodded. "However, since we're ordering all this extra stuff for you, you've got to eat your share 'cause I can't stuff myself silly tonight."

"Oh well, we don't have to eat it all. Left-over curry reheats perfectly fine."

"True. Although it's always a little spicier for some reason."

"Yeah, but you like it hot."

"Also true."

"But why can't you gorge yourself tonight?" Geoffrey asked. "Are you bringing in another prominent politician or something?"

"Detective work," Jason said. "I'm trying to solve a

murder." His expression was grim for a moment but then he eased up and gave his friend a little smile. "Still though, I'm not going to go chasing clues on an empty stomach. I'll just have to restrain myself a little, that's all. I might head out around seven or so."

"Hence the early dinner?" Geoffrey asked, realizing that his friend had intended that all along. "Jeez, you don't switch off very much these days, do you?"

"Geoffrey's got a point," Angie chimed in from the kitchen where she was now making some coffee.

"Yeah," Geoffrey continued. "You can't personally investigate every murder in Fringe City. That's what the police are for."

Angie shook her head and gave Geoffrey a knowing look. "That's exactly what I've been telling him."

Geoffrey nodded and turned back to his friend. "You should listen to the lady."

"You're both right," Jason told them. "But I don't think anyone's doing anything about this particular murder. Anyway, let's order. We'll have a nice dinner together and then Geoffrey, maybe you and Angie can watch a movie or something."

When he walked into a sleazy nightclub a few hours later, Jason was glad he'd had a proper meal before heading out. In the end, he had actually left after eight, as he realized that going out any earlier would have been a waste of time. Waiting was the name of the game that night and with the night club scene, it was likely the man he was looking for wouldn't come while the evening was too young anyway.

So Jason sat himself down at the bar and ordered a pint of lager. However, he took care to sip it slowly. He could hardly sit there and drink nothing of course, not without seriously pissing some people off, but he couldn't let himself slide too far under the influence either.

About an hour later, the man he was waiting for entered the club. He was in his late thirties, donned a leather jacket and had a shaved head with a distinctive tattoo behind his left temple. The man matched the description that pimp had given him but Jason needed more to act on. The pimp could just as easily been setting the man up as a fall guy. Jason had to make sure.

He left the place and outside, he pulled one of his grappling hooks out of a pocket and hauled himself to the roof of the building. He then pulled his bag out from behind its hiding place, got changed into his gear and waited. When the man emerged around another hour and a half later, he followed him while keeping to the rooftops. Geoffrey's new double-action grappling hooks worked like a charm for Jason as he went from building to building and he couldn't help thinking how much easier trailing Lamont would have been if he had the new gadgets back then.

The pimp was right about one thing though, Jason realized. The man was a regular. He walked straight to the brothel without so much as glancing at the other venues in the area or the girls waiting on the sidewalks. And the girls didn't even try to get his attention.

As his quarry neared the brothel, Jason saw it was to all appearances empty. The pimp must have cleared out. Then as he was contemplating his next move, Jason saw a familiar looking woman strolling around outside. It was Diane Reilly. So far, he had only seen her from a distance—although they had bumped into each other at Reggie Burges' so-called 'charity' ball without realizing it—but he instantly recognized the woman who had helped him out with the Black Baron and later on with Grigorie and Burges.

She had a patrolman with her as well, about thirty feet from where she was pacing around the sidewalk. He was probably just staying with their car because criminals in Fringe City would swipe anything if was left unattended too long. But he was alert and ready to assist at the first sign of trouble.

• • •

As the Sentinel's quarry headed up the final steps to the brothel, Diane marched over to him, holding up her badge. "Are you the owner of this establishment?"

"No," the man replied, giving her an appraising glance. "I was just interested in renting this place and I wanted to see if it was available."

Diane saw that the man was preparing to bolt, a sure sign he was hiding something. She nodded to the patrolman and stepped between the man and the road. "I'd like to ask you a few questions, sir."

The man also glanced at the patrolman. And then he was off, kicking open the door to the brothel and running inside.

"Damn it!" Diane muttered, shoving her badge away and drawing her gun. She waved to the patrolman and headed in, her partner racing over from the car while drawing his own weapon and radioing headquarters at the same time. When he got inside, he found Diane and gave her a questioning glance that she could only just see in the dim light. She shrugged in return. The patrolman flicked the light switch by the door a couple of times and nothing happened.

They then heard glass smash in one of the back rooms and the patrolman ran ahead.

"Careful!" Diane called out, running after him but her partner leapt through the broken window without looking and into the alleyway behind the building.

There was a gunshot and a scream.

Grimacing, Diane glanced out to check if the coast was clear before going through the window as well and dropping to the ground four feet below. Her partner had taken a shot to the chest and was writhing in pain, his face contorted in a pitiful grimace.

His assailant in the meantime was already sixty yards down the alley and running around a corner, but the chase was off. Her partner needed help right away.

"Hang in there," she said as she pulled out her radio. "Officer down! I need an ambulance right away!"

Meanwhile, the assailant ran as fast as he could. He risked a brief look back. Seeing no one behind him, he breathed a sigh of relief. Then a leg shot out from an alcove and he tripped, flying onto his face and rolling across the asphalt. He groaned, pressing the trigger of his gun in readiness to take whoever had tripped him out. But before he could fire, someone planted their heel sharply into his wrist tendon, making him drop the weapon.

The Sentinel then picked the gun up, emptied it and cracked him over the head with the butt.

• • •

Diane was administering first aid from a kit she'd had in the car when another patrol car pulled up with an ambulance behind it. "We'll take it from here," the first paramedic out of the vehicle said, the gratitude in his voice expressing what he didn't have time to say in words.

Diane stepped back as the paramedics placed her partner on a stretcher, checked whether he could be moved or not and got him into the ambulance with the kind of efficiency one rarely saw in other professions.

The cops who had arrived with the ambulance came over to her once the paramedics were clear.

"Are you okay, Captain?" one of them asked.

Diane nodded, wiping away some tears and brushing her hair back. "It's all right. I'm just a little shaken up, that's all. Don't worry."

"If you say so," the man replied. "Anyway, you just take it easy. We've got another patrol car on the way so we'll take it from here. What does the guy look like?"

"Leather jacket, shaved head with a distinctive tattoo on the side of his head." Diane pointed down the alleyway. "He went that way."

"All right, do you want a ride with us?"

"My car's out front."

"But you know, if you're feeling shaken up...?"

Diane nodded and gave him a smile. "I know. I'll be okay. But I appreciate it."

"All right," the man said reluctantly. "But if you change your mind, we're just a radio call away."

They jumped into the patrol car and drove off down the alley. And the ambulance was already pulling around the corner. Seconds later, Diane was alone... or at least she had thought she was.

The alley seemed rather dark after the flashing lights of the ambulance and the other patrol car disappeared but as her eyes readjusted to the gloom, she saw a man standing a few feet away, clad in some kind of Kevlar suit that largely concealed his features.

"Don't worry," the figure told her. "There's no need to be alarmed."

"It's okay," Diane replied and somehow it was. Somehow, she had known this moment would come. "I think I know who you are. And I know your voice. We've spoken a few times before, haven't we?"

"We have. It's nice to meet you at last. Although, believe me, I wish the circumstances were different."

"Me too," Diane said, fighting back sudden tears.

"How's your partner doing?"

"I don't know. He's alive and in the ambulance right now but he took a shot to the chest. That might well be fatal."

"I'm sorry."

"Me too."

"And I'm sorry I didn't get the perpetrator before he

could do any more harm."

Diane sighed, her gaze drifting down. "I know, but don't worry. We'll get him eventually."

"That wasn't what I meant."

Diane looked up in surprise. "What's that?"

"I meant I'm sorry I didn't get him before he shot your partner."

"You mean you've got him now?"

The Sentinel had until that point been standing partially behind a protrusion from the back of a building. At this point, he stepped out and dropped a bundle at Diane's feet. A man with a leather jacket, a shaved head and a distinctive tattoo on the side of his head, his ankles and wrists bound with wire. He was also as limp as a sack of grain.

"Is he dead?"

"He's just unconscious. I gave him a little something to make him easier to manage and if it works properly, he'll remain unconscious for another twenty hours."

"And if it doesn't?"

"Then it'll be on my head, not yours."

The Sentinel handed over the man's gun and the ammunition he'd emptied from it. "Here. These'll be safer with you."

Diane pulled out a handkerchief. "Put them here. I don't want to mess up the fingerprints."

"Good thinking."

"Thank god you've got gloves."

"Well, they come in handy." The Sentinel watched as Diane put the wrapped weapon and the bullets away in her jacket. "There's more. I have reason to suspect this man was responsible for the murder of a young woman who was found dead in this alley."

"Jesus. That's why my partner and I were here in the first place. We were investigating that very same crime."

"I didn't realize that anyone in the police cared."

"*I* care," Diane told him.

"Sorry, I didn't mean—"

"Forget it," Diane waved the apology away.

"Did Forensics find anything on the woman?"

"Fingerprints, traces of DNA... The usual. But they don't match any of our records."

"Run some tests on this man when you get him back to the station."

"I plan to."

"Also," the Sentinel added, hesitating, "I wonder if I could check up with you on this case later."

Diane raised her eyebrows. "How?

"I think I can trust you. Do you trust me?"

"I trust you."

"I've got a cell phone I don't use for personal calls. It's untraceable. The number won't reveal my identity to anyone who tries to track it and no one can triangulate my position from its signal."

"You were talking about trust just before, weren't you?"

"I do trust you. But you may have colleagues who'd try to shake this number from you. The new commissioner might make you hand it over to him. And if that happens, just do it. The number's useless as a means of tracking me down."

"I see. That's some pretty impressive technology you've got there."

"It's necessary," Jason replied, remembering how the Black Baron burnt his old place to the ground.

Diane nodded. "I understand."

They then exchanged their cell phone numbers.

"Can I contact you anytime?" Diane asked.

"I'd prefer it if you didn't. I might be in a tight spot, I might be busy or I might just be resting." Jason gave her a smile. "I am a regular man after all."

Diane shook her head. "Why do you do this then? It must be hell on you."

"You don't know the half of it," Jason replied. "However, I've probably said too much already. Why don't you fetch your car and I'll help you get this guy inside? Then you can call this in."

A ONE-MOB TOWN

THE MAN WAS DRESSED IN A SUIT TAILOR made in a fashion Mecca, and his car was polished within an inch of its life. If any Hollywood celebrity appeared in the neighborhood sporting such obvious wealth, they'd be robbed of everything they carried and dumped dead in a gutter somewhere but this man had no need to fear such things. He was scarier than any of the locals and they knew it.

He climbed in the back of his car beside two more similar men and closed the door behind him, shutting the neighborhood out with tinted bulletproof glass.

"Well?" one of his companions asked.

"Something's wrong here," he said, opening a brown paper bag. "Here. Have a look at this."

"This is good quality," his other companion said as he inspected the contents.

"Too good. It's the same grade as the stuff the boss was shipping in. And that's extremely hard to get."

"You're right," his companion agreed.

The man tapped the seats in front. "Lock the car.

We'll do this together."

As one, five men stepped out of the vehicle and walked over to a dealer, the man who had originally bought the drugs walking ahead while his friends stayed back.

"Pal, my friends and I were quite impressed by this stuff. Is there more where it came from?"

The dealer put his hands in his pockets to help him keep his cool. "Maybe, Joe. How much you want?"

"Say twenty pounds," said the man whose name was not Joe.

The dealer thought he'd hit the jackpot. "No problem, Joe. When do you want it?"

"By next Wednesday."

The dealer thought it over. "Come back on Tuesday night. Same time?" He looked thoughtful and swayed a little, trying to keep his excitement in check. "Say... You know the price. You really got that kind of money on you?"

"No discounts?" the man asked, raising an eyebrow.

"Hey, man," the dealer smiled nervously. "You know how it is, man. This stuff's hard to find, you know what I'm saying? I'll talk to my supplier but, hey, you know. No guarantees, man."

"What about the goods?"

"Like I told you, twenty pounds is easy."

"How easy? What if I wanted to get another twenty

pounds every week?"

The dealer's eyes lit up as he thought over the implications of that. "Say, you move this stuff fast, man. You want a steady supply, I'm your man. Hey, maybe a little discount might be all right after all."

"Sounds like you've got access to a pretty large stockpile," the man said, his voice now subtly altered. "It's yours?"

The dealer backed up a little at this, raising his hands in a defensive posture. "Hey, whoa... If I had direct access, do you think I'd be working this beat?"

"Who's your supplier then?"

"Hey, man. You know, trade secrets and all. If I give you my supplier, I mean, you'll just cut me out then, right? Besides, I mean my suppliers... They probably like you, right? They like their secrecy, you know?"

By now he realized just how much trouble he was in.

The man nodded to his friends. "Put him in the car."

It was very late when Jason finally arrived home but he was in good spirits. Angie was waiting for him, sipping a coffee on the lounge and watching late night TV when he came through the door. Geoffrey was reading some magazine that was supposedly about sail boarding but seemed to have a disproportionate number of pages dedicated to swimwear models. They both got up.

"How did you go?" Angie asked.

"I got the guy," he told her, "although there were some complications. And I think I've got an insider on the force now."

"You didn't give him anything that he might be able to use to pin your identity, I hope."

"Well, firstly, it's her, not him."

"Captain Reilly?"

"She was in the neighborhood."

"That was handy."

"Quite."

"And what was she doing there?"

Jason hesitated but there was no way out of it. "Investigating the same case I was."

Angie shook her head.

"Yeah, I know what you're going to say," Jason told her. "However, before you say it, I want to point out that I solved the case and that if it weren't for me, the guy would have got away."

"Maybe," Angie replied. "Maybe not. But now, we'll never know."

"Well, I helped her catch the guy sooner than she would have at any rate. But to answer your question—no, I didn't give her anything she could use to find out who I was. I gave her the number for that untraceable cell phone Geoffrey fixed up for me, and I got her cell number too so I can contact her directly and avoid any third parties." He nodded to his friend. "And thanks for that again."

Geoffrey however had other things on his mind. "No problem. But what about the double action grappling hooks?"

"Tried them out tonight. They worked a treat. I also tried out that that stun gas grenade."

"To get the guy?"

"Just to make it easier to tie him up and hand him over to the police," Jason said.

Angie stared at Jason in disbelief. "You threw a grenade in his face so it'd be easier to manage him?"

Jason shrugged. "Actually, I threw it in front of his face but that's basically how it was. But do you have any idea how hard it is to secure somebody while they're fully conscious and trying to smack your head in?"

"Yeah," Angie conceded. "It's just that the grenade thing seems a bit excessive to me, that's all."

"Well, maybe Geoffrey can make up a spray can of the stuff instead."

Geoffrey laughed. "Yeah, that might do the trick too. By the way, did the gas actually keep the guy unconscious for the whole twenty hours?"

Rather than replying, Jason simply let the question

hang in the air for a few moments.

"Ah," Geoffrey said, as his thought processes caught up with him. "Right."

"I always say you spend too much time in your lab, Geoffrey," Angie told him. "Now you've lost all concept of time."

"Yeah, it's a vampiric existence, all right," Geoffrey agreed.

"I'll tell you what," Jason told him. "I'll check with my police liaison later and ask about it."

"Do it," Geoffrey advised. "It's better to be sure. I don't want you lobbing one of those things into a room full of mobsters only to find out they're awake again after barely a minute."

"Me neither," Jason said.

"Oh, also if you want, I can make some more of them."

"Hey, I appreciate it, but I think the ones I've got should keep me going for a few more jobs at least."

"Well, I might make some more just in case. It's better to have too many than not enough."

"True, but I don't want you getting yourself into trouble with the faculty."

Geoffrey smiled. "I wouldn't worry about that. Besides, if anyone asks, I'll just tell them I'm working on an anesthetic."

. . .

The dealer looked around the room, crushed under the weight of all too real terror. He was surrounded by men who could and most likely would beat him to a pulp and leave him in a dumpster.

"Look, I don't want any trouble, guys," he pleaded, raising a hand in appeal. "I'll tell you anything you want to know. Please, just don't kill me."

"You're dealing stolen drugs," one of the men told him. "Our drugs."

"I didn't know, man," the dealer protested. "I swear to God, they didn't tell me nothing! I'm just a middleman, you've got to believe me!"

The man reached down and grabbed him by the scruff of the neck. "We know that, dipshit. We want your supplier."

"Okay, okay! Look, I told you I was going to tell you. It was Lamont's men! Lamont's got some guys on the force and the cops recently seized a ton of stock and now they're selling it off."

"And where are they keeping the stock?"

A few minutes later, the men conducting the interrogation entered a room upstairs where their boss was waiting. Danny Vincent was a man in his fifties, a little on the overweight side but with a lot of muscle under the extra pounds, and he didn't look like the kind of guy anyone in their right mind would want to cross. Right then, he was sitting behind a large ornate wooden desk with a glass of brandy in his hand and an impatient air about him.

"Well?" he asked.

"It's Lamont and his boys. They're selling off the drugs the cops took from us."

"Well, we figured that already. But where the hell are they stockpiling them? They wouldn't leave them in an evidence room."

"No, as far as the police who aren't on Lamont's payroll are aware, the drugs were all destroyed. Lamont's guys are keeping the goods in a gym that's supposedly undergoing renovations."

"Did you get an address off that little prick?"

"Yep."

"Lamont's done it this time," Vincent said. "He shoots up our guys, tries to bomb our subway warehouse and now he's selling our stuff? Go around to that gym and take out the lot of them."

"All right. What about our stuff?"

Vincent considered this for a moment. "If you can get any of it back before the cops turn up, grab it. But if not, forget it."

The men turned to leave.

"Oh, and get rid of the body," he added, almost as an afterthought.

Vincent's men jumped in their cars, a couple of them throwing the late drug dealer in the trunk of one before they set off. Twenty minutes later, the cars came screeching around a corner and to a screaming halt. Without stopping the engines, the men burst out with their guns at the ready and stormed into the seemingly closed gym.

As sudden as their onslaught was though, Lamont's men inside weren't slow to react. Some ran to the windows to cover the street below, while others took up positions above the stairs.

One of Vincent's men was the first down as the shooting started but although Lamont's men had the better defensive position, Vincent had more men on the street.

Soon, the shootout was so intense that for Vincent's men, the question of whether to recover any of their drugs or not turned out to be academic. Finally, any lingering doubts dissipated when the men heard sirens blaring not far off. Those among Vincent's boys who could make it scrambled into their cars and drove off as fast as they could, while the survivors among Lamont's men beat their own retreat out a back entrance.

Given the intensity of the shootout, it was little wonder when the cops got there that acting Commissioner Eric Hutchens was there as well, along with several more quite senior officers.

After inspecting the dead and the wounded gangsters, Hutchens looked at the massive piles of drugs stacked against the back wall, out of sight from the street.

"I don't believe it," one of his officers said. "This is the same stuff we hauled out of that subway station."

"Are you sure?" Hutchens asked, eyeing it all in a manner of calm appraisal.

"I was there," the officer replied, "so I'm pretty sure. The packaging's nothing fancy but the way it's wrapped, the size of the packages, the thickness of the plastic... You tend to notice these things when you work in narcotics long enough."

"I'll take your word for it," Hutchens said. "All right, I want to see the men who were in charge of disposing these drugs. Find out where they are right now, call them individually and give them whatever B.S. you want. But I want to see them all back at the station. I don't want them prepped."

. . .

Jason turned over the page of the book he was reading. Geoffrey had gone home half an hour earlier and he and Angie were just relaxing on the sofa for a little while before they went to bed. He heard a buzz and, checking his untraceable cell phone on the coffee table, he found a message waiting for him. A short text from Diane: *"DNA test positive. Also, Lamont's men and Vincent's men have just had a gunfight. 67 Kings Blvd. Large police force on scene."*

Jason frowned. "What's that?" Angie asked and Jason showed her the message.

"Well, you got your man at least," she said. "That's something, right?"

"I don't know now," Jason replied. "I mean, I guess it should be but when I read that, I just felt kind of empty. Sure, I got the guy. But that won't bring that woman back to life."

Angie thought about saying something but decided to wait.

"I wonder if she's got a family somewhere here in Fringe City and whether they know what happened," Jason told her. "According to that article I read, the original homicide report had her as unidentified."

Angie squeezed his hand and they were quiet for a few moments.

Jason shook himself out of the mood that had come over him and looked at the next part of Diane's message. "Well, it looks like Lamont hasn't wasted any time since he got out of prison. When was he acquitted again? Yesterday morning?"

He sighed and glanced at his watch. "How could it possibly still be only Friday night? It feels like a week since we finished work."

Angie looked at her own watch. "Well, technically it's Saturday morning now but I know what you mean."

Jason slid his hands onto the sofa and pushed himself up. "Well, whatever it may be technically, it's been a very long night."

"I'm glad you think so too," Angie told him. "Better get some rest then. Somehow I get the feeling that tomorrow night might be a late one as well."

"Tonight, technically," Jason reminded her.

Angie smiled. "Right."

Before getting ready for bed, Jason texted a simple *"Thanks"* back to Diane.

Eric Hutchens was not a happy man and with every mannerism and facial expression, he made sure the officers in the room in front of him knew it. "I don't know if I can make it any clearer than this, guys," he told them, "but you're in a world of trouble. And I don't care how much trouble you think that is, because it's more. And anyone who decides they don't want to cooperate with me now is going to have it much worse."

There were a couple of officers who had decided to play ignorant earlier but they now knew this wasn't a good card to play.

Hutchens paced back and forth, trying to keep his temper in check with only moderate success. "I want to know the names of everyone on the force you know who's moonlighting for Martin Lamont. I want to know who's in his direct pay. I want every last shred of information you can give me about his contacts. If any of you were in on this latest caper getting a cut of the profit, then you'd better come clean sooner rather than later. If you do, maybe I can argue for clemency on your behalf. And I also want to know who kept silent when they knew what was going on. We don't work for mob bosses here. Is that clear?"

Pacing around one of his establishments, Martin Lamont wasn't feeling charitable to the world at large either.

"Faulkner's going to be back on my case in a big way now," he told his men, "and that means we have to cut off the guys who were handling the operation tonight. They screwed up, they're on their own. Those are the rules. And you can tell them that if any of them try to pin the rest of us, jail time will be their best case scenario."

He took a breath to calm himself. "Now, I think it's time we brought in some outside help to take care of Vincent and his guys."

"What do you have in mind?" one of the men asked.

"If I can arrange it, you'll find out," Lamont told him. "But first, I'm going to need you to organize a prison break out."

When Jason got up the next morning—well, technically later that same morning—he felt like a new man. With the previous night a distant memory, he had a little breakfast and made some coffee for Angie and himself. Neither of them were feeling particularly energetic, but there was bright sunshine filtering through the windows and they were ready for a nice, lazy day.

"I think we ought to go shopping later though," Angie said when Jason told her his plan to just stay in.

"Well, I think I can manage that at least," he told her. "Are we out of anything?"

"Not yet but we're almost out of cereal."

"Let's stock up then. I might get some tzatziki and

Turkish bread as well and we'll have something nice and Mediterranean for lunch. And let's get some more tea and coffee."

"And fruit," Angie reminded him. "Got to look after our health."

"Hey, you know me. I love fruit. I just hate that flavorless out-of-season stuff that's been in a ship for two months, then a truck for one and deep storage for another three."

"Me too. But we've still got to *try* to look after our health, right?" Angie gave him a smile and flicked on the television. "Do you want to see what's on the local news?"

"Not really, but given the contents of Diane's last text, I probably should."

Angie found the channel they always watched... and what looked like a major story.

"—*it appears to have happened around five o'clock this morning,*" a reporter said, her voice earnest even by her profession's standards. Over her shoulder was a large concrete wall with a chunk missing in the middle. There was a lot of smoke and debris as well and in the background, the Fringe City fire brigade and the police were cleaning up the mess and holding back curious onlookers.

Then Jason noticed the rolls of barbed wire lining the wall. It was a prison. A sinking feeling set in as he guessed what this live bulletin was all about.

"The guards report that the masked men ushered Mr. Burges into a helicopter that headed west and an abandoned helicopter matching the description has been located on a private helipad several blocks away in that direction. Police are presently searching the premises but they say it's unlikely that they will find the masked men or Mr. Burges there. More likely than not, the men changed vehicles and—"

Jason turned the television off and stood up. "Come on, let's go and get the shopping done."

As he walked into the rather nice looking private bar, Burges eyed his surroundings in bewilderment and nervousness. He knew where he was and he didn't want to be there.

Martin Lamont was reclining in a chair with an empty seat across the table from him.

"Reggie," he beamed. "Good to see you again." He waved a hand to the empty seat. "Sit down."

Burges sat.

"Drink?" Lamont asked.

"Sure," Burges replied. "Um… Give me a bourbon. With ice. Lots of ice."

Lamont gave a nod to one of his men. "You heard the man. I'll have a scotch. Keep the ice." He turned back to Burges. "I want to make a deal, Reggie, and the fact that I got you out of the joint should show you that I'm willing to uphold my end of the bargain. You see, you're a man with his fingers in many pies and—"

"I was," Burges countered. "Not any more."

"Right," Lamont replied. "Not any more. However, you can be that man again with my help."

"How?" Burges asked, his suspicion on overdrive.

"I can give you your high flying lifestyle back," Lamont told him, putting the question aside, "and all I want in return is just one thing. The means to contact the Bandit."

Burges froze for a moment. "Why do you think I'd know how to find that maniac?"

"Simple deduction," Lamont replied with a smile that belied the man underneath. "The fact that the Bandit killed Commissioner Levings just before federal agents arrived to see if he was suppressing evidence that you were linked with Grigorie. That seemed a bit convenient to me. Not that I mind or anything. I think you did the right thing. However, you could have let me in on the secret."

Burges didn't say anything.

"Your bourbon," came a voice from behind him and a drink materialized in front. He didn't notice the hand withdrawing from the glass as he had his own hand around it instantly, taking a nervous swig.

"Thank you," Lamont said to the man as he took his

own drink and had a sip. "Anyway," he said as he put his glass down, "the reason I'm bringing this up, Reggie, is that I could use your acquaintance right now."

"The Bandit prizes his anonymity very highly," Burges warned him. "And you don't seek him out. If he wants to do business, then he finds you."

Then, just like that, Public Façade Lamont left the building and the uncouth bastard that he really was took his place and pulled out a gun. "Let me put it another way then, Reggie. You tell me how to contact this guy or I'll blow your damn head off."

It dawned on Burges that he didn't really have a great deal of choice in this matter. "All right, put the gun away. I can contact the Bandit and I'm still in credit with him."

Lamont raised an eyebrow. "So that's how it works with him, is it? However, I think you're forgetting the fact that all your assets were frozen when you were arrested. Including your imaginary offshore subsidiary company."

"Doesn't matter," Burges said. "I paid several million into an overseas account a while ago that the Bandit uses and he said that'd be good for two or three jobs. I've only used him once since then—that job with the commissioner—so I've still got one or two jobs left, depending on what the Bandit decides the next job is worth."

"Good," Lamont said, putting his gun away. "You can use the next job for me."

A little later, Jason and Angie arrived back home after their trip to the shops and started putting away the groceries. As Jason put the tea and coffee in the cupboard, he paused as something crossed his mind. He closed the cupboard and pulled out his untraceable cell phone.

"What are you doing?" Angie asked.

"I just had an idea," Jason replied, dialing Diane's number. "I think I might be able to get Burges back myself."

Things were understandably busy at police headquarters. Diane Reilly was fielding calls while processing the paperwork for the guy she'd brought in the night before. Then she noticed her cell phone vibrating. At first, she contemplated just letting it ring out—as she had lots to do—but then she thought the better of it and checked the number.

"Excuse me," she said to the officer beside her. She went out into a corridor where it was quieter. "I thought you only operated at night," she said as she answered the phone.

"I do," her friend replied. "But I want to know something. Are there any survivors from Lamont's side of that shooting last night?"

"There might be. What are you playing at?"

"It has to be Lamont's men who busted Burges out of prison this morning. He's the only one with a strong enough connection to the former mayor and the means to carry the thing off."

"The police are already checking that out."

"They won't find anything. You know that. Lamont's too good at covering his tracks. We need a comprehensive list of buildings, companies, licensed venues and so on that Lamont owns."

"I'm sure the department's taking care of that."

"And how thorough do you think they'll be? Do you trust them completely?"

Diane hesitated. "You're right. They might overlook something. Actually, come to think of it, I think they already have. By the way, that man I brought in last night is still unconscious. Are you sure he's going to wake up?"

"Pretty sure. But I'd like to check up on that later just in case. What about that patrolman who was with you? Is he all right?"

At this, Diane stifled a cry and held her hand to her face to wipe away sudden tears. "He—"

"I'm so sorry."

"Me too."

"Will you be okay?"

"I'll have to be."

"Because if you want to take some time—"

"If we want to get Burges back then I'll need to get on investigating Lamont's listed and unlisted holdings straightaway," Diane said. "Don't worry about me. I've been here before."

"Is everything okay?" Angie asked.

"That patrolman who was with Diane last night," Jason explained. "The one who was shot. He didn't make it."

"Oh, I'm sorry."

"We all are."

Angie then nodded to the television. "Also, you know how you were talking about Lamont just before? He's on the news now."

Jason turned around to see.

"—investigating the premises of several bars and restaurants under the ownership of Martin Lamont,"— while the reporter spoke, some footage of Lamont getting out of his car was playing—"who some believe is the head of one of Fringe City's largest crime syndicates, and who was alleged to have been in a close business relationship *with the former mayor."*

The footage cut to the reporter, who continued her spiel. *"These allegations have never been proven, but the question today is whether Lamont was involved with the early morning prison break out. However, in their search of Lamont's various establishments, the police have so far found no traces of Reggie Burges. Furthermore, Mr. Lamont has denied any involvement outright."*

The report then crossed to some more footage of Lamont, this time sitting in one of his bars. He waved away the media with a rehearsed charming smile, for a given value of charming.

"These rumors that Mr. Burges and I have some kind of business partnership," he said to the reporters around him. *"There's no truth to these rumors. It's like I've told you all before, I'm an honest businessman."*

Jason switched the TV off. "I sure hope Diane can find a chink in this guy's armor."

Sitting in his office, Faulkner was also watching the proceedings of the day unfold on the television when the phone rang.

"Faulkner," he answered.

"It's Diane. I need your help."

"What do you need?"

"I've got an idea that might help us get some leads

on Burges. I've got a few of Lamont's men down at the station who were involved in that shootout last night. A couple of them are prepared to play ball but only on the proviso they get something in return."

Faulkner sighed. "They want to cut deals. They know I can't guarantee anything, right?"

"I think these guys have probably all been in and out of the courtrooms enough times to know how it works."

"True. By the way, have you run this by the acting commissioner?"

"He's tied up checking out Lamont's holdings," Diane replied, "which both you and I know will just amount to a wild goose chase when it's all wrapped up. Anyway, Burges could be sneaking out of the country for all we know. I don't think we can wait until we can contact Hutchens. Every minute wasted is a minute that Lamont and Burges have over us."

"You sound pretty certain Lamont has him."

"You're not?" Diane asked.

"No, I think he has him too. But you already knew that or you wouldn't be calling me."

"So, can you help?"

"I'll be right over."

It took him half an hour to get to the station, which was not bad considering the traffic at that time of day.

"Sorry for keeping you waiting," he said as he came

into the holding cell where Diane was keeping Lamont's men. "I got here as fast as I could."

"No problem," Diane told him.

Faulkner looked at the men in front of him. "I hear you want to cut a deal."

Reggie Burges glanced around the penthouse. It was quite spacious, obviously expensive and it reflected the elegance of its sole occupant quite well. The woman who lived here was of a mature age but quite attractive—more attractive than many much younger women—and carried herself with what could be described as an aristocratic air. This was a woman who was used to the fine things in life, like the sensuous figure hugging dress she was wearing and the expensive white wine she was sipping from her slender glass.

Burges had a glass of that exquisite wine as well, but for the moment it remained untouched. The woman handed him the hand piece of her phone. "Make the call."

Burges took a deep breath and dialed the number.

The dial tone sounded twice before a man picked it up. "Allô?"

"It's Burges," the former mayor announced himself. "I have a new job for your brother."

"The last time I checked, you were in prison," the man replied. "How do I know this isn't some sort of entrapment operation?"

"I broke out. You're welcome to check with your brother if it'd make you feel better. Or check your own news channels. I might rate some airtime there."

"It could still be entrapment though. A highly sophisticated operation to make your story appear authentic enough to my brother. Also, you've used his services too recently. You know the rules. My brother doesn't like to operate too frequently. It's risky."

"All right," Burges said, going for broke. "I tell you what. If your brother does this one job then I won't bother him again. I'll waive any right to request his services for a third job as stipulated in our original agreement."

"Since we've already got your money," the other man pointed out, "he doesn't have to do a third job if he doesn't want to."

Burges began to sweat. He didn't want to hang up with nothing. However, he still had one last card he wanted to play. "All right," he said to the Bandit's brother. "Tell him this. Tell him it'll be fun."

There was a slight pause on the other end of the line. "Call me back in ten minutes."

. . .

"Thanks for all your help," Diane said as she and Charles Faulkner walked out of the police holding cell.

"Don't mention it," Faulkner replied. "I just hope it pays off. I don't like the idea of giving any of those guys in there slack, no matter how little it might end up being."

"Me neither," Diane concurred. "But we've got a lead on Burges and that's what we wanted." She looked out the window at the fading light. "Is the day over already?"

"The daylight hours at least," Faulkner said. "Somehow, I think the day's got a little while to go yet before we can all turn in."

"True," Diane replied, getting out her cell phone. "Anyway, thanks for all your help. I'll see you later."

"Good luck," Faulkner said as he left.

Diane then called her mysterious friend. "Hey, it's me."

"Have you got anything?"

"It might be nothing but it turns out Lamont has a sister here in Fringe City."

"I didn't know that."

"Me neither," Diane said. "Anyway, her name's Sophia Garcia. The Garcia's from her ex-husband and possibly, given the way Lamont's kind work, a late husband. Anyway, she's got a penthouse downtown and I've got the address right here. I don't suppose you've got a pen handy?"

On the other end of the line, Jason jotted down the information. "Got it."

"Now, I don't know what you've got planned but be careful. Being Lamont's sister, Sophia Garcia's probably got her own entourage of well-dressed thugs around her place."

As they spoke, Jason realized the aura of mystique he was going for wasn't really there with Diane. She wasn't speaking to him as if he were some mysterious figure of the night. She was speaking to him as a friend. And she was worried. It was a little weird for him as that wasn't what he was going for but in a way, it was good as it removed the need for charades.

"God, I shouldn't be giving you this information," Diane said. She must have been thinking the same thing. "You could get killed. Look, forget that address. I'm going to assemble a unit and do this by the book. Besides, I'll have to get the information to the acting commissioner anyway."

"You don't have to worry about me. I know what I'm doing."

"Look, you say that. But you're just one man. You'll be in over your head. Sophia's men will kill you."

"They can try," Jason replied, hanging up before Diane could argue the point further.

"Damn it," Diane muttered as the line went dead.

She had just placed her newfound friend in life-threatening danger. She knew he'd been there before of course—with the Black Baron, Lamont's men at the docks and that killer in the alleyway—but that didn't excuse it. She called over another officer.

"Get a squad together," she told him, "and bring along some back-up. A S.W.A.T. team. Tell acting Commissioner Hutchens about our new lead if you can as well. Hopefully he's got enough tact not to give Lamont any idea we're onto his sister."

At his desk in an empty room, Danny Vincent watched the live news updates on the hunt for Burges, relishing the slight possibility that Lamont might slip up somewhere so he could watch as the Fringe City police hauled his ass off to prison.

He reached for a drink when automatic gunfire erupted outside. One of his men threw open his door and leaned in, his weapon drawn. "Trouble downstairs, boss! Stay here!"

With that, he was gone and through the open door, Vincent saw him and several other men run down the hall to sort out whoever it was. Leaping to his feet, he ran over to the door as well and looked down the flight of stairs to the ground floor.

His men were crouched behind whatever cover they

could find, firing madly. Vincent wondered who would be mad enough to launch a frontal assault on his little base of operations. There were several successive rounds from outside and Vincent recoiled as two of his men were blown back from their positions with such force that they went sliding several yards across the floor, under the stairs and out of his sight. Whoever was down there was packing some seriously high-powered weapons.

Two of his men were still on the stairs, trying to cover the street from above.

"The door!" Vincent shouted. "Take them by surprise!"

The men nodded and rushed for the front entrance. But before they got there, an explosion ripped through it, taking them out in a shower of debris. For a few moments, Vincent's ears were ringing—the explosion had been so deafening—and he wondered if this was what shellshock was.

Then all he could see was splintered wood and smoke. Lots of smoke.

Sweating, he slammed the door and pushed a cabinet in front of it. He didn't want to wait to find out what the gas did. And given the scale of the assault, he now had a fair idea who it was down there.

"That son of a bitch," he muttered, fumbling with his desk drawer. "Son of a bitch..." He pulled out a prized automatic rifle and did his best to hold it steady. The sound of gunfire had ceased and now there was an eerie silence. Then he heard footsteps on the stairs. He swallowed and brushed some sweat off his forehead. No reassuring voice told him it was all clear. It was the worst case scenario.

"Come on, you prick," he muttered, trying to calm his nerves. "Come on in."

His adversary however made his own entrance, emerging from a cloud of smoke after blowing half the wall away with a grenade. Vincent froze. He'd never seen anyone like this in life. An armored figure carrying more weapons than he'd ever thought possible. He raised his gun but the Bandit shot first, with one burst of bullets that sent him staggering backwards, another burst that sent him sprawling over the desk and finally, a burst that sent him crashing through the back wall, buried in a pile of fiberboard, dust and woodchips.

The Bandit produced a flask and splashed its contents liberally around the room. Then he lit a match, dropped it and left.

"Goddamn it," Diane said, looking at the traffic ahead. "Is this mess moving or what?"

"I think we've hit peak hour," her partner said.

"Want to use the sirens?"

"Not yet," Diane replied. "I don't want to tip off Sophia. We're just two blocks away, right?"

"Yeah."

"Then we'll wait it out. This traffic's got to move some day."

Above a nearby subway station, Jason came out onto the street, fighting the urge to run. As he neared his destination, he used a grappling hook to ascend the building opposite Sophia's. It looked perfect: it wasn't fancy so it was unlikely to have alarms or security guards.

Then he geared up, adjusted his visor and used the zoom function to get a look at the roof above Sophia's penthouse. Diane had been right about the need for caution; there were several guards on the roof with automatic weapons. For a moment, Jason had second thoughts but he pushed them aside.

He then inspected his arsenal and fingered the gas grenades that rendered people unconscious. He still didn't know if the man he'd used one on the previous night would wake up again or not so he didn't know whether they'd be safe to use on Sophia's thugs. However, Geoffrey was sure they'd do the job without killing whoever he lobbed them at and that was good enough for him. He pulled out a couple from his bag.

Then he pulled out a double action grappling hook for getting over to Sophia's building, two smaller grappling hooks he used for binding criminals, his reverse periscope with the aural enhancement device and a simple slingshot.

It was the slingshot he used first. Grabbing a little piece of broken masonry, he loaded the kid's toy and shot the tiny projectile over the street and onto the far side of Sophia's roof. As he had hoped, the guards all migrated towards the sound the piece of stone made when it hit.

Then Jason was in action, shooting his double action grappling hook at Sophia's roof, while anchoring the other end on the roof where he was. He glided over the drop below and prepared for stage two. Once he reached the other side, he wasted no time lobbing one of his gas grenades at Sophia's guards. One of them fired a shot before he went down but the whole lot were out for the count in a matter of moments.

Jason tidied up his grappling hook, hooked it on his belt and set up his reverse periscope device to look into Sophia's penthouse. The attractive mature aged woman had drawn a nasty looking hand gun, he saw. As he watched, she motioned Burges to keep out of sight and moved towards the stairs leading to the roof.

Down by the building's main entrance, Jason saw

Diane's squad pulling up. He pulled out his untraceable and sent Diane a text: *"Rooftop guards unconscious. Sophia inside with Burges. I'm moving in."*

Diane read the text a moment later. "I don't know how he does it."

"What's that?" her partner asked.

"We've got help," she replied, nodding to the roof.

"The Sentinel's here?"

"He's seen Burges inside the penthouse," Diane said. "He's also taken out the guards on the roof and he's heading in. And so are we. Come on."

It was exhausting, Hutchens thought as he left another one of Lamont's establishments. And the worst part was that he had known it'd be a fruitless search right from the start. Lamont was too smart to hide the mayor anywhere where the cops would find him. But they still had to try.

"Commissioner!"

Hutchens turned to the officer who'd called him. The man was standing by a patrol car and waving a radio.

"Acting Commissioner," Hutchens said, walking over. "And after today's shambles, probably not for long. What's going on?"

"Captain Reilly's lead was good. She's found Burges and she's moving in with her squad."

"Well, I'll be damned," Hutchens said, feeling the fatigue of the day washing away. "You mean we might catch the son of a bitch after all? Let's go then."

"Wait. There's more," the officer told him. "A report came in from a patrol on the other side of town. Danny Vincent and his gang have been shot dead and his place burnt down. The fire brigade's there at the moment to keep the blaze from getting out of hand. But detectives on the scene found charred remains and they're certain the bodies are Vincent and his pals."

Hutchens reflected on this for a moment. "Well, I can't say I'm sorry about those pricks. We'll check it out later."

"There's something else though," the officer told him. "The detectives on the scene say the scale of the damage coupled with bullets from high powered weapons and grenade fragments suggests the Bandit's the most likely culprit."

Hutchens gritted his teeth. The Bandit's recent appearance at police headquarters was still very fresh in his memory, along with the memories of everyone else on the force. However, they had more pressing concerns right then.

"The Bandit can wait."

. . .

Back at the penthouse, the Sentinel made his move. Hooking one end of his grappling hook to the roof, he leapt off and swung in through the window with a loud crash, sending shards of glass all over the floor.

Sophia was quick, turning her gun on him and firing a couple of shots but the Sentinel rolled to his side and the shots went wide. His eyes then fell on Burges, running for the door, then—leaping to his feet—he grabbed the former mayor and slammed him headfirst into the floor.

Then, while Sophia was trying to get another shot in, the Sentinel shot a binding grappling hook around her wrists. She let out a startled cry and then another as he yanked the cord back, throwing the gun out of her hands and dragging her stumbling towards him till she tripped on her high heels and ended up on the floor just a few feet from Burges. Somehow though, she still managed to look elegant.

"Guns are dangerous things, Ms. Garcia," the Sentinel told her as he tightened the cord around her wrists, immobilizing her.

"Get your goddamn hands off me!" she muttered.

Ignoring her, he turned to Burges—who looked scared out of his wits—and hoisted him up by the collar of his shirt. "I didn't expect to see you again for some time, Mr. Burges. Now, let me make this very clear for you. The police will be here any minute and once they take you away, I don't expect to see you again."

Since his prison breakout had been more of a kidnapping than a rescue, Burges felt kind of gypped. But he nodded anyway.

The next day, Martin Lamont sat down in his favorite private bar and picked up the remote for his wall mounted television. The news unsurprisingly was all about Burges being taken away to prison. Lamont found some satisfaction in the fact that Vincent hadn't rated a report. It was a final triumph over his rival.

"Well, we don't have to worry about Burges now anyway," one of his men told him, thinking perhaps that his boss needed some cheering up. "We've got the details we need to contact the Bandit. Vincent and his men are all dead. It looks like we've come out on top again."

"I'm going to have to pay a lot of money to bail out Sophia though," Lamont said. "If I don't, I'll never hear the end of it. Do you think you can bring in our lawyers for me? I'm too tired to make the calls."

"I took the liberty already," the man replied. "They said they'll talk you through the game plan in the morning."

Lamont nodded. "Sounds good. Get me a scotch, will you?"

"Sure."

"Yeah, we'll be all right," he said. "I guess I'll probably face some charges as well as a conspirator or an accomplice with regards to harboring Burges but the lawyers will get me and Sophia off."

He smiled as his drink appeared and took a sip. "They always do."

On Friday afternoon of the following week, Jason and Angie were walking home with some tests and assignments to mark.

"Well," Angie said. "After we knock this down, it'll be a nice short waltz to the end of the term and then it'll be vacation time."

Jason nodded. "Yeah. It's not soon enough for my liking but at least it's coming."

"Yeah." Angie sighed. "I think we could all do with a break." She laughed. "I don't imagine you'll miss Gary much."

"No," Jason confessed. "Although I was really sorry he was off with the 'flu the past few days."

Angie laughed again. "Yeah, right."

They opened the door and put their gear on the

kitchen table and started sorting it all out. Jason then looked through the small pile of assignments he had. "Wow. This looks good. Three with just a poorly structured paragraph. Two that are exactly the same so I can fail them outright…"

"One for cheating, and one for aiding and abetting?" Angie asked.

"Yeah, and they're both crap anyway so it makes you wonder why the first kid copied the other one." He picked up another piece of paper. "Oh, this is just gold. Here's a word for word copy of a web page we actually looked at in class." He put it down with a shake of his head. "Well, there's one thing about those year 9s. They sure make my marking easy."

"That's great," Angie said. "Maybe you can help me with mine then."

Jason gave her a kiss. "I'd be happy to," he said. He then pulled out his untraceable. "Hold on. I think this thing was vibrating…" He flicked it on and looked at the screen. "Ah. Text from Diane."

"Sorry for the late update," the text read. *"Thought you could use a break. Thanks for everything. Also, the man you brought in last Friday regained consciousness about a day later. I remember you asked about that. And Sophia's thugs were fine after their little rest too. Thanks again."*

Jason smiled. "Well, Geoffrey will be pleased about that."

HUNT THE BANDIT

A FORTNIGHT LATER, THE FOLLOWING NEWS bulletin was aired:

"It's been a rather trying few weeks for everyone in Fringe City, even by our own standards but we've been given a little reprieve in the return of some normality.

"Thousands around the city were pleased by the court decision that put Alison St. Claire in office as our new Mayor, something investigators are now saying should have been the case all along, adding electoral fraud to the list of charges that have been laid against former mayor Reggie Burges. However, District Attorney Charles Faulkner says that regardless of whatever ruling the courts hand down on these charges, Burges will be in prison for a long time. And as he's been moved to a maximum security facility, police say there is no chance of a repeat of the prison break out of two weeks ago.

"Miss St. Claire in the meantime says that although she may be mayor, she wants to assure the citizens of Fringe City that she intends to earn *the right to represent them by doing everything in her power to make this city a better place*

to live.

"One of her first acts as mayor has been to make Eric Hutchens our official Police Commissioner, given the dedicated work he has been doing while acting in that capacity over the past few weeks.

"In other news, it appears that recently, the Sentinel has been stepping up his activities considerably. The mysterious figure who stopped the Black Baron, who first led police to Reggie Burges and who also captured him after his escape from prison is still at it with alleged criminals turning up bound and beaten around the city or knocked unconscious from what experts are claiming to be a sophisticated stun gas attack. While some observers have expressed alarm over the fact that the Sentinel's methods appear to be more brutal of late, there is no denying the fact that he is drastically changing the face of our city.

"Most recently, he has struck a blow against two of Fringe City's most notorious gangs. Residents unfortunate enough to be familiar with the Fallen Angels and the Red Berets will know about their gang war all too well. Both gangs have several hundred members and their ongoing street warfare has rendered large areas of the city no-go zones. However, this morning, several high-ranking members of each gang were found outside the main city courthouse.

"Each gang member was unconscious and tied up to a member from their rival gang while lists of each individual's

crimes, both proven and alleged, were found at the scene as well. Police also found a removal truck nearby which they believe the Sentinel used to transport the gang members to the courthouse. They found a note thanking the company for the use of its truck as well as some money to cover the cost of a two-day loan. The owner of the truck company says that as it was all for a good cause, he doesn't mind that the Sentinel borrowed it without asking.

"Police say the incident appears to be a warning to other gang members to disband. Furthermore, all the apprehended members are known felons and, if convicted, will face lengthy jail terms. And Police Commissioner Eric Hutchens, while he will not officially sanction citizens taking the law into their own hands, agrees that something did need to be done about these two gangs.

"In the meantime, Hutchens has been cleaning up corruption in the police force and says that things are finally looking up for Fringe City. However, he has stated in no uncertain terms that there is still a lot of work to be done. With the police force now operating more efficiently and crime down, he already has his sights set on his next goal: the apprehension of the Bandit.

"Any long term resident of Fringe City knows that we put up with a lot of madness and we've got far more than our share of killers and psychotics. It'd be hard to pick the worst of the lot, with options ranging from the Specter to Lady Vice, but the Bandit would certainly be a finalist. For the past few years, we have had to live with the knowledge that this mass-murderer hides among us and that he can appear without any warning—leaving a trail of death and destruction—then vanish without a trace.

"Well, now Eric Hutchens says he intends to put an end to his activities permanently but so far, it's nothing we haven't seen before. Commissioner Hutchens has begun his investigation by asking for anyone who has any information that may lead to his whereabouts to come forward and he has assured the public that the police will offer round-the-clock protection for anyone willing to do so. However, his predecessors have tried in much the same manner and failed so many are wondering why the Commissioner believes this latest attempt will be any different.

"In other news, thousands of people are heading out of Fringe City for the winter vacation, taking advantage of the season to visit some of this country's best ski slopes while others are heading south for warmer climes. Not that it gets that cold in Fringe City of course, as residents well know. However, many families at this time of year consider leaving Fringe City permanently and many real estate agents are asking, why not?

"Terry Higgens, head of one of the country's largest real estate agencies has just launched a massive advertising campaign specifically for residents of Fringe City who may be considering this. In his opinion, there has never been a better time to make the move. Whether you're thinking of *renting* or *buying, market prices across the country, while not favorable as such, are comparable to those locally."*

As Charles Faulkner entered the mayor's office the next day, he thought it said a lot about Alison St. Claire that she hadn't set up shop in Grand Central.

The mayor smiled at him. "The best D.A. on the coast. Are you late for anything, Mr. Faulkner?"

Faulkner returned the smile. "I try not to be."

"Well, thanks for coming in today," St. Claire told him and waved him to a seat. "Would you like me to have some coffee sent up?"

"Oh, I'm fine," Faulkner smiled, sitting down.

"Okay, then." St. Claire sat down as well. "Well, the first thing I really want to talk about is our friend, the Sentinel. I have to say I'm a bit worried by the recent blasé manner in which he's been carrying out his work. He seemed to have been more cautious when he first started out and now, it's as if he thinks he can do anything he wants."

"He's become more confident certainly," Faulkner agreed. "Almost brazen. That thing with those gang members for instance. That was a pretty public stunt."

"Although that was a bit more like his original style," St. Claire conceded. "Bringing the criminals in. Lately, Hutchens says his officers have been finding beaten crooks just lying in alley ways and dumpsters."

"I think he's just become more practical myself," Faulkner told her. "He can't bring in every criminal he knocks out. Also, he's probably beginning to understand his own limitations. He's just one man after all."

"We're sure about that?"

"Pretty sure," Faulkner said. "Although you do raise another possibility. I wouldn't be surprised if there were a few copycat vigilantes out there as well. He certainly wasn't responsible for all the beaten criminals that have been found at least. His style is to use stun gas."

"So the media's got its facts wrong?"

"In this instance, I think it has. Anyway, as for whether he's working solo or in tandem with others, we think he works alone. And we haven't seen him in two places at once yet."

"All right then. Tell me about his liaison on the force."

"Captain Reilly?" Faulkner asked. "Surely you've heard about her in the news. Mariane O'Hara at Fringe City Central thinks the world of her and Diane's certainly made a lot of headlines in the papers too."

"Yes, the heroic cop who worked out that the Black Baron was going to blow up the police station and got everyone out in time," St. Claire said. "I know the official stuff and I've no reason to doubt it. But what's your opinion?"

"I think she's a damn fine officer. I don't think she should take a fall for any of this. The Sentinel approached her, not the other way around. And he's been helping her get things done that she believes would not have been possible otherwise. I'd say from everything he's done for her and the public, it's perfectly understandable that she's decided to liaise with him."

"And you can vouch for her based on your relationship prior to the Sentinel's arrival on the scene, can't you?"

"Absolutely," Faulkner said. "For a long time, she was one of the only officers on the force I could trust. And she's always been willing to share information with me and pool resources as well."

"Has she told Hutchens about the Sentinel?"

"Only recently. Actually, it was pretty brave of her. God knows, he hasn't been the greatest supporter of our vigilante friend. But he seems to have come around recently. Although I don't think he knows I'm in on the whole thing yet."

"Well, we can tell him later," St. Claire replied. "But I don't want everyone knowing about this. If the press get even a scrap of this, they'll be all over us. Anyway... So for the time being, we're going to tacitly condone what he's doing?"

"For the time-being, I think so. You know, I don't like everything about his methods either. His rather destructive approach to fighting crime ruined a very important case for me recently."

"Yeah, you couldn't pin Lamont for trying to blow up Kingsford station because he destroyed the evidence. I remember."

"You've got a good memory," Faulkner replied. "Still, the point I wanted to make was that while he's a mixed blessing, I believe his heart's in the right place. Between our unofficial friend, Diane, Hutchens and myself, we might be able to get some good done in this town."

"All right," St. Claire agreed. "We'll keep it under wraps for the time being. I sure hope I'm doing the right thing though. Also, at some point, you and I should have a meeting with Hutchens. I want to talk about this Bandit thing. But not just yet. Let's give him some time to do whatever it is he's got in mind first."

Meanwhile, Jason found himself staring at a piece of paper in an almost comatose state. "Man, why did I leave the most difficult one of these till last?" he mumbled.

Angie leaned over to have a look at it. "What is it?

Oh god, I hate the "positive comments" box. I don't suppose you could say he has the decency to smoke his pot in the change-rooms instead of in class?"

"I'd thought of it," Jason replied. Then an idea struck him and he wrote something else down. "Wait, I've got it. 'His handwriting is usually legible.'"

"Done!" he announced with a healthy dose of euphoria as he finished the last of his term reports.

"Great. Now, let's get the hell out of this dump."

"Yes." Jason slid the reports in the appropriate tray, as did Angie with hers, and they headed out.

"All right!" Angie exclaimed. "Winter vacation! That's got to be worth a celebratory drink or two."

"I'd love to join you," Jason said. "But I've got something I want to check up on first.'

"I didn't say I wanted one with you," Angie told him. "I'm going out with the girls."

"Oh, thanks."

"However, I spend plenty of time with you, don't I?"

"You do."

"And who do I go to bed with at every night?"

"Well…"

"Well, most nights," she added. "Anyway, it isn't the girls."

"They can join us," Jason told her. "I don't mind."

"Hilarious, honey," Angie replied. "Come on. Let's

go home."

After Angie went out, Jason felt almost unaccountably restless and after trying to figure out the cause, he realized he wanted to put on his Kevlar costume again. He wanted to go out there and be the Sentinel. And for a moment, he wondered whether he could switch that part of himself off any more.

Trying not to think about it, he flicked on the TV and changed the channel until he could get some news. He found an extended segment on the Bandit that was running, detailing his sordid history and the terror he had unleashed on Fringe City.

After a minute of this, Jason climbed to his feet and picked up a folder he had on the kitchen counter. He pulled out two sheets of paper near the front of the folder and moved them to the back. One was on the Fallen Angels and the last was on the Red Berets. Then he pulled out another handful of papers that he'd stapled together, notes on the Bandit. For a moment, he flipped through them looking for some kind of inspiration but nothing jumped out. He put the papers away, along with the folder, then stood next to the counter thinking. He then pulled out his untraceable and made a call.

"We should talk," he said, trying to keep it

professional. Something that was getting harder with Diane. There was a brief reply. "Well," Jason said. "I think we should discuss exactly what we've got on the Bandit. Maybe we can work out some type of long term strategy."

He listened as Diane said something else.

"No, that's okay," he said. "All right. Tomorrow then. 8.00."

The next day, Angie was making herself a coffee when she heard a knock.

"Coming," she called out. She looked through the peephole and shook her head as she opened the door. "Geoffrey. Here's a surprise. Well, come on in."

He looked even more sheepish than usual, she thought to herself

"So, what's up?" she asked him as he wandered around the living room.

He scratched his head, trying to appear nonchalant, heightening his awkwardness. "Oh, that girl I met at that conference in Boston a few months ago has come to town to visit."

"So are you two going out then?" Angie asked, giving him an encouraging smile.

"Oh," Geoffrey said. "You know."

"With you?" Angie asked. "I never know. I'm not

fluent in Geoff-glish like Jason is."

"Oh, yeah… Jason," Geoffrey said, giving her the impression he had only just remembered what he was doing there. "Is he in?"

"He was, but he's gone out now." She sighed. "He's out a lot these days. I'm worried about him, Geoffrey. I think he's getting carried away with this whole thing. You should see him at work. He's so distracted and it's about all I can do to stop Gary from noticing. Thank god the vacation's finally come around. I honestly didn't think he was going to last another week."

"He knows what he's doing."

"I hope so. But I think he's getting in way over his head. Maybe you shouldn't give him all that gear he uses. It allows him to get himself into more trouble."

Geoffrey contemplated this for a moment, and it was amazing how quickly his awkwardness vanished with the change of topic. Right then, he looked as grown up as Angie had ever seen him. "Well, you know," he said, "the way I see it, he's dead serious about this thing of his so he's going to get himself into trouble with the gear or without it. At least if he has the gear, he can do this stuff a little more safely."

"Maybe you're right," Angie conceded. "Well, anyway. Um… Would you like a coffee? The pot's just boiled."

"I'll take a rain check," Geoffrey told her. "I was just

stopping by to say I'm going to be busy with Charlotte for the next few days. Oh, did Jason get those items I dropped off?"

"I don't know. I'll ask him next time I see him."

"Nah, don't worry about it," Geoffrey said, turning to leave.

"You're incorrigible," Angie told him. "More items? Sometimes, I don't know who's worse. You or Jason."

It was 8.00 p.m. Not the best time to be hanging around back alleys, Diane thought, wondering why the hell she had insisted on meeting the Sentinel there. Sure, she didn't want to be seen with him in the middle of a mall somewhere but there must have been somewhere a little less dangerous to wait. However, it was done and all she could do was hope there was no trouble.

Fortunately, she didn't have to wait long, as a familiar figure emerged from the darkness soon after she arrived. She gave him a grin. "We've got to stop meeting like this."

The Sentinel laughed at the little quip. "True."

"Well, where do you want to talk? It wouldn't be good for us to be caught chatting down here. I don't like the neighborhood much for starters."

"Me neither. How about the rooftops? Have you got

a good head for heights?"

"I'm pretty good," Diane said. "Although how exactly do you suggest we go about this?"

The Sentinel fired a grappling hook around a protrusion four storeys above them. "That's the first step," he explained. "Then you hang onto me."

"All right," Diane said, feeling a little awkward as they locked their arms around each other in what felt like an embrace. "By the way, I never kiss on a first date," she joked, trying to put herself at ease.

"I'll take it under advisement," the Sentinel replied. "Hopefully, you don't scream either. Otherwise, we might attract a lot of unwanted attention."

Diane frowned. "Why would I scream?"

"Let's just say the ride up may feel a little... sudden."

Diane braced herself. "Okay then."

She didn't scream as they shot up but she let out an audible gasp. The Sentinel hadn't been kidding about the speed of the ascent. The sensation put her in mind of rollercoasters. She hated those things.

"Well," she said when they were on the roof. "This is a little unusual for me, I have to say. I feel like a girl guide in a tree house."

"I understand," her friend replied. "I feel a bit like that myself when I do this sometimes."

Diane raised an eyebrow and smiled. "Like a girl

guide?"

Jason laughed a little. "Well, maybe not that but the bit about the tree house at least."

"Fair enough. By the way, Eric Hutchens loved that stunt with the gang members."

Jason seemed somewhat surprised by this. "Really? I thought the commissioner wouldn't be too keen on me taking matters into my own hands."

"Maybe not when he was acting commissioner. He didn't understand you then."

"He doesn't seem particularly keen on me now either."

"That's just on TV," Diane told him. "He can hardly go around publicly condoning what you do now, can he?"

"I see. So off the record, things were a bit different?"

"Off the record? He cracked up laughing when we saw those thugs trussed up outside the court house. Anyway, although Hutchens can't officially condone what you're doing, he's beginning to acknowledge the fact that Fringe City needs all the help it can get."

"That's what I've always thought," Jason said. "Kind of my motto really. Well, anyway. I suppose we'd better get down to business. What exactly do the police have on the Bandit?"

Diane sighed. "Not that much, to be honest. But Burges has decided that it might help him reduce the severity of his sentence if he comes clean and plays ball on some of his various dealings. I think you may have had a lot to do with that."

"Glad I could help."

"Well, he's scared stiff of having another run in with you. Right now, he'd divulge almost anything if we asked him to. However, we think he's holding back on something."

"Burges knows how to contact the Bandit," Jason said, following her. "He hired him for the hit on Commissioner Levings because Levings could have tipped the authorities off to the fact that he was working with Grigorie."

"Right."

"And then I suppose Lamont broke him out of prison because he wanted the Bandit for the job on Vincent."

"You're fast," Diane said.

"Well, I try to be."

"We tried to keep as much of that out of the news as possible. You know, there seemed to be enough hysteria around as it was."

"So is there any way to convince Burges to talk?" Jason asked.

"That's the problem," Diane told him. "He doesn't want to give us anything on the Bandit as it'd be a confession to hiring him. And being an accomplice to any job the Bandit's done might ruin any chance he'd have of an early parole."

"True. But since he's already been tied to Grigorie, has he got anything left to lose?"

"Probably not, but I doubt he'd see it that way."

"No, probably not."

"So," Diane asked, "any ideas?"

"Well, some… but they're all only semi-legal."

"What do you have in mind?"

"I just wondered if maybe I could give Burges a good scare. However, I guess I can't just waltz on into a maximum-security prison in my Sentinel gear."

"Your 'Sentinel' gear? My god, you're buying your own press."

"Sorry. I try not to get a big head when I read about myself in the paper, but you know how it is. You're a bit of a celebrity cop yourself."

"Yeah, tell me about it. The pay's not much better though. However, you're right. If you waltz on into the prison in your trademark 'Sentinel' gear, they won't let you out again, that's for sure."

"I don't suppose the police might be able to arrange an off-the-record visit…"

"You can get that idea out of your head right now," Diane told him. "After Hutchens made that big claim about cleaning out all the corruption in the system, the media would be all over him in a flash if so much as a hint got out that we're liaising with you."

"You really meant the police there, didn't you?" Jason asked. "Not just you."

"This won't work anymore if it's just between you and me," Diane told him. "The commissioner's got my back and although he doesn't know it, so does the new mayor and the district attorney."

"I suppose that should be a relief," Jason said, although he sounded unsure of what to make of it.

"It should be, yes," Diane replied. "It should be one less thing for you to worry about. Now, obviously, it's an unofficial sanction. I should point that out since we're having this conversation. We can't let the general public know about it. But as long as you don't push your vendetta on crime too far, we're on your side."

"What exactly is too far?"

"Hopefully, we'll never find out," Diane told him. "But I think you know what I mean."

"Sure," Jason replied. "I think I do. All right then. Let's get back to the Bandit. I've got an idea. Now his last job was getting rid of Danny Vincent's gang, which was to the direct benefit of Martin Lamont and it happened right after Lamont busted Burges out of prison."

"Yeah, we've already discussed that."

"But do you think Lamont would have asked Burges to contact the Bandit without obtaining the means to contact him directly himself?"

"Not likely," Diane replied. "Burges might not have wanted to share that information with Lamont, but Lamont wouldn't have passed up the opportunity to try to get it from him."

"And he could have succeeded. And if he did, then at least two people might know how to contact the Bandit."

"Well, Lamont for starters," Diane said.

"The obvious one," Jason agreed. "And?"

"His sister Sophia Garcia's the other. Since Burges was staying with her, if Lamont wanted him to make the call to the Bandit, then she would have been in the room with him at the time. So your plan is to shake these two down, is that it?"

"Something semi-legal, but nothing that crosses that metaphorical line of yours. Don't worry. It's not a line I want to cross either. But anyway, I think it's time to follow the trail. And since the term's pretty much wrapped up, I should have enough time to find out where it ends."

Diane looked a little surprised and Jason realized he had dropped his guard.

"Don't worry," Diane told him, giving him a smile. "I didn't hear that."

"Thanks," Jason said, smiling back. "Now, maybe you can get me started. Do you have any idea where I might find Lamont and his sister?"

"You clearly haven't been watching the news today."

"Well, I've been a little busy."

"It's just that the pair of them were in court this morning so the media's been keeping track of them all day," Diane explained. "Now, their high-flying law team's gotten them off again but Faulkner didn't make it easy for them. Or cheap. However, tonight, they're having a big party because it's Lamont's birthday."

"Uh huh." Jason nodded as he took it all in. "I don't suppose you know where they're hosting this party, by any chance?"

"Hey, honey," he said, his regular cell phone in hand as he walked down a bustling sidewalk.

"Hey, what's up?"

"Just calling to let you know I'll be a little later than I expected."

"Figured," Angie replied. "Oh, Geoffrey called round earlier. He said he might be busy during the next couple of days because that girl he met at that conference in Boston is staying with him."

"Oh, Charlotte? Yeah, Wolfman's told me about her."

"So, they're an item, are they?"

"Quite an item, I think," Jason said, glancing at the traffic before crossing a street. "Although, you never know with Geoffrey."

"No," Angie agreed. "Oh, he also wanted to know if you got the new items he left for you."

"Yeah, I got 'em. Might even try one out tonight."

"Sounds like there are a few people around," Angie said. "So I guess you can't divulge any more than that for the moment?"

"You know how it is."

"More like I don't know how it is. But I know what you mean at any rate."

Jason almost wished he could talk about what was going on right then, because he was beginning to feel a little apprehensive. Getting to Lamont was going to be a lot more difficult than breaking into his sister's apartment had been because now they both knew how he operated.

"Yeah, sorry about that. Anyway, I'll have to go pretty soon. No need to wait up."

"Funny. Before you called, I was about to ring you and tell you the exact same thing."

"Another drink with the girls?" Jason asked.

"Why, are you jealous?"

Jason laughed. "Maybe. Anyway, I'll see you later."

"Okay then."

"I love you, honey."

"I love you too."

He swallowed as he hung up. He was nearly there. As he came around the next corner, he saw the bright lights from the second floor of the elaborate establishment where Lamont was hosting his party. However, for the moment, he kept walking right past it and he didn't ascend an adjacent building either.

Instead, he chose another vantage-point further away. He then saw what he'd been worried about. Lamont had men on the roofs of the surrounding buildings as well... and they were carrying gas masks.

"Well, where there's a will, there's a way," Jason told himself. "Plan B."

He went back down to the street and pulled out his untraceable. "I'd like to report some prowlers," he said. "There are armed men on the top of the Global United Banking building, the Paris hotel, Verity Towers and the Opal apartment complex."

"Got it," Diane replied on the other end of the line. "They'll be out of your hair shortly. Sit tight."

Jason hung up and went for a cup of coffee from a café he spied on the nearest corner. About ten minutes later, as he was enjoying his drink, several S.W.A.T. vans drove past. He watched with a smile as they pulled up further along the street. The teams then leapt out and entered the four buildings he'd told Diane about.

Up on the roofs, Lamont's men got quite a surprise when the S.W.A.T. teams appeared, shouting at them to drop their weapons. And as they were all trespassing and carrying illegal firearms, there wasn't anything they could say in their defence.

Back in the café, Jason didn't have to wait too long before he was treated to the sight of Lamont's men being hauled off in a thoroughly undignified and, at least for him, quite entertaining manner. Soon the vans were gone, Lamont's men with them, and his phone vibrated.

"You move fast," he said, answering it.

"I try to. Anyway, it's all clear. Good luck."

"Thanks."

Jason then headed to the top of the Opal apartment complex, the closest of the other buildings to Lamont's establishment. Once he got there, he suited up and glided across to his destination.

After breaking in from the roof, he made his way down to the party. It wasn't difficult, since the rest of the building was deserted. Then, taking a breath, he strode straight into the large room, controlling the impulse to spin around as the metal detectors by the door went off.

As he entered, everyone in the room turned to look at him. Lamont certainly hadn't expected this, Jason knew. There he was, one of the crime boss's biggest enemies, standing alone in the lion's den.

He smiled at the stunned crowd, appreciating the fact that the musicians Lamont had hired had had the good grace to stop playing, lending his entrance the dramatic weight he thought it deserved.

"Good evening," he said. Then he lobbed a gas grenade into the middle of the crowd.

He stepped back as Lamont and his guests coughed, sputtered and collapsed, then pulled out his untraceable and called Geoffrey. "Hey, Wolfman. Are you busy?"

"What's up?"

"I just used one of the short term stun grenades."

"Did it work?"

"I've just knocked out close to a hundred people," Jason told him, looking around the room. "Actually, it might be more like two hundred."

"Damn. Did you lob it in a nightclub or something?"

"A party for Martin Lamont and his friends."

"You're insane!"

"Tell me about it. Anyway, remind me... How long have I got before these guys wake up?"

"Three hours," Geoffrey told him. "Um... That's what you wanted, isn't it?"

"Yeah, that's what I wanted. I just wanted to make sure," Jason said. "I don't want any of these people waking up until I'm well and truly gone."

"You should be okay. But I wouldn't hang around too long."

Jason smiled. "Not planning to. Later."

"See you."

Jason found Lamont and Sophia Garcia and dragged them away from the others. Then he went downstairs to find some transport. He felt a bit sorry when he lobbed another gas grenade at the chauffeurs standing around the limousines out the front though. They didn't look like bad types. But, presumably, they knew who they were working for.

Jason went inside again and dragged Lamont down and then went back for his sister. It felt wrong handling an unconscious woman into an elevator and out through a lobby, especially one in a thin backless evening dress. He just needed one by-passer to see him and draw the wrong conclusion and then his name would be as good as mud. Although it'd be as good a reason as any to retire the Sentinel, he thought with a shake of his head.

Once he'd gotten Sophia down, he took the keys from the nearest chauffer, opened up his limousine and hid Lamont and Ms. Garcia in the trunk. Then he went back to the room upstairs and lobbed another stun grenade at the sleeping occupants, one that would keep them under for a further twenty hours. The

Lamont establishment could afford to be closed for a day.

Then, with all that taken care of, he rappelled to the top of the Opal apartment complex and changed back into his plain clothes before returning to Lamont's establishment.

Once he got there, he threw his gear onto the back seat of the limousine he'd acquired and drove off. And about twenty five minutes later, he reached a quiet street running alongside a tall building that was under construction. No one else was around.

He smiled as he inspected the site. "Perfect."

When Lamont awoke, he was dazed, groggy and very confused. He then realized he was standing on a ledge in an unfamiliar place, high above the edge of the harbor.

"It's peaceful up here, isn't it?"

Lamont had a fair idea who was talking to him.

"The view's not bad either," the speaker continued. "Perhaps you'd like to take a closer look."

"Let's knock off the games," Lamont said. "You didn't bring me up here to kill me, so what *do* you want?"

"The Bandit," the Sentinel told him. "You know how to contact him. You're going to tell me."

"I don't know anything about that crazy son of a bitch."

"You're lying. The Bandit didn't just kill Danny Vincent and his men for the sport of it. No one would be happier to see Vincent dead than you."

"Let's be honest with each other, buddy. You wouldn't have been too sorry about Vincent either."

"I'm not. But let's cut the crap. It wasn't the police who paid the Bandit to knock off Vincent, and it sure as hell wasn't me."

"Hell, maybe he just knocked Vincent off for reasons of his own," Lamont sneered. "Anyway, you may try to play outside the rules but I know you liaise with the cops. Hell, you're probably on their payroll yourself. So I'd have to be pretty damn stupid to give you anything that'd incriminate me, wouldn't I? Now, you didn't kill me at the docks. You didn't kill Burges when you had the chance either, and you've had plenty of them. So as you said, let's cut the crap. This is all a big bluff. You're good, I'll give you that. But you're running out of tricks."

"Well, I'm not the one hanging by a thread over Fringe City harbor," the Sentinel told him. "And if you think this is a big bluff, then maybe you don't know me too well."

"Oh, I know you better than you think," Lamont said. "You talk the talk, but you need something else to shake up the underworld of Fringe City, and you ain't got it in you. So talk the talk all you want and we can shoot the breeze all night. I've got nothing better to do. But I can tell you right now that I'm not going to give you shit."

"You mean you won't talk about the Bandit then?"

"What do you *think* I mean?"

The Sentinel shrugged. "I was just making sure." He gagged Lamont, grabbed him by the scruff of his neck and hurled him over the ledge. "Happy birthday then."

As he walked away, he heard a brief muffled scream. Behind him, a wire rope secured around a pillar went taut and three storeys down, Lamont came to a halt.

Meanwhile, Sophia Garcia struggled in wire bonds as well. She was also gagged and, no matter how she struggled, she couldn't move away from the ledge she was on. And despite her usual ability to keep her cool, she was distraught.

"You shouldn't move so much," came a voice from behind, as gloved hands removed her gag. "It just makes the wire dig deeper. Anyway, it sure is nice to see you again, Sophia Garcia."

"What do you want this time?" she asked, her voice

mixed with emotions. Fear and annoyance competed for first place.

"I think you might be able to help me."

"Why do you think I'd want to?" Annoyance emerged victorious.

Jason remembered Diane's little joke from earlier that night. Somehow, it seemed quite fitting. "Because then we can stop meeting like this. I want to know how to contact the Bandit."

"Well, you should ask my brother then."

"I did. I'm hoping you'll be a bit more cooperative."

Sophia shivered. It was chilly up in this unfinished building, especially in a thin dress but it was fear more than cold that had her shaking. "Why do you think I know how to contact the Bandit?" she asked. "You've got no proof of that."

Jason shook his head. "I can't understand why anyone uses that line. 'You've got no proof' is as close to an admission of guilt as you can get without making a confession. However, since you asked, I'll indulge you. The first clue is the fact that the Bandit killed Danny Vincent and his men. The second clue is that it was to the direct benefit of your brother and that it happened right after he busted Burges out of prison. At the time, Burges was the only person Lamont knew for certain had the means to contact the Bandit. And as for the rest, it was pretty obvious. Lamont couldn't contact the Bandit himself as the police were combing his establishments and the media was in his face all day. So he had Burges stay with you, as very few people knew about you. And Burges contacted the Bandit from your place."

Tears welled in Sophia's eyes and Jason realized it was going to be a struggle to keep up the charade. Lamont had seen right through him; he wasn't cut out for this.

"If I tell you," Sophia pleaded, "will you promise to let me go? I'll tell you what you want to know. I'll tell you everything."

"I'll take you back home safe and sound," Jason replied. "But if you cross the line again, then you're going to be sorry."

The last part made Sophia really cry and for a moment, he hated himself. Really hated himself. He was glad Angie couldn't see him right then.

"I'm not going to do anything like that again," Sophia told him. "I'm done with all of it. Martin. His organization. Everything. The Burges thing was just a favor..." She sniffed a little, unable to speak for a moment. "Because Martin's my brother."

Jason didn't know he could feel more wretched but he did now. He knew she was telling the truth. For a moment, he wondered what he'd do if he had a sibling who was heading a crime syndicate. He thought about his own siblings, a younger brother in San Diego and an older sister living across the border in Vancouver. He couldn't imagine what he'd do if either of them asked him for a favor like the one Lamont had asked of Sophia. And he was glad he'd never find out.

"But I'm done," Sophia sobbed. "I'll never help him again. I promise!"

"All right," Jason said, trying to soothe her. He loosened her bonds, guided her away from the ledge and helped her sit down.

He listened as she talked about the Bandit for a few minutes. He even got out some paper and wrote some notes. Sophia didn't seem to notice but by then, he didn't care about projecting any illusions of mystique anyway.

"All right," he said when she was finished, putting a hand on her shoulder and giving her a small smile. "Let's get you home." He removed the top of one of the three-hour-variety stun grenades, taking caution to keep the contents covered so he didn't inadvertently knock himself out.

"Now, close your eyes," he said. "When you wake up, you'll be at home in bed."

Sophia didn't understand how this was all going to work but she nodded. "All right," she murmured, sniffling a little and wiping a few last stray tears away.

As she closed her eyes, Jason lifted the gas grenade

under her nose and moved his hand enough to let her inhale some of the contents. He watched as she went limp and then slid the grenade away across the floor where the remaining gas wouldn't affect him.

He brought Sophia down to the street by descending with the grappling hook he'd used when he had hauled her up, holding her limp body close to him. Once again, he was glad that Angie couldn't see him but this time for different reasons.

He then drove her in the limousine back to her apartment. As he carried her to the lobby, the doorman looked a little suspicious. Jason didn't blame him.

"The lady was at a function when she came over a bit faint," he explained. "I was on my way home when I got a call to go back and pick her up," he added to cover for the fact that he wasn't wearing fitting attire for a chauffeur.

"She's not... sick, is she?" the doorman asked, a funny expression on his face as he looked Sophia over.

Jason laughed. "She's not going to throw up all over the lobby if that's what you're worried about. I think it's just exhaustion. She slept for the entire ride in the limo."

The doorman noticed the dried tears and Sophia's smeared eyeliner. "Looks like the lady was upset," he remarked, helping Jason carry her to the elevator.

"Yeah," Jason said. "It might have something to do

with it."

"Jilted by a boyfriend perhaps," the doorman suggested as they got to the elevator.

"Maybe," Jason shrugged. He kept up the off-duty chauffer charade a little longer, just to be on the safe side. "Now, the nice young man at the function gave me the lady's key but he didn't give me her room number. But he said this lady's well-known in the building. You wouldn't happen to know the room, would you?"

"It's the penthouse." The doorman smiled. "Nicest apartment in the building."

"Well, at least she'll have a comfy place to sleep it off then."

"Um," the doorman hesitated. "I've got to keep an eye on the lobby…"

"Oh, no, that's fine," Jason waved the proffered apology away. "I can manage. Thanks."

It was a welcome relief when the elevator doors closed and an even more welcome one when he lay Sophia on her bed and pulled the covers over her. He'd taken her high heels off but had decided for decency's sake to stop there. She could always make herself comfortable after she woke up.

He shook his head as he contemplated how absurd the whole thing was, tucking a mobster's sister into bed. However, he couldn't help feeling sorry for her.

And she had told him what he wanted to know.

With a sigh, he put her key on the bedside table and left. He thanked the doorman again for his help on the way out, then drove the limousine somewhere out of the way and ditched it. Not long afterwards, he caught the train home, had a hot shower, went to bed and fell right asleep.

Meanwhile, Martin Lamont dangled upside down by his ankles, wide awake with no way of knowing when he'd be taken down.

It was 10 a.m. when Jason woke up and the morning sunlight was right in his face. Despite the fact she'd gotten home after him the night before, Angie was already up and about when he stumbled into the kitchen.

"Hey," he croaked as he got himself some cereal.

"Good morning," she said, giving him a kiss on the cheek. "I didn't wake you as it looked like you needed the rest."

"I appreciate it," Jason said, slumping into his seat.

"So what did you do last night?"

Jason tried to recollect the events. Two pertinent things stood out. He had thrown one of the most dangerous men in Fringe City off a building and he had tucked that same man's sister into bed.

"You wouldn't believe me if I told you," he replied. He shook his head before continuing. "However, I got a good lead on the Bandit at the end of it all. Burges contacted him through his brother in Canada and deposited money in a bank account in Zurich that the Bandit's brother monitored. And I guess the brother then transferred the money from this account to the Bandit's account in Fringe City.

"I got the telephone number Burges used to contact the brother, along with the number of the bank account in Zurich. I had a hunch that Lamont wanted to know how to set his own credit line up with the Bandit. Turned out I was right."

"That's pretty thin though." Angie frowned. "I mean, I'm not trying to downplay any of that, but I don't know if it's enough to track the Bandit. I'm no expert on international law but I don't know if the government could force a bank in Switzerland to hand over the transaction details of a private account."

"A private account that a criminal has paid into though," Jason pointed out.

"A criminal outside of Swiss jurisdiction."

"Yeah, okay. I see what you mean. But it gives the cops a place to start."

"Good," Angie said. "Give it to Diane and let them sort it out. Because this thing with the Bandit is also outside of your jurisdiction as far as I'm concerned."

"I plan to," Jason told her. "Trust me. Oh, and remind me to take Lamont down tonight."

"*What*?"

"Oh, he needed a lesson so he's spending the day hanging off an unfinished building by his ankles."

"Lamont. That's Martin Lamont, the head of the largest organized crime syndicate in Fringe City, right?"

Jason ate a spoonful of cereal. "That's the one."

Angie nodded and took a sip of coffee. "Right."

"By the way," Jason asked. "Would you like to get out of Fringe City for a few days?"

"What did you have in mind?"

"Oh, I thought you might enjoy a skiing trip in Canada."

"So you can go chasing the Bandit's brother? Forget it."

"Honey, I'm shocked. Why would you think I'd suggest such a thing? I just thought it'd be nice to get out of town for a little while."

"Yeah, I bet you did. Anyway, skiing trips are too expensive."

"Ah, well. It was worth a shot." Jason finished his cereal and climbed to his feet to wash up. "Oh, and I might go out for lunch today. Although I don't think I'll be long."

"Meeting someone?"

"Yeah. Another woman."

Angie shook her head at the dumb joke. "Not your police liaison?"

"You're pretty fast, Angie," Jason told her. "It's a shame you're not on the team. You might be a natural detective."

"It's not that hard to piece together with your extensive social network."

"True," Jason conceded. He put his bowl and spoon in the draining rack and got out his untraceable. "Anyway, I might give Diane a call now."

When Diane heard the suggestion, she had to take a moment to get her bearings back. "Sorry? You mean we'll just meet in a restaurant or a café somewhere in broad daylight and have lunch together?"

"It's as good a way to meet as any other," Jason reasoned. "Besides, even if you knew my first name and what I looked like, I'd say my identity would still be safe. I'm not exactly a front page celebrity."

"Well, your alter-ego's not doing too badly on that front," Diane pointed out, "but I take your point."

"And besides, I think the whole mystique thing's never really worked with you anyway."

"True, but then again… We're friends, right?"

"Yeah."

"Don't worry, though. I'm sure you're still scary to the underworld of Fringe City."

"Thanks."

With his out-of-town girlfriend Charlotte Gray beside him, Geoffrey walked into the lab where he did most of his work for the university. It wasn't exactly fancy, and was a little heavy on the concrete aesthetically speaking, but it had lots of space and everyone there was cool as far as he was concerned. And that was far more meaningful than working in a fancy looking building.

"Hey, Geoffrey!" one of his colleagues called out. He gave Charlotte a friendly nod but it was clear there were other things on his mind that superseded social formalities like introductions and suchlike. "I tried out that high-tensile wire you made. It works like a charm. So we should be able to complete those high speed tests now."

"Cool."

"And I noticed your little job with the wire release mechanism. That was good thinking. You know, we launched the thing without checking on that and man, we were seriously worried the wire would snap and send the damn thing crashing through the fan at the other end of the wind tunnel. Anyway, we all figure the next few rounds of drinks are on us."

Geoffrey grinned sheepishly. "Hey, I was just happy to help. The trick's just to play the release out a little bit instead of letting it instantly uncoil. I've made plenty of those kind of gadgets."

"Maybe but you probably saved the fan."

Geoffrey shrugged. "Well, that's good to know."

"Anyway, thanks for that," the other guy told him. "By the way, do you want the leftover wire?" He glanced at Charlotte again and gave Geoffrey a knowing look. "There's several hundred feet of it in the back room."

Geoffrey kept smiling. "Yeah, I'll find a use for it. My uncle's got a farm in Iowa. He'll find a use for every last inch of it."

"Well," the guy said. "I see you've got company so I might leave you to it. Anyway, we owe you a drink."

"Cheers."

Geoffrey then went to his desk where there were a few boxes about in various states from empty to stuffed. There was a bit of a cleanup underway. He taped down some of the boxes that were full and put some junk from his desk into the other ones. Charlotte in the meantime walked around the place looking at the various things her boyfriend was working on. Some odd looking gas canisters caught her attention.

She held one up, inspecting it. "What's this for?"

"I thought it might have some use as an alternative to current general anesthetics," Geoffrey told her. "Take a patient who's been operated on but is still in really terrible pain. Now, you could put them on morphine but you know, that's problematic. So maybe they could go under for a while until the pain's a little more tolerable. A general anesthetic might do the job, sure. But it could also be dangerous to keep a patient under something like that for extended periods of time. This gas, however, could theoretically safely keep someone under for a whole day or more."

Charlotte nodded. "Interesting. But then why are you compressing it in these oddly shaped containers? If these were punctured—and it doesn't look like it'd be difficult to do so—then the entire contents would explode in your face. Now, if I were to go back to your example of the patient, I'm not sure what good it'd do them if their doctor were rendered unconscious for the day."

"Well, it's a space-saving mechanism," Geoffrey replied, avoiding eye contact and reaching for another item from his desk. "But I take your point."

Charlotte frowned. When Geoffrey turned his back again, she took a couple of the canisters and hid them in her handbag.

. . .

A little bit before twelve, Diane Reilly walked into a downtown restaurant. The place was large enough that she could find a quiet corner and there was enough background chatter to mask a conversation without drowning it out. Her mystery friend had picked it well, and beating the lunchtime crowd had been a good idea.

She had barely seated when he appeared and sat across from her. "Hello."

She gave him an appraising gaze. "You know, you're not quite what I expected."

"What did you have in mind?" Jason asked.

"Now that you ask, I don't think I had anything in mind. But still. Anyway, it's nice to meet you at last. You know, properly meet you. It's amazing just sitting here with you in the middle of the day like this. You're just like the typical guy-next-door."

"I *am* the typical guy-next-door," Jason told her. "I didn't become the Sentinel by choice. Well, not exactly at any rate."

The kitchen door swung open and he heard a waiter approaching.

"But that's another story," he added.

"I think I know it," Diane said before the waiter arrived. They ordered their meal and, once the waiter had gone, resumed their conversation.

"We... ah... found Martin Lamont a couple of hours

ago," Diane told him. "He was hanging by a wire from the top of a half-completed building by the harbor, bound and gagged. You wouldn't happen to know anything about that, would you?"

"I was going to take him down tonight."

"Well, I guess you can take the evening off then." Diane said. "So he didn't talk then?"

"No. He thought it'd be more fun to play tough. So I decided a lesson was in order. How was he when your officers found him?"

"A nervous wreck apparently."

"Good."

"As for a complete update, all his guests are still unconscious and his thugs are being processed in the police holding cells. And since they were all armed while trespassing, they're going to be locked up for a while. So all in all, that was a good night's work. And with his manpower down, I'd say Lamont won't be bothering us again for a little while."

"So we might get some reprieve," Jason said. "Although he does have a pretty big operation."

"True. Oh, another thing. The guys the S.W.A.T. teams caught on the roofs all had gas masks with them."

"Yeah, I noticed."

"Criminals are fast learners," Diane told him. "You've got to work hard to keep one step ahead of them. By the way, I want to ask you something. And I don't want you to take it as condescending or anything like that. But have you had any training in this sort of thing or have you studied investigative techniques or something like that?"

Jason shrugged. "No. I just try to keep my wits about me. That's all."

"Don't you ever feel afraid?" Diane asked him, her voice showing equal traces of amazement and sympathy.

Jason thought about it. "I feel afraid every time I go out."

"Why do you do it?"

"Because it needs doing," he replied. "Now, this is where you and all your resources can take over. While Lamont didn't say much last night, his sister talked."

"His sister? Where's she now?"

"Safe and sound at home when I left her. Don't worry."

"*Your* home?"

"Her home."

"What—?"

"Well, I couldn't just leave her in an alley or risk going back to Lamont's establishment. Anyway, the point is she was forthcoming and cooperative."

"You think she was. She might have been trying to mislead you."

"I doubt it," Jason said. "She sounded genuine to me."

"So what did she give you?"

"Burges never contacted the Bandit directly."

"Well, that fits. I guess a man as wanted as the Bandit would probably feel safer having a middleman between him and his clients. So who is this person? Just one conduit?"

"Yeah. A brother in Canada. Also, Burges had a credit line with the Bandit or something like that. He deposited funds in a numbered account in Zurich that his brother monitored."

"Jesus, that'd be untraceable."

"Yeah, that's what my partner... I mean, that's what I thought." Jason smiled, hiding his embarrassment.

"It's a good thing *you're* not the Bandit," Diane told him. "You'd lead the police to your door within a week. So the Bandit's clients pay funds to an account overseas and his brother then funnels those funds to him here in Fringe City. The two of them have covered their bases pretty well, haven't they?" She thought for a moment. "Well, we can liaise with the CIA on this and if we can get the Swiss police to play ball as well, we might be able to trace transactions from that account that lead back here. And if we can trace a deposit from Burges, we might be able to force him to cooperate in this investigation too. We'll probably need a lot of third parties in this though, so I think I'll get Charles Faulkner in the loop too as he might be able to help."

"Well, that sounds all well and good. Although, if you're okay with it, I'd like to be kept in the loop too."

"You? The trick with you would be keeping you *out* of it."

Jason smiled. "Well, just let me know how you go with that telephone number in Canada. Also, it should be pretty easy now to get Burges to cooperate. Since the game is up, as they say."

"Yeah, I guess so."

Jason shook his head. "Actually, I almost felt sorry for him the last time I saw him and that's saying something."

"Hard to believe," Diane told him. "Now, it looks like the waiter's coming back with lunch so let's talk about something normal."

"Sure," Jason said. "Nice day, isn't it?"

"And perhaps something a little more interesting."

Alison St. Claire, the new mayor of Fringe City, smiled as she sat down to her meeting with Commissioner Eric Hutchens and Charles Faulkner. "Okay. Well, let's get started. Now Commissioner, about that spin you gave the media on the Bandit, what have you actually got?"

"Well, it was probably a bit premature, I admit," Hutchens replied. "In truth? All right. We haven't got much but I think the public needed the morale boost. We're trying to give people a bit of a hope. You know, let them know that things are changing."

"Well, we're going to need something," St. Claire said. "Otherwise, people are going to be despondent and disenfranchised again. Charles, you're the District Attorney. Is there any way we can persuade Burges to cooperate in the investigation?"

"It'd be difficult for him to provide information without incriminating himself," Faulkner replied.

St. Claire sighed. "All right. That's fine. Then Eric, what about your investigations into weapons smuggling? Are there any leads there?"

"Not yet. It's like a plague, that industry, and the Bandit doesn't have a monopoly on that kind of stuff. However, if we're talking off the record, one of my officers believes they may have a lead very shortly."

"How shortly?"

"Today, tomorrow," Hutchens guessed. "They might even have something already."

"And this would be the Sentinel, would it?" St. Claire asked. When Hutchens looked as though he was thinking up a story to cover his tracks, she waved a dismissive hand. "I have sources of my own,

Commissioner, but you needn't worry. I'm happy to keep it off the record too. I don't know where our mysterious friend came from but he's doing a lot of good work. And as long as he doesn't push things too far, I think we can turn a blind eye to the legality of his activities."

Hutchens glanced at Faulkner, wondering about the mayor saying this in front of the D.A without gauging his opinion first. Faulkner, sensing his anxiety, laughed with an embarrassed shake of his head. "Um… I'm one of the aforementioned sources."

"Well," Hutchens said, feigning injury to his pride, "thanks for letting me in the loop."

"Well, we could hardly have let you in earlier," St. Claire pointed out. "Up until very recently, you were still busily trying to catch the Sentinel."

"True," Hutchens conceded. Just then, his phone vibrated. "Ah, would you excuse me?"

He left the room.

A few moments later, they heard him finishing up the call. "—right? Okay. Ask Captain Reilly to meet us here and we'll take it from there."

He re-entered the room with a smile. "I must have known something. Ms. Mayor, we've got something."

THE PRICE WE PAY

ANOTHER EVENING ROLLED OVER THE CITY and Geoffrey was having a drink with Charlotte in a very nice establishment. Unfortunately, being Geoffrey, he lacked the necessary tact to pull off the touch of class he was aiming for.

"Now, this place is way out of my league," he said with a big grin and, with a sweeping gesture, indicating the expansive marble floor, the waterfall rolling down the glass façade by the entrance and the bar in the middle where they were seated, surrounded by many of Fringe City's movers and shakers. Behind the bar, four or five carpeted steps led to a wide lounge area where some musicians were playing some relaxing evening music off to one side.

"Way out of my league," Geoffrey said, downing a glass of wine. "But I splashed out just for you to create a good impression."

Charlotte laughed.

"What?"

She stroked his cheek and kissed him. "That's very

sweet, and I know, but you're not supposed to say that."

"Oh. Sorry."

"It's all right. It's just... It's a little unorthodox."

They both laughed a little but fell silent as they realized all the background noise around them had stopped. Even the musicians had stopped playing as well. Everyone in the place was looking towards the lounge area, eyes wide in fear.

From a staff entrance used by the musicians, a rather alluring woman walked towards the assembled patrons, hips swinging with every step. Flanking her were several other women, all very striking themselves, carrying guns. In silence, they formed a perimeter around everyone there, herding them away from the bar and into a group near the entrance.

Once they were done, the woman who led the group of party crashers stood in front of the frightened people, eyeing them all as if she were taking a measure of their terror.

Without a word, she raised her arms and nodded to two of her ladies who stepped over and took her figure hugging coat, revealing an outfit that was largely lace and leather. As her two helpers stepped away, her arms remained in an outstretched position. Then a third women stepped out and handed her a short riding crop. Only then did the leader of the group lower her arms. She paced for a moment, looking as though she enjoyed the attention of the patrons—the looks of terror and some of the mixed emotions from the men. She smiled at some of them, while playfully slapping the riding crop on the side of her thigh.

Those who paid close attention noticed the riding crop was basically a prop. The more wary patrons had their eyes on the woman's extraordinary fingernails, each sharpened to a tapered point.

"Oh my god," Charlotte murmured, clutching Geoffrey's arm. "Is that…?"

"Lady Vice," Geoffrey said through stiff lips. "Man, she hasn't been seen for months." He stopped talking to avoid bringing any attention to himself.

"I believe," Lady Vice announced in a voice as smooth as velvet, "this business with Commissioner Hutchens vowing to bring in the Bandit is taking up far too much of our airtime, considering the fact that the second-rate artist only ever appears for a minute then disappears." She smiled again. "Considering he knows nothing about working an audience"

She walked over to a young woman and held her around the waist. "Mariane. My sweet, sweet Mariane. I thought you might like a new story to run with tomorrow night. In fact, I'll even give you an exclusive interview after we're done here. What do say?"

"That's Mariane O'Hara," Geoffrey whispered to

Charlotte. "She's from Fringe City Central."

Mariane chose not to reply. For a few heartbeats, she tried to hold Lady Vice's gaze without breaking down but tears began to well in her eyes.

"Don't worry, darling," Lady Vice told her, smiling. "I need you to put me back in the headlines, don't I?" She gave her a kiss that Mariane was too frightened to resist. "You'll survive the evening." Then she glanced at the rest of the crowd. "Even if no one else does."

Stepping away from the reporter, Lady Vice looked at one of her ladies and pointed to a young couple. The lady strode over, her gun ready at her hip and waved the couple over to her boss.

"I'd rather not have to kill any innocent people tonight," Lady Vice announced, pacing around the terrified pair and inspecting the fingernails on one hand. "It's such a messy business. I'm sure you feel the same way. So unless you want bloodshed on your..." She chuckled. "—well, *my* hands—you will hand over your cell phones, followed by your wallets and handbags. Then we might have a look at all you ladies and see if there's any nice jewelry here tonight."

She began to dance around the couple, easing up to man and teasing him with her riding crop. "And if you don't—" She slashed her nails through the air, a mere inch from an artery on the side of the man's neck, causing him to visibly flinch and his partner to scream.

Lady Vice laughed and shoved the man back into the crowd before turning to his partner, who was now in tears. "Oh, poor dear." She danced around her some more, putting her arms around her waist. In a way, she calmed her down as the woman was too terrified now to make another sound.

Without taking her eyes off her, Lady Vice wrapped a limber leg around her and locked it in place. "We'll start with the cell phones," she announced to the gathered group.

Everyone was quick to oblige, although one other woman began to break down, protesting and trying to back away. Lady Vice turned away from the woman in her embrace and frowned. After releasing her from her arms with exaggerated reluctance, she walked towards the commotion, pointing to the hysterical guest with her riding crop.

Two of her ladies nodded. They calmly pinned the woman to the floor and stretched one of her arms out.

From his vantage point, Geoffrey shuddered and turned Charlotte's head away. "Don't look." He felt Charlotte's wet tears on his shirt and noticed his own eyes were glazing over. He saw Lady Vice standing over the woman and lifting one stiletto heel over the underside of her wrist and the vital artery there. Then he shut his eyes too.

"Such smooth skin," Lady Vice murmured, moving

her foot away and crouching down in front of the woman. She kissed her and smiled. "There's no need to carry on like that now, is there?"

The woman nodded hurriedly, unable to speak.

"There's a good girl," Lady Vice told her, standing up again. She nodded to her ladies. "Help the poor lady up, why don't you? She's come over a little faint."

Her girls laughed, lifted the now quiet woman to her feet and took her phone away. Geoffrey opened his eyes. "It's okay," he whispered to Charlotte.

Lady Vice in the meantime walked back to the woman she'd been holding before and held her again in the same embrace.

"Well, that's better," she said. "All right, ladies. As you were."

Her group then resumed their task of collecting the cell phones.

Geoffrey grimaced. At that moment, he would give anything to call Jason and get him to kick Lady Vice's ass but by making them give up their cell phones first, she was preventing anyone from calling for help. He scowled as he handed over his own phone, feeling impotent. Beside him though, Charlotte's expression had changed to one of determination. She no longer held onto Geoffrey. One of her hands was free and with whitened knuckles, she gripped her handbag by her side with her remaining hand. And all the while, she watched Lady Vice and her gang like a hawk.

As the women finished collecting the cell phones, they placed them down behind their boss who smiled at it all. Turning away from the hostage in her arms, she kissed one of the women who'd carried the cell phones over then turned back to the crowd. "Now, ladies and gentlemen, your wallets and handbags."

Once again, the ladies circulated amongst the crowd to make the collection. Beside Geoffrey, Charlotte watched them, biting her lip in anticipation. Then when one of the ladies was close enough, she threw a small item at the floor in front of her, one of the gas canisters she had taken from Geoffrey's desk at the university. The canister exploded and as the contents sprayed out, the lady collapsed, along with a handful of the other patrons there.

Another one of Lady Vice's girls came rushing over to the commotion and collapsed too as she came into the range of the effects of the gas. Charlotte seized the advantage, running over to her as the gas dissipated. She grabbed the woman's gun and pointed it at her, while everyone in the room stared.

Lady Vice still had her female hostage in her embrace though and wasn't going to be beaten so easily. She clutched the woman even closer and gave Charlotte a smile. "You've got spunk, babe. I'll give you that. I'll tell you what. If you put the gun down, I won't hurt this lovely young lady you're endangering here."

"Let her go, Lady Vice," Charlotte said, her voice wavering but not demanding any less attention for it, "or I'll blow your own girls away." Then she pointed the gun at her. "Or maybe I'll just shoot you instead. How would you like that, you deranged bitch?"

Her adversary's smile vanished. "You haven't got in you."

"I will," Charlotte said, keeping her voice steady.

Lady Vice stared at her for another few moments and then relented, releasing her hostage who ran back to the relative safety of the crowd..

Then Lady Vice turned to those among her girls who were still upright. "All right. Let's go. We can tell when we're not wanted." She grabbed her coat and others followed, several carrying their unconscious companions. "Oh, and Mariane," she called out over her shoulder. "You'll give me proper coverage, won't you?"

Mariane O'Hara didn't answer of course.

Then with all eyes watching her, Lady Vice walked out the way she had entered, with swinging hips and not one backwards glance.

Charlotte realized that luck had saved her more than anything else. The bitch had been right. She didn't have it in her to pull the trigger. She watched Lady

Vice's retreating back, knowing that it was possible to lift the gun even then, even if it was just to injure her enough so she couldn't get away. However, she couldn't, and in a way, she was glad.

Then, when Lady Vice and her girls disappeared from sight, Geoffrey rushed over to her, helping her before she collapsed.

"I... I can't believe I did that," Charlotte murmured.

"I can't believe you did that either," Geoffrey said. "But you were amazing."

Behind them, the other patrons were beginning to come out of their various states of shock.

"Where did you—?" a man stammered, looking at Charlotte and Geoffrey with a hint of suspicion and eyeing the unconscious bodies on the floor, including several innocent patrons.

"The hospital where she works," Geoffrey explained, knowing full well where the gas canister had come from. But that was a private matter for later. He had to almost carry Charlotte then and she looked woozy. "General anesthetic," he added. "Wears off after a day."

He leaned close enough to Charlotte to whisper without being overheard. "Come on. Let's get out of here before we discover there's a real doctor or nurse in the room."

However, by then, Charlotte had fainted.

Geoffrey got moving, scooping up his and Charlotte's cell phones on the way out.

"Wait, you can't just leave!" someone exclaimed. "We should wait for the police or the—"

However, Geoffrey was out the door before anyone could stop him.

"Taxi!" he shouted at the line of yellow cabs heading past.

Within a few seconds, he had clambered in with Charlotte and they were away.

About half an hour later, they were back at his place. Charlotte was awake again and they were both having some coffee to help them relax and calm their nerves. However even then, Charlotte's hands were still shaking and small drops of coffee splashed over the rim of her cup.

"How can you live here?" she exclaimed. "The Bandit? The Black Baron? Lady Vice?" She started crying then, angrily, put the coffee down and swiped at her tears. "I mean, I care about our future and I think you care too. And you've got an offer in *Boston* for god's sake! Why don't you come back with me?"

"All right," Geoffrey said.

"And all my family are there too," Charlotte continued. "And you'd be closer to your own parents than you are here. I mean we could be happy—"

"I'll come with you to Boston," Geoffrey told her, placing his hands on her shoulders. "After what happened tonight, I don't want to live here anymore either. I'll get all my gear from the university, pack up tomorrow and we can take a late train out together."

Charlotte looked up, the reflection of the kitchen light broken up in her tear glazed eyes. "You're serious?"

"I am."

"And you can really turn your back on your life as the Sentinel?"

"You think I'm the Sentinel?"

"That's what those gas canisters were for," Charlotte told him. "Exactly what I used them for tonight."

Geoffrey sighed. "Yeah, that's what they're for. Although I thought I sold my line about them being used for anesthetics a little better than that."

"Honey, you had a stack of these things. Light canisters that would explode easily if you threw them at the ground. How long did you think it'd take me to join the dots on that?"

"Um…"

"Does anyone else at the faculty know about it?"

"Pretty much everyone, I think," Geoffrey admitted with another sigh. "However, they all turn a blind eye.

But I don't tell Jason that. I tell him it's a huge secret. He likes it more that way."

"Jason?" Charlotte asked with a laugh of disbelief. "Your friend from the Education faculty? *He's* the Sentinel?"

"Yeah. You worked out half of it but not the whole story. I'm not the field operative. I'm just the equipment officer. I mean, you saw me tonight. I completely froze up. I'm not the heroic type."

Charlotte squeezed his hand. "Thank god for that."

In a private bar in another part of town, Martin Lamont was pacing like a caged lion. "I want that prick dead."

"Um," one of the men ventured, hesitating before getting his point out. "But he seems to always mop the floor with us."

"That's *why* I want him dead," Lamont replied, slamming his fist on the bar top.

"Maybe we could put the Bandit on him," someone suggested.

Lamont shook his head. "No. The Bandit's like a shotgun. You need something to point him at. Besides, if he's got any sense, he'll want to lie low until this crap with the new commissioner blows over. I want you guys to sort this out."

"But how will we find this guy?"

"I'm glad you asked," Lamont said, reaching behind the bar and pulling out a photograph of an attractive dark skinned woman. "This woman. Captain Diane Reilly. She's very well regarded on the force and her record is outstanding. It's probably the cleanest record any cop in this town has, except for one thing. She's become an unofficial liaison to our man. In fact, it seems that off the record, the cops are quite happy to let our friend do all their dirty work. But she's your lead. Stay on her and we'll find the Sentinel."

When morning came round, Jason and Angie watched one of the numerous reports on the incident with Lady Vice. It was the headline story for Fringe City Central and while Mariane O'Hara was usually their anchor for these situations, another reporter was filling in.

"—including Fringe City Central's very own Mariane O'Hara, who is presently taking time off to recover from the traumatic incident. And all our thoughts are with Mariane and her loved ones during this difficult time.

"This is the first major incident involving Lady Vice for several months, a reprieve however that feels all too short. Although this woman so far has never actually committed a murder nor resorted to the wholesale slaughter that symbolizes Fringe City's number one public enemy at present, there is nonetheless something very chilling about *the way she draws out her crimes. In the words of several witnesses, this is a woman who 'savors' what she does. Fortunately so far, no deaths have been involved in these robberies but nevertheless, patrons in the establishment feared for their lives. And lives were at risk."*

"You know, I'd honestly forgotten about her," Jason said.

"Yeah, me too." Angie handed him a cup. "Here. Coffee."

"Mm." Jason took a sip. "Thanks."

"No worries," Angie replied, taking a sip from her own. "You know, I think they've got to stop reporting this woman's crimes. This is why she does what she does. I mean, her whole problem is the fact that she's an attention-seeking nut job, right? So giving her this coverage is only going to encourage her to strike again. She doesn't do anything for money or jewelry. It's all about having her time in the spotlight. You know, the costumes and the pseudo-lesbian dancing and whatnot. It's a goddamn show, that's what it is."

"Yeah," Jason agreed. "But by that same token, if they don't cover her crimes, then she might commit more of them to get the attention she craves. I mean, if she feels like she's not getting enough attention, isn't that going to make her try to rectify the situation?"

"Maybe. But I wish they'd—" Angie stopped mid-sentence. "Jason, look!"

The TV was now showing footage of thin metal fragments around some unconscious people on a marble floor.

"Trace elements reveal that in fact it is the same type of gas used by the Sentinel for rendering his various underworld targets unconscious. Then after knocking out two members of Lady Vice's entourage, along with a handful of other patrons, the woman took a gun from one of them and convinced Lady Vice to release the woman she was holding hostage. Lady Vice left the building shortly after.

"And this remarkable young woman left the premises minutes afterwards as well, assisted by the man who had been accompanying her. Some witness report that the woman had fainted shortly after Lady Vice's departure and that she had to be carried out. However, whether this is true or not, both the woman and the man who was with her were unable to be found by the time police arrived on the scene.

"Despite the fact that the gas she used was identical to the stun gas that the Sentinel is known to employ, the reason why seems unclear. Several possible theories have since been put forth however. One is that the man accompanying *her was the Sentinel but given the fact that she had the equipment to deal with Lady Vice when he did not, this is somewhat questionable. However, the* second *theory may carry somewhat more weight and that is that there may be several people operating under the Sentinel's guise, rather than just one man as has been believed to be the case so far."*

"Charlotte and Geoffrey," Jason murmured. "I got a text from Geoffrey last night saying something had happened but it didn't go into a lot of details. He certainly didn't tell me anything like this had happened. It sounds like Charlotte's pretty shaken too."

"Poor girl," Angie said. "It was a good thing she had the gas canisters with her though."

"True. Although, I wonder why she had them." Jason thought for a moment. "Actually, it's probably a good idea to carry a few with us when we go out in our civilian gear ourselves, come to think of it. In fact, I might just grab a few before my next meeting with Diane. I'll put a couple in your handbag too."

"Our 'civilian gear'?" Angie asked. "There you go again, with your pseudo military speak."

"Sorry."

"By the way, have you tried calling Geoffrey? I mean, I know he didn't tell you exactly what happened but you knew that *something* had happened, right?"

"I've tried a few times," Jason told her. "But I can't get a hold of him. There's something going on there with him and Charlotte. I wonder if it's because he's brought Charlotte into his confidence on our crime fighting thing perhaps. Although, I guess he has now."

"Civilian gear… crime fighting thing." Angie tried to smile but the attempt to lift her mood didn't last.

"Poor Charlotte," she murmured.

Jason got a call from Diane the following day. And although he'd tried to get back to Geoffrey, he hadn't managed to get in touch with him so when he came into the restaurant, he had a lot of things on his mind.

The place was a little smaller than the last rendezvous they'd used, but it was similar in all the ways that counted. Again, they met a little before the lunchtime rush.

Unsurprisingly, the conversation started with Lady Vice rather than the Bandit.

"I wasn't there," Jason said.

Diane was taken aback. "But the woman who turned the tables on her... She was using your gas canisters, wasn't she?"

"She was, although I'm not sure exactly why she had them."

"You've been compromised?"

"No, no," Jason said. "She's a friend. Anyway, it was lucky she had them. Otherwise someone might have been killed."

"Maybe," Diane said. "Maybe not. Although you never know with Lady Vice."

"Or any of Fringe City's celebrity psychotics. They're all ticking time-bombs."

"Yeah. Anyway, I shouldn't pry," Diane said. "Sorry."

Jason waved a dismissive hand. "Don't worry. I'd have been surprised if you didn't ask."

"Still," Diane said, "that was a damn brave thing she did. She must be a remarkable woman."

"I've heard it on good authority that she is," Jason replied before Diane reached the wrong conclusion.

"Sorry. Prying again."

"That's all right. However, let's get to business. The Bandit."

Diane sat up. "Okay," she said, taking a breath before getting started. "Here's what's been happening over the past two days. Now, some good news. The Swiss actually played ball. When our people explained how serious the problem of the Bandit was, they agreed to suspend the account so now his funds are frozen. Nothing can go in or out. Also, we were allowed to see all the past transactions on it and now we've got the proof we needed that Burges was doing business with this guy."

"Excellent," Jason said. "So now he can stop pretending he wasn't."

"Yes. I think he realizes now that it's actually in his best interests to cooperate with us."

"And you've got some good people too. I would never have thought you'd get so much. I mean, I hoped you would but I have to admit I had my doubts. And these people move fast too."

"Yeah," Diane agreed. "There are good people in the system. Not as many as I'd like but more than we realize."

"Well, that'll make things a little easier for us, I imagine. By the way, how much was in that account? If you don't mind me knowing."

"And assuming I know? But yeah, I found out. There's about forty-eight million."

"Jesus. So how did the Bandit access his funds?"

"This is where it gets really complex. You know how we thought his brother wired the funds to him here in Fringe City? He doesn't."

"Then how does he get his money?"

"The Bandit flies to Zurich when he wants his cash and withdraws his funds directly."

"Does that mean the account's in his name?"

Diane shook her head. "No such luck. He set it up in his brother's name."

"How did your people figure that?"

"The Swiss authorities examined video surveillance from the bank—which these fancy banks keep for a very long time—and they identified the man accessing the funds. Then they compared the images they acquired with photos they had of the man who had opened the account."

"The brother in Canada."

"Right. And when they compared the images, they found there was a pretty clear family resemblance between them but they clearly weren't photos of the same man."

"So, the brother in Canada. Who's he then?"

"His name's Daniel Kowolski. Also, Daniel's an American by birth and he gave incomplete information in all his visa applications so the Canadians have no idea what his brother's name is either. According to their records, he doesn't have a brother."

"He falsified documents then?"

"What? No. Nothing that fancy. He just didn't tell Canadian Immigration, that's all. And I'm not even sure they ask for that kind of information anyway."

Jason nodded. "Fair enough. So do the Canadians have Daniel then?"

"No. The authorities there issued a warrant for his arrest and went around to his place, but he appears to have gone missing."

"Where was his place?"

"Just outside Toronto. Also, his face is now plastered all over the city and is on the news 24/7. There's a massive man hunt for him."

"He's gone to ground then."

"So it seems," Diane said.

Jason nodded. "So what measures are being put in

place to contain the Bandit back home?"

"That's a tricky one. We've got *some* measures set up. The name Kowolski for starters will trigger a flag if anyone with it crosses a regulated border or tries to board a plane but there are a lot of Kowolskis. Basically, that's being left to the discretion of border control officers. They've all got pictures of Daniel Kowolski and the clearest image of his brother the Swiss authorities could get and it's up to them when a flag is triggered to decide whether the Kowolski in front of them bears any resemblance to either of them. But there's not much else. Anyway, that's the latest news."

It was strange, Jason thought as he left the restaurant. It was a lot on the one hand, but yet it felt like very little. With a sigh, he reached for his cell phone. It was time to try Geoffrey again.

However, before his hand reached his pocket, he was grabbed from behind and thrown into the back of a car. He couldn't move as someone was holding him and whoever it was had a lot of strength behind his grip. An imposing man was sitting beside him as well, while another man and the driver of the vehicle were in front.

Just as quickly as the ordeal had started, the car

stopped and the men climbed out and drew their guns. When they opened the back door though, Jason didn't just sit there. For the next few moments, he was fuelled by fear, desperation and the desire above all else to get out of there alive and back home to Angie. And if that meant fighting dirty, then he'd use every trick in the book.

First, he elbowed the thug who was holding him, jabbing him with a painful thrust to the groin that had him instantly keel over.

Then, not stopping to let his brain catch up, he kicked the thug closest to the car as well, knocking him far enough away to give him a moment to reach into his pocket for the gas grenade he'd started keeping there. He then threw the canister at the thugs outside, hitting one of them on the bridge of his nose so hard that it exploded right then and there in his face. Then Jason shoved the incapacitated thug beside him out of the vehicle was well, making sure he got a nice good dose of the stuff.

That done, Jason slammed the door closest to the gas, opened the door on the other side of the car and scrambled away to avoid the effects of the stuff.

He took several moments to catch his breath and for a little while, he paced back and forth trying to calm his nerves. "Jesus Christ..." he muttered, looking at the four unconscious men on the pavement.

After a couple of minutes, he was a little more composed but still badly shaken up. And he was angry.

Once the gas had cleared, he pulled the license plates off the car and stuffed them into his bag, which was on the back seat. Then he dragged his unconscious would-be assailants along the alley, took off their jackets and tied the men up with the sleeves. After that, he hoisted the lot of them one by one into a dumpster and slammed the lid shut.

Then there was one last idea he had in mind to get back at these bastards who'd tried to kill him. He walked back to the car, climbed in the front and drove for several blocks. Then he parked it in a tow-away zone, climbed out and threw away the keys.

Shortly afterwards, Geoffrey's cell phone rang for the sixth time in five minutes. He checked the number and gave Charlotte an apologetic look before answering it. "Hi, Jason."

"Where the hell have you been? I've been trying to get in touch with you all day."

"Are you all right? You sound—"

"I got jumped by a carload of mobsters, probably Lamont's men," Jason told him. "It was only by sheer luck I had a couple of gas grenades with me. I took a cue from Charlotte. Still though…"

"Holy crap." Geoffrey took a moment to process it all. "Yeah, I can imagine. Does Angie know?"

"Not yet and you're going to tell her either. She'd completely freak if she found out. Especially with what happened to you guys yesterday night. Why didn't you say anything to me about it?"

"I didn't have time to go into the details. I'm kind of busy."

"Busy?"

"Yeah, busy. But all right. I won't say anything to Angie if you don't want me to. But I think you should tell her."

"Fine. But can you come on over? I think we've got to talk. Bring Charlotte."

"Why?"

"No one's in trouble, Geoffrey. But we need to talk."

Geoffrey sighed. "You're right. We *do* need to talk."

Martin Lamont was pacing in his bar. Again. "They should have called back by now."

"Maybe they're planning to give you the good news in person," one of his men suggested.

"I doubt it," Lamont replied. "Call Sergeant Green. It looks like we'll have to do this the hard way."

"What about that thing in the news with Lady

Vice?" the other man asked. "It sounds like that girl who stopped her probably knows the Sentinel."

"Good for her. But we don't know a thing about her. Captain Reilly's our lead and she's our only lead."

"All right," the man replied. "I'll call Green. Pity though. Captain Reilly *is* rather easy on the eyes."

Elsewhere, Jason and Geoffrey had their talk with Angie and Charlotte beside them. As they spoke, Angie looked at Jason with more concern than he'd ever seen in her before. For a while, she was speechless.

"I can't believe it, Jason," she managed at last.

"Yeah, I was a bit shaken up by the whole thing, to tell you the truth," he replied. "I guess when I'm out on the job, I'm prepared. I've got a plan. I've got all my gear. But the main difference is I'm in control."

"Still..." Geoffrey said. "Jesus, Jason. You could have been killed."

"I could be killed every time I go out," Jason reminded him. "But yeah, it was a close call."

"It's a good thing you took those gas canisters with you."

"Yeah. Although that was lucky too. I only had them because of Charlotte."

"Well, I'm glad something good came out of all of

that," Geoffrey said.

"Actually, I put some in Angie's handbag as well," Jason told him. "From now on, we're not going anywhere without them. I reckon they're probably the best self-defence gear someone could have in this city."

"Maybe I should market this stuff," Geoffrey commented, trying to lighten the leaden mood. "Still, getting distracted here... You think it was Lamont's men?"

"I'm sure of it. Jeez, I'm a goddamn idiot. Lamont told me he knew I was liaising with the police just the other night and I didn't think twice about it. He's clearly got an insider on the force or something. I just wasn't paying attention. Anyway, I'll check it out with Diane. I took the license plates off the car so she can run them through their records."

"What, you didn't have a pen?"

"No," Jason said. "But also it means they'll have a hard time getting their car back from the impound."

"Nice," Geoffrey replied with a nod of approval. "So how can I help you get back at these guys?"

"Leave that with me," Jason told him. "That's not what I wanted to talk to you about. The Bandit. The authorities have identified his brother, and the guy assists him in getting his various assignments and payments. Now we don't know the Bandit's identity yet, but the brother's an American born man living in

Canada. Goes by the name of Daniel Kowolski."

"The Bandit again?" Geoffrey asked in disbelief. "What about Lady Vice?"

"Trust me, she's on my list of people to sort out," Jason promised him. "But I haven't got anything on her yet. With the Bandit, I have."

At this, Angie held Charlotte's arm. "Come on. Why don't we leave them to it?"

"Yeah," Charlotte agreed, her voice soft and somewhat distant.

Angie guided her to the sofa for their own private chat, while Jason and Geoffrey kept going.

"I think you're getting too caught up in this," Geoffrey told his friend. "I understand. Really, I do. You're all fired up, you've got these leads and you want to follow them to their ends. But I don't see where I can help you. Tracking down fugitives in foreign countries isn't quite the same as manufacturing grappling hooks."

Jason sighed. "I suppose you're right. I'm sorry."

"Face it, Jason," Geoffrey told him. "They won't find Daniel. If he's got any sense—and it sounds like he does—he'll just disappear and start a new life for himself in South America or somewhere and then no one'll ever see him again. And as for his brother, he'll just lie low for a while until he works out another way to run his show. I know you've worked hard on this and I wish I could do something but I can't help you on this one. And I'm sorry to leave you and Angie this way. I'd rather leave on a high note."

Jason frowned. "What are you talking about?"

"Charlotte and I are going to Boston," Geoffrey told him. "I've got some contacts there and you know I've got that open-ended offer to be an associate professor. So I've decided to accept it before someone smartens up and it's withdrawn."

"Well," Jason replied, clearly stunned but also trying his best to be supportive, "this is a bit sudden but it'd be good for you. I think—"

"I'm going to marry Charlotte as well," Geoffrey told him. "So I'm not going to be coming back."

The two of them then saw that Angie and Charlotte were now listening in on the conversation. Jason swallowed. "Well... Wow. You know I'd be lying if I said I wasn't a bit choked up about all this. But yeah. I'm happy for you. You know, both of you. And yeah. Moving to Boston is the right thing, definitely. It's a good idea, and um... Well, I'm sure everything will all work out well."

"I do feel a little bad about all this, though," Geoffrey told him. "I think that's why I was avoiding your calls since the other night. I know there's still a lot of work to do in Fringe City—"

"Yeah, there'll always be a lot of work here," Jason

told him. "But you can't get so focused on the big picture that you forget about yourself. We're not martyrs and I don't think we should *be* martyrs. And right now, you've got to just be Geoffrey Stevens."

Geoffrey nodded for a little while. "Thanks, man," he said. He then reached for his pocket and pulled out a CD. "Oh, yeah. Almost forgot. Here."

"What's this?" Jason asked, taking the disk.

"I made it up last night," Geoffrey explained. "It's got a whole lot of information to help you with your work. I've given you instructions on how to manufacture some of your gear and some details about where you can get certain items and components. I didn't want to tell you, but there are a few people in the lab who know about this and—"

"What?"

"Relax. They're cool. They all admire what you're doing and they'd never rat on you."

"Jeez, I hope not."

"Anyway, I've included some contact details for a few of them. They said they'd be happy to help you out with anything if you need it. Also, you can always contact me in Boston too. I can still arrange for things to be sent here if it'll help you out any. Anyway, that's all it is."

"Thanks, man," Jason said. "I appreciate it."

"You probably won't need anything for a while

anyway," Geoffrey told him, beginning to babble a little. "Your grappling hooks should keep you going for a while as long as you keep them in good condition and don't lose any. And you've got a good supply of those gas canisters. Just don't keep any on the top shelf where they might fall off."

Jason laughed a little. "Thanks. Good advice." He appreciated everything but he was starting to feel a little emotional. "Um, when are you leaving?" he asked. Getting the question out had been more difficult than he'd thought it would be.

"Tonight," Geoffrey said. "We're heading out on a 9.30 train."

"All right. I'll come and see you guys off."

"You don't have to."

"I want to."

"Are you all right?" Angie asked after Geoffrey and Charlotte had gone.

Jason nodded, sitting down on the sofa and leaning back. "Yeah, I'm fine."

"It's just that with getting mugged and your best friend leaving town all on the same day, I thought you might… You know."

Jason sighed. "I don't… know."

"I'm here for you, Jason," Angie said, sliding across

to him. "That's what I'm trying to tell you."

"I know that," Jason told her. "I appreciate it. But I'm all right."

"I know but you don't have to tough this out on your own."

"Yeah, I know."

"And there's another thing too," Angie said. "I think working so closely with Diane Reilly's turned out to be a liability for you."

"I trust her," Jason told her. "I completely trust her. And she's been very helpful for me."

"I know that, and I'm not saying anything against her, but if you're certain that Lamont was behind this, then it's like you said to Geoffrey; he must have some cops on his payroll."

"I'm sure it's Lamont. And I know he had someone on the force because the bastard told me when he said he knew I was liaising with the police. I was just too stupid to make the connection."

"Well, don't be too hard on yourself," Angie told him. "You know, between this ongoing campaign of yours against the city's underworld and doing the end of term reporting, I'm amazed you're able to keep track of anything at all."

Jason smiled. "Thanks. Anyway, like I said to Geoffrey, I'll find out whether or not it was Lamont's men by getting Diane to run a check on those license plates I took. Maybe it wasn't him. But if it was, then I'm going to make that son of a bitch sorry he was ever born."

Angie shook her head and gripped his hands. "No, Jason. Jason. Honey, why don't you leave this one to the police? Well, the ones who aren't in Lamont's wallet at any rate. These mobsters are serious. After what happened today, you should know that better than anyone. These guys won't think twice about killing you."

"I've held my own so far," Jason said, "including today."

"You've been lucky," Angie insisted. "You're not a fighter, you're not some kind of super-fit athlete, and you're not particularly big or unusually strong."

"Thanks. I'll try not to take that the wrong way."

"That's not what I meant," Angie chided him gently. "I'm worried about you. Don't you worry sometimes when you're out there?"

Jason couldn't help but notice that the conversation closely mirrored the one he had had with Diane in their first restaurant meeting. "I worry every time I head out," he told Angie, which was more or less what he'd told Diane at the time. "However, someone's got to do it or everyone in the city will have to go on wondering whether one of the nut jobs we put up with here will come barging into their favorite restaurant one day, just like Lady Vice the other night."

Angie held him closer. "I can't talk you out of this, can I?" she murmured. "Don't worry. I'm on your side. And when the men in white come to drag you away, I'll come with you. But you're not going after Lamont tonight. Leave him to the police."

For a moment, they were quiet, letting their troubles fade away. And in that moment, the outside world didn't matter anymore. They had each other.

Then slowly, Angie unbuttoned her blouse. Wordlessly, she cast it aside and reached behind her back to unbuckle her bra strap.

It was at this moment that Jason's untraceable began vibrating. It sounded much louder than usual.

He sighed. "I'm sorry, honey."

"It's okay," Angie murmured. "Go on."

Jason picked it up and froze. The voice on the other end was not Diane's.

"I want the Sentinel," a man said.

"Who is this?" Jason asked, keeping his guard up.

Angie did her bra clip back up and listened, just as anxious to find out what was going on as Jason was.

"I'm God as far as you're concerned," the man replied. "And I tell you, you'd better know who the Sentinel is or your lovely young friend from the police force won't be feeling too crash hot."

Jason's stomach sunk. "I want to speak to her," he

said, fighting to keep his voice under control.

The man acquiesced and Jason heard Diane's voice on the other end. "Richard," she said and Jason thought it sounded convincing enough to fool her captors into believing it was his real name. "Richard, I'm so sorry."

"It's okay," Jason told her. "Listen. I'm going to get you out of this."

The phone was taken from Diane. Jason heard her scream something and then the sound was muffled, as if her captors had gagged her.

"You want the Sentinel?" Jason asked, a slow fire beginning to burn within him. "Fine. But I'm not giving his name over the phone to you. I want to see Diane and make sure you let her go first. What do you say?"

He glanced at Angie and saw her wordless protests. He tried to give her the most reassuring look he could manage. "We meet up," he told the speaker on the other end. "I give you a name and you give me Diane. You can tell me not to call the police or try any funny business. I can say I agree and then try to pull something anyway. And as for yourself, you can set up whatever trap you want and then when we meet up, we can see whose underhanded subterfuge works best."

The man on the other end laughed, possibly even

impressed. "Fair enough. Then let's simplify the proceedings." However, the moment of respect for his enemy passed, indicated by a new hard tone in his voice. "We know you're the Sentinel and we know you're not going to deliberately walk into a trap. But we don't think you're going to abandon this young woman either so here's the deal. Diane's at 667 Farlane Avenue and at midnight, I'm going to shoot her in the head. You have until then to show up. Oh, and if we see any cop cars before then, she's going to be just as dead. So, as you so eloquently put it, let's see whose underhanded subterfuge works best. See you soon, 'Richard'."

With that, the call was over and Jason stood up, watching his hands shake.

"Jason!" Angie exclaimed. "What are you doing? Call the police."

"They'll kill Diane if the police are involved. It's like you said, these men are serious."

"And if you go, they'll kill you both!" Angie cried. "God... There's got to be a way you can fix this without putting your life on the line."

Jason paused and gave her a thoughtful look. "You know, you're right." He reached for her and kissed her. "I love you, Angie."

Then he got his gear from the corner of the room, while Angie watched baffled.

"Now what are you doing?" she asked him.

Jason smiled. "I'm going to see another woman."

When she saw the familiar figure standing by her balcony window, Sophia Garcia gasped. "What have I done now?" she exclaimed. "I swear, I've hardly even left the house since I last saw you."

"I know," Jason told her. "And believe it or not, I am sorry for scaring you like that. But I need your help."

"Again?" Sophia asked in disbelief. "Why? And what are you going to do if I don't help you? Throw me out the window? What the hell do you want from me?" She burst into tears. "I haven't done anything, I swear. I've hardly even called my brother since you left me!"

"Please," Jason said, putting a hand on her shoulder. "Please. Sophia, I don't want to coerce you into doing anything you don't want to but I've got no-one else to turn to."

Teary eyed, she looked up. "What?"

"I really need your help," Jason said. "A young woman's life depends on it."

Sophia brushed her tears away. "What's that?"

"I need you to save someone's life."

"My brother's involved, isn't he?"

Jason nodded. "His men are holding her at 667 Farlane Avenue and they're threatening to kill her unless I show up and take a bullet to the head or whatever it is that'll make them satisfied."

"All right," Sophia said, taking a deep breath. "How long have we got?"

At 667 Farlane Avenue, a phone rang. A scowling man sitting in a wooden chair picked it up. "Who's this?"

"It's Sophia," came the voice from the other end. "You guys are in big trouble."

"What are you talking about?" the man asked.

"Hutchens and his men are crawling all over Martin's place and they've practically got him under house arrest. Is the woman all right?"

The thug glanced over his shoulder at Diane, who was crouched on the floor in a corner of the room. She was in obvious distress but she was unharmed. "Yeah. We haven't touched her."

"Thank god for that. I don't know what the hell you guys have done but you've compromised everyone. There wasn't supposed to be anything that could pin this back on Martin."

"It wasn't us!" the thug protested. "Our boy on the force must have squealed."

"Fine," Sophia snapped. "We can work out who

screwed up later. Frankly, I don't care. Take it up with Martin if we manage to get out of this mess. But just get her out of there. Blindfold her and let her go somewhere back near the police headquarters or something. And don't go back to that address either. It's dead now. We'll have to have it scrubbed from the books."

"All right, all right," the thug replied and hung up. He looked at another man sitting across from him. "Damn it. We were so close."

"We've got to let her go?"

"Yeah. Otherwise the boss is going to get it," the thug said. "If she doesn't show up alive and well soon, we're all going to be dead. Come on. Let's get her out of here before the Sentinel comes. Because that'd just be a perfect way to end the evening, wouldn't it?"

They grabbed Diane by her wrists and hauled her up. "Come on, sweetheart. It looks like it's your lucky day."

"It's done," Sophia told Jason, hanging up the phone. She walked into her kitchen. "Although, I suppose you'd like to wait here to make sure, right? I know I would."

"Thanks," Jason replied. "I couldn't have done it without you."

Sophia shrugged, reaching for a bottle of white wine. "I don't suppose you'd like a drink?" she asked, pouring herself a glass.

"That'd be nice," Jason told her. "But just water for me, thanks."

"Suit yourself," she said, pouring some for him from a water pitcher and sliding the glass towards him. She laughed but with sadness in her eyes. "Look at us. One minute, you've got me strung up on a building ledge and the next, we're having drinks at my place. I imagine we'll be sleeping together before the night is up." She sighed. "I know you'll probably think it's funny but right now, I feel closer to you than all the other men I've met."

Jason drank some water. "Well, I wouldn't say that's funny," he told her. "But it does seem a little odd."

"Is it?" Sophia asked him. "You're the only man I've ever dropped my guard in front of. And since you came to me begging for help, you're the only man who's dropped his guard in front of me."

"Sophia," Jason said, taking care not to injure her feelings, which seemed delicate right then to say the least. "It's good that you've turned over a new leaf and all but I don't think you and I…"

Sophia gave him a pathetic smile and sculled the wine in her glass. "Of course. I've got my checkered history and my moron of an ex-husband and I guess you've got someone of your own anyway." She raised her eyebrows. "That police woman?"

Jason shook his head. "No. I like her a lot though."

"That girl who stood up to Lady Vice?"

"Not her either."

Sophia nodded. "Someone perfectly normal then."

Jason's untraceable vibrated. "I guess this is my friend," he said.

"Well, I suppose you'd better answer it then."

"Hello?" Jason asked, holding the phone close to his ear.

"It's me," Diane replied.

"Are you all right? Are you safe?"

"They let me out a few blocks away, I think. Anyway, they're gone now."

"Well, don't hang around in the middle of nowhere though," Jason told her. "Have you got any money on you for a cab fare?"

"A little," Diane told him. "But enough."

"All right then. Well, go straight to the police headquarters and tell Hutchens what happened."

"I plan to. What about you? You're not going to do anything stupid, are you?"

Jason sighed. "No. I sure feel like it. But I'm not going to go busting anyone's head in. Don't worry about me."

"We'll sort this out," Diane assured him.

Jason smiled. "I know. Anyway, I'll call you later." He hung up and turned back to Sophia. "Well then, she's safe."

"I'm glad to hear it. How's she holding up after all that?"

"She sounded a little rattled, but I think she's okay."

Sophia nodded, looking teary again.

"Thank you, Sophia," Jason said, "for everything. Hopefully, with any luck, you won't have to see me again."

"What if I'd like to?" she blurted.

Jason paused, taken quite by surprise.

"You know, I could help you," Sophia told him. "I mean, that police woman of yours has her finger on the pulse. I'm sure she gives you the heads up on things that you'd never find out about otherwise, right? Well, I bet I could keep you up to date on things that neither of you know about."

"I nearly lost that woman tonight because she helped me," Jason told her.

"I know," Sophia replied. "But can't the people you're trying to protect make their own choices?" She sighed. "But if you don't want me to get involved in your work, you could always just stop by. The sisters of notorious crime bosses get lonely too sometimes."

"Maybe," Jason said. "But it could never lead to

anything."

"I know that," Sophia said, more tears welling in her eyes. "I'm not stupid. But I could do with some company, that's all." She hung her head for a moment then turned back to him. "So will I see you again?"

"Maybe," Jason repeated. "Look, Sophia... Are you going to be all right?"

"Yeah." She nodded and brushed some tears away. Then she forced a smile. "Yeah, I'll be fine."

"Thanks for everything you did tonight, Sophia. You saved my friend's life."

"I just did what I had to do."

"Well, I guess I'll be going then. Goodnight."

Jason stepped out onto the balcony and ascended to the roof with one of his grappling hooks.

"Good luck," Sophia murmured after he'd left. She then rubbed her temples and sat down on her sofa in a slump. "Goddamn it, Martin," she said to herself. "You goddamn son of a bitch."

Across town, Geoffrey and Charlotte got on their train. As they took their reserved seats, Geoffrey had one last look out the window for Jason but he was nowhere to be seen. He tried to give Charlotte a reassuring smile but it was more than he could manage. She squeezed his hand as the train pulled away from the station.

. . .

About twenty minutes later, Sophia Garcia pulled up in a nice car outside Lamont's favorite establishment and walked in.

Two of his thugs were standing in the foyer. She glared at them. "Where's my brother?"

The nearest thug gave her a stare that was as defiant as permitted, given Sophia's relationship to his boss. It wasn't rude enough to take offence at but it skirted the line. "He's in the bar."

"Wait outside," Sophia told them. "He and I have some personal business to settle. Is he alone?"

"Yeah."

"Good."

"But he said he was not to be disturbed."

"I'm family." Sophia marched on past, swinging open the door to the bar.

Lamont looked up in surprise, his collar loosened, his tie on the seat beside him and a brandy in his hand "Sophia? What's going on?"

In answer to the question, Sophia raised a hand gun with a silencer attached and shot him in the chest. Lamont fell back on the floor, his wound fatal. However, he still had a breath of life in him. He gave her a baffled look. "Why?" he stammered.

"Because I'm sick of all the trouble you make for the

rest of us," she told him and shot him in the head. "And I'm sick of you."

With the deed done, Sophia turned on her heels and walked back out, swinging the door shut behind her. As she passed the thugs outside, she knew that they knew what had taken place inside.

"Yeah, that's right," she told them. "I had some personal business to settle and it's settled. Feel free to divide what's left amongst yourselves however you want. I don't care."

Then, leaving the stunned men behind, she walked outside, climbed into her car and drove away.

In another part of town, Jason arrived home. Angie hugged him as he came through the door, relieved that he was all right.

"What happened?" she asked, helping him inside.

"Everything's fine," he said. "Diane's okay and I didn't have to go anywhere near that address where they were keeping her. You made a good point earlier tonight. I don't have to risk my life every time I go out. I realized tonight there are other ways sometimes besides throwing myself in harm's way."

"I'm glad I could help, but how did you...?" She stopped. "What's wrong?"

Jason had trailed off.

"It's 10.20," he told her.

"Oh…"

"I missed seeing Geoffrey off."

"So Lamont's men jumped you as well?" Diane asked.

"Yeah but I got away," Jason told her. The two of them were once again in a restaurant together, and once again it was before the lunchtime rush. "So I think that's why they decided to use you to get to me," Jason explained. He sighed. "I'm really sorry about everything. I had no idea this relationship would put us in this kind of danger."

"I did," Diane confessed, her gaze flitting down. "It was something I worried about from the beginning. Anyway, we'll just have to be on our guard more. Fortunately, I don't think any of Lamont's competitors knew about our liaising with each other. Lamont had someone on the force. That's all."

"Had?"

"Had," Diane confirmed. "We got an anonymous tip that it was Sergeant Green and it checked out. The man had several suspiciously large deposits made in his bank account over the past year or so."

"Let's just hope there aren't any more mobsters on your payroll. A little while ago, Hutchens said he had cleared them out and he was wrong."

"Yeah," Diane said. "Still though, we won't have to worry about Lamont again at least." She watched Jason for some kind of reaction but there was none. "He was found dead in the back of his car this morning. His boys said it was a drive-by shooting but the coroner's not convinced. You wouldn't happen to know anything about it, would you?"

Jason shook his head. "It wasn't me. I wanted to put a stop to his activities as much as anyone but I don't kill people."

"I didn't think it was you," Diane said. "But I imagine you have your suspicions though."

"I do," Jason admitted. "But if it's all the same, I'd rather keep them to myself."

Diane nodded, leaning back. "All right," she said, dropping the subject and starting a new one. "Apparently, in the midst of all that excitement last night, we missed some news on the Bandit case. It turns out that the Australian Federal Police sent us a transcript of an interview they had with a man from Melbourne."

"And?"

"The man saw photos of Daniel Kowolski and his brother in the news over there and told police that he recognized them from a joint unit of British, Australian and American soldiers that he served with in Iraq. Various inquiries have been made to the relevant people and everything the man said has been confirmed."

"So now we know who the Bandit is?"

"Yeah. His name's Andy Kowolski. And it's a fairly distinctive name too because it's not Andrew on the birth certificate as is the norm. It's just Andy."

"So how many Andy Kowolskis do we have in the States then?"

"With his middle name as well, just the one," Diane said. "Here in Fringe City. The police raided his place at about half past one this morning." She took a sip of coffee before breaking the rest of the news. "It was cleared out."

Jason nodded. "And his brother?"

"God knows."

"And I don't suppose anything's turned up that might help you guys find Lady Vice?" he asked.

"Not a scrap," Diane said with a sigh. "But there you go. That's another hard fact of this business for you. You can't win them all."

FAIR GAME

NEW GIRL IN TOWN

THE GROUP MOVED IN ON THE WAREHOUSE.

"There are two guys on the roof," one of them said, instructing two of his companions to head up there. "Take the stairs on the alley side and take them out from behind."

"Right."

As the pair headed off, he turned to the rest of his group. "All right. We'll take out the four guys around the back. Murdoch and Travis, you wait here. As soon as you hear the guns, you blast the front lock and head on in. With luck, we can clear these guys out and grab all the money before the cops even make it to the neighborhood. Are you ready?"

The group got to work. However, as the two men on roof duty reached the stairs on the alley side, they ran into a snag. One moment, they were making their way up the steps. The next, they stepped on some mesh and were hauled off their feet in a net.

On the roof, the two men they had been planning to take out heard the trap go off—but as they started to head over to investigate, they collapsed with tranquillizer darts in their backs.

Outside, Murdoch and Travis decided that gun shots or no gun shots, they were going to make their move. With a mutual nod, they lunged forward and fell on their faces. There were tranquillizer darts in their backs as well.

Meanwhile, their friends behind the building discovered that all the opposition had been taken out already. Dead or unconscious, it was hard to tell.

"Looks like someone beat us to the job," one of them said, glancing at his boss.

His boss frowned. "Don't be so certain." He turned and glared at one member of the group, the only woman among them. "Hey, sugar. You told us this was a sure thing."

The woman smiled. "It is."

She watched as the man and his friends fell to the ground. There were tranquillizer darts in their backs as well, just as there had been with the others.

Another woman emerged with a dart gun. "All right. The trucks should be here any minute."

"Good," the first woman replied as more of her female friends appeared, also carrying dart guns.

Once the trucks arrived, a pair of them, the women ferried money out of the warehouse and loaded the first of them up. Then they put the unconscious members of the two mob groups in the back of the other one.

The mobsters from both groups woke up in a brightly lit warehouse, tied up in front of a large stash of money. They were surrounded by a group of fetching women but not the kinds of girls one brought home to mother. Standing in the middle of the group, lavishing the attention, was Lady Vice.

"No doubt, you're all wondering why you're here," she told them. "You guys," she said, indicating one group, "have taken what you thought to be your fair share of Lamont's organization and you had one of his money launderers to help you out. Unfortunately, everyone else who wanted their piece of the organization came after your launderer, forcing you to recover whatever cash you could before they got him and then you stockpiled it in that warehouse back there. Kind of desperate really."

"We found out where your stash was pretty easily," she continued, walking around a little and playing with her riding crop. "We just got a hold of one of your guys and he was smart enough to realize that his life was more valuable to him than your operation. Rather sensible man, I thought. In fact, I gave him a job in my organization."

She then turned to the other group. "And Castella's boys. You ought to count yourselves lucky to be here." She sighed. "Unfortunately, your boss won't be joining us though. He and I had a little talk and we didn't see eye to eye. You know how it is. I believe a clean-up team scraped him off the street this morning. Although as it turns out, we didn't need him, right O'Reilly?"

The leader of the group glowered.

"I mean, why play right hand man to Castella when you can take a cut of Lamont's stock and set up shop on your own?" Lady Vice's voice was lilting and playful. "So you got all the guys you needed and set this scheme in motion." She shook her head in amusement. "And yet you never stopped to wonder why the mole I planted in your group told you about the money these guys had stashed in their warehouse instead of going after it herself. So anyway, you bought the bait, turned up at the address at the right time..." She then addressed both groups. "And from this happy string of events, you've all made it to this meeting."

"So now we can listen to you gloat about how clever you are?" one of the men asked, annoyed.

"Not at all," Lady Vice told him. "This is a recruiting drive. Basically, Lamont's organization has broken off into a bunch of small groups while the rest of the groups in this town were already small to begin with. Well, there was Vincent's gang but the Bandit took care of them. So there you go. A whole lot of small groups and a big power vacuum. And you've all gone stupid in this vacuum and have been fighting each other over the scraps. However, if you keep up these idiotic games, whatever assets you have will just dwindle down to nothing and you'll all be picked off one by one. Probably shot. Maybe incarcerated. But you'll be finished either way. However, if you work together, you could make one of the most powerful syndicates in the country. I've already started working on this. In fact, the money we've retrieved tonight is being added to the group fund. And unlike you guys, no one knows who's laundering my money and I've got the brains to keep it that way."

"We get it, Lady Vice," another mobster told her. "You're consolidating all the groups you can get, along with all the cash, assets and holdings you can get your hands on and you're offering us the chance to join you."

"Glad you joined the dots," Lady Vice told him. "I'd hate to have been delivering this spiel to empty air."

"However, I can't see what's in it for us," the man said. "The way I see it, you're just ripping off the lot of us and then to add insult to injury, you're asking us to work for you so you can keep skimming profit for you and your girls. Well, what if we want out?"

Lady Vice smiled. "You can ask Castella how that worked out for him."

The following day, the mid-morning sunlight spilled over the calm sparkling water of the Caribbean and some of its more tranquil tourist islands. On one of these, Jason and Angie were slouching about on their beach towels, their hair wet, the sun warm on their skin... And the air... There was something wonderful about the air outside built-up city areas. It was invigorating.

Angie sighed. "Aren't you glad we came here instead of going skiing? I think a bit of sunshine and warmer weather's done me a world of good."

"Yeah," Jason agreed, lying back on his towel.

Right then, life was good.

In the Fringe City Police Headquarters, Captain Diane Reilly was touching base with Commissioner Eric Hutchens. "I don't like it. I think there's something going on with the lot of them. You heard about what happened to Castella, right?"

Hutchens shrugged. "I didn't shed any tears. The man was a killer. Nasty way to go though, thirty-seven storeys down and all that, but still. Not exactly a nice guy. Anyway, I know what you're implying but I don't think any of this is particularly unexpected. The various factions of Lamont's former organization are trying to snatch what they can and members of the smaller groups around the city are doing the same thing. I'd be more worried if something like this wasn't happening."

"Yeah, I get that," Diane agreed, "but I'm also getting reports of members of various organizations seemingly working together as well. Is it possible that someone might just be recruiting all the different groups?"

"You mean, knocking off the various bosses and hiring the thugs who work for 'em?" Hutchens asked. "That's a cheerful thought. Well, if you want to follow up these reports, that's fine with me. I'll assign you what people I can but on the understanding that they may be needed elsewhere down the line. Just draw me up a list of what you need and I'll see what I can do."

"Thanks, Commissioner."

"Has our mystery friend got anything on this?"

Diane hesitated. "I haven't heard much from him lately."

"He's isolated himself from us, hasn't he?"

"I think so. We worked well together but... Well, it was probably the right thing to do."

"True," Hutchens said. "And no doubt he's looking

out for your interests just as much as his. Anyway, that shouldn't change the way we do things now, should it? We'll work on fixing this city from our end and he'll work from his."

The man was Cooper and while he had a fairly comfortable life, he didn't have a job as such. Not as most people interpreted the term anyway. He had however had a very long night and a lot like people who did honest work for their livings, he felt tired at the end of such days.

He sat down at his desk, loosened his tie, opened a drawer, pulled out a scotch and poured himself a stiff drink. As he raised the glass to his lips, he paused. A man was standing in front of the door to his office.

Cooper's hand lashed for his gun and in less than a heartbeat he had fired off a round at the visitor. A cowboy of the old west would have been proud of a draw that quick. However, for all of that, the man in the doorway only staggered a bit.

"What kind of way is that to greet a visitor?" he asked as he straightened himself. He grabbed a chair near the door, pulled it up in front of Cooper's desk and then took the scotch bottle from his hand. "Have you got another glass?"

Cooper found one, deciding that if the Bandit asked

you for a glass, then you'd *better* give him one. The Bandit removed the lower part of his mask to enjoy his drink.

"So I take it you're not here to kill me then?" Cooper asked.

"Of course not," the Bandit scoffed. "There isn't any money on you. You don't have enemies in high enough places, it seems."

"So what's your interest in me then?"

"I think we can help each other," the Bandit explained. "The cops have raided my place and frozen my assets, so I need more money. And I figure if I can pull off the right job, I can get enough to keep my head above water for a while."

"I don't have any jobs for you," Cooper told him. "And right now, I'm trying to keep a low profile. The last thing I need is the kind of attention one of your jobs stirs up."

"Right," the Bandit told him. "And exactly how long do you think this happy state of affairs is going to last? Lady Vice is going after the whole pot. She's already finished sweeping up what was left of Lamont's group. Castella's guys are pretty much all accounted for now and the cops scraped Castella himself off the street this morning. So exactly how much time do you think you have before she comes for you?"

Cooper swallowed. "So if I give you a million or so, you'll take her out for me?"

"If you give me ten million, yes. She won't be a problem anymore."

"I don't have ten million to spare."

"I think you do," the Bandit told him, finishing his drink and getting up. "And I'll be back to collect it tomorrow. You'll thank me later, trust me."

The kid was nineteen with all the confidence that came from imagining he was making his mark on the world. For regular folk, it was meaningless. For him, it was real. He looked at the smoking barrel of the sawn-off shotgun in his hand. He looked at the three dead rival gang members lying in the alley in front of him. He looked at the four other gang members behind him. The three younger ones who idolized him and the older guy he had just beaten in one-upmanship. That guy had hidden behind a dumpster when those three punks had come round the corner and the younger kids had seen it. However, the nineteen year old kid had stood his ground. Who knew? When he got back to the headquarters, a promotion might be in order.

"Taught those sons of bitches whose turf this is," he boasted to the others, twirling his weapon around. Then he stopped. There was someone else standing behind the rest of his gang, a little way back in the shadows. The others turned around to look at him too.

"Hey, asshole!" the nineteen year old kid shouted. "This don't concern you! Beat it!"

The figure didn't move. There was something about him that made the kid feel uneasy. In moments, he began to feel it—the cold sweat, the tightening of the chest—and he was afraid the others would notice if he didn't do something. They were all waiting for him to take charge and he had to show them he was boss.

"Hey, didn't you hear me?" he tried again, the bravado in his voice forced and less convincing now. "Are you looking for trouble?"

"I seem to have *found* it," the stranger replied.

"Take this prick!" one of the younger members called out, fumbling around for his own gun.

"I don't run from trouble," the figure said, unfazed by the sudden flurry of activity in front of him as the gang members reached for their weapons. "I clean it up."

As one, the kids started shooting. But the stranger moved like lightning. They saw flashes of an armored suit and there was a spark as a bullet ricocheted off a plate on his shoulder. One of the kids screamed, gasping for a moment, and collapsed. Another was down a moment later.

"What the hell?!" the leader screamed out, trying to

track their assailant. "It's the Sentinel! He's cracked!"

The older guy went down. The other remaining member tried to make a run for it and then the leader saw what was going on. The Sentinel was using a short blade.

"Wait a minute..." he protested, backing away. He was the last one left now, which looked intentional on the part of his assailant. "Wait a minute... You don't kill! You *never* kill!"

"The Sentinel never kills," the stranger said, thrusting the blade through his ribcage. Then he pulled it out and gave the gang member enough room to crumble to the ground.

The stranger wiped his blade and sheathed it. "I don't have a problem with it."

Hutchens waved Diane to a chair. "Morning, Captain."

"Good morning, Commissioner," she said, sitting down. "You look tired. You didn't sleep last night?"

Hutchens rubbed his temples, loosened his tie a little and sat across from her. "It's that obvious?"

Diane smiled. "Don't worry. You hide it better than most, sir."

"Thanks," Hutchens replied. He poured himself a coffee that had just been made from a plunger, then got some milk from the fridge beside his desk. "You want one of these?"

"Thanks, but I've just had one."

"Fair enough," Hutchens replied, putting the milk back and sitting down.

"So what's going on?"

Hutchens frowned. "Maybe nothing. But we found eight dead gang members in an alley last night. Three from one gang and five from a rival one. The first three had been killed by someone from the other group, so there was nothing odd there. They'd been shot and the weapon that had been used was still at the scene. So that was straightforward enough. The tricky part though is what happened to the other lot. Every one of them had been stabbed. Which is odd for a number of reasons. If they killed the other guys first—and Forensics is pretty sure they did—then how did *they* all end up dead? Also, every one of these kids had a gun. So if it was a regular rumble or whatever the hell they call these things, then it wouldn't make sense for someone to bring a knife."

"It's odd," Diane agreed. "But I get the impression you're going somewhere with all this. Are you asking if this could have been our off-the-record friend?"

Hutchens sighed. "Yeah... I guess that's what I'm asking. I don't want to ask, believe me, but it's just that it looks like this is the work of a third party."

"It wasn't him," Diane said.

"You sound very sure," Hutchens remarked.

"Well, it couldn't have been him."

Hutchens sighed again. "Look Diane, I know he's your friend but we don't know what he's capable of. I mean, a man who turns to that kind of thing... He could crack, you know."

"Sure," Diane agreed. "But that's not what I meant."

"Well, what did you mean then?"

"I meant he wouldn't be capable of what you described. The Sentinel couldn't single-handedly take down five gang members in a fight. He probably couldn't take down one."

Hutchens frowned. "I don't follow."

"He's not a fighter. He uses stealth. And he uses other tricks like the stun gas and so on. He plans his appearances carefully and he does it because he has to."

"You're kidding, right?"

"Not at all."

"Jesus... He's got no training in anything like this? Amateur boxing? Nothing?"

"Not a thing."

Hutchens shook his head. "It's a wonder he doesn't get himself killed."

"As I said. He tries to be careful."

"Well..." The commissioner took a sip of his coffee. "It was good of you to tell me. However, it does kind of change things a little. If you want my advice, if you really care about this friend of yours you should try to talk him out of this evening job of his."

"I think you're right," Diane agreed. "And I think I have tried before but I'll try harder. Although to tell you the truth, I haven't been in touch with him for a while."

"Yeah, you told me," Hutchens replied, taking a breath. "Well, I hope he's okay." He took another sip of coffee and put it down. "So, how's your investigation into these mobs going?"

"Well, we've found a number of banks that some of the groups were using, some directly and some through intermediaries. And a whole lot of them have just recently pulled all their funds."

"Interesting."

"Yeah. We don't know what it means yet though, but we're still working on it."

O'Reilly eyed the warehouse in front of him with disdain. "Always warehouses with you, honey," he muttered. "Always abandoned."

"Do you really want to go in there?" the man beside him asked him, his expression dubious.

O'Reilly grimaced. "If we can get this bitch, we might be able to find out where she's stockpiling the money she stole."

"It's just this stinks of a trap."

"Of course it does," O'Reilly replied. "But if we want to find this bitch, then coming along to her goddamn rendezvous and secret meetings are the only way. It isn't as though she's given us a proper address."

"True," his companion admitted. "Yeah, I see how she works all right. She's going to call everyone in one by one, saying she's got a special job for 'em and then her girls are going to blow them away."

"Not," O'Reilly corrected him, "if we blow them away first though. Then we'll turn the tables on that bitch, make her beg for her life and get every last cent she's hoarded."

They watched the warehouse for a few more moments.

"Where are all the girls though?" O'Reilly's companion asked. "Do you think they know we're onto them?"

O'Reilly frowned. "I'm not sure." He nodded to the other men around him, five of them in all. "Get ready."

He edged his way closer to the entrance of the warehouse, trying to get into a position where he could see inside without getting too close. Then he let out a few shots of cover fire that echoed inside the building. At this, the other men rushed in hoping to take Lady

Vice and her girls by surprise.

As they ran towards the entrance, they heard the odd high-pitched whistles of tiny objects piercing through the air. Before any of them realized what was happening, they were all down with tranquilizer darts embedded in their arms and necks.

Shortly after nightfall the following day, the small operator known as Cooper was pacing back and forth in his office when he saw a familiar figure in the doorway.

"Well?" the visitor asked.

"I had a feeling you might be turning up," Cooper said, relieved. "Drink?"

"I'm fine."

"I have to wonder about your timing though."

"That's why I'm the best," the Bandit said. "Ask around. I often know what my clients need before they do. In this case, I knew because I've been keeping an eye on you."

"You saw Lady Vice's people?"

"I did."

"And you didn't do anything?"

"You haven't paid me to do anything yet," the Bandit reminded him. "Anyway, it looked like you handled yourself okay. What did you tell them?"

Cooper waved his hands. "They're moving in on my funds. They said I can join them and contribute the funds to the organization's and benefit from the whole thing."

"That's a lie," the Bandit said. "No one's going to benefit from this except for Lady Vice and her girls. She's playing the rest of the syndicates for fools."

"I don't think they're fools," Cooper said. "They're just trying to save their skins."

"It's too late for that."

"Why didn't you offer your services to them then?"

"By the time I figured out what Lady Vice was up to, it was too late—as I said. She had their funds. But she doesn't have your funds yet."

"How do you know all this stuff?"

"That's information," the Bandit told him. "And information's expensive. Also, it's not my trade."

"Right, I forgot."

"So you managed to keep your funds for a little while longer, I take it?"

"I told them I'd cooperate, but that I'd have to re-route my funds from some foreign accounts and that it would take a little while."

"Good thinking."

"Well, it's bought me a little time," Cooper said. "But I doubt it's very much."

"You're right about that."

"So, this is the part where I give you ten million and you sort this all out?"

"That's entirely your choice, Mr. Cooper."

Cooper shrugged. "Well, I made up my mind the moment those bitches left today, so you can have it. But I wonder... When you take out Lady Vice and her girls, maybe we could get our hands on that pile of accumulated funds they've gathered from all the other syndicates and split it."

"Two points," the Bandit said. "First off, Lady Vice is smart. A hell of a lot smarter than anyone in the remaining syndicates. Smarter than you. Maybe smarter than me."

"And how do you know that?"

"That's information again but the way she's neutered the last remaining syndicates in the city overnight should tell you she's a pretty capable woman."

"True. So then she's smart. What about it?"

"The point is that her money won't be easy to find. Second point. If I could find it, then I wouldn't be asking you for money now, would I?"

"You've got me there," Cooper conceded.

"Now," the Bandit said, "I take it that you expect to see Lady Vice's girls again soon?"

"Yeah, I'll see them soon," Cooper told him. "The lady herself is expecting me to come and see her somewhere downtown tomorrow night."

"And why does she think you'll meet her?"

"Because she thinks I'll be interested in seeing how the conglomerate's funds will be distributed so the cops will never find it." Cooper shrugged. "She might be on to something. Cops have been showing up at some of the various banks around town that my rivals use."

"She's ripped off Castella's boys and the largest group that came out of Lamont's organization," the Bandit said. "And I'd say since then, she's anonymously fed the cops bits and pieces to get them coming after the other syndicates in the city."

"She wouldn't tip them off, would she?"

"Why not?"

"Because it's self-defeating," Cooper said. "That's why. How can she possibly hope to acquire the funds of the various remaining syndicates if she tells the cops the names of the banks where those funds are being kept?"

"Because it's getting the exact results she wants," the Bandit told him. "You want information so much. Here. The last dregs of the syndicates are pulling all their cash like scared rabbits and stashing it in physical locations where they believe it'll be safe. And just like she did when some of Lamont's old boys tried that trick, Lady Vice is finding these stashes and making off with them. And if it weren't for my warning, she'd probably have you hooked now as well. Now, you wouldn't pull your cash like the others. You're smarter than that. But as a fellow professional, you'd be curious to see how she was managing to deal with the problem and don't tell me you wouldn't. If I hadn't warned you, you would walk into her trap tomorrow, no two ways about it."

"Maybe I would," Cooper admitted. "Although we'll never know now. However, if she's able to find all the money stashes around the city so easily, why are the rest of the groups still pulling their funds and stockpiling them for her?"

"Because the cops are moving in on their banks too fast for them to think of anything better. And some of them would be too stupid to think of anything else anyway. There's a reason none of you guys could make any headway when Lamont was running things."

"I resent that."

The Bandit shrugged. "Resent it all you want. But Lamont controlled more than half the city and at best, the rest of you controlled the odd neighborhood here and there. There are only a handful of ways you can look at that."

Cooper glowered. "You're a prick, you know that?"

"I've been called worse things. Anyway, tomorrow night. Let's sort out the particulars."

• • •

Outside on the street, a woman sat in her car, watching the building. With her hair tied back and thick rimmed glasses, she didn't look remarkable, nor likely to attract a lot of attention. The Bandit certainly didn't notice her when he left.

As night fell on Fringe City, a number of girls sat by a second storey window, watching a building across the street. The building where Lady Vice had told Cooper to meet her. The time for the meeting had been and gone, and a couple of the girls were beginning to have their doubts, but most of them seemed confident their quarry would show.

Then ten minutes after Cooper was supposed to have arrived, a familiar figure rushed at the door of the place and lobbed a grenade at it. As it blew to pieces, he moved in with a large automatic in each hand.

"Like clockwork," one of the girls commented.

"Yes," another agreed, picking up a small remote control and flicking a switch. "Observe, ladies. The Bandit."

With a thundering crash, the building exploded outwards, sending the Bandit flying back with the burning debris and rolling out into the middle of the street.

As one, the group of women climbed to their feet. None of them were dressed in their typical attire. They wore plain shirts, jeans and the odd cardigan or two. Nobody was going to notice anything out of the ordinary when they walked out the other side of the building.

"Oh, I can't wait to see Cooper's face tomorrow," one of the girls said.

"Home sweet home," Jason announced as he and Angie stepped back into their apartment after their brief trip away. Angie reached for the zipper of their suitcase as he closed the door.

"Ah, leave it," he told her. "I'll unpack later. Why don't you relax on the sofa and I'll get us some coffee?"

"Okay," Angie said, stretching out and switching on the TV. "Shall we see if all hell broke loose while you were away?"

"Yeah, why not?" Jason replied, putting on some water to boil.

Angie flicked through the channels until she came across a story on Fringe City Central. There was footage of a burning building at night. The fire brigade were there, along with the police, but the focus of the camera was a man on a stretcher.

"- has been confirmed," a reporter was saying, "that the Bandit is still alive but has sustained critical, possibly life-threatening injuries from the blast and that he was rushed to hospital shortly after police arrived on the scene last night."

"What's that?" Jason called out from the kitchen.

"It looks like the police have caught the Bandit," Angie told him.

"How?"

"Damn good question."

In a hotel room in Chicago, Daniel Kowolski shook his head as he watched the same report. "Andy," he murmured. "Why? You've thrown away everything." He hung his head in his hands in a moment of utter impotent frustration. "Goddamn it."

Then resting his chin in his palm for a moment, he thought and made a decision. He stretched over to the bedside table and picked up the phone. "Hey, man," he said into the receiver, "how do you dial out?" There was a short reply. "Thanks," he said. "Thanks a lot."

He dialed a number and waited. "Hey, it's Daniel. I need to get a few guys together. Who've you got we can trust?"

There was a question from the other end.

"Nothing special," Daniel replied. "They just have

to be good with a gun, and not afraid to take some heat." He listened for a moment. "Great. Oh, where? Well, just come down to Fringe City separately. I'll find somewhere out of the way where we can meet up. Call me back when you've got the group together and we'll talk over the details. Here's the number. Have you got a pen?"

LAST MAN STANDING

CARL CRESTON WAS ONE MOB BOSS WHO wasn't going to be roped into Lady Vice's schemes.

One moment, he was in his office on the twenty-third floor, threatening someone over the phone. The next, there was the sound of gunfire followed by one of his men crashing through his door, dead from a knife wound. Creston pulled out his gun before another man appeared, lunging through the doorway at him. Creston got off a couple of shots but they went wide. Then his assailant held him in a wrist lock and hurled him through the window.

When all was said and done, Creston wasn't going to be roped into *anyone*'s schemes.

Diane took a sip of coffee and put her cup down. "You know," she said, "I don't mean this in an unkind way, but I kind of hoped you wouldn't call me again."

"I know what you mean," Jason replied. "I've been thinking of getting out of this a lot lately. And actually,

I appreciate the fact that you know..." He shrugged, feeling a little embarrassed before he finished. "Well, I mean... I appreciate the fact you care about me. That you want me to get out of this for my own good."

"You should get out," Diane told him. "You know that."

"Yeah, I know," Jason said. "And believe me, I'm working on it. For a moment there though, this whole thing really felt addictive."

Diane nodded. "I can understand that. But oh, well. Let's talk. You obviously want to, or you wouldn't have called me. Are you up to anything?"

"Me? No. No, I'm taking it easy to tell you the truth. But I just want to be kept in the loop a little bit longer, that's all. You know, to ease out of this thing gently."

Diane smiled, nodding. "I guess I can live with that. Well, what can I tell you? I presume you saw the news about the Bandit?"

"Yeah. So he's in a hospital at the moment, presumably under guard?"

"Yeah. Although he's not going anywhere. He's in very bad shape." Diane sighed. "You know, I was there when he shot up the police station but I still felt sorry for him when I saw him."

"That bad?"

"Have you ever seen someone injured by an explosion?"

"I can't say I have," Jason admitted.

"Well, believe me, you don't want to. He had burns all over his side, bits of metal and all sorts of other things embedded in him..." She shook her head.

"So what exactly happened?"

"The rest of us are as much in the dark as you are," Diane told him. "The Bandit was on a job, but someone was clearly expecting him and set up a trap. But as to who he was working for, who he was trying to take out and by extension who set the trap... no one knows a thing."

"Someone in one of the syndicates perhaps," Jason suggested.

"I doubt it," Diane said. "We've rounded most of them up now. Oh, something happened with one mob boss though. Last night, a nasty mid-sized operator by the name of Creston was thrown out of the twenty-third floor of a building."

"That can't be too good for his health," Jason remarked. "Any idea who did it?"

Diane hesitated. "I think someone else out there is waging their own little vigilante war. But they're being a little less delicate about it than you were."

"Well, I suspected there were a few others having a crack at my job when criminals started turning up battered and bruised a while back. But this newcomer... They're on their own killing spree?"

HAMISH SPIERS

Diane shrugged. "Possibly. There were five gang members killed recently and along with Creston, six members of his entourage were found dead throughout the building as well. And they all died from knife wounds."

"And there's a connection?"

"Well, the guys working on the cases seem to think so."

"But you weren't involved in either of the investigations though."

"Well," Diane told him, "this may come as a shock to you but I'm not actually personally involved in every police case in the city."

Jason grinned. "Hard to believe, but fair enough." He then noticed a woman across the café looking at him over her book. He smiled at her and she blushed and went back to her reading. He turned back to Diane. "So what are you doing these days?"

"Not that much," Diane said. "Because some other Fringe City citizen's now knocking syndicate members out cold and tipping us off to their locations." She raised her eyebrows. "You woudn't happen to know anything about that, would you?"

Jason shrugged. "Not me. I haven't knocked out a mob boss for a while now. I wonder who it is?"

"They use tranquilizer darts, whoever they are, so they're not Captain Psychopath. But other than that, we don't know the first thing about them."

When Diane left the café, Jason felt a little awkward. Sometimes on reflection, it seemed as though Fringe City's criminals were cleaning themselves up. The Bandit had taken out Danny Vincent's mob. Sophia Garcia had taken care of Martin Lamont. Now, the remaining syndicates were more or less finished, someone had incapacitated the Bandit and landed him in police custody. And some new vigilante was finishing up what was left.

"Maybe I should retire," he murmured to himself as he walked up the steps to his apartment building.

He then paused, feeling a sense of déjà vu. There was a woman across the street and he had a funny feeling he'd seen her before, but he couldn't place her. Shrugging, he went inside.

The next evening, he was watching TV with Angie when she noticed he looked a bit distracted.

"What's wrong?" she asked.

"Huh?"

"You've seemed a bit funny since you saw your friend Diane."

Jason shrugged. "Have I?"

"Yeah, you seem a bit out of it."

"It's weird," Jason admitted. "I haven't got decked out in my crime fighting gear since before we left on our trip."

"But that's good, right?" Angie asked.

"Yeah, but it's..."

Angie frowned. "Like withdrawal symptoms or something?"

"I guess," Jason said. "I mean, I want to put the Sentinel behind me. And who knows? Maybe I might even call Cassie and see if I can find out more about those jobs in Portland."

"It'd be nice to get out of this place." Angie sighed. "Although sometimes it's hard to leave the place you call home, no matter what it's like."

"Well, it's home," Jason pointed out, squeezing her hand. He smiled. "Also you were describing the same problem I have. We want to get out of here eventually, but we're just not ready to make the move yet."

"So you're not ready to put the Sentinel behind you yet, is that it?"

"I guess so," Jason told her. "I'm nearly there, I think, but not quite all the way."

The following evening, he was in his Kevlar gear again, standing on Sophia Garcia's balcony.

She was somewhat calmer than when he'd seen her last. And when she turned away from the TV by chance and saw him, she showed no sign of alarm at all. She smiled and stood up, adjusting the towel around her hair and tightening her bathrobe. For a woman of her age, Jason thought, she looked pretty fetching in one.

She slid the balcony door open and shivered a little from the change in temperature. Jason stepped in and closed the door behind him.

"You missed me, did you?" she asked.

"I guess I did," Jason replied.

"But of course, this could never lead to anything," she said, reminding him of what he'd said the last time. She walked back to the lounge, her hands trailing over the furniture. "So, would you like to watch a movie or something?"

Jason smiled. "I can't drop by all the time just to say hi."

"I know," Sophia told him, sitting down and gesturing for him to sit in the lounge chair across from her. "So," she asked. "What's going on?"

Jason tried to make himself a little more comfortable. "Well, it's a little embarrassing actually," he confessed, "but that was basically the question I wanted to ask you."

"'What's going on?'?"

"Yeah."

Sophia's eyes flicked around the room for a moment. "I don't suppose you could be more specific by any chance?"

"Um... I just wanted to find out if there's anything I should know."

"I'm sorry," Sophia said. "I think it's my fault for suggesting I could help you keep your finger on the pulse. But the truth is I've been out of the loop a bit."

Jason nodded. "I think I understand."

"You do?"

"Well, I guessed what happened," he told her. "You know, with your brother. But you needn't worry. Your secret's safe with me."

"I know."

"You didn't have to do it though, you know."

"I know that too," Sophia told him. "But you shouldn't feel as though you were in any way responsible. Our worlds are different places. But I think things are better this way. Since..." She paused to recompose herself. Then she smiled but it was a little forced. "Well, you know. Things have been better recently."

She reached over to him and grasped his hands. "I couldn't have turned my back on Martin any other way. He wouldn't have let me."

"I'm not judging you," Jason told her.

"And everyone tried to put him away," she continued. "And everyone failed. Martin weaseled his way out of everything. But maybe I'm no different to that new vigilante out there."

"Come again?"

"Oh, there's this new vigilante making a reputation for himself," Sophia explained, letting go of his hands. "A bit of a mystery man. He's got a bit of your tech apparently…" She shook her head. "Where do all you guys get your Kevlar suits from? Is there a Kevlar suit aisle in the toy section of every department store or something?"

"Well, mine's a trade secret," Jason said. "But I don't know about the Bandit's or this other guy's. What else can you tell me about him? He kills people rather than bringing them in?"

"Yeah, he's pretty ruthless. Word on the street is he threw Creston out of a high-rise window the other day. Oh, right, you probably don't know Creston."

"Headed a mid-sized operation."

"Oh, you *do* know him?"

"Not well. I just heard the name recently, to tell the truth."

"Well," Sophia said, "there's some news for you at any rate. Although, what this guy's deal is is anyone's guess. I think he killed Castella earlier too."

"Um… I don't think I know him."

"His organization was a little larger than Creston's." Sophia frowned. "You know, there's this rumor running round that Lady Vice took the credit for knocking off Castella. And that's weird too."

"Well, it doesn't sound like her style," Jason agreed. "She's never killed before, right?"

"Not that. It's obvious she didn't kill Castella. Well, at least that's what I think. But why would she try and convince people she had?"

Jason shrugged. "Beats me. What about the remaining syndicates?"

"The dregs," Sophia said. "There's not much left of them now. But I don't know what they're up to any more than you do, really."

"Well, I know you've been cut out of things but you've probably heard *some* rumors, right?"

Sophia shook her head. "No one tells me much these days at all. I just heard about this new vigilante from one of the nicer guys who organized Martin's security. And I use the term 'nicer' in its loosest interpretation. Other than that, the only real vibe I'm getting is that everything's pretty quiet now."

"Too quiet?" Jason suggested with a hint of a grin.

"Well," Sophia said, "that's the question, isn't?"

Jason nodded and stood up. "I suppose. Well, I guess I'd better get going now and let you enjoy your evening."

Sophia got up as well to open the balcony door for him. "It was good to see you again."

"It was good to see you too," Jason told her. "You're looking well." He paused by the door for a moment. "By the way... With all your money and everything, why are you still hanging around Fringe City? Why don't you move to New York or someplace, or try your luck on the west coast?"

Sophia shrugged. "Well, you know how it is. This is home."

A couple of days later, Angie was coming out of the local shops when she saw a woman whose eyes lit up as they met hers. The woman threw her hands out in a gesture of surprise. "Angela Morris?"

Angie smiled. While the woman seemed to recognize her, Angie couldn't place her for the life of her. "Yeah. I'm sorry ..."

"Gwendolyn Taylor," the woman replied. "I was in your cohort back at West Ridge University. We did a few classes together." She sighed. "You probably don't remember, I know. I was a fairly quiet student."

Angie looked at her with a little bit of pity. She was probably quite attractive but she seemed to hide her features as if she were unaware of them. And with her hair tied back in a bun, her thick rimmed glasses and her plain cardigan, she looked quite the mousy type. It wasn't too much of a stretch to imagine she'd been quiet back at university.

"Oh," Angie waved a hand. "I have a terrible memory. I don't even remember the girls I sat with the whole time, to be honest."

"Jennifer and the others?" Gwendolyn asked.

"Yeah, you see?" Angie asked. "I can't remember who Jennifer was."

"The one with the long dark hair."

"It's hopeless," Angie told her with an embarrassed smile. "It's like I said, I have a terrible memory."

"That's all right," Gwendolyn said. "Say, would you like to have a coffee or something sometime? Maybe we could catch up."

Diane switched off the light in her office. It seemed another day had passed without incident. She could get used to this. She shut the door, said goodnight to a few of the officers on the later shift and headed outside. As she came out of the building though, she discovered a bit of a commotion.

A large group of officers were gathered around in a circle, while some others headed past her inside with an air of urgency. Meanwhile, curious onlookers walked over to the circle to see what was going on.

Against her better instincts, Diane joined them. But generally things that drew a whole lot of cops together like that weren't good.

"What's going on?" she asked.

One of the cops in the crowd pointed at the ground where a man lay dead.

"Someone dumped him here," the officer explained.

"There's a note tied to him," Diane observed.

"Yeah," the other officer replied. "The guy who wrote it claims this is the Specter."

"The Specter?" Diane asked. "That serial killer who's announced his sprees in advance every year for the six years straight but has still eluded the best people we've got on the force? *That* guy?"

"That's what the note says," the officer replied, although his own doubt was evident in his voice. "And with almost a year since his last appearance too."

"And did this guy leave a name on his note? Some kind of alias or street name?"

"Yeah, he did actually," the officer replied. "Orion."

"The hunter," Diane murmured. "That tells us a lot about him."

"Yeah. And he ain't the Sentinel."

"No," Diane agreed. "He's not."

The next day, she received a short text:

"Forensics took DNA samples from the body to correlate with evidence collected from various Specter killings. Orion's claim's been verified."

Diane read the message again, thinking over the implications. The Specter was one of the worst killers Fringe City had put up with in recent years and it was good to know he was finally accounted for. However, there was a more frightening aspect to what had happened and it wasn't just that this new vigilante was killing.

"Well," Jason said as he watched the evening news. "That changes things."

"Yeah," Angie agreed. "Although I have to say I've got mixed feelings about the whole thing. Yeah, the Specter was pretty scary but I can't say I feel too comfortable with the idea that there's a vigilante out there whose solution to crime is to just kill off every criminal in the phone book one by one."

"You misunderstood what I meant," Jason said. "I wasn't talking about the fact that this guy's taken out one of Fringe City's most wanted. I meant that this 'Orion' character is more dangerous than I thought."

"Well, obviously he's dangerous," Angie said, frowning. "He's a brute who sounds like he's physically formidable and he likes to deal with crime by stabbing people and throwing them out of high-rises."

"Yes, but that's the obvious part," Jason pointed out. "It's scary, sure, but it's not the part that really scares me. What really gets me is *this*. Before, I thought this guy was basically a thug with a misguided sense of morality. But this guy's just found a serial-killer that no-one on the police force could find. And he did it without any assistance from the department and almost a whole year after the last Specter killings. Think about that. He's an outsider who can single-handedly solve a cold case that the police couldn't. So, not only is he physically formidable, he's smart too."

Jason sighed. "He's stronger than me, Angie. He can handle himself better in a fight than any of the various criminals he's taken down already—and I bet none of those guys were pushovers—and he's smarter than me."

"But does it matter?" Angie said. "You're not going head to head with this guy. You're out of it. Let the police deal with him."

"Damn it! Sophia!" Jason exclaimed.

"What's Sophia got to do with anything right now?"

Jason got up and begun pacing back and forth. "You said it yourself. This guy seems to be systematically going through a list. So far, that list has covered mid-level syndicates, teenage gang members and a serial killer whose identity was a complete mystery to everyone else in the city. That's pretty extensive. Do you think he'd leave off the sister of one of the most notorious mob figures Fringe City ever saw?"

"I don't know," Angie said. "What's Sophia done? I mean, yeah, she killed Martin Lamont, but that's not exactly public knowledge and seeing how Orion operates, he'd be more likely to give her a medal for it."

"She's connected to Fringe City's underworld."

"That's a pretty loose connection now though," Angie told him. "You said so yourself."

"It won't make a difference as far as Orion's concerned," Jason countered. "I mean, what did those teenager gang members do? Sure, some of them had probably killed people and at least one of them *definitely* had. But the younger kids who were found in that alley were probably only in those gangs because they were too stupid to know better. Orion didn't seem to make a distinction."

Angie nodded. "All right," she said, keeping her voice controlled. "Let's say you're right. What exactly can you do to protect this woman?"

"Maybe nothing," Jason told her, "but I'd like to at least warn her to be careful. And secondly, just in case, I'm going to give her the number for my untraceable."

Angie frowned. "You shouldn't go giving that out

to too many people."

"I don't like it any more than you do. But under the circumstances, I think it might be a good idea. Besides, it's an untraceable."

"Well, if it makes you feel better, go for it. But what will you do if she does call you?"

Jason shrugged. "Well, hopefully, she'd call the police first and I'd just be there as back-up. She doesn't have any outstanding warrants or convictions, so there's no reason why she can't call the cops. And if I am needed for some reason, I won't get into a round of fisticuffs with this guy. I'll hit him with some stun gas instead."

"I hope you know what you're doing," Angie told him

"Yeah," Jason replied. "That makes two of us."

Andy Kowolski, better known throughout the country as the Bandit, lay immobile on his hospital bed breathing through a respirator mask. A machine to the side of the bed monitored his vital functions, while a nurse checked his charts and his doctor discussed his condition with a senior police officer. There were two other police officers in the room and four were circling the hospital outside. There was little to be concerned about from the Bandit however; he was heavily sedated, and just to be safe, he was restrained to his bed. The concern was danger from the outside and that's where it came from.

The police had of course taken care to withhold the name of the hospital where Andy Kowolski was being treated; and even within the building, only those who were directly concerned with his treatment knew he was there. Nevertheless, with a little investigative work, Daniel Kowolski had found it. Moving through the parking lot, he nodded to the other members of his team, giving them the signal to spread out. There weren't as many cars in the lot as he would have liked but there were still enough to give him cover.

He frowned at the police officer pacing around the near side of the building. He was irritatingly alert for someone who'd been on guard duty for five hours straight. No overweight security guard having a smoke in a corner, this guy. He was looking everywhere on his lap and the other officers circling the building were the same. Daniel Kowolski gritted his teeth.

It was the constant moving, he knew. If they were staying still, they wouldn't be anywhere near that alert. They were seeing everything with fresh eyes.

He fixed the silencer to his weapon then looked to his right to see if he could make eye contact with one of his own men. He could. He made a couple of short gestures to signal the plan.

Then an officer came around the front of the building from the side and the officer who was already there gave him a nod before circling around the other side. Before he disappeared from sight though, Daniel's man shot him. The second officer turned to shoot back but before he could get his own shot off, Daniel took him out.

He and the other man then ran across the parking lot and another member of the team joined them. Then one more came around from the other side of the building.

"I got the guy on the north wall," he said as he jogged over to them, "but the prick by the east wall got Jones and he's calling for back-up."

"Let him," Daniel replied. "If the guys inside were watching the cameras, they're probably ahead of him anyway."

They charged into the hospital foyer, startling everyone inside. For good measure, Daniel twisted off his silencer and fired a couple of shots in the ceiling. Then they left the screaming people behind them and scrambled into an elevator.

"Hey, can they lock these things down?" one of the group asked as Daniel punched in the fourth floor.

"No idea," Daniel replied, watching the numbers light up above the door. "But I doubt they'll have the time. Now get down!"

They all crouched before the doors opened, and Daniel and the guy on his right laid down some quick cover fire. There was a scream and through the smoke, Daniel saw a police officer go down, clutching at his chest.

Seeing another moving towards him, Daniel hit the button for the sixth floor and the doors slid shut. As one, his gang climbed up.

"There are two others," he said.

The door opened and he ushered his group out then held the lift doors open. He nodded to two of his men. "Take the stairs and watch out. I'd bet one of those officers is on 'em now. We'll go back down."

With that, he climbed back into the elevator with the remaining guy. "Got your grenade handy?" he muttered as he hit the fourth floor button again.

"Ready," the man said. He released the pin before the doors opened, judging the time it would take with the confidence of expertise. When the doors opened and he lobbed it outside, it exploded on impact. As luck would have it, one of the remaining officers was a foot away from the centre of the blast.

As Daniel and his partner stepped out of the elevator, the others appeared from the stairwell.

"Well?" he asked them, looking around to make sure there weren't any other cops around.

"We got the guy on the stairs," one of them replied.

"Did you get any more?"

"Yeah. Got one with the grenade."

"So, three total. That might be all of them."

"Seems to be all of them," Daniel said. "But stay sharp. Come on."

They pressed on, noticing that this section of the hospital was very quiet. Perhaps the other patients had been relocated so they wouldn't be disturbed by the police presence around Andy Kowolski.

As they entered the room, the doctor was sending the nurse away.

Daniel pointed his gun at her. "Back inside. Now."

The doctor raised his hands. "I know you're here for the man inside this room. But you must understand that he is in a very critical condition. By attempting to move him, you might kill him."

"You're just going to have to make sure that doesn't happen," Daniel told him.

"Believe it or not, I'm doing my very best for this man," the doctor said. "My business is in the preservation of life." He then nodded to the woman beside him. "And that also includes the people I work with. You're not going to harm this nurse."

Daniel smiled. "No, but I'm not letting her go either. You said it yourself. My brother's in a critical condition."

"Your brother?"

"My brother. And you said he's in a critical condition. He's going to need all the help he can get."

"But there's no need to involve this nurse in this," the doctor insisted. "If you really wish to move him—and I strongly advise you don't—then I will go with you. But let this woman go."

Daniel thought over his options.

"Daniel?" one of the men asked, getting anxious.

"Shut up, I'm thinking," Daniel told him. He turned back to the doctor. "Your nurse stays, as do you." He looked at the machines his brother was hooked up to along with the medical implements about the place. These were things he did not understand. "We can't move him, you're right. So we'll hole up in here."

"Hey, Daniel, what the hell?" his partner exclaimed.

"We were going to have to hole up somewhere eventually," Daniel replied. "And the cops would find us, right? So we may as well just save ourselves the trouble and stay here. Besides, if we go somewhere else, then I just know this doctor here's going to start telling me he needs this, that and the other thing and I won't have the medical expertise to tell if he's lying or not."

"What about food and all that stuff?"

Daniel looked out the window and smiled as the first police cars pulled into the parking lot. "We'll get those sons of bitches out there to send it up." He laughed as he pictured it. "Yeah, they'll be all 'What are your demands?' and we'll be like 'twelve cheeseburgers.'"

He clapped his partner on the shoulder. "We'll be fine. Don't worry about it." He then gestured to the window. "Besides, it's a moot point anyway. Where do you think those pretty lights are coming from?"

One of the others rushed over to have a look. "Oh, shit!" he cried, banging his fists on the windowsill. "We're going to be holed up here for months!"

Daniel sat down in a chair at the end of his brother's bed and lit up a cigarette. "Yeah, it'll be fun."

The doctor positioned himself between Daniel and the nurse and looked straight at him. "There's no smoking allowed inside this building, sir," he said, keeping his voice steady.

"Ask me if I give a damn," Daniel replied, not bothering to look at him.

The doctor didn't budge. "Your brother might."

Daniel almost jumped out of his chair, jabbing the cigarette out on the leg of his trousers. He looked at his brother lying there with the machine monitoring him as he breathed in and out through his respirator mask.

"Damn it!" he shouted, kicking over the chair. He turned to two of the men. "Go and see what you can do about disabling the lifts and blocking the stairs, then we'll talk about taking shifts."

He then turned back to the doctor and tried his best to be civil. It was a skill he'd been able to manage once, back before his parents had been killed in a car crash and he and Andy had started off down the slippery slide of teenage delinquency.

He sighed. "All right, doctor. You seem pretty straight so don't sugarcoat this or nothing. But how long will it take before my brother can recover enough to walk around on his own?"

"I can't answer that," the doctor replied. "At the moment, I don't even know if we can save his life."

Daniel nodded. Then walking past the others to the window, he turned his head away so they couldn't see him cry.

Meanwhile, more police arrived along with representatives of the other emergency services. A police helicopter flew overhead, search lights sweeping over the neighborhood while news vans circled the parking lot and camera crews jostled to get the best positions for live coverage of the siege.

"Jason," Angie said, introducing the woman who had just come through the door, "this is Gwendolyn."

"Nice to meet you, Gwendolyn," Jason greeted her.

Gwendolyn gave him a bashful smile. "Nice to meet you too."

"Angie's told me you guys went to university together."

"Yeah, although we didn't really know each other then," Gwendolyn said. "We were just in a few of the same classes, that's all."

"But you don't teach now, right?" Jason asked her as Angie closed the door.

Gwendolyn smiled. "I couldn't handle the stress. I'm an accountant now actually."

"Wow. And is it really as boring as everyone says?"

"Every bit of it." Gwendolyn laughed. "But I'll take that boredom over stress any day."

"I can understand that," Jason admitted.

"Me too," Angie said. "Well, anyway, why don't we all sit down at the table? I think that tuna casserole needs another ten minutes or so, and then we can eat. In the meantime... Gwendolyn, would you like something to drink?"

After dinner, the three of them sat down in the living room and were talking over coffee when Jason's untraceable rang.

"Excuse me," he said, getting up to answer it. Diane had never rung before when a guest had been over, so he knew he'd have to be discreet.

He walked into the corner of the kitchen. "Hi," he

answered, keeping his voice at a murmur.

It wasn't Diane.

"It's me," a woman whispered on the other end of the line.

Angie, Jason noticed, had suggested to Gwendolyn that they watch some TV together at that point, giving him a bit of ambient noise in the background to mask his conversation. She was a gem, he thought to himself.

"What's going on?" he asked.

"The power's been cut to the building. I've tried calling the police and they say they'll get try to get a unit out here... but I got the impression they're short on staff tonight."

"All right," Jason told her. "Hide under some furniture or something, keep out of sight and I'll be there as soon as I can."

He hung up and grabbed his bag. "Sorry, honey," he said to Angie. "I have to go out for a little bit. Got to help Sophia out because her babysitter didn't show up. You know, kids home alone and all that jazz."

"Okay," Angie replied. She nodded towards the television. "By the way, have you seen this, Jason?"

He looked at the footage of police cars and emergency vehicles surrounding a building. "What's that, a hospital or something?"

"It's a siege apparently," Angie said. "A group of men have broken into the building to get the Bandit out. Now, they're inside holding a doctor and a nurse hostage."

"When did this happen?"

Angie shrugged. "About an hour ago, I think. Anyway, if her kids are waiting, you'd better head on over."

"Yeah, sorry about that." He gave Gwendolyn a friendly nod. "It was nice to meet you, Gwendolyn. Hopefully, I'll see you again soon."

She smiled. "Yeah, that'd be nice."

As he went out the door, Gwendolyn turned back to Angie. "He's nice, your husband."

"Actually, he's just my partner at the moment," Angie explained. "We're not married yet."

"You guys planning on officially tying the knot some day?" Gwendolyn asked.

Angie smiled. "We'd like to. It's just hard finding the time to organize it." She reached for the remote. "This hospital siege isn't the most cheerful thing on TV, is it? Would you like to watch a movie or something? I've got a few DVDs. Well, most of them are Jason's but they're not *all* guns and explosions."

Gwendolyn shrugged. "Guns and explosions are fine with me."

Half an hour later, Jason reached Sophia's place. He

hoped she was still alive because half an hour was a long time in a situation like that. Hurrying, he went behind the building and shot a grappling hook at the roof and hauled himself up.

Once he reached the top, he started getting suited up, terrified of what he was going to see once he got into the apartment.

"Who are you?" came a voice from behind.

Jason whirled round and saw a man in a Kevlar armored suit not too dissimilar to his own.

"So you're the Sentinel," the man said. "You can't be too crash hot if I can sneak up on you that easily. Are you protecting the woman who lives in the penthouse down there?"

"You're not going to hurt her."

"So you *did* tip her off. Do you want to tell me why you did that?"

"This woman doesn't deserve to die."

"Everyone dies eventually."

"I'm not here to spout philosophy with you," Jason told the man, who was undoubtedly Orion. "But this woman's not with the mob any more. She even helped me save another woman's life. I'm not trying to get in your way but—"

"You're in my way right now. That woman's not in her apartment. And there'd be no reason for her to suspect that the blackout was anything out of the ordinary unless someone told her so."

"I warned her you might come after her," Jason said, staring at Orion's mask. If it filtered the effects of the stun gas, then he might well have no way of taking him down. His only way out then in all likelihood was to talk Orion out of his plan.

"That was a mistake, my friend," Orion replied. "I've had no problem with you so far. It'd be a pity for that to change."

"We're not the same," Jason said. "But we want the same thing, right?"

"We do, but let's be honest with each other. Your way wasn't working."

"What? What about all the things that have happened since—?"

"Blind stupid luck," Orion said. "You didn't put Burges away. He did that himself when he murdered his assistant to cover his tracks. And if the Bandit hadn't taken out Danny Vincent and his boys, you would have had another syndicate in the city every bit as bad as Lamont's. And now, Lady Vice has blown the Bandit away—"

"Lady Vice?"

"Lady Vice, but unsurprisingly, I'm the only one who seems to know that. But you see it now, don't you? You've just hung around in the background while these people have killed each other off and incriminated themselves and then you've taken all the credit for it."

"I think that's a bit unfair."

"I think it's perfectly fair. And I think what galls you is the fact that you know it too. If you had just killed Burges at the get-go, you wouldn't have had half the problems you've had. But anyway, that's water over the dam. Now, where's Sophia Garcia?"

There was a click.

"Never mind," Orion said. "Ms. Garcia, you don't want to try that, believe me. I've taken out men in the past few weeks armed with far more substantial weapons than that little Derringer you're carrying."

Sophia still held her gun pointed at Orion's back but with less confidence than she had a moment before.

"Damn it, Sophia," Jason said. "You should have stayed out of sight."

"He was going to hurt you. I could see it," Sophia said. "This man's trained to kill. It's in his poise. Like he's coiled up and ready to spring."

"Fascinating, Ms. Garcia," Orion said.

"Why are you here?" she asked him.

"To kill you, my dear," Orion replied. "I was simply asking your friend where you were."

"Sophia killed Lamont," Jason blurted out. "Her own brother."

"And why are you telling me this?"

"She did it because as long as Lamont lived, he would continue killing innocent people. She did it because she thought it was the only way to stop him. By your own logic, you should be thanking her."

Orion seemed to relax a little. "Interesting. And her action was acceptable to you?"

Jason realized that any moral high ground he held was now slipping away. "It doesn't matter if it's acceptable to me or not," he said, choosing his words carefully. "She was faced with a difficult situation and she made a tough choice. Was it the right choice? I don't know but who am I to judge?"

"Yet I think you've judged me," Orion said. "And the scales tilted rather differently."

"I couldn't kill because I couldn't live with myself if I did," Jason said. "I think taking a life must change you—it must—and I don't want to go through that."

"I thought as much. But, my god, you are a paradox. Now that I've met you, I can't understand why a man with your sensitivities would involve yourself in the problem of dealing with Fringe City's underworld. Have a good look at me, Sentinel. I'm what you need to be to do your work." Orion then turned around. "Ms. Garcia. Put the gun away already. You're embarrassing yourself. I won't kill you. Your friend's persuaded me on that front."

Sophia put it away.

"Anyway," Orion said, turning back to Jason, "now that we've all agreed to be civil, what were you going to say next?"

"Your way is too extreme," Jason said. "Can't you see that? The innocent are going to be hurt. I mean, take tonight. And when you killed those gang members recently, you got a killer or two but what about the others? What was their crime?"

"One of association," Orion told him. "They would have killed soon enough. Think of it as preventative medicine."

"Well, you asked me," Jason said. "I told you."

"Indeed," Orion replied. "I like you but I think you're too soft for this business. I'll let Sophia live though. You have my word and that's as good as any promise. However, leave this city to me from now on. Your work's finished. Go back to your loved ones and allow the professionals to handle these things."

He started to turn away. "Well, I believe I've dallied here too long as it is. Fringe City's finest have a problem at Graceville Hospital and I'm going to solve it for them."

"Wait a minute!" Jason exclaimed. "The siege? You can't go in there. They've got hostages."

"I'm aware of this."

"Well, let's compromise," Jason said. "Let me come with you."

"You? You'll slow me down."

Jason moved towards him. "I can't let you go in there and endanger the lives of those hostages."

Without warning, Orion whirled around, delivering a brutal blow to Jason's side that sent him keeling over in agony. Water came to his eyes and the pain was almost literally blinding. A memory flashed by him, a boy in the grade above him beating him up back in elementary school. He felt that same sense of vulnerability now and that same realization that as much as he would like to be, he wasn't the tough type. He wasn't a bruiser like that older boy back in school and he wasn't a fighter like Orion.

"Well, I'll need you out of the way then," Orion told him before looking at Sophia. She had cried out when Jason had gone down. "Don't be alarmed, Ms. Garcia. There'll be some bruising but no internal damage. He'll feel all right in an hour or so."

He then disappeared down the fire escape.

With Orion gone, Sophia ran over to Jason and turned him over. "Are you okay?" she cried. "Here, come on. Let's help you up."

She assisted him into a sitting position and sat behind him, letting him lean back for support. It somewhat alleviated the pain, Jason found, and eventually, the blinding extremity of it seemed to subside.

He winced a little as he tried to make himself more comfortable. "Ahhh…"

"Don't move. Don't move," Sophia calmed him. "Relax."

Jason did so.

"You came to save me," she said, shaking her head. "And I don't even know your name."

"It's Jason," he replied, wincing again.

"Jason," Sophia repeated. "Jason, do you think maybe I should try to get you downstairs? Maybe you can rest on the sofa or something."

Jason tried to get up. "The sofa? I have to get to the Graceville Hospital and stop that crazy son of a bitch before he gets someone killed."

"Jason," Sophia said, holding him down. "That crazy son of a bitch is too dangerous. And the way he moves… I'd bet he's had some military training somewhere and it wasn't the basic course."

"You're probably right," Jason said, "But he's going to get someone killed if he goes down there, I just know it."

"Warn that woman on the force," Sophia told him. "Your lady friend."

"All right," Jason murmured.

"And then I'm going to take you home."

"You can't."

"What?" Sophia asked him, giving him a wry look.

"That whole mysterious figure of the night act? I thought we were past that."

Jason sighed. "Yeah. All right. I don't think it's working with anyone anymore." He tried to stretch but his side still hurt like crazy. "Sophia…"

"Yes?"

"Could you get my bag?"

"Your bag?"

"Yeah, since we're done with the whole mystery thing as you put it, I always head out with a bag. And if I'm going to call Diane… Sorry, I mean, if I'm going to call that police officer I know whose name is absolutely not Diane, then I'm going to need my phone. And it's in my bag."

"Where's your bag?"

Jason waved a hand in the general direction. "Over there somewhere."

Sophia had a look around. "Found it," she said, bringing it over. She looked a bit surprised when Jason opened it up. "You keep your regular clothes in there?"

"Of course," he said. "I can't go leaving the house dressed like this, now can I? The neighbors might figure out my secret. There've got to be a *few* people at least who don't know it." He fumbled around in it until he found his untraceable and dialed Diane's number.

"Hi. Um, Jason, I'm kind of busy at the moment."

"Graceville Hospital?" he asked, groaning from a sudden shot of pain.

"Yeah. Everyone's here," Diane replied. "Are you all right? Are you hurt?"

"I'm okay," he managed, "but you've got trouble on the way."

"What's going on?"

"I just had a friendly chat with our new neighborhood vigilante Orion."

"Are you serious?"

"Yep," Jason told her in a mock cheerful tone. "We had a good old chat, we did." He flicked his left wrist to get some life back into numb fingers. "Yeah. He told me I was finished and that he'd solve Fringe City's problems from now on. You know, he's a generous guy."

"Jason…"

"And well, anyway, I tried to stop him but I think he's busted my kidneys. And now he's on his way down to Graceville Hospital to solve that little problem you've got there." He smiled. "Isn't that terrific?"

"Oh, my god," Diane murmured. "All right. We'll keep an eye out for him. Now, Jason, this guy assaulted you?"

"Oh, don't worry. I don't think he wanted to kill me. Just wanted to make me feel like crap for the next day or so."

"Do you need any help? Maybe we can get a car out there or something?"

Jason gave Sophia a wry look. "No thanks. I think I've trashed my mysterious figure of the night persona enough for one night."

"Jason…"

"No, I'm fine," he said, dropping the sarcasm. He realized he was acting strange. "I'm with a friend right now. You just concentrate on keeping Orion out of that hospital."

"I don't see how he can get in, but I'll tell everyone to stay alert."

"Diane," Jason told her. "Be careful. He's smart."

"Yeah," Diane replied. "That's what I'm afraid of. All right, I'd better go. Take care of yourself."

"Yeah," Jason murmured. "You too." He sighed as he hung up. "All right, Sophia."

She gave him a little smile as she held up his shirt from the bag. "Now since your mystery persona's so thoroughly and completely trashed, do you want to get changed downstairs before you go home?"

When they reached Jason's apartment, Sophia had to help him out of the car and into the elevator.

"Oh, crap," Jason muttered as they reached his floor.

"What?" Sophia asked.

"My partner's got a friend over," he said. "Um, I told her that I was babysitting your kids and you're a single mother."

"No problem," Sophia told him. "You slipped on the stairs. I got a call and came straight home and another friend of mine came back with me to help out with the kids."

"That was fast."

Sophia shrugged. "It wasn't hard."

Jason put the key in the lock and opened the door.

"Jason!" Angie said, getting up and rushing over. Gwendolyn hovered behind her.

"Hi, Angie," Sophia said, slipping effortlessly into her role play. "I'm so sorry. He slipped on the stairs in front of the building."

"It's all right," Jason told her, hobbling inside with Sophia's assistance until Angie could take over and help him over to the sofa. "It's more embarrassing than anything else. Really."

"Thanks, Sophia," Angie said.

"It was the least I could do," Sophia told her. She was good, Jason thought as he listened. The woman was a born actress. "Oh, I feel terrible. If I hadn't called him up to babysit for me, this would never have happened."

"Who's looking after the kids?" Angie asked her,

joining in the improvised performance.

"Vivian gave me a ride back from the party as soon as I'd heard what happened," Sophia explained, "and she's looking after them until I get back." She hesitated. "Actually, I'd better be heading back soon, I think. I'm really sorry about this."

"No, it's all right," Angie said. "Thanks for driving him home."

Sophia blushed. "Oh, as I said, it was the least I could do. And if you need anything, just give me a call, all right?"

"Thanks, Sophia," Jason called out as she left. With a groan, he sat down on the lounge.

Angie put his bag down in a corner of the room and then joined him, while Gwendolyn stood around looking awkward.

"Perhaps I should go too," she said.

"It's all right," Angie said, waving to the spare seat beside her.

"Is it bad?" Gwendolyn asked Jason as she sat down.

Jason smiled. "No, it's all right. I'm just stiff, that's all. I guess there might be some nasty bruises there in the morning but I'm fine." He tried to forget the thought of Orion breaking into a room full of armed men and hostages. "What's this?" he asked, pointing to the TV.

"Oh, some kind of panel talk show," Angie explained. "The first guest was kind of funny but this lady's a bit full of herself. We were watching a DVD earlier but it's finished now. Do you want to watch something else?"

"I'm good," Jason told her. "You guys watch whatever you want."

Angie got up. "Okay. Tell you what, I'll make you a coffee. I think I could do with another one myself. How about you, Gwendolyn?"

At the Graceville Hospital, Hutchens paced back and forth waiting for one of his officers who was on the radio. "They haven't said anything," the man said when he came back. "No demands. Nothing. Oh, they did tell us all to screw ourselves, but that was about it."

"So they honestly think they can just sit up there for months and get out at the end of it?" Hutchens asked. "In all my years of service, I've never seen anything like this."

"Sir!" someone shouted out.

Hutchens turned around. "What?"

"That chopper shouldn't be there!"

"What the—?" Hutchens watched as a police helicopter moved slowly towards the hospital roof.

A number of officers around him had drawn their

own conclusions as well and were looking his way.

"Orion's either commandeered or hijacked one of our aircraft!" Hutchens called out. "Snipers?"

One of the snipers looked through his scope and shook his head. "It's no good, sir. It's a hijacking. If we took a shot, we might hit the pilot. And the guy's wearing some kind of armor."

"All right." Hutchens pulled out his radio. "This is Commissioner Hutchens to anyone in the air. Orion has hijacked one of our aircraft and it looks like it's landing on the roof of the hospital. If you hurry, you might be able to take him out when he makes his exit."

"I read you," someone replied. "Give us forty seconds."

Which was soon, Hutchens knew, but it might not be soon enough. The hijacked helicopter was at that point right on top of the building. Then, moments later, the body of the vehicle was out of sight below the line of the roof and only the rotating blades and part of the cockpit were visible. Overhead, another helicopter appeared and several shots were fired from within it.

"Well?" Hutchens asked, fearing the worst.

"It's no good, sir," his man in the helicopter replied. "He's inside the building."

"Goodnight, Gwendolyn," Angie said as her friend

walked down the hallway to the elevator. She closed the door and turned to Jason. "So, what happened really then?"

"It was Orion," Jason told her, walking under his own steam again. "We talked at first. I managed to talk him out of hurting Sophia. We kept things rather civil for the most part and for a moment, I thought we were actually getting through to each other."

"So what went wrong?"

"What went wrong?" Jason said, sitting back on the lounge and picking up the remote. "What went wrong was that he told me he was going down to Graceville Hospital to single-handedly end the siege. Knowing his way of doing things, I tried to stop him."

"Jason, this guy kills with little more than brute strength and a knife."

"Trust me," Jason said, rubbing his side, "he doesn't need the knife. Anyway, I didn't try to physically restrain him or anything stupid. I tried to reason with him instead and when that didn't work, I just told him flat out that I wasn't going to let him."

"Well that was a brilliant idea," Angie muttered in disbelief. "And he snapped, did he?"

"Yeah," Jason muttered back, feeling as though he had now copped two beatings in the same evening. "He gave me a good blow to the side. But apparently, I'll be just fine so don't worry. He said something about no internal damage etcetera. He basically just wanted to make sure I wouldn't follow him." He found a news channel on the TV. "Which is why I need to see what's happened," he continued. "I mean I called Diane and gave her a heads up but—"

"Which is what you should have done in the first place," Angie said. "After that nut job had gone."

"Yeah, well, we all make mistakes sometimes," Jason told her, getting sick of the lecture. "So I screwed up? Fine. I know that. But I think it's fair to say I've learned my lesson, don't you think?"

"Thank god Sophia had the sense to drive you home," Angie said. She sighed and put her arm around his shoulder. "I'm sorry, Jason. You know, I just realized something. Before I met her tonight, Sophia was always just Martin Lamont's sister to me. But she's saved Diane and tonight, she stopped you from charging off after Orion. Tonight, I've realized she's a good person."

She leaned in close and held Jason's hand. "And if it weren't for you, Orion would have killed her. So yeah. You did screw up a little but you did a good thing tonight. And I'm proud of you."

She kissed him and for a moment, they held each other. It was only then that they heard the report on the TV.

"Yes, that's right, Mariane. The Special Weapons and

Tactical unit that went into the hospital exited the building about ten minutes ago."

"And what's been confirmed so far? We've heard several reports that indicate that Andy Kowolski is dead. What can you tell us?"

"This has been confirmed. Now the men who were in the building... there have been some rumors about them too but we can dispel them right now. The leader of the gang was in fact Mr. Kowolski's brother Daniel Kowolski, while the other men have yet to be identified."

"And I understand that there were a lot of innocent casualties in all of this."

"Yes, there were. Now that police have been able to get in closer, it's been confirmed that three officers outside the building were killed when Daniel and the other men accompanied him broke into the hospital and a further three were killed inside. The tragedy however was compounded by the actions of the vigilante known as Orion when, during the struggle with Daniel and his companions, one of the two hostages—twenty-four year old nurse Danielle Sutherland—was killed in the cross fire."

"And... uh... what about the other hostage?"

"Well, Mariane, obviously he's very distraught over what happened, but he is otherwise unharmed. He may have minor injuries, but that's not certain. Now, Orion... Wait."

The camera panned away from the reporter to Commissioner Hutchens, as he approached the line of reporters waiting just beyond the police barricades.

"It appears that the commissioner is making a statement."

A microphone with the Fringe City Central logo appeared in the centre of the frame, along with a dozen other microphones.

"Ladies and gentlemen," Hutchens began, *"as you are all aware, the siege is over and Andy Kowolski is dead, along with his brother and the men who were accompanying him. The tragedy obviously extends well beyond that, as I'm sure many of you have heard as well. We have lost seven others this evening, one nurse and six police officers."*

For a moment, the commissioner froze, unable to speak. He brushed a hand over one eye and took a moment to compose himself before continuing. *"A more detailed statement will be issued and made available to the public at a later point in time. This is not what I wish to discuss right now."* He swallowed. *"The loss of the six police officers is a tragedy that nothing could have prevented. While we can learn from hindsight, it cannot undo what is done in a situation like this. However, the loss of that young nurse's life could have been prevented. And it came about because of the reckless interference by the vigilante known to us as 'Orion'. And I wish to say a few words about this matter.*

"Firstly, to dispel a rumor. It is not our belief that this man is the same vigilante known to many as the Sentinel.

However, in saying this, I want to make it clear that while we do distinguish between individuals who choose to take the law into their own hands, we do not condone any of their actions in any way shape or form—and we implore each and every citizen out there to trust in your police force instead of taking such radical measures. Crime has decreased drastically *in this city over the past year and with your support and goodwill, we can make Fringe City a wonderful place to live. There is no need for these types of so-called heroics.*

"And to dispel another rumor. I wish to make it known that we are in no way associated with the Sentinel on any level whatsoever. As such, we can make no suppositions on his current whereabouts either. It is my hope however that perhaps at least one *vigilante has seen the error of his ways and has stepped back to allow the police of this city to do their jobs.*

"Because as we can see today, this kind of reckless interference with the hard work our police do can have tragic consequences. Orion may not have fired the weapon that killed Danielle Sutherland but he shares the responsibility for her death with the man who did. And for this reason, we will do everything *in our power to bring this man to justice."*

"Jason," Angie said.

Jason didn't seem to hear her. His eyes, moist with tears, were fixed on the screen in front of him.

"Jason," Angie repeated. She clasped his hands in her own when he turned to face her. "This wasn't your fault."

Jason shook his head. "Why did he do it? I told him there were hostages. He wouldn't listen."

"You couldn't have stopped him, Jason," Angie said. "You're not responsible for this."

SHADES OF GRAY

MAYOR ALISON ST. CLAIRE LISTENED AS Commissioner Hutchens finished.

"We've got problems," she said. "Don't we?"

"Yeah."

The mayor sighed. "And things were really beginning to look up."

"They were," Hutchens said.

Sitting between Hutchens and Charles Faulkner, Diane stirred. "I'm not sure about that. There's something going on with the mobs we don't know about."

"What's that?" St. Claire asked. She looked very tired, Diane thought. Looking after a city with the problems Fringe City had probably wasn't good for one's health. At least, doing it properly wasn't.

"The syndicates are lying very low and investigations into their holdings show that they're all pulling their funds out of their banks."

"Maybe they figure we're onto them," St. Claire suggested. "Maybe they're keeping their money in physical locations somewhere. Or maybe they're using offshore banks."

"Sure," Diane said. "But all the remaining syndicates at once? It's a little weird."

"Well," the mayor said, "we'll worry about it when we have to. Now, if we can get back to Orion for a moment, I understand that our unofficial friend who Hutchens publicly disowned last night had a run in with him shortly before that disaster at the hospital."

"Yes," Diane told her, sitting up and addressing the others as well. "I spoke with our friend this morning."

"What was he doing talking to Orion?" Faulkner asked.

"He was protecting someone from him."

Faulkner clasped and unclasped his hands. "I think you'd better give us the whole thing from the start."

"Our friend believed that Orion was systematically hunting down underworld figures with little regard for their particular crimes. The woman the Sentinel was protecting was related to a prominent syndicate leader—"

"Sophia Garcia," Faulkner said, nodding to himself.

"I didn't say that," Diane said. "Anyway, the Sentinel warned her that this man might target her and he received a call last night. She told him that her power had been cut and that she suspected Orion might have been behind it."

At this, Hutchens nodded as well, as if a piece of a puzzle had fallen into place. "Right. There was a memo on the notice board when I came into the office this morning. The woman called the station too and it was reported as a prank call. I'll fix it up later."

"Anyway," Diane continued, "the woman managed to hide in the building somewhere until the Sentinel got there. And he arrived right when Orion did. He said he talked Orion out of hurting the woman but then Orion said he had to go to the siege and sort it out." She paused. "The Sentinel tried to stop him from going but was incapacitated—" She waved a dismissive hand when she saw the concerned looks around her. "Oh, he's fine. Orion just slowed him down enough to stop him from following him to the hospital. Then our friend called me to tell me that Orion was on his way, which is how we knew to keep an eye out for him. And, well, the rest you know."

For a moment, no one said anything. "Um, there was something else as well," Diane added. "During their talk, Orion told the Sentinel that the person who had set the blast that took out the Bandit was Lady Vice."

"How did he figure that?" Faulkner asked.

Diane shrugged. "Orion didn't tell him. But that does bring us to another point. Now this is just a hunch but I'm not sure if Lady Vice is exactly what she seems to be."

"What do you mean?"

"Well, she targets these rich establishments, and amasses quite decent takings but nothing that will help her retire on an island somewhere. She also seems to desperately want people to pay attention to her, hence the performances. You know, the costumes, the erotic dancing and kissing girls and all that, but I've noticed a few things. She keeps people scared pretty well, and people always respond as if their lives are in fact threatened, but she hasn't killed anyone during these robberies. Not once. And neither have her girls."

"So she's not the killer we think?" St. Claire asked, trying to work out where Diane was going with this.

"I didn't say that," Diane said. "She had no problem blowing the Bandit away, if we can believe Orion. But I suspect she wouldn't kill an ordinary citizen."

"But she'd rob them."

"Yes, but I think she'd do that selectively as well," Diane replied. "Who knows? Maybe she robs the wealthier citizens in town because she fancies herself as some kind of champion of the poor."

St. Claire frowned. "Do you think she might be stealing from the syndicates as well?"

"I'm not sure," Diane admitted, impressed by how quickly the mayor caught onto her theory. "But I think it's possible. There's something else too. A while ago, a mid-level crime boss called Castella was thrown out of a window. I think in hindsight it was probably Orion, since he did the same thing to another mob boss. A guy called Creston."

Hutchens nodded. "And some of Castella's men were found dead from knife wounds, just like Creston's."

"But the Sentinel told me he'd heard a rumor that Lady Vice had taken credit for Castella. And I think that makes sense. It would have helped cement her reputation among the syndicates as a woman to fear."

"Allowing her to prey on them more easily," St. Claire said, following along. "Clever." She leaned back with a sigh. "Although it doesn't get us anywhere. So, what do we do about this? We can't have this woman terrorizing the city. And while I can't say I'm too sorry about the Bandit, if Lady Vice is blowing people away like that, then she's no different from Orion."

"Well, she hasn't killed any innocent people yet," Hutchens murmured.

"And she doesn't seem to claim the moral imperative that Orion seems to," Faulkner added.

St. Claire frowned. "I hate our jobs sometimes. There are so many gray areas to deal with."

Faulkner smiled. "Well, the world isn't black and white."

"No," St. Claire said, "but it'd be a hell of a lot easier

if it were. I still don't like the idea of this woman running around out there causing trouble though."

"Yeah, but I'm not sure how we'd go about finding her," Diane said. "I mean how would we do it? Head into every adult store in town and review their security footage to see who buys fetish gear?" She trailed off as she noticed the awkward silence in the room and the way the others avoided her gaze, St. Claire included. Diane chuckled. "All right. Forget that." In the end, they all had a little laugh.

"Well," St. Claire started again, recovering first, "I'm not sure how you'd bring Lady Vice in either." She hesitated. "Although to tell you the truth... I know that officially we *should* bring her in but if all she's doing now is cleaning up the city's underworld, I almost feel like we should just *let* her." She waved her hand in a half-hearted apologetic gesture to Faulkner. "Sorry, Charles."

Faulkner gave her an understanding smile. "It's all right, Ms. Mayor. Sometimes, I feel the same way about these things."

"Yeah," Diane joined in. "We all want to see the city cleaned up. And as long as the good people are safe and the bad guys are taken care of, we'd be happy. However, we can't let innocent people get caught in the cross fire."

"Right," Hutchens agreed, his tone grim. "So the

biggest problem right now is Orion. That nurse is dead now because of him. And all *she* ever did was help people, even those people the rest of us wouldn't give a damn about. Like the Bandit."

Silence settled on the office once more.

"All right," St. Claire said at last. "So what's important now is to bring in this loose cannon who's running around there before he gets any more bystanders killed." She looked at Hutchens. "Is there anything that either Mr. Faulkner or I can do to help?"

Hutchens sighed. He'd never felt this tired before in his life. "I wish there were, Ms. Mayor."

Faulkner spoke next. "Um, Diane. I wonder. On the phone, you told me that Orion had a Kevlar suit similar to what the Sentinel uses. And the police at the hospital who saw him reported this as well."

"The Bandit had a Kevlar suit too," Diane said. "Maybe they're available at all the local convenience stores."

Faulkner smiled. "Yes, maybe. But assuming they're not, where could someone like Orion get one?"

Diane shrugged. "I have no idea how you work Kevlar, but who knows? Maybe he could have swiped some S.W.A.T. armor and made some modifications to make it less bulky and allow him more freedom of movement."

Faulkner smiled. "Well, it might be nothing but I

just thought I'd mention it."

Gwendolyn weaved past the other people on the sidewalk. Thankfully, there were just enough. There were enough that she could walk unnoticed but there weren't so many that they would slow her down or block Sophia Garcia from her view.

The woman was about fifty yards ahead of her and while it was possible Sophia wouldn't recognize her after having seen her the previous night, Gwendolyn didn't want to take any chances.

Finally, Sophia stepped into a restaurant and Gwendolyn gave a sigh of relief. If she'd hailed a taxi, it would have made her job considerably more difficult.

She waited a little bit before heading in since the most important thing about staging coincidental meetings was that they were supposed to appear coincidental. Walking into the restaurant a second after Sophia would rather break that illusion.

When she did enter though, Gwendolyn slipped into her role with ease. She looked around for an empty table until her eyes met Sophia's. Then she gave her a look of recognition followed by surprise and walked over to her.

"Sophia?" she asked, maintaining an air of nervous

uncertainty.

Sophia gave her an awkward smile as she tried to place her. "Yeah... Have we...?"

Gwendolyn gave a laugh, sounding embarrassed. "Oh, I'm sorry. We didn't really meet. It's just, I saw you last night at Angie's place and I thought I recognized you. I'm Gwendolyn. Gwendolyn Taylor."

"Sophia Garcia," the woman replied. "Um... I haven't ordered anything yet. Would you like to join me?"

Gwendolyn smiled, slipping in her role as the rather shy but friendly woman Angie had met outside her local shops. She nodded, a little too quickly as befitted the performance. "Okay."

Ten minutes passed. They talked, they ordered and then they talked some more. For a little moment, Sophia turned away, her handbag on the table in front of her. With deft movements, Gwendolyn removed Sophia's cell phone and slid it into her own handbag before Sophia turned back.

"Oh," she said. "Would you excuse me one moment? I just need to go to the ladies room."

"Sure," Sophia replied.

"I won't be long."

Once she was out of Sophia's sight, Gwendolyn pulled out the phone and searched through the numbers stored there. There wasn't anything as obvious as *'The Sentinel'* or anything and it was clear that Sophia hadn't known his name was Jason when she had put his number in. But Gwendolyn knew it was in there somewhere. Then she found it. So simple, so elegant and so Sophia Garcia: *"My friend"*.

Gwendolyn pulled out her own phone, typed in the number and saved it. Then, deciding that she'd better look as though something were different when she got back to the table, she applied some additional make-up.

"Hello again," she said as she slid back into her seat at the table. "So, what were you saying before?"

"Oh, I was just saying that, you know," Sophia continued, "Jason's a good friend. He's a very good friend. So, did you know him back in university as well or was that just Angie?"

"Oh, I was mostly in Angie's classes," Gwendolyn said. "I don't remember Jason from university. Although, actually, I didn't really know either of them back then to tell you the truth." She glanced at the window. "Say, do you know that guy?"

Sophia looked. There was a man a few yards from the window with his back to the street.

"I thought he was looking at us," Gwendolyn said as she put Sophia's phone back where she'd found it.

Sophia shrugged. "I think he's just waiting for someone." She turned back. "I wouldn't worry about him."

"Yeah," Gwendolyn said. "You're probably right."

Meanwhile, their mutual friend was sitting down in a restaurant as well, opposite his regular dining partner Diane.

"I wish I could give you more," he said. "But anyway, that's how it all happened. As I told you on the phone."

Diane smiled. "No, it's all right. Anyway, it's good to see you're okay though. I was worried about you last night. But I think now Sophia's safe, there's no real sense in getting yourself involved any more. And actually, since Hutchens has to bring Orion in, it's probably better for *everyone* if you lie low."

Jason nodded. "Right, 'cause he can hardly go around condemning vigilantism while turning a blind eye to me."

"Jason," Diane said, seeing that he was a little upset, "he didn't mean what he said about you last night. You know that."

"Yeah. Sure. I know that."

"He had to say it."

Jason sighed. "Yeah, I understand. Anyway, it's not that. I've just got a lot on my mind right now."

"I know the feeling." Diane said. She reached over

and put a hand on his shoulder. "Jason, this thing with Orion. Don't let it get personal. You didn't get that girl killed last night."

Jason nodded. "Yeah, I know. Angie said the same thing."

"Angie?"

"Yeah, here goes another piece of my mystery persona. Angie's my partner."

"How long have you been together?"

"Seven years."

"Married?"

"In every sense of the word really. But just not in name."

"Why don't you tie the knot officially?"

Jason shrugged. "I don't know. We've always wanted to but we've just been too busy."

"I think you should make the time," Diane told him, smiling. She then shook her head. "Oh, I'm sorry. I shouldn't have called you today. It's just that we've got *nothing* on Orion."

Jason gave her a thoughtful gaze. "I think he's had military training at some stage," he offered.

Diane frowned. "What makes you say that?"

"What kind of guy can deliver a blow that can render you unable to move properly for the better part of an hour, while knowing that it won't cause any lasting internal damage? They don't teach you that in school."

Diane was quiet for a moment.

"What?" Jason asked.

"And what kind of guy has enough forensic expertise to solve a cold case that nobody else could?" she asked. "And could a guy with that level of expertise in one field of science have enough technical know-how to also modify S.W.A.T. armor to make his own custom Kevlar suit?"

"Do you think—?" Jason started but Diane cut him off.

"I think I've probably done enough thinking out loud, that's what I think," she told him. "And when I say that I don't want you to be involved in this anymore, I mean that as your friend."

"I understand," Jason replied. "And speaking as your friend, I appreciate it."

Commissioner Hutchens awoke with a start. "Wha—?" It took him a moment to gauge his surroundings and work out where he was. He had fallen asleep at his desk and Diane was standing in his doorway.

Hutchens looked down in embarrassment and sighed. "I'm sorry. I've never fallen asleep at my desk before."

Diane gave him a little smile. "It's been a long day

for all of us, sir. Anyway, it's after midnight."

"Jesus. I must have been here for hours."

"Yeah, well I was surprised to see you still here," Diane told him. "So, anyway, I thought I'd better wake you up."

"Sure..." Hutchens said, blinking. "Hang on, why are *you* still here? You were on the day shift."

"I was doing some research," Diane replied. "Actually, since you're still here, maybe you might like to see this." She handed him a folder.

"What is it?" Hutchens asked, struggling to focus his weary eyes.

Diane sat down. "I think it's the real identity of Orion."

"How did you—?" Hutchens shook his head.

"The Sentinel thought that Orion might have had military training of some kind," Diane explained. "And his reasoning seemed sound." She rested her elbows on the table and Hutchens saw dark circles under her eyes. "Also, to work out who the Specter was, he must have had a substantial knowledge of forensics and of wider investigative techniques too. He'd be good at science in general, I think, but I thought he must have been interested in police work at some stage given the forensics expertise."

She stifled a yawn and blinked. "So, um... So anyway, I wondered why he wasn't on the payroll and, well, to cut a long story short, I came up with a theory that he was someone who had tried to become a police officer at some stage but had failed. Also, if he had made some friends in the process, it's possible he could have acquired some S.W.A.T. armor from one of them and modified it for his costume.

"So I spent the afternoon trawling through old applications looking for any matches on an applicant who had military experience, forensic training and finally, who had been turned down, and I came across the one you've got there now."

"Why was he turned down?" Hutchens asked, the folder still closed in his hands.

"He failed his psych evaluation," Diane said. "His examiners thought he exhibited too much aggression. I thought that was rather telling. Actually, the report indicated that he would have made an exemplary police officer otherwise."

Hutchens turned the folder over and looked at the name of the applicant. "Derek Bradley," he read out loud. "Interesting name."

"Derek Bradley. Post-graduate qualifications in forensic science, a dual under-graduate degree in physics and engineering and to top it all off, he also enlisted in the armed forces and had a short stint as a Navy SEAL."

Hutchens took a deep breath, then he put the folder

in a desk drawer and locked it. "Jeez. Well, if he's not Orion, then he's a pretty strong contender for prime suspect." He stepped out from behind his desk and put a hand on Diane's shoulder. "You know, Diane. It's late and I guess you'll probably put this down to the fact that I'm tired and that it's been an emotional couple of days for everyone ... but I mean every word of what I'm about to tell you. I've never worked with a finer officer. Ever." He shook his head. "Here I was sleeping at my desk, while you were blazing a trailhead into the investigation all day and now you may well have cracked it."

"It's kind of you to say so," Diane replied. "But I think there's a little bit of fatigue and emotion coming through, don't you think?"

Hutchens laughed a little. "I don't know. Maybe you're right."

"Anyway, you can have a look at the file in the morning," Diane told him. "Do you need a ride home? Would you like me to arrange a lift?"

Hutchens slumped his shoulders, still exhausted despite the hours of sleep at his desk. "Just find someone on duty in there who'll give us both a ride and I'll give 'em the rest of the night off."

Gwendolyn and a group of female friends were

celebrating in her apartment.

"I think a toast is in order," one of her friends, Sonya, announced. "We've just seen McGraw hauled off on the evening news. With O'Reilly and Cooper out of the picture as well, that's it. We have officially cleared out the syndicates of Fringe City. So here's to us."

The toast was echoed with rejoinders around the room.

"And," Sonya added, "to the woman who made it all possible. Our sensuous but dangerous femme fatale, Lady Vice."

"To Lady Vice!"

"There you go, Gwendolyn," Sonya said as everyone went back to their own conversations. "The planning, the groundwork, the public heists to build up the 'Lady Vice' myth... We did it."

Gwendolyn pursed her lips for a moment. "We did. And I think it certainly deserves some celebration but we're not in the clear yet."

Sonya frowned. "What are you talking about?"

"We've got a new problem that needs to be taken care of, something that wasn't in the original plan." Gwendolyn hesitated. The others weren't going to like this. "One last job."

"Wait a minute," one of the other women called out, overhearing the remark.

The room went silent.

"Gwendolyn," the woman told her, "McGraw was it. That was the end goal of the plan. Actually, since Lamont's sister knocked him off and pushed the schedule ahead by a good six months, it went better than perfectly."

Gwendolyn smiled. Perhaps it was a good idea to lighten the mood a little first. "Well, that's technically impossible. Right, Claudia?"

Claudia laughed. "Yeah, Gwendolyn's right, Kathy."

"Nerds. Both of you," Kathy scoffed but without any sting.

"Hey, you're talking about one of our best Lady Vices there," Claudia said, nodding at Gwendolyn. "One of the sexiest bad girls in Fringe City."

"Well, Gwen's got the hips and the thighs to pull it off, but she's not Lady Vice at the moment, she isn't."

"Even with her firm but supple… ?"

"Shut up, Claudia," Kathy said, rolling her eyes. "You know, sometimes I wondered whether the whole lesbian act really *was* an act for you."

"And what would be wrong if it wasn't?" Claudia asked.

"Yeah," Sonya said, playing along. "I find that statement homophobic, Kathy."

"All right," Kathy replied, chuckling. "There'd be

nothing wrong. At all."

"Don't worry, Kath," Claudia told her, giving her a playful slap on the arm. "I just like embarrassing you."

"Anyway," Sonya said. "I think Gwendolyn wanted to make a point, Kathy."

"Yeah, I know, but I disagree."

"You haven't heard it yet, Kathy," Gwendolyn said.

"You said we've got some more work to do," Kathy told her. "I disagree with that."

"Hang on a second," Sonya reminded her. "The job's not finished yet anyway. We're not keeping all that mob money, remember? We've got to think about how we can use it to help the disadvantaged communities in the city."

"It's out of my expertise," Kathy countered. Then she relented. "But yeah, I'll help. Of course. I just meant I was through putting our necks at risk."

"Our necks are still at risk," Gwendolyn said, getting back to business. "Along with the necks of other innocent people as well. And we've got to carry off one more public heist to solve the problem."

"Orion," Sonya agreed. "Right. He doesn't know we're on his side. No one knows we were actually trying to help the city."

"Yeah," Kathy said. "Thankless work."

"But the point is he's going to come after us," Sonya said.

"But then..." one of the other girls joined in. "Well... I take it the plan is to pull this other heist as a trap to lure Orion in, right?"

"Yeah, basically," Gwendolyn said.

"But then we'll bring ourselves back into the public eye again and we'll be public enemy number one," the girl told her. "I don't like that. At the moment, everything's all nicely wrapped up. No one really understood our deal but if we don't do anything else, we can now just fade away."

"We can't, Deborah," Gwendolyn explained. "Orion won't let us fade away. He found the Specter didn't he? And it'd been almost a year since his last killing spree."

"But the Specter was different," Deborah said.

"Yeah," another girl, Belinda, joined in.

"That'll make no difference to him," Gwendolyn told them. "You know, he tried to kill Sophia Garcia as well. And that was just because she'd done a small job for Martin Lamont."

"She was an accomplice to the murder of Danny Vincent and his gang," Belinda pointed out. "She helped Lamont get Burges to contact the Bandit."

"Something she probably didn't have a choice in," Gwendolyn countered.

"Hey, how do you know that Orion tried to kill her?" Deborah asked.

"Because the Sentinel saved her life," Gwendolyn said, taking a moment to brace herself for the shock waves. "And I'm friends with him and his partner." She waited while the group absorbed that in stunned silence and then continued. "Also, he's best friends with Captain Diane Reilly, a woman with close ties to the commissioner, the D.A. and even the mayor. In fact, it was by following her that I found the Sentinel."

"And how did you get from following him to being friends?"

Gwendolyn shrugged. "I found out who his partner was and then did a little bit of work on finding out about her background. Then I arranged a chance meeting and pretended I'd been one of her classmates back in university. Anyway, the point I wanted to make is that Orion will have no qualms about trying to track us down and we need to set a trap for him. And I intend to get the Sentinel to help us."

"Right," Kathy said, her tone doubtful. "But I'm under the impression he's friends with Gwendolyn Taylor here, not Lady Vice."

"That won't matter," Gwendolyn told her.

"You'll approach him like this then?" Kathy asked her. "As yourself?"

"No," Gwendolyn said. "I'm going to call the untraceable cell phone that he uses and talk to him as Lady Vice. I want to be able to go back to being

Gwendolyn Taylor with these people when it's all finished."

"But he won't listen to you as Lady Vice," Kathy said.

"I'll persuade him," Gwendolyn replied. "I'll tell him everything I need to to make him come around."

"And he can take out Orion?" Sonya asked her.

Gwendolyn hesitated. "Well, no. Not by himself. Orion's too dangerous."

"What?" Kathy asked. Even Sonya and Claudia, the most supportive pair in the group, seemed a little taken aback by that.

"If I follow you, Gwendolyn," Sonya said, "and I know how you think so I *do*, then it sounds like you're going to put a lot on the line here."

"You're right."

"Derek Bradley isn't on a single residential record in the city limits," Hutchens said the following morning. He and Diane, along with a dozen others had been on the case since they'd come into work the previous day.

"He's not on a single residential record in the entire country," Diane corrected him, sitting across from him at the table with the rest of the team, "which means wherever he is, he's living under an alias."

"Anyway," Hutchens said, "it sounds like he

probably *is* the guy we're looking for. But if we've got no idea where he's hiding, that's not going to help us much."

Another officer sighed. "So I guess we're going to have to just go through the residential records, looking for any names that aren't in the national census or are registered for other locations around the city or the country. Man. That could take ages."

"Maybe," Hutchens shrugged. "Maybe not. I'll talk to someone on the I.T. side of things and see if they can make a program that can automate the process." He rubbed his eyes. "Anyway, thanks everyone. You've done good work. In fact, I'll tell you what. Lunch is on me. Come on."

"Hey, man, it's been a while."

"Yeah," Jason agreed. "Sorry about that."

On the other end of the line, there was a short pause. "So…" Geoffrey said. "Everything good with you?"

"Yeah, yeah. We're fine. Um, I'm sorry I couldn't make it to see you off."

"Forget it."

"No, no. I wanted to be there. But something came up," Jason told him. "Actually, a lot of things have come up in the past little while."

"I know," Geoffrey said. "I still keep tabs on the place. And now you've got that nut job Orion running loose down there as well. That thing at the hospital was all over the news up here."

"I think it was all over the news everywhere."

"Sorry, man. I've got to go. Charlotte's back. Take care of yourself, all right?"

Jason swallowed. It wasn't too long ago that he and Geoffrey were the best of friends and already, he could feel them drifting apart. It was amazing how thoroughly a little bit of time and distance could separate people.

"Yeah," he replied. "I've got to go too. I'll talk to you later."

"Okay, man. See ya."

Geoffrey hung up first and for a little while, Jason just stood on the spot. He might have stayed there even longer if it hadn't been for the faint vibrations of his untraceable. He picked it up. "Hey, it's me."

"Well, it is a pleasure to speak to you at last," a woman on the other end of the line said, her voice exhibiting an elegance and sensuousness that even someone like Sophia Garcia would envy. And yet, after hearing just that one sentence, Jason was left with a strange impression of familiarity. He had heard this voice before, he knew. He just didn't know where.

"You would perhaps know me best as Lady Vice,"

the woman told him.

"How did you get this number?" Jason asked her, a numb sensation coming over him.

"I got it without harming anyone you care about," Lady Vice assured him.

"I'll take your word on it," Jason said. "What do you want?"

"I want your help. We need to bring in Orion. I can set the bait and you know the people who can trap him. Captain Diane Reilly is well connected. We can do this."

"But why would we work with you?" Jason asked. "You're worse than Orion is."

"Am I? How many people have I killed, Jason?"

"How do you know my name?"

"You haven't answered my question."

"And you haven't answered mine."

"I learned your name when I found your number."

And then, like a weight crashing to the ground, it all fell into place.

"Gwendolyn," Jason murmured.

The woman on the other end of the line sighed. "All right. It's me. I'm sorry, Jason. I didn't want you to know."

"I lost my best friend because of you," Jason told her.

"I never would have killed—"

"Oh, you didn't kill him," he said. "But with that latest act of yours, you scared him out of town. He and his fiancé live in Boston now."

"I'm sorry. Maybe, this'll be easier if I come over."

"I can't see how. You terrorized my friends."

"I know," Gwendolyn replied. "And I'm sorry. But my true targets were always the city's syndicates."

Jason waited since Gwendolyn was going somewhere with this.

"These men have left families in poverty and destitution. They've created armies of drug addicts. They've butchered and killed police officers, informers and anyone down on their luck wanting to get out of the vicious cycles these men have dragged them into. Along with the women I work with, I made a pact to rid the city of them."

Jason sighed. He could certainly relate to that. "But what of the shows? The prancing around in the leather get-up and terrorizing innocent people?"

"A necessary evil, I'm afraid," Gwendolyn explained. "Our campaign against the syndicates of the city required the creation of an illusion we could use to manipulate the city's syndicates when the time was right. We tried only to terrorize people who could afford to be terrorized, of course, but the illusion had to look real. To everyone. And Jason, you became the catalyst that allowed us to get our work done sooner rather than later. Because now, there are no crime syndicates operating in Fringe City."

So that was why the mobs had been quiet. Gwendolyn and her friends had found some way to take them out of the game.

Jason nodded, regaining his composure. "All right. What do you want me to do?"

"Well, first of all, I want you to promise that you won't tell Angie about this. Maybe later, when the time is right, we'll both tell her but now is definitely not the time and, believe it or not, I really like Angie."

"It's not hard to believe." Jason sighed. "I really like Angie too. Although, you didn't go to university with her, did you?"

"No," Gwendolyn said. "But I needed a way to get into your social circle."

"I don't like the fact you manipulated us, Gwendolyn. Particularly her."

"I know," Gwendolyn told him. "I didn't want to, believe me, but when I realized what Orion's long-term plans were, I had to do something."

"Wait a minute, you've been planning this moment since you first knew about Orion?"

"Well, since I first knew how dangerous he was. Orion threw a spanner in the works in terms of our overall scheme to bring this city back onto its feet and I knew I needed to work on a contingency plan right away. And Jason, you're a part of that plan."

"Thanks for asking me first."

"Well, I'm asking you now. Will you help?"

SHOWTIME

THE GRAND BALLROOM ON THE TOP FLOOR OF the Sapphire Hotel was alive with bright lights as the private function got started. As the small group of well-dressed people danced away, a handful of them noticed the alluring women walking onto the stage beside the musicians. And if those particular women were part of the show, then the band had the wrong venue.

Lady Vice edged up to the female singer, who froze when she saw who was standing beside her. Lady Vice smiled and took her microphone. "Take a hike, dear." She nodded to the rest of the band. "All of you."

The musicians beat a hasty retreat through the stage exit. Some of those on the dance floor tried to get out as well but they found their way barred by more of Lady Vice's girls, with these women carrying guns.

"Good evening, ladies and gentlemen," Lady Vice announced, raising the microphone. Not that she needed it with this particular girl's natural voice projection.

"What the hell do you want?" one of the bolder guests asked, stepping in front of the group.

"For the moment?" Lady Vice said. "All I want is for you to wait quietly. The police should be here shortly to hear our demands."

On the top floor of the building opposite the hotel, another of Lady Vice's girls answered a call on her cell phone. "Tricia."

"The band's gone and the others are in place."

Tricia nodded. "All right. I'll make the call." She hung up and dialed a new number. "Is this Fringe City Central?"

There was a short reply on the other end.

"I'm calling across the road from the Sapphire Hotel. Someone said the cops are on their way and that Lady Vice is holding some guests hostage on the top floor."

There was another brief response.

"Well, I hear sirens but I can't see any police here. But you could call them." Tricia smiled as she listened. "You're welcome," she said. After hanging up, she turned to the S.W.A.T. commander beside her. "Well, we should get our coverage soon."

"Right," the commander said, getting out his radio. "Now, let's give 'em something to cover." He flicked the radio on. "All positions, move in and assemble outside the building. Commander Harrington, you're going to be our face on the TV. Good luck, everyone."

"This is Mariane O'Hara," Fringe City's most popular reporter announced to the camera, walking backwards past the police cars with their flashing lights, "and I'm reporting live from outside the Sapphire Hotel, where it is believed that—even as we speak—Lady Vice is holding a group of people hostage in the ballroom on the top floor."

She stepped over to a police officer. "I'm standing here with Commander Harrington, who is currently the senior officer on the scene. Commander, what can you tell us about what's happening here tonight?"

"All I know," Harrington replied, enjoying his little moment in the sun, "is that there are a number of people up there in that ballroom and we've got to be careful how we handle things or we could endanger those people."

"Now, has Lady Vice issued any demands?"

"Not yet, but I imagine she'll be arranging some means to communicate with us shortly. At the moment however, all we can do is wait."

· · ·

Up in the ballroom, Hutchens noticed some of the other officers around him getting twitchy. "Let's stay in role, people," he cautioned them, giving a little nod to Lady Vice. "We're terrified hostages, remember?" He reached for the little microphone under his collar. "Position two, what's going on out there?"

"Mariane's interviewing Harrington. Other reporters are in position. We've got coverage from half a dozen news services out here. Any prediction on Orion's ETA?"

"We don't even know if he'll take the bait," Hutchens replied. "But keep it tight anyway. I'd better get back to role playing."

Jason watched the hotel from an adjoining rooftop. He remembered that when Orion had left Sophia's place, he had used the fire escape which meant he didn't have the kind of gadgets he used for getting around. Not for the first time that evening, Jason wondered how airtight Gwendolyn's plan really was. However, since everyone was involved now, it had to work.

"Think, damn it, think," he muttered to himself. He wished he had some of those S.W.A.T. guys to talk to. Or anyone. "He's not going to come in from the roof," he said, thinking out loud. "He can't." He pulled out his radio and flicked it on. "Hello?"

"Who's this?" came an abrupt reply.

"The Sentinel. I'm going to swing across to the hotel. Don't shoot me."

"You listen to me, you little son of a bitch. I don't like any of this but I'm going along with it because that's what we arranged. So stick to the plan. If you go across now and Orion's down there watching, you'll ruin everything."

"Jesus, buddy, calm down," Jason told him, trying to keep himself under control. "I thought we were on the same side here. I don't think Orion's going to come in from the roof. He's going to come up from under the building."

"That's nice, hot shot, but the entrance to the underground parking lot's in full view of at least fifty armed officers. So keep quiet and stay put."

Jason switched off the radio. "Screw him," he muttered to himself. Getting in position, he fired one end of his double sided grappling hook at the hotel roof and the other at the roof he was standing on. Then he slid across. No one was going to shoot him, he knew, but that S.W.A.T. guy was going to be pissed. However, Jason could live with that.

He retracted the cord the moment he was across. The little police radio he was carrying beeped. "Look, buddy, I—"

It wasn't his hot tempered friend in the other

building. "I just got a call from the S.W.A.T. commander across the street," Diane murmured. "Would you mind telling me what you're doing?"

"I think Orion's going to come from under the building."

"How? Go in through the sewers and blow a hole in the underground car park?"

"I hadn't thought of that," Jason admitted. "Thanks."

"Jason—"

"I've got to go." He flicked the radio off and headed for the rooftop stairs.

From her position with the back-up officers on the floor below the ballroom, Diane flicked the radio to another frequency. "This is Captain Reilly."

"Go ahead."

"Send a group down into the underground car park, but tell them to be discreet. I don't want them scaring the quarry off but we believe Orion might attempt to make his entrance from down there."

"Got it."

"Oh, and Captain? Do it quietly."

"Understood."

• • •

Angie frowned as she watched the live reports on the television. There was something very strange about it all. Jason had been rather vague about what he was up to before he'd gone out and now there was this massive emergency downtown.

She then noticed something she'd missed earlier. Jason's untraceable was sitting on the kitchen bench. Forgetting about the news for a moment, she walked over to the kitchen and picked it up. She held it for a moment, looking at it. Jason had never left on one of his Sentinel errands before without taking the blasted thing with him. Something was definitely up. She played with the buttons for a moment, looking at recent calls. One of the numbers brought about a sense of déjà vu that was too strong to just be a feeling. Angie then got her own phone and compared the numbers in her contact list. It didn't take long to work out why the number had triggered the response. It was Gwendolyn's.

Then Angie starting seeing her friend in a new light. For instance, Gwendolyn always tied her hair back, hiding its length and luxurious texture. And although she didn't seem to know how to flaunt it, she had quite a figure as well…

Angie sighed. "Of course she knows how to flaunt it, you idiot." She sat back on the sofa in a slump. It wasn't hard to paint the rest of the picture now she had started. She pictured Gwendolyn in contacts, her hair hanging loose around her shoulders, dark lipstick and eyeliner, a leather corset hugging her midriff. It wasn't hard at all, and the picture was that of Lady Vice.

This was her new best friend and while Angie had rather been under the impression that this woman was a dangerous psychotic, she was apparently great friends with Jason. Gwendolyn, as her cheerful self, might have called Jason on his regular cell phone. However, of the two personas the woman adopted, only Lady Vice would have cause to call him on his untraceable. It also meant that not only was Gwendolyn not what she seemed but Lady Vice wasn't either. Whatever was going on though, one thing was certain. Both Jason and Gwendolyn had some explaining to do.

Flinging the untraceable to the other side of the sofa, Angie settled back to watching the live news bulletin. However, she couldn't stop the wheels from turning inside her head. They were working together on something and if the Lady Vice persona was just an act with an ulterior motive...

"Jesus," she whispered. "It's a trap for Orion." With that realization, any thoughts of reprimand dissipated. All she wanted now was for Jason and Gwendolyn to come back safe and sound.

• • •

A faint vibration through the floor was Jason's first warning. He kept heading down. Then he heard gunshots. He called Diane on the radio. "Hey!"

"What's that noise?" she asked. "He's here?"

"He's downstairs. You can hear the gunfire. Listen, why don't you get the hotel staff to lock the elevators down? Then I can pin him on the stairs."

"Jason, you're back-up, remember? Observe and advise. What do you think you're doing putting yourself in danger like this?"

"I'm just trying to stop this man."

"Think about Angie. Or think about me if that doesn't work, 'cause I'll have to think about what to tell her when you don't come back."

Jason paused on the stairs. Somewhere below him, he heard a door open and light footsteps. He had him. He could feel it. And yet...

"Jason," Diane's voice cut through the fog that had come over him.

"Jason?"

Beads of sweat broke out on his forehead, rubbing beneath his helmet and sliding down the inside of his visor.

"I'm here," he replied.

"A S.W.A.T. team's on the stairwell above you and the unit in the parking lot is on its way."

"I thought they were down," Jason said.

"So did I. But another officer was just talking to them then. Orion hot-wired a car and blocked the basement entrance to the stairwell. You heard the unit blasting their way through it. And now they're heading for the ground floor entrance."

"Okay. Um…"

"Jason. I'm saying this as your friend."

"Yes?"

"Get off that stairwell right *now*!"

He didn't know whether it was the words or the way Diane had said them but Jason found himself opening the nearest door before he even realized he was doing. And as he closed it behind him, he breathed a sigh of relief. He didn't know exactly how the S.W.A.T. units were going to pin Orion in place. It was unlikely that a man of his expertise was just going to sit on the stairwell between two of those units and wait for them to catch him. He'd probably duck out a door and then try to pry open an elevator and haul his way up the cables. Some cute Navy SEAL, action movie crap or something like that. However, Jason realized it wasn't his problem.

Gwendolyn had provided the bait. Jason had figured out which way Orion would try to get through the trap and the rest was now up to the police.

. . .

"I don't suppose I have to tell you all that I want absolutely no record of this," St. Claire said after everything was said and done. She looked around at everyone in the ballroom. The ones who'd been there originally to play the roles of frightened guests had done pretty well, she thought. Herself included. Although now there were a few more people present.

"Anyway, we have Orion in custody now," she said. "Although he did give our S.W.A.T. teams a good run for their money."

"Navy SEAL training, I suppose," Hutchens suggested, "and a bit of creativity on the side."

"Yes," Faulkner agreed. He'd played another one of the guests as well. "And as agreed, I'll argue for some psychiatric counseling for the man when he appears in court. I can't help feeling sorry for him when we're all a little guilty of the same type of law-bending."

"Now, now, Charles..." St. Claire started.

Faulkner sighed. "No. We're all as bad as each other now. But anyway, let's wrap this up so we can move on to making a brighter future for the people of this city."

"Agreed," the mayor said. She looked at Sonya, who was playing Lady Vice that evening, at Jason, and then the commissioner. "Eric, what kind of bullshit are we going to give the media about all this?"

"Got it covered," Hutchens replied, looking up as he

recalled what he had worked out earlier. "Lady Vice and her gang used a hostage to get down the stairwell to the basement once they realized the police weren't going to negotiate with them. They found the hole that Orion had made breaking into the parking lot and escaped through it, letting the hostage go."

"And of course, for reasons of privacy, the identities of the hostages will not be released and no one will be giving interviews," St. Claire added.

"Right," Hutchens told her. "Now, some people saw the Sentinel on the scene but we weren't aware of it. And if he was, we couldn't find any evidence of his having been here."

"Good enough for me." St. Claire turned to Sonya. "Now, miss, officially Lady Vice is still going to be at large but I'm not going to see her or her girls in the news again, am I?"

"No, Ms. Mayor."

"Good. So keep those costumes in your bedrooms."

Sonya smiled. "Okay."

"Now, the Sentinel," St. Claire said, taking a slow step. "It's nice to finally meet you. However, I'd be very grateful if you could keep yourself out of the papers too. If you want to hang on to *your* costume for sentimental reasons, that's fine, but keep it in a cupboard out of sight."

"Sure."

"And if you want to go swinging around with your fancy grappling hooks, do it someplace else."

Jason nodded. "Got it."

"Um, Ms. Mayor…"

St. Claire turned around and saw another one of Lady Vice's girls standing next to Jason. "Yes?"

"I'm sorry about those people we robbed to build up our street reputation," Gwendolyn said. "However—"

The mayor nodded. "Yes, I've been filled in on the details. You used it to acquire the funds of all the syndicates and drive them out of town."

Which was one way of saying it, Gwendolyn supposed. "Well, yes. But, um, what I wanted to say was that my friends and I never spent a cent of the money we stole during our publicity stunts. We never used the jewelry, we never made a call on a cell phone that didn't belong to us and we didn't touch any of the credit cards."

The mayor sighed. "I think I know what you're going to say, and it's kind of you, but we can hardly return that stuff without people getting suspicious."

"Maybe you can find a hidden stash somewhere and say that while Lady Vice left the premises before the police could arrive, some of the items that she'd stolen were left behind. Don't give specifics, and don't let anyone catch onto the fact that *everything* her gang ever stole was still there. Just put an announcement in the paper or something so that people can come in and see if anything belonging to them was recovered. Then maybe in a month or so, you can start contacting various individual owners directly."

"I suppose that might work," St. Claire conceded. "Eric?"

"Yeah?"

"Maybe later, we can see about moving all of these things into the police headquarters somewhere."

"No problem."

"Now," St. Claire said, turning back to Gwendolyn, "these syndicate funds."

"Two hundred and twelve million, four hundred and sixty-two thousand dollars," Gwendolyn told her. "And a little bit more in the hundreds and the tens columns."

St. Claire tried to find her voice. Tried and failed.

"That was what you were going to ask me, wasn't it?"

"Yeah," St. Claire said, finally able to speak again. "That's a lot of money."

"It's going back into the community," Gwendolyn told her. "All of it."

"I'm sorry?"

"Look, these syndicates bled neighborhoods across the city dry and they ruined thousands of people's lives. We want to use the money to help those people."

"How?"

"Charities and various projects and suchlike."

"I think charities have to account for where their funds come from though," St. Claire pointed out.

"Various anonymous donations," Gwendolyn told her. "Through a number of small organizations over a period of several years. We've got it worked out."

"Well…"

"If they need any help down the line, Ms. Mayor," Faulkner said, stepping in and giving her a cheerful smile, "I'd be happy to lend my services. Strictly on my own time of course."

Jason met Diane the following day.

"I just wanted to thank you. You know. For helping me let go."

"So the Sentinel's gone for good?" Diane asked.

"Yeah, I'd say so."

"I'm glad to hear it."

"I'm glad to say goodbye to him too, to be honest."

"Although *we* don't have to say goodbye," Diane said.

"I didn't say we had to."

"But you were going to." Diane smiled. "I think I've got you fairly well pegged now, Jason."

"Yeah, you're right. I sometimes act as if my life's a movie."

"Yeah, well. Acknowledging the problem's the first step."

"Yeah, that's true. And you know, I'd like to keep in touch."

"I'd like to keep in touch too," Diane told him. "And I hope that when you and Angie finally decide to tie the knot, that you don't forget to invite me to the wedding."

"I won't." Jason was quiet for a moment. Then his lips formed a smile.

He *had* been imagining his life as a movie, imagining that friends had left when they hadn't. Geoffrey hadn't given him the proverbial cold shoulder over the phone. He'd just been too busy to talk to him. And Diane's comment had reminded him about the letter he and Angie had just got from Geoffrey, inviting them to his wedding in Boston. Things hadn't ended up too badly after all.

"Jason?"

He snapped out of his introspective mood. "Oh, I was just thinking about something."

"Yeah. That was kind of obvious."

"Diane?"

Both Diane and Jason turned to the newcomer. The man had been on his way to another table when he'd seen them.

"Oh, hi, Nathan," Diane greeted him. "How are you?"

"Great. Great. You on your lunch break?"

"No, it's my day off."

Nathan smiled. "Cool. I'm on an early afternoon-evening shift so I've got to grab something to bite." He nodded at Jason. "Hi there."

"Hey."

"Oh, Nathan," Diane said. "This is Jason. He's a friend of mine. He works in a high school."

"My condolences," Nathan said to Jason, shaking his hand. "My sister works at a high school too. It sounds crazier than police work."

"I imagine it's a close call," Jason said, giving Diane a knowing smile.

"Yeah, you may be right," Nathan grinned. "Anyway, I've got to run." He gave Diane a friendly pat on the shoulder. "See you next week, Diane. Nice to meet you, Jason."

"You too, Nathan."

"See you, Nathan," Diane called out. She watched him leave then turned back to Jason. "Well, I'm hungry. How about you?"

. . .

After lunch with Diane, it was dinner at home with Angie and Gwendolyn. He and Gwendolyn came clean with the whole thing of course. In the end, there was no way they could keep that secret.

"Well, I'm glad you guys told me all of that," Angie said. "Although, to tell you the truth, it wasn't exactly a revelation anymore."

"You knew?" Jason asked.

"I joined the dots," Angie said. "It wasn't too hard."

Jason shook his head. "I've said it before. You could have been a great detective."

Gwendolyn then reached over and held Angie's hands in her own. "Oh, Angie. I'm sorry I lied to you. But I really needed Jason's help to pull everything off last night. But you know, I feel as though you and I have become really close. And I don't want to ruin that."

For a moment, Angie felt like flinging her hands away. For a moment, she contemplated telling her— and Jason—to get out of her life and go and live together somewhere else. They'd make a great couple, she thought to herself. The Sentinel and Lady Vice.

However, the moment passed and when she saw the sincerity in Gwendolyn's eyes, she was ashamed she had even thought that. Gwendolyn and Jason had come clean. They hadn't tried to hide what had happened from her. And while Gwendolyn had done some things that she could never do, she was still the kind and caring Gwendolyn who had so endeared herself to her when they'd first met. And the fact that the story about being in university together wasn't true didn't matter either. She liked Gwendolyn and Gwendolyn liked her and as far as friendship was concerned, that was all that mattered.

"It's all right," Angie told her, squeezing her hand. Sudden tears came to her eyes and she pulled her friend to her in a tight embrace. Gwendolyn was crying too. "It's all right."

When, a few hours later, they said goodnight and Gwendolyn left, Angie turned to Jason. "You know, I was thinking. It might be good to stay here a little longer. I thought maybe we could help Gwendolyn out with her community work."

"Yeah," Jason said. "I was thinking the same thing too actually." He took her hands in his own. "And something else."

"What's that?"

"I've decided that busy or not, come this spring, I want to get married. Do what we should've done seven years ago."

"Yeah," Angie told him with a smile. "Me too". She kissed him and wrapped her arms around him. "Although, we made those vows a long time ago, didn't we?"

"I don't remember saying anything."

"We didn't say anything out loud," Angie told him. "But there's never been anyone else for me but you."

"There's never been anyone else for me either," Jason said. "I think from the very first moment I saw you, I knew you were the one I wanted to spend the rest of my life with."

Angie smiled. "Oh. I actually waited until I knew you a little better before I let those kinds of thoughts into my head."

Jason laughed.

"Come on," she told him. "Let's go to bed."

"Yeah, okay."

When they entered the bedroom, Jason caught a glimpse of the bag that contained his Sentinel gear, sitting at the bottom of the cupboard. He couldn't imagine throwing any of it out. The thought never crossed his mind. However, if all it ever did was gather dust, it wouldn't matter anymore. With a smile, he closed the cupboard and turned away. It was time to sleep, and Angie was waiting for him.